Rudolph Hering, E. Ganquillet, Wilhelm R. Kutter, John Cresson
Trautwine

A General Formula for the Uniform Flow of Water in Rivers and

Other Channels

by E. Ganguillet and W.R. Kutter. Tr. from the German, with numerous additions,

including tables, diagrams, and the elements of over 1200 gaugings of rivers, small

channels

Rudolph Hering, E. Ganguillet, Wilhelm R. Kutter, John Cresson Trautwine

A General Formula for the Uniform Flow of Water in Rivers and Other Channels
by E. Ganguillet and W.R. Kutter. Tr. from the German, with numerous additions, including
tables, diagrams, and the elements of over 1200 gaugings of rivers, small channels

ISBN/EAN: 9783337734602

Printed in Europe, USA, Canada, Australia, Japan

Cover: Foto ©Andreas Hilbeck / pixelio.de

More available books at **www.hansebooks.com**

A GENERAL FORMULA

FOR THE UNIFORM

FLOW OF WATER

IN

RIVERS AND OTHER CHANNELS;

BY

E. GANGUILLET and W. R. KUTTER,

ENGINEERS IN BERNE, SWITZERLAND.

— —

TRANSLATED FROM THE GERMAN, WITH NUMEROUS ADDITIONS, INCLUDING TABLES, DIAGRAMS, AND

THE ELEMENTS OF OVER 1200 GAUGINGS

OF RIVERS, SMALL CHANNELS AND PIPES,

In English Measure,

BY

RUDOLPH HERING and JOHN C. TRAUTWINE, JR.

M. AM. SOC. C. E., M. INST. C. E.   ASSOC. AM. SOC. C. E., ASSOC. INST. C. E.

NEW YORK:
JOHN WILEY & SONS,
15 ASTOR PLACE.
LONDON: E. & F. N. SPON.
1889.

AUTHORS' PREFACE.

THE present treatise* appeared in the "Zeitschrift des Oesterreichischen Ingenieur- und Architecten-Vereins" in 1869. At that time but a few separate copies were prepared and distributed among professional co-laborers. A considerable inquiry for such copies soon arose, and, as no more were to be had, the volume of the "Zeitschrift" was taken instead, which also has long since been exhausted. As the demand continued, and as our formula has come into use in Germany and Italy, and is recommended by M. Achille Bazaine to French engineers,+ the Direction of Public Works of the Canton of Berne (virtually. the Government Counsellor, Mr. Kilian) decided to have our treatise republished in an octavo edition. We have added to it a supplement, from which it will be seen that since the establishment of the formula no reason has appeared for modifying it in any way.

BERNE. January 1877.

---

* Versuch zur Aufstellung einer neuen allgemeinen Formel für die gleichförmige Bewegung des Wassers in Canälen und Flüssen.

+ See Mémoires de la Société des Ingénieurs civils. Paris, 1876.

AUTHORS' PREFACE TO THE PRESENT TRANSLATION.

THE present translation of the second edition (1877) of our treatise "Versuch zur Aufstellung einer neuen allgemeinen Formel für die gleichförmige Bewegung des Wassers in Canälen und Flüssen" is authorized by us.

A number of articles upon the subject have been issued from time to time by Mr. Kutter, among which is a series of tables of velocities and discharges, demanded by professors of agricultural engineering in Germany for the use of their schools. On the expediency of publishing these tables, however, the writer has expressed himself as follows on page 13 of his latest work:[*] "These tables were calculated at the request of Professor Dünkelberg of Bonn, who had recognized the insufficiency of the constant coefficient c in the general formula $v = c\sqrt{RS}$ for the design of small canals in earth; and were published in his Journal 'Der Cultur-Ingenieur,' vol. ii., in the year 1870. The author has, however, repeatedly insisted that it is better to use the new general formula itself, and the graphic process which forms its basis, neither of which offers the slightest difficulty."

The tables, together with the accompanying text, were translated into English in 1876 by Jackson from the Journal referred to, but without authority from the author. They were contained also in the (authorized) Italian translation by B. Dal Bosco of Mr. Kutter's work "Die neuen Formeln für die Bewegung des Wassers." But it is hardly necessary to say that the development and presentation of the formula,

---

[*] "Bewegung des Wassers in Canälen und Flüssen," 2d ed. Berlin, 1885.

established both experimentally and mathematically, and now generally known and used, have a value superior to that of incomplete tables, which can find but a limited application since they serve only for canals in earth and for only three widely differing degrees of roughness of wet perimeter ($n = 0.025$, $n = 0.030$, and $n = 0.035$).

The motive to our investigations and studies was the demonstrated uncertainty of the older coefficients, contained in the formulæ of deProny, Eytelwein, and others, and the nearly simultaneous publication of the works of M. Bazin and of Messrs. Humphreys and Abbot, both containing new formulæ based upon the results of very important gaugings made under exactly opposite conditions, namely, in small artificial channels on the one hand, and in the Mississippi and its tributaries on the other.

The last-named work contained a request that the new American formula suggested in it should be tested by application to European channels with steep slopes. The result of our investigations in response to this request was published in Kutter's " Kurzer Bericht," * and consisted in the demonstration of the inapplicability of the new American formula to channels with great descent.

In studying the subject we made continual use of the graphic method, and were eventually led to the recognition of the elements affecting the flow of water, and thus to the development of our general formula.

The Department of Public Works of the Canton of Berne was directed to take part in the Centennial World's Exhibition in Philadelphia in 1876, and we were desirous of acquainting the American engineers with the results of our researches in connection with the Mississippi investigation. At the close of the Exhibition our entire exhibit was presented to the War Department of the United States, and is probably still in its possession.

Mr. Kutter conducted not only the graphic investigations

---

* Kurzer Bericht über die neuen Theorien der Bewegung des Wassers, etc. Bern, 1868.

and the great mass of calculations, but also the writing of the treatise, while Mr. Ganguillet took upon himself the algebraic and analytical portion of the task.

We hope that the present translation may contribute towards the development and advancement of hydraulic knowledge in America and wherever the English language prevails.

E. GANGUILLET, *Chief Engineer.*

W. R. KUTTER, *Engineer.*

BERNE, February 18, 1888.

TRANSLATORS' PREFACE.

IT is perhaps unnecessary to enlarge upon the great usefulness of a mathematical expression which determines with
approximate correctness the velocity of water flowing in regular
channels of any size and shape, and under all usual conditions.
It has been said that a single formula satisfying a requirement
so general in its character would not be practical. But when
we consider that the laws of flowing water must be the same
whether the channel is large or small, slightly inclined or
precipitous, and that it is impracticable, if not impossible, to fix
exact limits of conditions up to which one formula and beyond
which another one applies, it seems reasonable to seek for such
a general expression, particularly when extreme accuracy is not
required.

Until Humphreys and Abbot gauged the Mississippi River
and Darcy and Bazin gauged a large number of small channels,
differing in the nature of their perimeter, there was no satisfactory basis for a general formula. But with the aid of these
gaugings, and of others made by our authors of mountain
streams of nearly uniform cross-section and great descent,
they believed themselves to be in possession of the necessary
data for the development of a general formula for the flow of
water in the regular reaches of rivers and smaller channels.

Some misapprehension still appears to exist as to the claims
of the authors. They have been regarded as holding their
formula to be scientifically perfect, and to cover both possible
and impossible conditions of flow. In the work here translated
they expressly disclaim any such assumption, and insist that
it is purely and essentially empirical, and must not be expected
to apply to cases beyond the range of the data from which it
has been derived ; and we are glad of the opportunity to dis-

abuse any English and American readers of this misconception, and also to present to them the process of reasoning which led to the formula which is now regarded by most hydraulicians as the best that has been reached up to the present time.

It belongs to the general class of "slope-formulæ," and its application is therefore of course limited to cases where the slope of the water-surface can be ascertained with a degree of accuracy sufficient for the given case. In large rivers this is very difficult, if not impossible, on account of the very light slopes and of the irregularities of the water-surface, both longitudinally and transversely. During the passage of flood-waves, in fact, the slope sometimes entirely loses its value for determining velocities, because during a rising and falling of a river the inclination of the water-surface and mean radius may be the same, while the respective mean velocities are different.

For important questions in large rivers, slope-formulæ are therefore generally discarded, and other means adopted for ascertaining the discharge. Indeed, it seems doubtful whether any general formula can be made applicable to very large streams, from the many irregularities and other features peculiar to each one. A special equation for the particular site, dependent in the main only upon the mean depth and deduced from gaugings made for the respective section, appears to be the best method of estimating their discharge. But for smaller streams and for artificial channels a slope-formula offers the only practical or at least most useful method of presenting the conditions of flow.

As, however, time and means are not always at hand for accurately gauging a large river, and as in such cases a slope-formula may often give an acceptable approximation, we have included in our Table I a list of those gaugings of large streams where the slope was carefully determined. They are useful, further, in closely indicating certain extreme values to which a general slope-formula should conform.

As the relation $v = c \sqrt{RS}$ will most likely remain its fundamental expression, the coefficient c, which varies with different conditions, will hereafter require the most careful attention of hydraulicians. A number of authors have endeavored to establish laws for its variation, and among them Ganguillet and Kutter appear so far to have been the most successful. More recently Mr. Hamilton Smith, Jr., following the same lines as our authors, has endeavored to generalize the variation of c, but without giving it a mathematical form. He acknowledges its dependence upon R, S, and a coefficient of roughness (J), but leaves its determination, except in a few instances, for extremely regular conditions, to the judgment of the practical engineer. Our authors endeavored to give a mathematical expression for the variation of c with R and S, and thus confine the exercise of judgment to a selection of a proper value for n (coefficient of roughness), which is found to be nearly constant for the varying conditions of flow occurring in one and the same channel. This renders the choice of a coefficient for a given case a much simpler matter, and reduces the liability to err in judgment.

Our authors, we believe, were the first to notice certain opposite effects in the variation of the coefficient c with the slope. Their own investigations led them to make the assumption, which is embodied in their formula, that these effects depended upon the size of the channel, and that the point of change was found to be in one whose mean radius was about one meter. They, however, recognized the insufficiency of the data upon which this assumption and the convenient limit of one meter are based, and admitted that the point of change might be variable. The collection of gaugings in Table I indicates that where the perimeter is very rough, this point of change is found in a channel whose mean radius is less than one meter, and *vice versa*. The gaugings also indicate that, as pointed out by the authors on p. 99, a given difference of roughness has less effect upon the coefficient c in large rivers than in small channels, which feature is likewise not represented in the formula.

The present volume is the first published translation of Ganguillet and Kutter's chief work: " Versuch zur Aufstellung

einer neuen allgemeinen Formel für die gleichförmige Bewegung des Wassers in Canälen und Flüssen," Berne, 1877. Mr.
Lowis D'A. Jackson's work, " The New Formula for the Mean
Velocity of Discharge of Rivers and Canals," London, 1876,
was translated chiefly from articles published in the " Cultur-
Ingenieur" and in the " Zeitschrift des Oesterreichischen Ingenieur und Architecten Vereins."

The first part of the present work is devoted chiefly to historical matter, and to a glance at the status of our knowledge
concerning the laws of flowing water. The second part treats
of the establishment of the new formula, and shows its close
agreement with a large number of experimental results obtained
under widely different conditions. In a supplement the authors
add a more direct method of deriving their formula "to satisfy
those who prefer mathematical brevity," and sketch the development of a second general formula, which assumes that the
effect of slope upon the coefficient c is the same in small channels as in large streams, but which they consider inferior to the
first one.

Great pains have been taken to give a faithful representation of the authors' ideas rather than a scrupulous translation
of their words and expressions. While, therefore, we have condensed the text in a number of instances, we have in others
added to or amended it, and have inserted new figures and
elaborated the older ones wherever we thought it conducive
to greater clearness.

In the Appendices I to IV we give a number of extracts
from sundry works of Mr. Kutter bearing upon the subject,
and in order to make the volume as useful as possible we have
added still other matter, as follows :

Appendix V contains simple directions for constructing the
diagram which is used for a graphical solution of the formula.

Appendix VI contains Kutter's modification of Bazin's
general formula, which may prove useful for some special purposes on account of its comparative simplicity.

In Appendix VII will be found a number of formulæ and
data concerning the relation between the mean and surface
velocities in streams.

Appendix VIII gives the views of a number of investigators in regard to the velocities beyond which a scouring of the bed takes place in channels formed of different materials.

Appendix IX gives an account of Harlacher's method of ascertaining the discharge of rivers.

In Table I, designed to facilitate the selection of the coefficient of roughness *n*, we have collected the hydraulic elements of over 1200 gaugings, made in some 300 different channels and pipes under varying conditions of mean hydraulic depth and of slope. In the original work the corresponding table is confined to 81 gaugings, being average values for 81 different channels, to fewer elements, and to a scanty description, if any, of the character of the channels. The data have been collected from the original publications where practicable. The Irawadi gaugings not being published in the shape required for our table, Mr. Robert Gordon, their author, has very kindly recompiled them for us. We have endeavored to present a complete description, wherever available, of the physical characteristics of the pipes and watercourses, in order to assist judgment as much as possible in the selection of the coefficients of resistance. We believe that this collection is the most complete and comprehensive one published at the present time.

The following is a list of the authorities referred to in this Table :

Couplet.—Mémoires de l'Académie des Sciences. Paris, 1732.

Bossut.—Traité théorique et Experimental d'Hydrodynamique. Paris, 1786.

Dubuat.—Principes d'Hydraulique. Paris, 1786.

Provis.—Proc. Inst. C. E. London, 1838.

La Nicca.—Die Rheinkorrection im Domleschgerthal. 1839.

Bidder.—Proc. Inst. C. E. London, 1853.

Leslie.—Proc. Inst. C. E. London, 1855.

Rittinger.—Zeitschrift des Ing. u. Arch. Vereins. Vienna, 1855.

Darcy.—Recherches experimentales relatives au mouvement de l'eau dans les tuyaux. Paris, 1857.

Humphreys & Abbot.—Report upon the Physics and Hydraulics of the Mississippi River. Philadelphia, 1861.

Darcy & Bazin.—Recherches Hydrauliques. Paris, 1865.

Gauckler.—Etudes théoriques et pratiques sur l'écoulement et le mouvement des eaux.   Paris, 1867.

Grebenau.—Zusätze zur Uebersetzung des Werkes von Humphreys & Abbot.   München, 1867.

Kutter.—Die Neue Theorie, etc.   Förster's Allgemeine Bauzeitung. Vienna, 1868.

Bornemann.—Civil Ingenieur, Vol. XV.   Leipzig, 1869.

Gale.—Proc. Inst. C. E. in Scotland.   1869.

Lampe.—Civil Ingenieur, Vol. XIX.   Leipzig, 1873.

Kutter.—Die Neuen Formeln, etc.   Vienna, 1877.

Kutter.—Versuch zur Aufstellung, etc.   Berne, 2d ed., 1877.

Fanning.—Treatise on Hydraulic and Water Supply Engineering.   New York, 1877.

Darrach.—Trans. Am. Soc. C. E.   New York, 1878.

Iben.—Druckhöhen Verlust.   Hamburg, 1880.

Cunningham.—Roorkee Hydraulic Experiments.   Roorkee, 1881.

Mississippi River Commission.—Reports for 1881 and 1882.

Harlacher.—Hydrometrische Arbeiten bei Tetschen.   Prag, 1883.

Kutter.—Bewegung des Wassers, etc.   Berlin, 1885.

Stearns.—Trans. Amer. Soc. C. E.   New York, 1885.

Seddon.—Journal Ass'n of Engineering Societies.   New York, 1886.

H. Smith, Jr.—Hydraulics.   New York, 1886.

Missouri River Commission.—Unpublished data, through kindness of the President of Com.   1887.

Herschel.—Trans. Am. Soc. C. E.   New York, 1887.

Brush.—Trans. Am. Soc. C. E.   New York, 1888.

Gordon.—Irawadi Gaugings: Private Communication.   1888.

Epper.—Swiss Gaugings: Private Communication.   1888.

Tables II, III, and IV contain the computed values of different elements of the formula by means of which its numerical solution, otherwise quite laborious, is rendered very simple for all conditions occurring in practice. And Table V gives the conversion of such units of measure as are likely to occur in hydraulic problems.

Although we have preserved the original metric measures throughout the text, we thought it well to add English measures at a number of places. The tables, however, are confined to English measure. To have undertaken to add metric equivalents would have rendered them cumbersome, and perhaps somewhat confusing. The diagram, by which the use of the formula is so greatly simplified, we have given both in metric and English measure, the latter being drawn to a larger scale. It should be mounted on card-board, and care taken to avoid distortion.

We have appended no tables of velocities given by the formula. Such tables, to be of any value, would fill a large and expensive volume, and, as the authors say, are rendered unnecessary by the use of the diagram, from which all of the elements, including the velocity, can be easily found.

While engaged upon this work we were much grieved to learn of the sudden death of Mr. Kutter, who had shown great interest in the forthcoming translation. Through the kindness of Mrs. Kutter we have received some notes from which our short biographical sketch is compiled.

In presenting this translation to English and American engineers we trust that it will serve not only as a faithful record in our own language of these valuable researches in hydraulics, but also as a useful guide and hand-book to the practical engineer in determining the hydraulic elements of flowing water.

We also trust that it may be useful to students, in giving a concise historical account of the progress made in ascertaining the laws of flow in streams, and particularly because it presents an instructive analysis of a method of deducing an empirical formula from observed facts, an operation which will be more frequently required and performed in the future, as we add to the store of scientific data in the various branches of experimental knowledge.

RUDOLPH HERING,
JOHN C. TRAUTWINE, JR.

December, 1888.

MEMOIR OF W. R. KUTTER.

WILHELM R. KUTTER was born August 23, 1818, in Ravensburg, near Lake Constance, in the kingdom of Würtemberg. His ancestors belonged to one of the most distinguished families of the country. They had acquired much wealth by the manufacture of paper, but lost it all during the Napoleonic wars.

As a boy he manifested a strong love of nature and great clearness of understanding. He was industrious and acquired orderly habits. His collections of minerals and other natural objects were arranged with scrupulous care; and in later life the neatness and beauty of his many plans, topographical maps, and landscape sketches bore witness also to some artistic talent.

At the age of 13 he left his father's home to enter the service of an uncle in Switzerland for the purpose of learning surveying, and made rapid progress. Toward the close of this apprenticeship, his uncle proposed to instruct him in the conversion of irregular figures into triangles of equal area, and was surprised to find that his pupil had already discovered the method for himself. At 17, Kutter had taken pupils in surveying and mathematics, and from this time forward earned his own living.

He soon after entered the Technical Bureau of Berne, and studied the designing of highways, under the direction of banished Polish officers, whose society was of great value to him, especially as he acquired from them his thorough knowledge of the French language.

Upon the dissolution of the Bureau, in 1839, Kutter continued his studies and was employed mainly on a number of extensive and difficult projects for Alpine roads, all of which he successfully executed. He made, in all, 120 designs of this kind, most of which were carried out.

His knowledge of forestry caused him to be frequently employed as arbitrator in cases of dispute on matters of valuation or partition, etc.; an office which his integrity, and fidelity to his convictions, his mild and courteous demeanor, enabled him to discharge to the satisfaction of all concerned. He was regarded as an authority in matters of forestry, and published some works upon the subject.

The correction of the streams of the Jura, in which he was subsequently engaged, naturally led him to the study of hydraulics, and finally, with the valued co-operation of his warm friend Chief Engineer Ganguillet, to the elaboration of the now well-known " Formula of Ganguillet and Kutter," of which the present work is an exposition.

His knowledge of the several branches of learning referred to was gained through his own persistent study and observation, without the advantages of attendance at technical schools.

In 1851 Kutter was appointed Secretary of the Department of Public Works of the Canton of Berne, and in this capacity, up to the time of his death, faithfully served the country of his adoption.

He was twice married, and was the father of 18 children, 10 of whom survive him. He thus had upon his shoulders not only the heavy burden of his professional work, but also the care of a very large family, a responsibility which he bore most creditably, leaving his survivors, though without means, yet also without debt.

He died on Sunday, May 6, 1888, mourned not only by his family, but by many personal friends, to whom his modesty, his quiet manner, and his amiability had warmly endeared him.

The following is a list of his writings, so far as known to us:

SCIENTIFIC WORKS OF W. R. KUTTER.

Die Juragewässer-Correktion im Jahr 1853. Mit Zeichnungen. Von W. R. Kutter.

Studien über die Tieferlegung des Bielersees, mit Benützung desselben als Reservoir für die Hochwasser der Aare. Mit Zeichnungen. Von W. R. Kutter. 1865. Manuscript.

Kurzer Bericht über die neuen Theorien der Bewegungen des Wassers in Flüssen und Canälen von Darcy und Bazin und von Humphreys und Abbot, nebst einer Coefficienten-Scala zum Gebrauche für den schweizerischen Ingenieur. Bearbeitet von W. R. Kutter, Ingenieur und Secretär der Direktion. Bern, 1868.

Die neue Theorie der Bewegung des Wassers in Flüssen und Canälen von Humphreys und Abbot, in Beziehung auf die schweizerischen und andere Gewässer mit stärkeren Gefällen. Mit Zeichnungen. Von W. R. Kutter. 1868.

Abhandlungen aus der Zeitschrift: Der Culturingenieur. Braunschweig, 1868 bis 1871.

1. Die neue amerikanische Theorie der Bewegung des Wassers in Flüssen und Canälen.

2. Die neuen Formeln für die Bestimmung der mittleren Geschwindigkeit des Wassers in Canälen und Flüssen, nebst mehreren Coefficienten-Scalen zum praktischen Gebrauche.

3. Mittlere Geschwindigkeiten und Wassermengen per Secunde in Gräben und Flüssen mit verschiedener Rauheit des benetzten Umfanges und mit verschiedenen Gefällen und Querschnittsformen. Für den praktischen Gebrauch bearbeitet.

4. Neue Formeln für die Bewegung des Wassers in Canälen und Flüssen.

5. Das Verhältniss zwischen Sohlenbreite und Gefälle geschiebeführender Canäle und Flüsse.

Versuch zur Aufstellung einer neuen allgemeinen Formel für die gleichförmige Bewegung des Wassers in Canälen und Flüssen, gestützt auf die Resultate der in Frankreich vorgenommenen umfangreichen und sorgfältigen Untersuchungen und der in Nord Amerika ausgeführten grossartigen Strommessungen. Mit graphischen Darstellungen. Von E. Ganguillet und W. R. Kutter. (Zeitschrift des österreichischen Ingenieurund Architecten Vereins. Wien, 1869.) Separat Abdruck. Bern, 1877.

Von den mathematischen Gesetzen welche sich beim Wachsthum des Bauholzes finden lassen. Vortrag von W. R. Kutter. Bern, 1870.

Die neuen Formeln für die Bewegung des Wassers in Canälen und regelmässigen Fluss-strecken. Von Humphreys und Abbot; von H. Bazin; von Ph. Gauckler; und von E. Ganguillet und W. R. Kutter. Mit Zeichnungen und graphischen Darstellungen. Von W. R. Kutter. (Allgemeine Bauzeitung. Wien, 1871.) Zweite Auflage, 1877.

Einfluss der Störungen der gleichförmigen Bewegung des Wassers auf die Geschwindigkeit desselben, und etwas über die *Geschiebeführung in Canälen und Flüssen.* Mit Zeichnungen. Von W. R. Kutter. (Allgemeine Bauzeitung. Wien, 1873.)

Bewegung des Wassers in Canälen und Flüssen. Tabellen und Beiträge. Von W. R. Kutter. Berlin, 1885.

NOTATION.

v = the mean velocity, in feet per second or in meters per second,

$= \dfrac{\text{discharge per second}}{\text{area of cross-section}}$.

R = the mean hydraulic radius or depth, in feet or in meters,

$= \dfrac{\text{area of cross-section}}{\text{wet perimeter of cross-section}}$.

S = the slope of the water surface, being the same for all measures,

= the sine of the angle of slope,

$= \dfrac{\text{fall of the surface in a given length}}{\text{given length}}$.

c = the variable coefficient in the formula $v = c\sqrt{RS}$, differing for different measures.

n = the coefficient of roughness of the wet perimeter, varying generally between .009 and .040, and being the same for all measures.

a = a constant = 41.66 for English measure,

= 23.0 for metric measure.

l = a constant = $\sqrt{3.2809 \text{ feet}}$ = 1.81132 for English measure,

= $\sqrt{1 \text{ meter}}$ = 1.0 for metric measure.

m = the "constant" of a certain hyperbola used in constructing the formulas = .0028075 for English measure,

= .00155 for metric measure.

x = the variable abscissa ⎫ of the slope curves, located by the
 intersections of the asymptotes
 of the hyperbolæ whose abscissæ
y = the variable ordinate ⎭ are $\sqrt{R}$ and whose ordinates are c.

NOTE.—The values a, l, m, x and y are established by the authors in constructing the formula. Their signification is fully explained in the text.

CONTENTS.

PART I.

GENERAL REMARKS—HISTORICAL MATTER—LATEST RESEARCHES AND THEIR RESULTS.

PART II.

ESTABLISHMENT OF A GENERAL FORMULA FOR THE UNIFORM FLOW OF WATER IN RIVERS AND OTHER CHANNELS.

TABLES FOR PRACTICAL USE.

PLATES.

" Si mon ouvrage n'a pas le mérite d'étendre autant que je l'aurais désiré les limites d'une science aussi importante, j'espère qu'il servira du moins à mieux diriger les efforts des savants, à encourager ceux qui se livrent aux observations, et à les convaincre par mon exemple qu'on peut, avec les talents les plus ordinaires, contribuer aux progrès de la philosophie naturelle, et marquer les écarts des hommes de génie."

BERNARD, Nouveaux principes d'hydraulique, 1787.

[If my book has not the merit of extending the limits of a very important science as much as I should have desired, I hope that it will serve at least to direct the efforts of students to better purpose, to encourage those who devote themselves to observations, and to convince them through my own example, that with the most ordinary talents, one can contribute to the progress of natural philosophy, and record the achievements of men of genius.

BERNARD, *New Principles of Hydraulics*, 1787.]

A GENERAL FORMULA FOR THE UNIFORM FLOW OF WATER.

PART I.

GENERAL REMARKS—HISTORICAL MATTER—LATEST RESEARCHES AND THEIR RESULTS.

1. Principles hitherto assumed.

The movement of water in canals and rivers has for a long time been the subject of scientific investigation and research, engaging the attention of the most noted hydraulicians. Italy is the cradle of hydraulics, and the Po is presumably the stream which gave the first impulse to its study. Investigators at first sought to express the laws of the flow of water by means of mathematical principles, and busied themselves with hypotheses more or less entitled to claim agreement with the actual phenomena.

Galileo, who, at about the beginning of the seventeenth century, discovered the laws of falling bodies, is said to have been the first investigator who turned his attention to those of the flow of water in rivers. How far he remained from arriving at the truth, however, is evidenced by the following circumstance, related by M. Bernard :* It was proposed to straighten

---

* " Nouveaux principes d'hydraulique." Paris, 1787.

the course of the tortuous river Vicentio, whose floods were causing damage. Galileo opposed this project and maintained that in two channels having the same total fall, the velocity of the water would be the same, whatever might be the respective lengths of the channels; also, that the windings of a river, unless they formed very sharp angles, caused very little or no retardation of its flow. An engineer, Bartolotti, who had written upon the necessity for the rectification of the river Vicentio, was unable to refute Galileo, because he could not actually demonstrate the incorrectness of his views. The rectification was not undertaken, and, says Bernard, "Galileo had the misfortune to accomplish the triumph of his opinion to the prejudice of truth."

Brunings [*] tells us that Galileo declared he had "found less difficulty in the discovery of the motions of the planets, in spite of their amazing distances, than in his investigations of the flow of water in rivers, which took place before his very eyes."

Castelli, a student of Galileo, in his work which appeared in 1628, under the auspices of Pope Urban VIII., for the first time introduced the velocity as an element in the movement of the flowing water. Another of Galileo's students, the renowned Torricelli, then discovered that, except for the resistance, the velocity of jets of water flowing from small openings was equal to that of bodies falling in space, from the same height as that causing the flow; in other words, the velocities are proportional to the square roots of the heights. From this fact he deduced the fundamental theory of hydraulics: "that, neglecting the resistances, the square of the velocity of water is proportional to the head of pressure." He concluded also that the acceleration of the velocity of water on inclines is dependent upon the rate of slope, i.e. the hydraulic gradient.

The work of Guglielmini, the greatest master of the Italian school, appeared at the close of the seventeenth century. This philosopher accepted Torricelli's theorem and developed the

---

[*] "Abhandlung über die Geschwindigkeit des fliessenden Wassers."

so-called parabolic theory of flow in rivers, which in brief is as follows: "A particle of water x feet below the surface tends to move with the same velocity which it would have when flowing from an opening in the side of the reservoir at x feet below the surface, namely, with the velocity acquired when falling x feet in space, and expressed by the formula $v = \sqrt{2gx}$. Draw through the given point a vertical line and regard it as the axis of a parabola, whose apex is at the surface and whose parameter is equal to four times the distance through which a falling body passes in the first second. Then, the corresponding ordinate of the parabola represents the velocity of the particle."

According to this theory the velocity of the water in a river must be greatest at the bottom and zero at the surface, whereas the contrary is generally the case. We thus see to what conclusions abstract theorizing in hydraulics led even the greatest philosophers in those days.

In a treatise laid before the Paris Academy of Sciences by Pitot in 1732, the error of the above theory is demonstrated by means of a series of measurements, which this savant had carried out with the so-called "Pitot's tube" invented by him. At about the same time Daniel Bernouilli first applied the principle of *vis viva* to the theory of the motion of water. This marked the beginning of a new epoch in the history of hydraulics.

The first attempt to discover the law by which the velocity of water depends upon the fall and the cross-section of the channel was, according to Hagen, made by Brahms,* who observed that the acceleration which we should expect in accordance with the law of gravity does not take place in streams, but that the water in them acquires a constant velocity. He points to the friction of the water against the wet perimeter as the force which opposes the acceleration, and assumes that its resistance is proportional to the mean radius R, i.e., to the area of cross-section divided by the wet perimeter.

---

* "Anfangsgründe der Deich- und Wasserbaukunst." Aurich, about 1753.

Brahms and Chezy * are to be regarded as the authors of the well-known formula

$$v = c \sqrt{\frac{a}{p} \times \frac{h}{l}} = c \sqrt{RS},$$

or

$$\text{velocity} = \text{a coefficient } c \times \sqrt{\frac{\text{area of cross-section}}{\text{wet perimeter}} \times \frac{\text{head or fall}}{\text{length}}}$$

$$= \text{a coefficient } c \times \sqrt{\text{hydraulic radius} \times \text{slope}}.$$

More than a century ago, Michelotti and Bossut established the true principle that the formulæ for the movement of water must be ascertained from the results of observation, and not by abstract reasoning. Dubuat (1779), who recognized the truth of this proposition, undertook to investigate the laws of flowing water by means of thorough experiments, for which purpose he carried out very careful measurements, not only on the Canal du Jard and the River Haine in France, but also in specially constructed wooden channels of small dimensions. The results thus obtained he summed up in these two laws:

1. The force which sets the water in motion is derived solely from the inclination of the water surface.

2. When the motion is uniform the resistance which the water meets, or the retarding force, is equal to the accelerating force.

Dubuat also ascertained that the resistance is independent of the weight or pressure of the water, so that its friction upon the walls of pipes and channels is entirely different in its nature from that existing between solid bodies.

De Prony † arrives at the following conclusions, among others :

" The particles of water in a vertical line in the cross-section of a stream move with different velocities, which diminish from the surface to the bottom."

---

* A celebrated French engineer. 1775.
† Recherches physico-mathématiques, 1790.

" The surface, bottom, and mean velocities stand in a certain relation to each other, which Dubuat, strange to say, finds to be independent of the size and form of the cross-section."

" A layer of water adheres to the walls of the pipe or channel, and is therefore to be regarded as the wall proper which surrounds the flowing mass. According to Dubuat's experiments the adhesive attraction of the walls seems to cease at this layer, so that differences in the material of the walls produce no perceptible change in the resistance."

" The particles of water attract each other mutually, and are themselves attracted by the walls of the channel. These attractions (resistances) may, in general, be expressed by means of two different values, which, however, are supposed to be of the same nature and comparable with each other."

2. The earlier formulæ.

Coulomb's investigations indicated that the resistance offered by the perimeter of a channel is represented by two values, the first of which is proportional to the velocity and the second to the square of the same. Upon this principle de Prony based his celebrated formula,

$$RS = av + bv^2,$$

in which a and b are coefficients of friction to be deduced from the results of experiments.

From thirty measurements by Dubuat and one by Chezy, de Prony found, for metric measure,

$$a = 0.000044;$$
$$b = 0.000309.$$

Somewhat later, Eytelwein, after comparing the above thirty-one experiments with fifty-five others by German hydraulicians (Brunings, Woltmann and Funk), suggested

$$a = 0.000024;$$
$$b = 0.000366.$$

Many authors held that it would be permissible to simplify the formula by neglecting the value av, which is very small for rivers and for mean velocities over 1 meter per second; and in 1775 Chezy, in harmony with Brahms (1753), had already established the following formula:

$$RS = bv^2,$$

and assumed, in meters,

$$b = 0.0004,$$

whilst Eytelwein eventually adopted

$$b = 0.000386.$$

The Italian hydraulicians took

$$b = 0.0004,$$

while in Germany and Switzerland Eytelwein's formula for velocity, in the form suggested by Brahms, has been in use until recently.   It gives

$$v = 50.9 \sqrt{RS} \text{ for metric measure };$$

$$v = 92.2 \sqrt{RS} \text{ for English feet.}$$

Without stopping to discuss also the formulæ of Dupuit, St. Venant and others, based upon the above-mentioned principles, we merely remark that in all these formulæ the coefficients are *constant* values.

Rühlmann and Weisbach give, for the formula

$$v = c \sqrt{RS}.$$

the following values of c, deduced from de Prony's formula, and varying with v:

Meters per Second.		Feet per Second.	
v	c	v	c
0.1	36.4	.4	68.6
0.2	43.4	.6	76.4
0.3	46.7	.8	81.1
0.4	48.8	1.0	84.7
0.5	50.1	1.2	87.1
0.75	52.1	1.5	89.6
1.00	53.2	2.0	92.3
1.25	53.8	2.5	94.4
1.50	54.3	3.0	95.6
2.00	54.9	3.5	96.5
		4.0	97.2
		4.5	97.8
		5.0	98.5
		5.5	98.8
		6.0	99.1
		7.0	99.5

3. The foregoing formulæ recognize no influence of the roughness of the wet perimeter, or of the degree of slope, upon their coefficients.

According to Dubuat and de Prony, and all of the ancient and modern hydraulicians, differences in roughness of the wet perimeter, or in the slope, had no effect upon the variation of the coefficients; and from the beginning of the present century up to within recent years, but few experiments were added to determine these coefficients with greater exactness. Yet their inadequacy has steadily become more apparent; the breaking of dams and levees in regulated rivers (of which we will mention only the case of the Rhone at Lyons) have given rise to just suspicions as to the reliability of the formulæ upon which the construction of these works was founded, and engineers have begun to modify them somewhat in practice, yet without any safe guide.

4. Insufficiency of the earlier formulæ.

The French engineer Vallés [*] ascribes to the unqualified confidence in these formulæ, the incorrect design of the cross-section of many canals in France, and the resulting calamities in times of freshets. Indeed, if we suppose, for instance, that for any mountain stream which is to be dammed up, the cross-section between the dams has been calculated by de Prony's or Eytelwein's formulæ; then this section must be too small, because the coefficients of the formulæ are too large for such cases. The consequences are breaches and floods with their inevitable results. German hydraulicians, such as Hagen, Dr. Bauernfeind and others, have also expressed doubts as to the reliability of the formulæ referred to, and of their coefficients.

Attempts have been made here (Switzerland), in the case of streams carrying much detritus, to introduce a modification in the formulæ to the extent of taking, for the wet perimeter, the length of a line following the projecting portions of all the stones on the bottom and all irregularities of the banks. Others had already attempted to make a corresponding modification on account of aquatic plants. It was of course impossible to devise means for accurately determining the length of such a line, and it was assumed as being equal to 1.4 to 1.8 times the nominal perimeter, according to the dimensions of the stones, etc. Such increase in the length assumed for the wet perimeter of course reduced proportionally the value of the mean radius R.

In the Rhine, Defontaine found the greatest velocity at the surface, and a great decrease as the bottom was approached, a circumstance which he ascribes to the rocky nature of the bed of the stream.[†]

The cast-iron pipes used for the water-supply of the town of Grenoble gave, after only six years' use, less than half their original discharge, and it was found upon investigation that

---

[*] " Etudes sur les inondations."
[†] See Annales des Ponts et Chaussées, 1833.

the diminution was caused by tubercular incrustations which had formed upon the inner surfaces of the pipes.* Similar experiences were met with in supplying water to Toulouse. It may have been this consideration which led the Romans to give the preference to stone in constructing their aqueducts.

All this points to the conclusion that hydraulic formulæ must contain variable and not fixed coefficients of velocity.

5. Darcy and Bazin's new and comprehensive investigations.

In the midst of the prevailing uncertainty, it was reserved for a man whose great learning, power of penetration and talent for research specially fitted him for the task, to open the way to a wholly new understanding of the subject. In using water-pipes at Dijon, the renowned H. Darcy, Inspecteur général des ponts et chaussées, to whom that city is indebted for her excellent water-supply, had noticed, as already observed by others, that those pipes which presented the smoothest inner surface furnished the greatest quantity of water in a given time ; or in other words, that the greatest velocity was found in the smoothest pipes. He argued rightly that a similar phenomenon must occur in open channels, and undertook to make a series of extended and thorough experiments upon this point. Through the results of a number of measurements made by his colleague Baumgarten upon canals near Marseilles, he thoroughly satisfied himself of the correctness of his proposition, and then, by the authority of the government, constructed on the Canal de Bourgogne, near Dijon, a special canal for experimental purposes, 596.5 meters long, 2 meters wide, and 1 meter deep. It received its water from the Canal de Bourgogne, level No. 57, and discharged it into the river l'Ouche. A double reservoir was placed at the entrance to this canal, and the wall of the lower reservoir was provided with twelve square openings of precisely equal size, edged with copper. Their discharge, for each level of the water in the reservoir, had previously been

---

* See remarks upon this subject in " Annales des Ponts et Chaussées " by Fournet (1834), Gras (1835), and Payen (1837); also Kirkwood in Reports Brooklyn, 1865.— *Trans.*

obtained by a large number of careful observations. The special canal itself was furnished successively with very different linings; namely, neat cement, cement with one third sand, boards, bricks, fine and coarse pebbles fixed in place, and laths nailed transversely to the direction of flow 0.01 and 0.05 meter apart. Its form, dimensions and grade were also varied in the different experiments, the grades between 0.001 and 0.009 per unit of length. For all these manifold degrees of roughness, and of forms and slopes, careful measurements of the flow were made by means of Pitot's tube, which had been materially improved by Darcy (tube jaugeur de Darcy), but chiefly by dividing the area of the wet cross-sections into the volume discharged by the canal in a given time, which volume had been previously measured, as noted above. The results were grouped in series containing generally twelve experiments each. In addition to this, the results of river measurements by Dubuat, Brunings, Woltmann, Funk, Poirée, Emmery, Leveillé and others were collected for comparison. The Mississippi and other recent American measurements were not yet known in Europe.

The preliminary arrangements had just been made by Darcy, when death called him from the midst of his fruitful and beneficent labors. The execution of these comprehensive experiments now fell upon his assistant, H. Bazin, Ingénieur des ponts et chaussées.

It was he who arranged and conducted the gaugings and extended them to several branches of the Canal de Bourgogne, who collected and digested the numerous results, and who wrote that most remarkable work, " Recherches hydrauliques," the fruit of years of investigation and study; a work which the Academy of Sciences in Paris received with the most unqualified approval, and for which they have since awarded a valuable prize.

6. Bazin's results.

The principal facts developed by the researches of Bazin with reference to the uniform flow of water are the following:

1. The coefficients (*c*) of the formulæ for the determination of the mean velocity of water in canals and rivers of uniform

flow, vary with the degree of roughness of the wetted surface. This opposes the assumption of de Prony that the perimeter of the flowing mass is formed by a film of water adjoining the walls and bottom of the channel, and that hence the nature of the walls and bottom has no effect upon the friction.

2. These coefficients (c) vary much more nearly with the hydraulic mean depth (R) than with the mean velocity (v).

Bazin, it is true, observed that in the main the coefficient c (in the expression $v = c \sqrt{RS}$) increased with an increase of slope, the coefficients α and β of *his* formula* *decreasing* with such increase, but did not find this variation of sufficient importance to be specially taken into account. He also observed that a semicircular form of cross-section gives a greater value of c than a rectangular form.

7. A new formula.

The knowledge thus gained was of the greatest importance, and led naturally to the introduction of a new formula. M. Bazin established four categories, corresponding to different observed degrees of roughness of wetted perimeter, and for each of these suggested two "interpolated" coefficients, which vary with the four degrees of roughness. Thus, in the abbreviated formula of de Prony, $RS = bv^2$, he put

$$b = \alpha + \frac{\beta}{R},$$

in which α and β are constant for any one category. Hence the general formula of M. Bazin is

$$RS = \left(\alpha + \frac{\beta}{R}\right)v^2,$$

or

$$v = \sqrt{\frac{RS}{\alpha + \frac{\beta}{R}}} = \sqrt{\frac{1}{\alpha + \frac{\beta}{R}}} \sqrt{RS}.$$

---

* $v = \sqrt{\dfrac{RS}{\alpha + \dfrac{\beta}{R}}} = \sqrt{\dfrac{1}{\alpha + \dfrac{\beta}{R}}} \sqrt{RS}$, so that $c = \sqrt{\dfrac{1}{\alpha + \dfrac{\beta}{R}}}$.

The coefficients α and β were deduced, largely by graphic processes, from the results of the measurements of flow. The expression $RS = \left(\alpha + \dfrac{\beta}{R}\right)v^2$, or $\dfrac{RS}{v^2} = \alpha + \dfrac{\beta}{R}$, is the equation of a straight line cq, Fig. 1, whose abscissæ are the values of $\dfrac{1}{R}$ and whose ordinates are those of $\dfrac{RS}{v^2}$, or $\dfrac{1}{c^2}$, which M. Bazin designated as A.

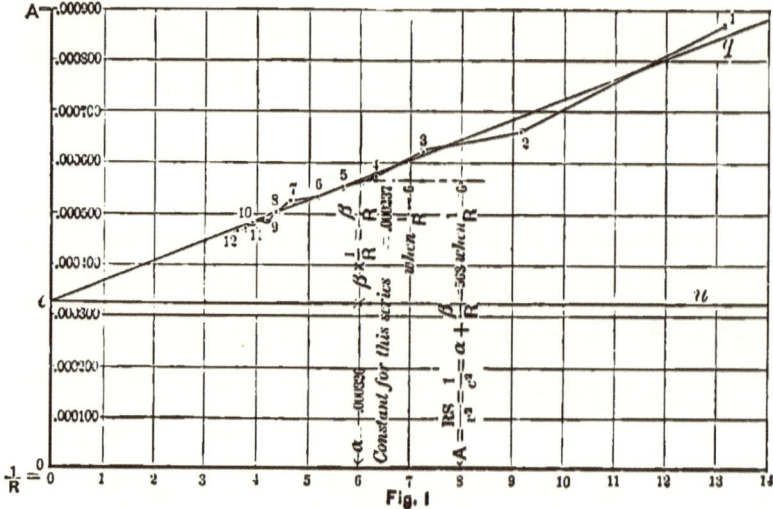

Fig. 1

Bazin's Series No. 4. Rectangular channel lined with fine gravel. Slope = .0049. Abscissæ and ordinates as follows:

Experiment No.	Abscissa $\dfrac{1}{R}$.	Ordinate $A = \dfrac{RS}{v^2} = \dfrac{1}{c^2} = \alpha + \dfrac{\beta}{R}$.
1	13.14	.000862
2	9.20	.000661
3	7.28	.000625
4	6.31	.000567
5	5.58	.000550
6	5.00	.000528
7	4.60	.000523
8	4.40	.000504
9	4.18	.000481
10	3.94	.000483
11	3.77	.000475
12	3.61	.000472

Plotting each series in this way, and drawing through its points a line *cq* averaging them as nearly as possible, the value of α is given by the distance *oc* from the axis of abscissæ to the point *c* where *cq* meets the axis of ordinates, while β is the tangent $\dfrac{A-\alpha}{\frac{1}{R}}$ of the angle *qcu*,* equal to that between the averaging line *cq* and the axis of abscissæ.

The experimental or "interpolated" coefficients thus obtained for the four categories are as follows:

Category.	Channels.	α for English Measure.	α for Metric Measure.	β
I.	{ Cement............ } { Carefully planed wood. }	.000046	.00015	.0000045
II.	{ Smooth ashlar......... } { Brick................ } { Unplaned wood........ }	.000058	.00019	.0000133
III.	Rubble masonry.......	.000073	.00024	.0000600
IV.	Earth	.000085	.00028	.0003500

With regard to the establishment of four categories, we may observe that still others might have been assumed if it had been considered necessary. For streams carrying detritus and boulders we have thought it well to add a fifth category, based upon a number of gaugings of such streams, viz.:

Category.	Channels.	α for English Measure.	α for Metric Measure.	β
V.	Carrying detritus and coarse gravel.......	.000122	.00040	.0007000

8. Humphreys and Abbot's Mississippi gaugings.

A few years before M. Bazin made his valuable researches, expert engineers in North America (chief among whom were Captain A. A. Humphreys and Lieut. L. H. Abbot) were engaged, by direction of their government, in ascertaining the extent and the physical characteristics of the region inundated

---

* Since the ordinates are plotted to a much larger scale than are the abscissæ, the angle is of course greatly exaggerated in the diagram.— *Trans.*

by the lower Mississippi, from the Ohio to below New Orleans, in order to elaborate a project for the regulation of the river and its tributaries.

The territory subject to overflow by the Mississippi, next to the largest stream in the world, has an area approximately equal to that of Germany or France.   Its bed has here a mean breadth of from 1000 to 1500 meters (3000 to 5000 feet), and a maximum depth of 45 meters (150 feet).   Below the mouth of the Ohio the difference i level between the extremes of high and low water reaches 15 meters (about 50 feet), and the maximum discharge is given at about 33,000 cubic meters (1,220,000 cubic feet) per second.

This "Commission" appeared to distrust the existing formulæ, and rightly considered it necessary to determine by direct observation the laws of flow in this river.   For about ten years, 1850–1860, it was occupied in collecting hydrometric, geological and physical data, as well as in surveying the territory.   The comparatively high mean velocity (about 2 meters, equal 6.6 feet, per second) of the colossal mass of water, and the extraordinarily great depths, rendered the investigations exceptionally difficult, but the American engineers accomplished them with the best results.   For the measurement of the velocities at a given point, at so great a depth below the surface as here occurred, Woltmann's tachometer (current-meter) would have been of as little service as Pitot's tube.   Double floats were therefore used, consisting of a light body floating upon the surface, and a heavier one suspended from it by a slender hempen cord and remaining at a fixed depth.

The line indicating the path of the float was determined by means of two theodolites, set up at the ends of a base line on shore, and the time in which the float passed over the given distance was accurately observed.   Lines for cross-sections were staked off in selected reaches where the flow was regular.   Each cross-section was divided by a number of vertical planes reaching from the surface to the bottom, and in each of these planes the velocity was repeatedly measured at various depths, until not the slightest doubt remained as to the accuracy of the results.   From the resulting mass of evidence the elements were obtained from which Humphreys and Abbot derived their new formula.

9. The velocities found to vary as the abscissæ of a parabola.

The results of these measurements were contrary to Guglielmi's theory. It appeared that the velocities in a longitudinal vertical plane, when represented as in Fig. 2 by horizon

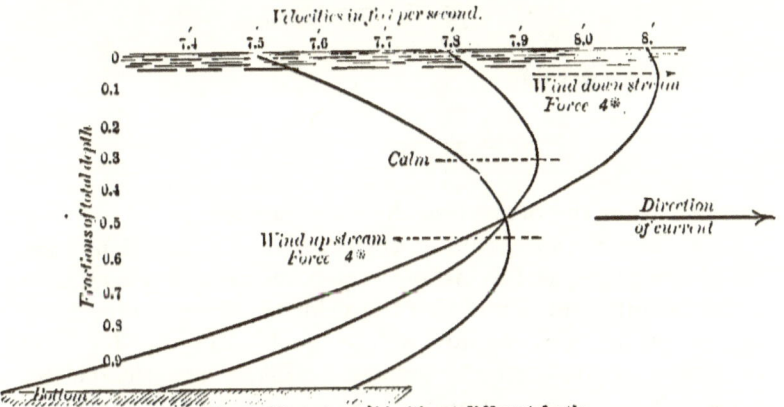

Fig. 2. *Mississippi Velocities at different depths.*
*The scale of wind-forces ranges from 0(calm)
to 10 (hurricane).*

tal lines drawn at their respective depths, form the abscissæ
of a parabolic curve, with its axis parallel to the surface and
situated at the depth of the maximum velocity. This depth,
when the air is still, is about 0.3 of the entire depth below the
surface. A down-stream wind brings the axis (or point of
greatest velocity) nearly to the surface, while with an up-stream
wind it is found below the mean depth. The velocities in horizontal planes also were found to give parabolic curves with
their vertices at the point of greatest velocity.

M. Bazin, and, still earlier, Boileau, Hennoque, Defontaine
and others, had already discovered that the velocities in a vertical plane decrease approximately in accordance with the law
of the parabola, and that the greatest velocity is found, as a
rule, somewhat below the surface.

10. The friction at the surface.

Humphreys and Abbot believed further that they had ascertained and could demonstrate, from the observed phenomena, that the water was exposed to as great a friction at the surface as at the wet perimeter of the cross-section. In their new formula, therefore, instead of the value

$$R = \frac{A}{P} = \frac{\text{area of cross-section}}{\text{wet perimeter}},$$

they placed the value

$$R_1 = \frac{A}{P + W},$$

in which W is the breadth of the water surface.

This assumption would be correct if it were found by careful observations, as for instance upon rectangular channels of equal breadth and depth, that the velocities at the bottom and at the surface were approximately equal. But the degree of roughness of the bottom must also be taken into account, because differences in this respect, as we have seen, exert a great influence upon the friction; an influence which cannot, in all cases, be just equal to that of the friction at the surface. But Humphreys and Abbot found the velocities greater at the surface than at the bottom; hence their assumption appears untenable. In regard to this matter M. Bazin also made very careful and thorough experiments, but without recognizing any influence of the air upon the flow of the water, i.e., he observed no retarding friction at the surface, although he states* that when the breadth and depth of the channel are equal, the greatest velocity is found at about mid-depth; from which we might conclude that in this case the equality of the surface and bottom velocities was due to the effect of the sides, and not to a surface friction equal to that at the bottom. However, such an influence of the air, if it exists, would not be

---

* " Recherches hydrauliques," p. 152.

so readily observed in small channels as in a stream like the Mississippi. M. Bazin nevertheless assumes, with Humphreys and Abbot, that the reduction of velocity at the surface may be due to effects caused by irregularities of the bottom and transmitted to the surface, where they appear as disturbing movements. But whether or not so marked an influence of this kind exists in the Mississippi we must leave in abeyance. It certainly is not impossible. The only effect of such an influence upon the formulæ is that the experimental coefficients must be arranged in accordance with it, and this has been done in the new formula of Humphreys and Abbot. For the method by which it was deduced, and for its mathematical development, we refer the reader to the original work of Humphreys and Abbot * to the German translation by Grebenau, entitled " Theorie der Bewegung des Wassers in Canälen und Flüssen, etc.," Munich, 1867, and to a French *résumé* by Fournie, Paris, 1867.

11. The new American formula.

The American formula of Humphreys and Abbot is as follows :*

For English measures.

$$v = \left(\sqrt{0.0081m + \sqrt{225R_1 \sqrt{S}}} - 0.09 \sqrt{m} \right)^2 ;$$

For metric measures,

$$v = \left(\sqrt{0.0025m + \sqrt{68.72R_1 \sqrt{S}}} - 0.05 \sqrt{m} \right)^2 ;$$

in which

$$m = \frac{1.69}{\sqrt{R} + 1.5}, \text{ for English measure,}$$

$$= \frac{0.933}{\sqrt{R} + 0.457}, \text{ for metric measure,}$$

$\left. \right\}$ in small streams ;

* " Report upon the Physics and Hydraulics of the Mississippi River," p. 312.

$m = 0.1856$ for English measure, ⎫ for rivers* whose mean
                                    ⎬   radius exceeds 12 or
   $= 0.1025$ for metric measure, ⎭   15 feet ;

$$R_1 = \frac{A}{P+W} .$$

If we omit from this complicated formula the two very small values at the beginning and at the end of the second member of the equation, and in the remaining middle term substitute $0.5R$ for R_1, which in most cases may be done without detriment, W being generally nearly $= P$, we obtain the much simpler formula for metric measure :

$$v = \beta \sqrt{68.72 \times 0.5R} \times \sqrt[4]{S},$$

or

$$v = \beta \, 5.86 \sqrt{R} \times \sqrt[4]{S};$$

or, still simpler,

$$v = k \sqrt{R} \sqrt[4]{S}.$$

In the last expression, k is $= 5.86\beta$, β being the coefficient of correction which takes the place of the two terms omitted from the second member of the equation, and varying, according to the value of R, only between 0.85 and 0.97 in metric measure, and between 1.54 and 1.76 in English measure.

This new American formula, adapted to the measurement of the Mississippi and its tributaries, agrees also with the results of careful gaugings by Grebenau of streams in Rhenish Bavaria, and in general with those obtained in cases where the slope is small.   But Humphreys and Abbot, and their transla-

---

* Humphreys and Abbot, in their Report, say: This makes the numerical value of the term involving b so small that, for any but theoretically small velocities, it may be neglected, thus reducing the equation to

$$v = \left(\sqrt[4]{225R_1} \sqrt{S} - .0388 \right)^2. \qquad —\text{Trans.}$$

tor Grebenau, desire that it should be tested also upon streams
with steep slopes. For this purpose we selected the " Wildbachschalen" near Lake Thun and the "Alpbachschale" at
Meiringen, and availed ourselves of occasions of considerable
discharge. The " Wildbachschalen" are channels of semicircular cross-section, built of rubble masonry, from 4 to 10
meters wide at the top and 150 to 500 meters long. They
were constructed to safely carry off the surplus water of floods,
together with boulders and rock fragments from the moun-
tains. Their very steep slope justified us in expecting a result which should be decisive as a test of the formula. Repeated measurements were carefully made in the summer of
1867 by means of floats, and the mean velocities determined in
accordance with M. Bazin's coefficients $\dfrac{v}{v_{max}}$, which vary with
the values of R and with the degree of roughness.[*]

The following table exhibits the observed mean velocities
in comparison with those obtained by means of the American
formula of Humphreys and Abbot. The fifth and sixth items
are from M. Bazin's measurements in the spillway of the Gros-
bois Reservoir, built of masonry and rectangular in form.

CHANNEL.	Slope, S.	Mean radius, R, in meters.	Velocity, in meters per second.	
			Observed.	By the American formula.
1. Grünnbachschale at Merligen.	0.083 to 0.107	0.108 to 0.197	3.6 to 5.8	0.9 to 1.3
2. Gerbebachschale at Merligen..	0.112 to 0.237	0.059	2.6 to 3.1	0.7 to 0.8
3. Gontenbachschale at Gonten..	0.042 to 0.046	0.098 to 0.112	2.9 to 3.3	0.7 to 0.8
4. Alpbachschale at Meiringen...	0.023 to 0.032	0.209 to 0.229	2.4 to 2.6	0.9 to 1.0
5. M. Bazin, Series No. 32...	0.101	0.100 to 0.202	3.7 to 6.4	0.9 to 1.3
6. M. Bazin, Series No. 33........	0.037	0.129 to 0.260	2.8 to 4.6	0.8 to 1.1

From a comprehensive investigation of the results of several hundred measurements, it appeared that the coefficient k
of the abbreviated American formula, which varies only between the extremes 5.0 and 5.7, should, in order to accord with

---

[*] See Appendix VII.— *Trans.*

the experimental results, vary between 5.0 and 33.0. It increases with increase of the slope. These results show ,that the formula of Humphreys and Abbot is not applicable to streams with steep slopes, as indeed became very evident from a comparison of a great number of Swiss and other measurements, notably those of M. Bazin.

The American formula is specially adapted to streams with a gentle slope, and is not to be recommended for general application. Nevertheless it is the outcome of most important studies, and will always retain its high value in its own field.

12. The American formula compared with that of M. Bazin. Variation of the coefficients.

In order to compare the American formula with that of M. Bazin, let us begin with the simple form $v = c\sqrt{RS}$, confining our attention to the velocity coefficient c.

From M. Bazin's formula,

$$v = \sqrt{\frac{RS}{\alpha + \dfrac{\beta}{R}}} \, ,$$

we have

$$c = \sqrt{\frac{1}{\alpha + \dfrac{\beta}{R}}} \, ;$$

while from the simplified formula of Humphreys and Abbot,

$$v = k\sqrt{R} \sqrt[4]{S},$$

we have

$$c = \frac{k}{\sqrt[4]{S}} \, .$$

Hence, according to M. Bazin's formula, c varies with the degree of roughness of the wetted perimeter and with the value of R. In Humphreys and Abbot's, on the contrary, c varies very slightly with the value of R, as already remarked, and also inversely with the fourth root of the slope.

13. Remarks on the two formulæ.

The measurements of M. Bazin were conducted with such care and precision that we should not be justified in entertaining any doubt as to the general correctness of their results. Similarly we must accept with confidence the results of the American observations, for when we consider the great difficulties to be overcome, the rational methods of procedure, and the very numerous repetitions of the measurements, we can hardly expect that results of much greater exactness will ever be obtained in such cases. Hagen[*] remarks that the gaugings of Humphreys and Abbot are among the best hydrometric records known, and are of special value in view of the great size of the river upon which they were made. We may state, however, that in such a stream the mean velocity cannot be obtained " within $\frac{1}{1000}$ of an inch;" an exactness of about one inch is as much as may be expected. In view of the great reliability of these two series of observations we cannot but be surprised at the divergence between the two formulæ respectively derived from them. It is, however, to be borne in mind that they spring, as it were, from extreme cases ; M. Bazin's investigations having been confined to small channels, where the effects of the different degrees of roughness of wet perimeter were very perceptible, while the American engineers experimented upon a great river, where these effects could not be observed, but where those due to a variation in slope were all the more evident. Humphreys and Abbot devote a very elaborate discussion to this feature of the case, and to the precise determination of the slope.

The two formulæ are not equally entitled to general application. That of M. Bazin is indeed as inapplicable to the Mississippi, as that of Humphreys and Abbot is to channels with steep slopes ; but it contains the basis of a formula which can

---

[*] Erbkam's Bauzeitung, 1868, vol. i. p. 63.

be generally applied, simply by introducing the effect of the change of slope, while the American formula cannot be thus generalized.

With regard to the coefficients α and β of M. Bazin's formula, we observe that there could be established between them, in connection with R, a relation remaining constant for all degrees of roughness, and thus rendering it possible to replace them by a *single* variable coefficient.

14. Summary of results.

The results of the latest investigations upon channels and streams with uniform flow of water may therefore be summed up in the following statements:

The coefficient c in the formula

$$v = c \sqrt{RS}$$

varies: (1) with the degree of roughness of the wetted perimeter, decreasing with the increase of the roughness ; (2) with the value of the mean radius R, increasing with its increase ; (3) with the slope, decreasing with its increase in large streams, and increasing with its increase in small channels. The latter feature is fully discussed farther on.

The formula of M. Bazin contains the first and second of these variations, while that of Humphreys and Abbot contains but one of the two variations with the slope noted under (3), and an almost imperceptible variation with R. Thus, both formulæ embrace but partially the variations which appear from the results of the investigations, and therefore neither is universally applicable. A general formula, however, is obtainable by taking proper account of all the observed forces affecting the flow.

15. The problem of establishing a generally applicable formula.

Basing our argument upon the above-established facts, we have endeavored, first, to construct a formula which shall satisfy the results of the measurements of M. Bazin as well as those of

Humphreys and Abbot, and then to introduce into it a single variable coefficient for the expression of the degree of roughness of the wet perimeter. In other words, we have tried to give for the several values of these degrees a mutual relation with the value of the mean radius R, and thus to express the universality of the influence of roughness upon the mean velocity of water flowing in channels of nearly uniform cross-section.

A formula in which the coefficient c is no longer constant, but is subject to many different variations, cannot be as simple as those heretofore in use. It should, however, remain as simple as possible. In this connection Bernard* remarks :

"As the physical conditions of rivers are not uniform, the formulæ which are employed to represent their flow must necessarily, if they are to be trustworthy, include all the observed irregularities. One can easily judge that a theory embracing so many factors must be unusually complex, and that it loses correctness and precision in proportion as it is simplified."

---

* " Nouveaux principes d'hydrauliques," p. 57.

PART II.

ESTABLISHMENT OF A GENERAL FORMULA FOR THE UNIFORM
FLOW OF WATER IN RIVERS AND OTHER CHANNELS.

16. Basis of the general formula.

Since the formula of M. Bazin possesses the characteristics
of a general formula, we have made it the basis of our own,
and have endeavored to embody in it the effects of the slope
as well as a relation between the coefficients of roughness.

17. Equations of three different hyperbolæ for determining the coefficient c in the formula $v = c\sqrt{RS}$.

Beginning with the fundamental formula, $v = c\sqrt{RS}$, and
seeking a fitting expression which shall determine the coefficient c^* and at the same time satisfy the above-named requirements, we obtain first, from the formula of M. Bazin,

$$v = \sqrt{\dfrac{RS}{\alpha + \dfrac{\beta}{R}}} = \sqrt{\dfrac{1}{\alpha + \dfrac{\beta}{R}}}\,\sqrt{RS},$$

the value

$$c = \sqrt{\dfrac{1}{\alpha + \dfrac{\beta}{R}}}\;;$$

---

*Our coefficient c coincides with the value $\dfrac{1}{\sqrt{A}}$ in M. Bazin's " Recherches
hydrauliques," where $\dfrac{RS}{v^2} = A$.

or, if we make $\frac{1}{\alpha} = y'$, and $\frac{\beta}{\alpha} = x'$,

$$c = \sqrt{\frac{y'}{1 + \frac{x'}{R}}} \quad \cdots \quad \cdots \quad (1)$$

But we might also express the value c by means of such formulæ as

$$c = \frac{y}{1 + \frac{x}{\sqrt{R}}} \quad \cdots \quad \cdots \quad *(2)$$

or

$$c = \frac{y''}{1 + \frac{x''}{R}} \quad \cdots \quad \cdots \quad (3)$$

This modification, however, is justifiable only if we obtain by means of formula (2) or (3) at least as correct results as by that of M. Bazin (1). Thorough investigations have shown that formula (2) really gives the value of c at least as correctly as that of M. Bazin, and better than formula (3).†

Each of the three formulæ is the equation of an equilateral hyperbola, i.e., of one whose asymptotes intersect at right angles. These hyperbolæ are referred to co-ordinates parallel with the asymptotes and pass through the origin of co-ordinates. The co-ordinates are :‡

---

* The authors, in the process of developing their formula, at first (p. 33) assumed y and x, y' and x', etc., to be constant quantities, and therefore designated them by a and b, a' and b', etc., until (p. 36) they were recognized as variables and then called y and x. To secure greater uniformity in notation, we have taken the liberty of using the letters y and x, etc., from the outset, as above; and as formula (2) is the one finally adopted, it has been given the letters without accents.—*Trans.*

† See Art. 19, p. 31.

‡ In Plate I, opposite p. 30, where the three formulæ are compared, the abscissæ are the values of R, and the ordinates those of c, the values of c ($= \sqrt{c^2}$) for formula (1) and those of R ($= \sqrt{R^2}$) for formula (2) having been calculated, in order that the comparison might be properly made.—*Trans.*

Formula (1): abscissæ R, ordinates c^2.

Formula (2): abscissæ $\sqrt{R}$, ordinates c.

Formula (3): abscissæ R, ordinates c.

In Fig. 3 we represent, by way of example, the hyperbola of formula (2). In it $dm = bh = y$ is the distance of the horizontal asymptote du' from the axis mp' of abscissæ, and

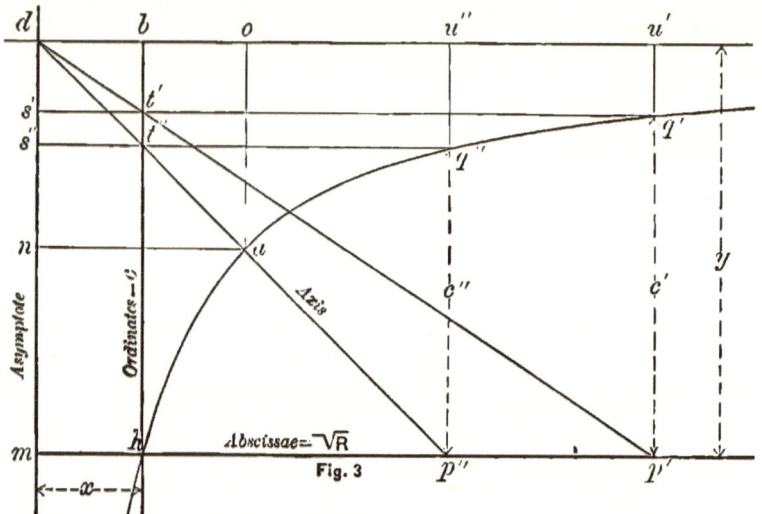

Fig. 3

$bd = hm = x$ is the distance of the vertical asymptote dm from the axis bh of ordinates. Thus, if we make $\sqrt{R} = \infty$, the corresponding value of c is $= dm = y$; and if $\sqrt{R} = -x$, then

$$c = \frac{y}{1 + \dfrac{x}{-x}} = \frac{y}{0} = \infty.$$ Let hp' be the abscissa, and $p'q' = c'$

the ordinate of a point q' in the hyperbola. If from the point a, in which the equilateral hyperbola is intersected by its axis dp'', we draw the perpendiculars an and ao to the asymptotes, we obtain, as is well known, a square $doan$, whose area is the constant which determines the equilateral hyperbola, haq', and is equal to the area of any rectangle comprised between the asymptotes and two perpendiculars drawn to them from any one given point in the hyperbola. For example, *doan = dblhm = du'q's'*. Hence, if we draw a straight line *dp'* from the intersection *d* of the asymptotes to any given point *p'* in the axis of abscissæ, then the point *t'*, in which *dp'* intersects the axis *bh* of ordinates, indicates the height of the ordinate *p'q' = c'* of the hyperbola at the point *p'*.* In this way an equilateral hyperbola may be easily constructed.

18. Comparison of the three formulæ.

We must now endeavor to ascertain which of the three formulæ, (1), (2) and (3), gives the smallest variations from the experimental values of *c*, and is therefore the most suitable.

The curves given by the formulæ for any series of gaugings must pass through the origin of co-ordinates, *h*, Fig. 4, and through at least two of the experimental values of *c* in that series, and will depart more or less from the remaining ones. Let *c'* and *c''* represent the two given values of *c*, and let *R'* and *R''* represent the corresponding values of *R*. From the general expression

$$c = \frac{y}{1 + \dfrac{x}{R}}$$

(in which, for the present comparison, *c* gives the values of c^2 or *c*, and *R* the values of *R* or $\sqrt{R}$) we thus obtain the following equations for the values of *y* and *x* in the three formulæ†:

$$x = \frac{c'^2 - c''^2}{\dfrac{c''^2}{R''} - \dfrac{c'^2}{R'}} \quad \text{and} \quad y = c'^2\left(1 + \frac{x}{R'}\right); \quad . \quad . \quad (1)$$

---

* *Demonstration.*—Since $du'' \times ds'' = du' \times ds'$, we have

$du' : du'' = mp' : mp'' = ds'' : ds' = bt'' : bt' = u''q'' : u'q' = y - c'' : y - c'$.

We see, also, that $c' = y - ds' = y - y \times \dfrac{s't'}{mp'} = y - y \times \dfrac{x}{\sqrt{R} + x}$;

or, multiplying and dividing by $1 + \dfrac{x}{\sqrt{R}}$,

$$c' = \frac{y}{1 + \dfrac{x}{\sqrt{R}}} ,$$

as in equation (2).

† See demonstration on next page.

† *Demonstration.*—In Fig. 4 let

$y =$ the vertical distance from the axis of abscissæ to the horizontal asymptote;
$x =$ the horizontal distance from the axis of ordinates to the vertical asymptote.

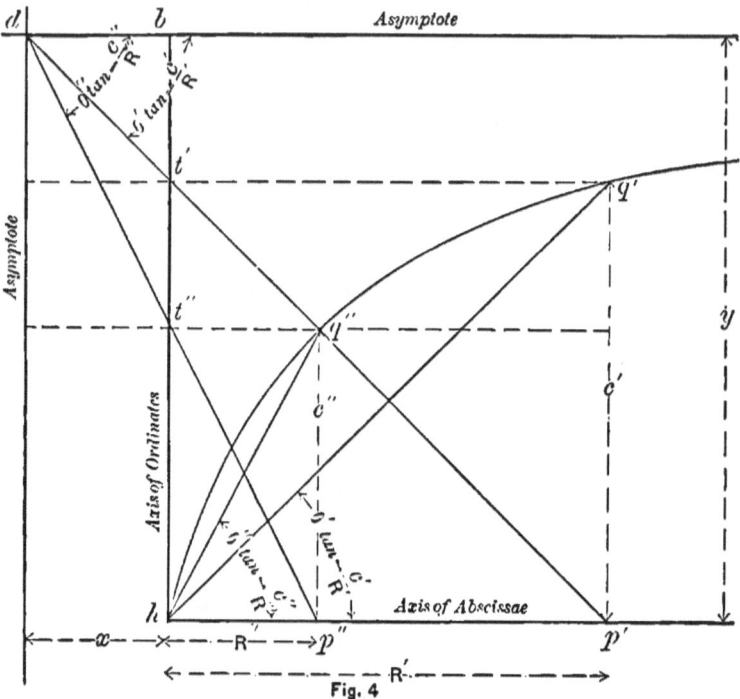

Fig. 4

From the origin of co-ordinates, h, draw hq'' and hq' through the two points q'' and q', which correspond to the given values, c'' and c', of c, and through which the hyperbola is to pass. These lines form respectively with the axis of abscissæ, angles θ'' $\left(\text{tangent} = \dfrac{c''}{R''}\right)$ and θ' $\left(\text{tangent} = \dfrac{c'}{R'}\right)$. Now if lines dp'' and dp' be drawn from the center d to the points p'' and p', whose abscissæ are respectively R'' and R', they will form the same angles with the horizontal asymptote, viz., θ'' $\left(\text{tangent} = \dfrac{c''}{R''}\right)$ and θ' $\left(\text{tangent} = \dfrac{c'}{R'}\right)$.

From the figure, we have

$$x = bd = \frac{bt''}{\tan \theta''} = \frac{bt'}{\tan \theta'} = \frac{bt''}{\dfrac{c''}{R''}} = \frac{bt'}{\dfrac{c'}{R'}} = \frac{bt'' - bt'}{\dfrac{c''}{R''} - \dfrac{c'}{R'}} = \frac{c' - c''}{\dfrac{c''}{R''} - \dfrac{c'}{R'}}.$$

And, since $c = \dfrac{y}{1 + \dfrac{x}{R}}$,
$\qquad y = c \left(1 + \dfrac{x}{R}\right) = c' \left(1 + \dfrac{x}{R'}\right)$ \qquad —*Trans.*

$$x = \frac{c' - c''}{\dfrac{c''}{\sqrt{R''}} - \dfrac{c'}{\sqrt{R'}}} \quad \text{and} \quad y = c'\left(1 + \frac{x}{\sqrt{R'}}\right); \quad \cdot \quad (2)$$

$$x = \frac{c' - c''}{\dfrac{c''}{R''} - \dfrac{c'}{R'}} \quad \text{and} \quad y = c'\left(1 + \frac{x}{R'}\right); \quad \cdot \cdot \quad (3)$$

or, in general, for all three formulæ:

$$x = \frac{c' - c''}{\dfrac{c''}{R''} - \dfrac{c'}{R'}} \quad \text{and} \quad y = c'\left(1 + \frac{x}{R'}\right).$$

19. Demonstration that formula (2) gives at least as correct results as M. Bazin's formula (1).

In the following table the values of c obtained by the three formulæ on page 25, from eight of M. Bazin's series of gaugings, are compared with each other and with the actual value of c deduced from the experiments. Plate I shows graphically the same comparison for six of the series.

COMPARISON OF THE THREE FORMULÆ,

$$(1)\ldots c = \sqrt{\frac{y}{1 + \frac{x}{R}}} \; , \quad (2)\ldots c = \frac{y}{1 + \frac{x}{\sqrt{R}}} \; , \quad (3)\ldots c = \frac{y''}{1 + \frac{x''}{R}} \; ,$$

with the results of eight of M. Bazin's series of gaugings.

Series No.	Actual Gauging.	Formula (1).		Formula (2).		Formula (3).	
	c	c	Difference.	c	Difference.	c	Difference.
24	73.0	73.0	0.0	73.0	0.0	73.0	0.0
	76.8	77.6	+ 0.8	77.2	+ 0.4	77.8	+ 1.0
	78.2	80.0	+ 0.8	79.7	+ 1.5	80.1	+ 1.9
	81.4	81.4	0.0	81.2	− 0.2	81.5	+ 0.1
	82.2	82.5	+ 0.3	82.4	+ 0.2	82.6	+ 0.4
	83.3	83.3	0.0	83.3	0.0	83.3	0.0
	83.1	84.0	+ 0.9	84.1	+ 1.0	83.9	+ 0.8
	84.3	84.6	+ 0.3	84.7	+ 0.4	84.4	+ 0.1
	86.4	84.9	− 1.5	85.2	− 1.2	84.7	− 1.7
	86.9	85.2	− 1.7	85.7	− 1.2	85.1	− 1.8
	87.4	85.6	− 1.8	86.1	− 1.3	85.4	− 2.0
	87.9	85.7	− 2.2	86.2	− 1.7	85.5	− 2.4
			10.3		9.1		12.2

COMPARISON OF THE THREE FORMULÆ—*Continued.*

| Series No. | Actual Gauging. | Values of the Coefficient c, for Metric Measure, according to— | | | | | |
| | | Formula (1). | | Formula (2). | | Formula (3). | |
	c	c	Difference.	c	Difference.	c	Difference.
2	63.3	63.3	0.0	63.3	0.0	63.3	0 0
	68.0	67.7	− 0.3	67.7	− 0.9	68.0	0.0
	69.0	70.0	+ 1.0	69.2	+ 0.2	70.3	+ 0.3
	71.9	71.2	− 0.7	70.5	− 1.4	71.5	− 0.4
	71.9	72.2	+ 0.3	71.6	− 0.3	72.4	+ 0.5
	73.4	72.9	− 0.5	72.4	− 1.0	73.1	− 0.3
	73.6	73.5	− 0.1	73.0	− 0.6	73.6	0.0
	74.0	73.9	− 0.1	73 5	− 0.5	74.0	0.0
	74.5	74.3	− 0.2	74.0	− 0.5	74.3	− 0.2
	74.5	74.6	+ 0.1	74.4	− 0.1	74.6	+ 0.1
	74.9	74.8	− 0.1	74.8	− 0.1	74.9	0.0
	75.1	75.1	0.0	75.1	0.0	75.1	0.0
			3.4		5.6		1.8
26	59.4	59.4	0.0	59.4	0.0	59.4	0.0
	62.9	64.2	+ 1.3	63.7	+ 0.8	64.5	+ 1.6
	66.5	66.4	− 0.1	65.7	− 0.8	66.6	+ 0.3
	67.9	68.1	+ 0.2	67.6	− 0.3	68.5	+ 0.6
	68.0	69.4	+ 1.4	68.9	+ 0.9	69.7	+ 1.7
	69.5	70.3	+ 0.8	69.9	+ 0.4	70.6	+ 1.1
	68.8	71.1	+ 2.3	70.7	+ 1.9	71.3	+ 2.5
	70.7	71.6	+ 0.9	71.3	+ 0.6	71.8	+ 1.1
	70.7	72.2	+ 1.5	71.9	+ 1.2	72.3	+ 1.6
	72.0	72.6	+ 0.6	72.4	+ 0.4	72.7	+ 0.7
	72.0	73.0	+ 1.0	72.9	+ 0.9	73.0	+ 1.0
	73.1	73.3	+ 0.2	73.2	+ 0.1	73.3	+ 0.2
	73.5	73.5	0.0	73.5	0.0	73.5	0.0
			10.3		8.3		12.4
6	49.8	49.8	0.0	49.8	0.0	49.8	0.0
	52.3	54.8	+ 2.5	53.8	+ 1.5	54.7	+ 2.4
	55.0	57.3	+ 2.3	56.6	+ 1.6	57.7	+ 2.7
	57.0	58.9	+ 1.9	58.2	+ 1.2	59.3	+ 2.3
	57.2	60.2	+ 2.8	59.5	+ 2.3	60.4	+ 3.2
	60.2	60.8	+ 0.6	60.3	+ 0.1	61.1	+ 0.9
	60.7	61.9	+ 1.2	61.5	+ 0.8	62.1	+ 1.4
	60.7	62.2	+ 1 5	61.7	+ 1.0	62.3	+ 1.6
	61.9	62.6	+ 0.7	62.3	+ 0.4	62.6	+ 0.7
	62.2	63.0	+ 0.8	62.8	+ 0.6	62.8	+ 0.6
	63.7	63.2	− 0.5	63.2	− 0.5	63.0	− 0.7
	63.6	63.6	0.0	63.6	0.0	63.6	0.0
			14.8		10.0		16.5

PLATE I.

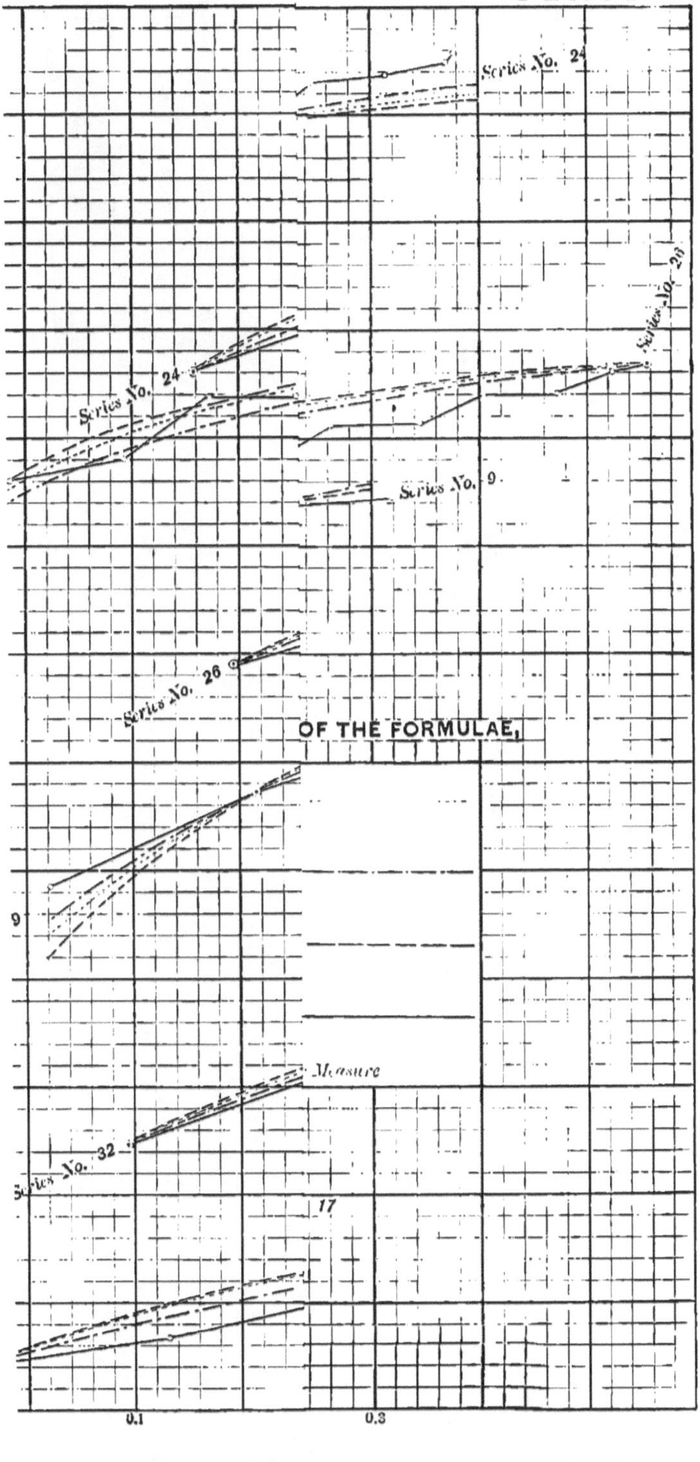

Series No. 24

Series No. 28

Series No. 24

Series No. 9

Series No. 26

OF THE FORMULAE,

9

Measure

Series No. 32

17

0.1   0.3

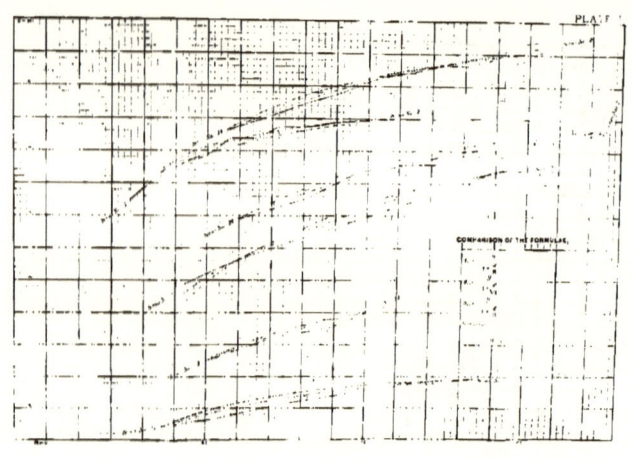

COMPARISON OF THE FORMULAE.

COMPARISON OF THE THREE FORMULÆ.—*Continued.*

Series No.	Actual Gauging.	Values of the Coefficient c, for Metric Measure, according to—					
		Formula (1).		Formula (2).		Formula (3).	
	c	c	Difference.	c	Difference.	c	Difference.
9	49.3	47.2	− 2.1	47.9	− 1.4	46.2	− 3.1
	53.7	53.7	0.0	53.7	0.0	53.7	0.0
	58.2	59.9	+ 1.7	59.5	+ 1.3	60.2	+ 2.0
	61.6	63.0	+ 1.4	62.7	+ 1.1	63.3	+ 1.7
	64.2	65.0	+ 0.8	64.9	+ 0.7	65.2	+ 1.0
	66.5	66.5	0.0	66.5	0.0	66.5	0.0
	67.2	67.8	+ 0.6	67.9	+ 0.7	67.6	+ 0.4
			6.6		5.2		8.2
32	37.5	37.5	0.0	37.5	0.0	37.5	0.0
	41.2	41.5	+ 0.3	41.4	+ 0.2	41.7	+ 0.5
	42.7	43.8	+ 1.1	43.7	+ 1.0	43.9	+ 1.2
	45.1	45.1	0.0	45.1	0.0	45.1	0.0
			1.4		1.2		1.7
33	39.9	39.9	0.0	39.9	0.0	39.9	0.0
	44.9	43.9	+ 2.0	43.8	+ 1.9	44.1	+ 2.2
	45.1	45.8	+ 0.7	45.6	+ 0.5	45.9	+ 0.8
	47.0	47.0	0.0	47.0	0.0	47.0	0.0
			2.7		2.4		3.0
17	26.9	26.9	0.0	26.9	0.0	26.9	0.0
	28.3	29.8	+ 1.5	29.4	+ 1.1	29.9	+ 1.6
	30.8	32.0	+ 1.2	31.6	+ 0.8	32.1	+ 1.3
	32.3	33.1	+ 0.8	32.8	+ 0.5	33.2	+ 0.9
	33.4	33.8	+ 0.4	33.6	+ 0.2	33.9	+ 0.5
	34.0	34.3	+ 0.3	34.2	+ 0.2	34.3	+ 0.3
	34.7	34.7	0.0	34.7	0.0	34.7	0.0
			4.2		2.8		4.6

TOTALS OF DIFFERENCES.

24			10.3		9.1		12.2
2			3.4		5.6		1.8
26			10.3		8.3		12.4
6			14.8		10.0		16.5
9			6.6		5.2		8.2
32			1.4		1.2		1.7
33			2.7		2.4		3.0
17			4.2		2.8		4.6
	Totals..		53.7		44.6		60.4

From the totals of these differences between the actual values of c and those obtained from the three formulæ, it appears that No. (2), from which our principal formula is derived, gives the best results, at least for the eight series here compared, as shown also by the graphic representation in Plate I. In a few cases, however, for instance in series Nos. 3, 10 and 21, formula (1) gives better results than (2).

We remark here that our series of values for c do not always agree with M. Bazin's corresponding series of values for $\dfrac{1}{\sqrt{A}}$ *. The discrepancies are due to the following circumstance : With respect to the tables on page 353 *et seq.* of his work, the headings " Calcul des principaux éléments de chaque expérience pour la partie du courant comprise entre les profils No. ... et No. ..." (principal elements of each experiment for the section between stations No. ... and No. ...), inform us which stretch of channel was selected in each case, in order to use the most nearly uniform flow observed, for the determination of these principal elements. Now it seemed to us that for this purpose we should use the slopes of these selected lengths rather than the average slope of the entire canal, from which M. Bazin deduced his values of $\dfrac{1}{\sqrt{A}}$ or c. We therefore calculated from the given level readings upon the bottom, at the respective stations, the slopes of the water surfaces between them, and from these slopes, from the values of R and from the observed mean velocities v, we obtained the values of c by the formula $c = \dfrac{v}{\sqrt{RS}}$.

---

* " Recherches hydrauliques," pages 330 to 350.

20. Relation between the coefficients of roughness, and their connection with the mean radius R. General applicability of the formula.

In M. Bazin's formula

$$v = \sqrt{\dfrac{RS}{\alpha + \dfrac{\beta}{R}}}$$

the values α and β, as we have seen, have been specially determined for each of the four categories of roughness, but no general mutual relation between them was established. It would seem, however, to be natural and proper to assume such a relation. But one variable coefficient would then be introduced, and the formula would thus be rendered more generally applicable. Mr. Gauckler[*] makes the same demand upon a formula of this kind, when he remarks that a formula with coefficients varying with the degree of roughness of wetted perimeter, and at the same time with the mean hydraulic depth R, is not satisfactory, but rather proves that its general form does not correspond with observed phenomena. He holds that a simple algebraical relation exists; that a single coefficient, varying with the degree of roughness and having a certain relation to R, can be introduced, and that the natural phenomenon of the movement of water is thereby stated in its full universality.

It was our purpose, at first, to proceed upon the assumption that the value y in the formula

$$c = \dfrac{y \cdot}{1 + \dfrac{x}{\sqrt{R}}}$$

was constant, or independent of the degree of roughness, and to express the variation of x by means of the function $x = ny$, or $x = n^2 y$ (n designating the *nature* of the surface); so that

---

[*] " Etudes théoriques et pratiques sur le mouvement des eaux," page 232. Annales des ponts et chaussées, 1868.

when $R = \infty$, the effect of variation in roughness should become zero, the desired relation between R and the degree of roughness being thus established. Under this assumption, the hyperbolæ, hk', hk'', hk''', etc., Fig. 5, whose ordinates give

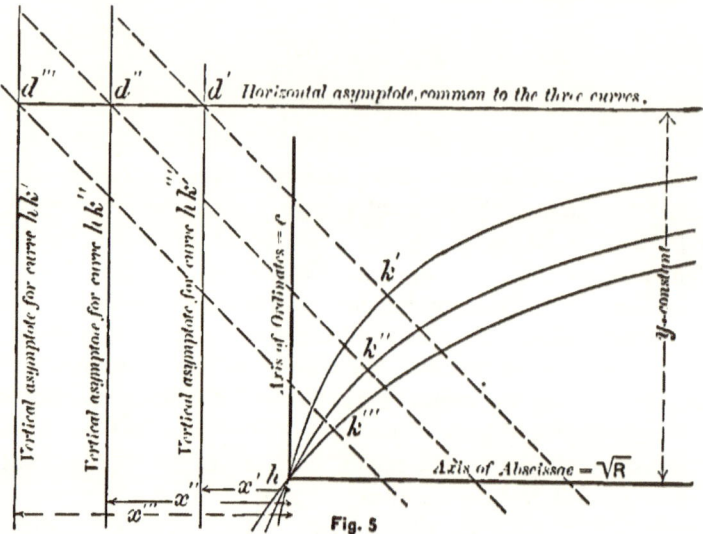

Fig. 5

the values of c for three series of gaugings, while they have different vertical asymptotes (x varying with the degree n of roughness) have a common horizontal asymptote, $d'''d'$.

In order to test the correctness of this assumption, we made use of the following graphic process:

From the formula

$$c = \frac{y}{1 + \dfrac{x}{\sqrt{R}}}$$

we have, dividing by y.

$$c = \frac{1}{\dfrac{1}{y} + \dfrac{x}{y}\dfrac{1}{\sqrt{R}}}$$

and, taking the reciprocals of these values,

$$\frac{1}{c} = \frac{1}{y} + \frac{x}{y} \cdot \frac{1}{\sqrt{R}}.$$

This is the equation of a straight line cq, Fig. 6, whose abscissæ are the values of $\dfrac{1}{\sqrt{R}}$, whose ordinates are the values of $\dfrac{1}{c}$, and in which $\dfrac{1}{y}$ is the distance oe between the axis of abscissæ

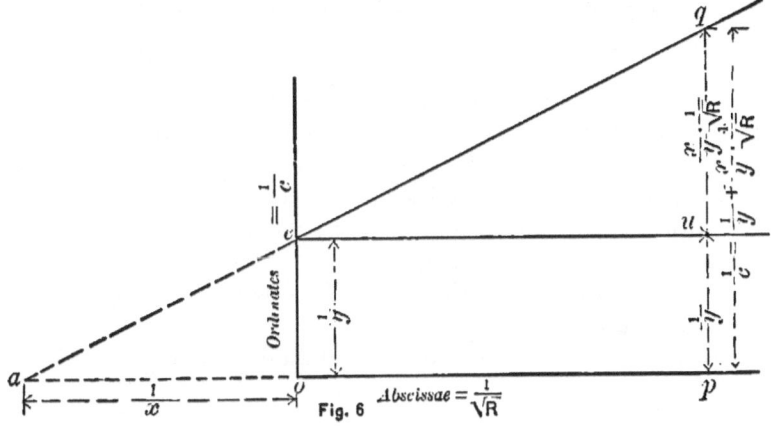

Fig. 6 $Abscissae = \dfrac{1}{\sqrt{R}}$

and the point e where the straight line cq intersects the axis of ordinates.

Also,

$$\frac{\dfrac{1}{c} - \dfrac{1}{y}}{\dfrac{1}{\sqrt{R}}} = \frac{\dfrac{1}{y}}{\dfrac{1}{x}} = \frac{x}{y} \,,$$

which is the tangent of the angle qap at a.[*]

---

[*] If, therefore, we take $\dfrac{1}{\sqrt{R}} = op$, we have

$$\frac{x}{y} \cdot \frac{1}{\sqrt{R}} = uq, \text{ and}$$

$$\frac{1}{c} = \frac{1}{y} + \frac{x}{y} \cdot \frac{1}{\sqrt{R}} = pu + uq = pq.$$

— *Trans.*

We plotted the experimental results of M. Bazin, taking the values of $\dfrac{1}{\sqrt{R}}$ as abscissæ and those of $\dfrac{1}{c}$ as ordinates; and through the points so obtained for each series, having a uniform slope and character of bed, we drew a straight line, averaging them as nearly as possible and corresponding to cq in Fig. 6.

We proceeded in the same way with a number of series of gaugings of the Seine, Saône, Weser, Rhine-delta in Holland, Linth Canal, etc. If our assumption were correct, the averaging lines should intersect the axis of ordinates at one and the same height, indicating a common value of $\dfrac{1}{y}$ for all the gaugings. This, however, was not the case. On the contrary, the straight lines cut the axis of ordinates at very different heights. In particular, the lines representing experiments upon flow in rivers differed widely in this respect from those for artificial channels, especially when the latter had a smooth perimeter.

We thus found that the value of y could not be constant, but that it must vary with x.

In order to establish a mutual relation between the values y and x, we might put

$$y = \frac{a}{\sqrt{n}} \quad \text{and} \quad x = ny = a\sqrt{n},$$

or

$$y = \frac{a}{n} \quad \text{and} \quad x = n^2 y = an,$$

in which expressions the coefficient a is constant and n varies with the degree of roughness. But repeated trials finally induced us to assume the following relation, as best meeting the requirements of the case :

$$y = a + \frac{l}{n} \quad \text{and} \quad x = an = ny - l,$$

in which a and l are constant, and n is the only variable.

We thus obtain, neglecting for the present the influence of the slope, the formula

$$c = \frac{y}{1 + \dfrac{x}{\sqrt{R}}} = \frac{a + \dfrac{l}{n}}{1 + \dfrac{an}{\sqrt{R}}} \quad \ldots \ldots \quad (4)$$

Farther on we shall justify this expression and the introduction of the value l in the formula.

We shall endeavor by means of Fig. A on Plate V to show graphically the construction of the formula.

Let bg, on the axis bh' of ordinates, represent the constant value a, and $h'i' = gk$, on any one of the axes of abscissæ, the constant value l. Through the point g draw straight lines, forming, with the axis of ordinates, angles whose tangents are $n', n'', n''', n''''.*$ Extend these straight lines to the vertical line $i'k$ and to the horizontal line pq; and through the points i', i'', i''', i'''', draw horizontal lines cutting the axis bh' of ordinates in the points h', h'', h''', h''''. We thus obtain, for example, for four degrees of roughness of wetted perimeter,

$$\text{tang} (gi'k) = \text{tang} (bgd') = n',$$
$$\text{tang} (gi''k) = \text{tang} (bgd'') = n'',$$
$$\text{tang} (gi'''k) = \text{tang} (bgd''') = n''',$$
$$\text{tang} (gi''''k) = \text{tang} (bgd'''') = n'''';$$

further,

$$gh' = \frac{l}{n'},$$

$$gh'' = \frac{l}{n''},$$

$$gh''' = \frac{l}{n'''},$$

$$gh'''' = \frac{l}{n''''}.$$

---

* For the coefficient n, in any given case, the authors take the quotient arising from dividing a fixed value l, of $\sqrt{R}$ by the special value c_l, of c for the given degree of roughness and for the value of $\sqrt{R}$ corresponding to l, so that $n = \dfrac{l}{c_l}$. Since the value of c for any value of $\sqrt{R}$ (and therefore the value c_l for $\sqrt{R} = l$) decreases when the roughness increases, the above quotient varies with the roughness and thus forms a proper measure for it.—*Trans.*

Hence we have the values of y corresponding to the four assumed degrees of roughness

$$y' = a + \frac{l}{n'} \quad = bg + gh' \quad = bh',$$

$$y'' = a + \frac{l}{n''} = bg + gh'' \quad = bh'',$$

$$y''' = a + \frac{l}{n'''} = bg + gh''' = bh''',$$

$$y'''' = a + \frac{l}{n''''} = bg + gh'''' = bh'''';$$

and finally the corresponding values of x,

$$x' = an' \quad = bd',$$
$$x'' = an'' \quad = bd'',$$
$$x''' = an''' \quad = bd''',$$
$$x'''' = an'''' = bd''''.$$

The horizontal lines passing through the points h', h'', h''', h'''', are the axes of abscissæ of the four equilateral hyperbolæ* $h'k$, $h''k$, $h'''k$, $h''''k$, whose ordinates give the values of c for the four assumed degrees of roughness, n', n'', n''', n''''; and the points d', d'', d''', d'''' are the centers of these hyperbolæ, or the intersections of their asymptotes. The hyperbolæ pass respectively through the origins h', h'', h''', h'''', of co-ordinates and through the common point k.

21. The effect of variation of the slope upon that of the coefficient c.

We have thus found that in our formula (4),

$$c = \frac{y}{1 + \frac{x}{\sqrt{R}}} = \frac{a + \frac{l}{n}}{1 + \frac{an}{\sqrt{R}}},$$

the values of y and x vary with the degree of roughness of wetted perimeter, a variation which is also embodied in M.

---

* To avoid crowding the figure, we show only the upper and lower hyperbolæ, $h''''k$ and $h'k$.—*Trans.*

Bazin's formulæ, yet without any relation between the corresponding coefficients. But in the above formula we have not yet expressed the influence of the slope upon the variation of the coefficient c.

From the observations on the Mississippi, its tributaries, etc., it appears that the value c increases with a decreasing slope. The results of the gaugings are given in the following table,* in which we have included also the deduced values of

$$c = \frac{v}{\sqrt{RS}} .$$

HUMPHREYS AND ABBOT'S MISSISSIPPI GAUGINGS,

Showing increase of c with *decrease* of slope.

(Metric measure.)

Number of Observation.		Locality.	Mean Radius, R.	Slope, S.	Mean Velocity. v.	c.
G. & K.'s Nos.	H. & A.'s Nos.					
1	8	Vicksburg, Miss............	9.407	.00000227	1.074	73 9
2	9	"	15 886	.00003029	1.694	77.2
3	10	"	17.484	.00004811	1.926	66 4
4	6	"	19.538	.00006170	2.118	60 0
5	7	"	19 666	.00004305	2.080	71.0
6	5	Columbus, Ky.	20.081	.00006800	2.121	57.4
7	1	Carrolton, La.............	21.953	.00002051	1 807	85.1
8	2	"	22.085	.00001713	1.794	92.7
9	3	"	22.413	.00000342	1.229	140.4
10	4	"	22 673	.00000384	1.212	129.9

Selecting those of the Mississippi gaugings having approximately equal values of R (Nos. 4 to 10 inclusive), we plotted the values of S as abscissæ and those of c as ordinates, Fig. 7, and obtained a curve convex toward the axis of abscissæ, and closely resembling an equilateral hyperbola.

On the other hand, M. Bazin's results, especially those of the comparable series Nos. 6 to 11,† and also those of the comparable series Nos. 32 and 33, 3 and 39, 21 and 22, etc.,† exhibit

---

* For more extended data, in English measure, concerning the Mississippi gaugings, see Appendix, Table I.—*Trans.*

† For extended data, in English measure, see Appendix, Table I.—*Trans.*

an influence of the variation of slope upon the variation of c which is the reverse of that just noticed in the case of the Mississippi: namely, an increase instead of a decrease of c

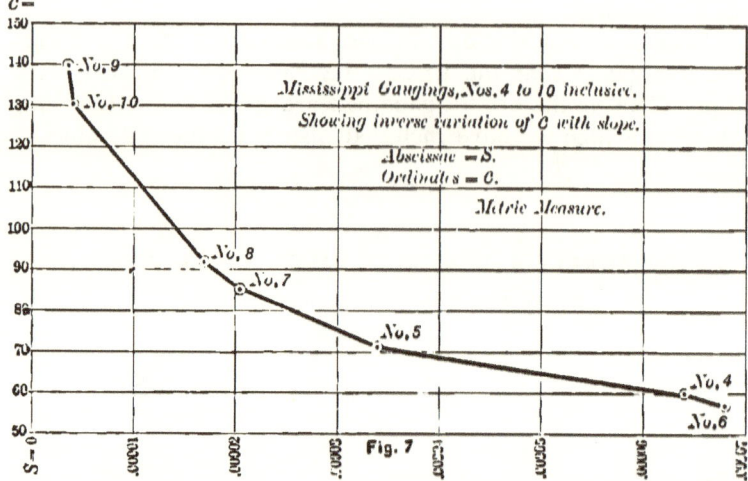

with increase of slope, as will appear, for instance, from the results of two series given in the following table, in which we have included, as before, the values of $c = \dfrac{v}{\sqrt{RS}}$

BAZIN'S SERIES Nos. 6 and 8,

Showing increase of c with *increase* of slope.

(Metric measure.)

SERIES No. 6.				SERIES No. 8.			
R	S	v	c	R	S	v	c
0.073	0.002214	0.635	47.8	0.045	0.008163	1.074	56.2
0.111	"	0.319	52.3	0.070	"	1.348	56.3
0.133	"	0.962	55.0	0.088	"	1.594	59.4
0.161	"	1.076	57.0	0.104	"	1.776	60.9
0.183	"	1.152	57.2	0.120	"	1.902	60.8
0.198	"	1.259	60.2	0.131	"	2.053	62.7
0.215	"	1.324	60.7	0.142	"	2.186	64.2
0.231	"	1.374	60.7	0.154	"	2.268	63.9
0.244	"	1.440	61.9	0.165	"	2.357	64.2
0.258	"	1.487	62.2	0.174	"	2.447	64.8
0.268	"	1.552	63.7	0.184	"	2.518	64.9
0.281	"	1.587	63.6	0.192	"	2.612	66.0

If we plot the values c for six similar values of R of the six comparable series Nos. 6 to 11 (rectangular channels lined with boards) as ordinates, and the slopes S as abscissæ, the points representing equal values of R form curves concave toward the axis of abscissæ.

In Fig. 8 are shown those corresponding to $R = .73$ to .88.

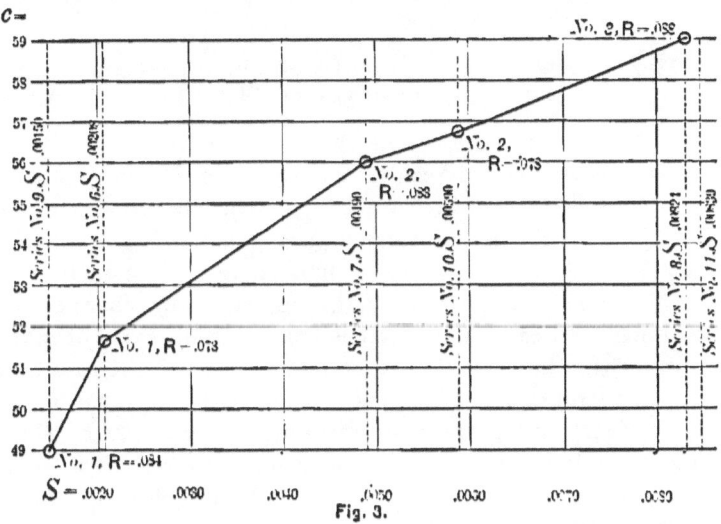

Fig. 8.

M. Bazin has indeed demonstrated this effect, but he did not regard it as of sufficient moment to require recognition in his formula. Upon this point he expresses himself as follows:[*]

"The form $\alpha + \dfrac{\beta}{R}$ is superior to the form $\alpha + \dfrac{\beta}{v}$,[†] because the two coefficients vary inversely as the slope; i.e., when S is increased α also increases, but β, on the contrary, diminishes. A sort of compensation is therefore established by which the formulæ for various slopes, though apparently differing, never-

---

[*] "Recherches hydrauliques," page 91.
[†] This form through v includes the slope.—*Trans.*

theless give almost identical values for A* within the ordinary limits of application, and consequently they can conveniently be replaced by a single formula with average coefficients."

If, however, in channels of exactly similar character and dimensions, but of different slopes, the value c increases with increase of slope, the formula should, we think, contain such a variation, provided it is recognized as a dominant one, as the results of series Nos. 6 to 11 and others appear to justify.

22. The nature of the influence of change of slope upon the variation of the coefficient c.

The effect of slope upon the variation of c presents, as regards the Mississippi results and those of M. Bazin, an apparent contradiction, which we are as little able to explain by natural laws as the much more surprising paradox contained in series Nos. 28 and 29, where at first there was an increase of the value c with that of the fall, and, after the channel had been lined with canvas, an increase of c with decrease of fall.

From what has just been said, and in view of the results of the latest gaugings, we are justified in assuming that in the case of rivers the value c increases with a *decrease* of slope, while in small channels c increases with an *increase* of slope. In Art. 26 we shall discuss the whereabouts of the point of transition from one system to the other.†

23. Establishment of the general formula.

In order to satisfy the condition that the coefficient c in large streams shall decrease with increase of slope, we must devise a formula which, when the slopes S are taken as abscissæ and the values of c as ordinates, shall give the equation of a curve convex toward the axis of abscissæ. We have already observed, in Art. 21, that such of the Mississippi gaug-

---

* A represents the value $\dfrac{R.S}{v^2}$, and $\dfrac{1}{\sqrt{A}}$ the coefficient c.—*Trans.*

† See footnote at beginning of Appendix II.

ings as are comparable for this purpose* correspond to such a curve. In our formula (4),

$$c = \frac{y}{1 + \dfrac{x}{\sqrt{R}}} ,$$

if $R = \infty$, c becomes $= y$. The variation of the coefficient y with the slope must therefore follow a similarly curved hyperbola ; and we are justified in assuming for y an expression of the form

$$y = y_1 + \frac{m}{S} ,$$

in which y_1 is the value $a + \dfrac{l}{n}$ given to y in Art. 20. where the effect of S is neglected, and in which m is a coefficient to be referred to presently. We thus obtain

$$y = a + \frac{l}{n} + \frac{m}{S} ;$$

and by substituting this value in the formula, $x = ny - l$, Art. 20, we obtain further

$$x = n\left(a + \frac{l}{n} + \frac{m}{S}\right) - l$$
$$= \left(a + \frac{m}{S}\right)n.$$

Substituting these values of y and x in formula (4), we obtain, for c, the general formula

$$c = \frac{a + \dfrac{l}{n} + \dfrac{m}{S}}{1 + \left(a + \dfrac{m}{S}\right)\dfrac{n}{\sqrt{R}}} \quad . \quad . \quad . \quad . \quad . \quad (5)$$

---

* Nos. 4 to 10, because they have nearly the same mean radius, R.—*Trans.*

As already observed, the effect of variation of slope upon the variation of c in smaller streams is the reverse of that just noticed. For the discussion of the transition from one of these effects to the opposite one, and for the determination of the constant values a, l and m in the expression

$$y = a + \frac{l}{n} + \frac{m}{S} ,$$

we can find the necessary data by examining the relation between the Mississippi results and those of other streams.

24. Relation between the Mississippi results and those obtained from other streams, with regard to the influence of the variation of slope.

In order to compare the effect of variation of slope in the Mississippi with that in smaller streams, we must select from the latter as many cases as possible where the slopes correspond to those of the former. We find such cases in the series obtained from the Seine at Poissy, etc., from the Saône at Raconnay, from the river Haine, and from the Canal du Jard, in which streams we may also assume approximately the same degree of roughness of wetted perimeter. Nearly all other data of which we know are obtained from streams having steeper slopes.

Since in our formula (4)

$$c = \frac{y}{1 + \dfrac{x}{\imath R}} = \frac{1}{\dfrac{1}{y} + \dfrac{x}{y \sqrt{R}}} .$$

and since, therefore,

$$\frac{1}{c} = \frac{1}{y} + \frac{x}{y} \cdot \frac{1}{\imath R} ,$$

we see that, if the reciprocals of $\imath R$ are plotted as abscissæ and the reciprocals of c as ordinates, the points obtained will lie in a straight line.

PLATE II.

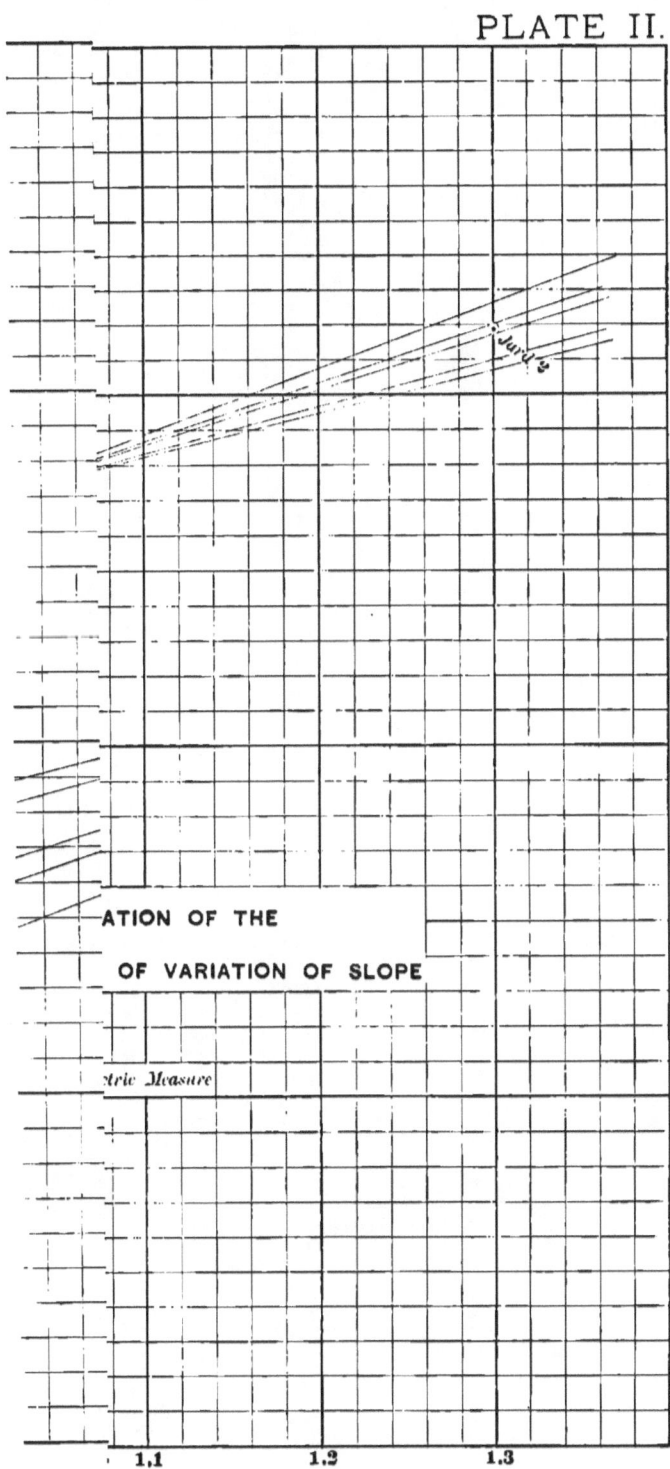

ATION OF THE

OF VARIATION OF SLOPE

tric Measure

1,1   1,2   1,3

PLATE 11

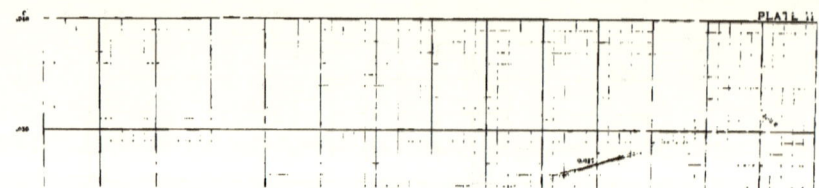

We accordingly plotted the Mississippi experiments and those of the other streams referred to, and joined by straight lines such points as pertained to approximately equal slopes (see Fig. 9, Plate II). We were able thus to connect five points from the Mississippi with points from other streams, and found that the directions of these five straight lines indicated unmistakably that they would, if sufficiently extended, intersect at a certain distance from the axis of ordinates. We accordingly produced these lines, and found that their intersections nearly coincided in a point whose abscissa $\frac{1}{R}$ was $= 1.00$ m. and whose ordinate $\frac{1}{c}$ was $= 0.027$ in metric measure. The following is a list of the points thus plotted : those from the smaller streams being placed respectively opposite to such Mississippi results as have approximately the same slope and are therefore connected with them in the figure.

Missis-sippi. $S =$		$S =$		$S =$
No. 6, .00006800	Seine at Poissy. etc., No. 4, .00006000	Seine at Poissy, etc., No. 9, .00007500		
No. 4, .00006379	" " " No. 7, .00006200	" " " No. 8, .00006700		
No. 3, .00004811	" " " No. 6, .00005400			
No. 5, .00004365	" " " No. 3, .00005700	Saône at Raconnay........ .00004000		
No. 2, .00003029	River Haine...... .... .00003030	Canal du Jard,* No. 2, .0000362		

The above-named Mississippi gaugings are those corresponding to the steepest slopes. For the remaining five, viz.,

$$\text{Mississippi No. } 1. \; S = .00002227,$$
$$\text{" " } 7, \quad .00002051,$$
$$\text{" " } 8, \quad .00001713,$$
$$\text{" " } 10, \quad .00000384.$$
$$\text{" " } 9, \quad .00000342,$$

---

* By some error the authors have confounded Nos. 2 and 3 of the gaugings on the Canal du Jard. The co-ordinates for No. 2 (slope = .0000362) plotted in our Plate II were taken by them as being those of No. 3 (slope = .0000458) and wrongly joined with Mississippi No. 3 (slope = .00004811) and Seine No. 6 (slope = .00005400).— *Trans.*

we found no gaugings for similar slopes from other streams, and accordingly joined their five points with the intersection already found, whose abscissa $\dfrac{1}{\sqrt{R}} = 1.00$ meter, and the lines thus obtained conformed very well with the first five lines, as will be seen from Fig. 9, Plate II.

23. Deductions from the foregoing results.

When the variation of slope causes a variation of c, the straight lines formed by the points of comparable series for dissimilar slopes, whose ordinates $= \dfrac{1}{c}$, must intersect.

It will be observed that in Fig. 9 the straight line corresponding to the steepest slope occupies the highest position in the diagram, and therefore gives the greatest values of $\dfrac{1}{c}$ or the smallest values of c, while the line corresponding to the least slope has the lowest place, and thus gives the smallest values of $\dfrac{1}{c}$ or the greatest values of c. Our expression thus embodies the principle that in large streams the value of c generally *decreases* with increase of slope, as was seen in the case of the Mississippi. But it also embodies the second proposition, that in small streams the value of c generally *increases* with the slope, as appears from many observations by M. Bazin. For, if the above ten straight lines be produced beyond their point of intersection $\left(\dfrac{1}{\sqrt{R}} = 1.00 \text{ meter} \right)$, they will evidently occupy relative positions which are the opposite of their former ones, so that the greater values of $\dfrac{1}{c}$, or smaller values of c, correspond to the upper lines which represent the lesser slopes, and the smaller values of $\dfrac{1}{c}$ correspond to the steeper slopes.

But while we have shown the correctness of our assumption, with regard to the influence of the slope upon the variation of c in the case of large streams, we have still to examine whether and in how far it is borne out in small channels; in other words, whether also in the latter cases the straight lines, whose abscissæ are the values of $\dfrac{1}{\sqrt{R}}$ and whose ordinates are the values of $\dfrac{1}{c}$, intersect, and whether all the points of intersection have the same abscissæ as those found above for large streams.

For this examination we selected from M. Bazin's gaugings five pairs of series, the two series of each pair being alike in roughness and cross-section, but very different as to slope. As before, we plotted $\dfrac{1}{\sqrt{R}}$ as abscissæ, and $\dfrac{1}{c}$ as ordinates, and then drew a straight line through the points of each series, averaging them as nearly as possible. These lines were also found to intersect at points whose abscissæ are approximately $\dfrac{1}{\sqrt{R}} = 1$ meter, as follows:

No. of Series.	Slope, S	Abscissa $= \dfrac{1}{\sqrt{R}}$.
6	0.0022136	} 1.06
8	0.0051629	}
9	0.0014678	} 1.12
11	0.0053805	}
12	0.0014678	} 1.00
14	0.0055618	}
15	0.0014678	} 0.68
17	0.0055618	}
32	0.1007600	} 1.00
33	0.0365560	}

From the foregoing we conclude that when gaugings of similar channels with different slopes are plotted as in Fig. 9, Plate II, the lines for the several series intersect in points whose abscissæ are approximately $\dfrac{1}{\sqrt{R}} = 1$ meter.

26. Determination of the constant value l in the expression

$$y = a + \frac{l}{n} + \frac{m}{S}.$$

Relying upon the indications of the graphic processes described in Arts. 24 and 25, and realizing that a strictly exact determination of the transition-point between the two opposite effects of slope would be of no great value, we assumed for its abscissa $\dfrac{1}{\sqrt{R}} = 1.00$ meter, which gives the value l * in

the expression

$$y = a + \frac{l}{n} + \frac{m}{S},$$

namely, for metric measure,

$$l = 1.00.$$

---

* The two curves in Fig. 10 represent two series of gaugings having the same degree of roughness and the same range of R, but different slopes.

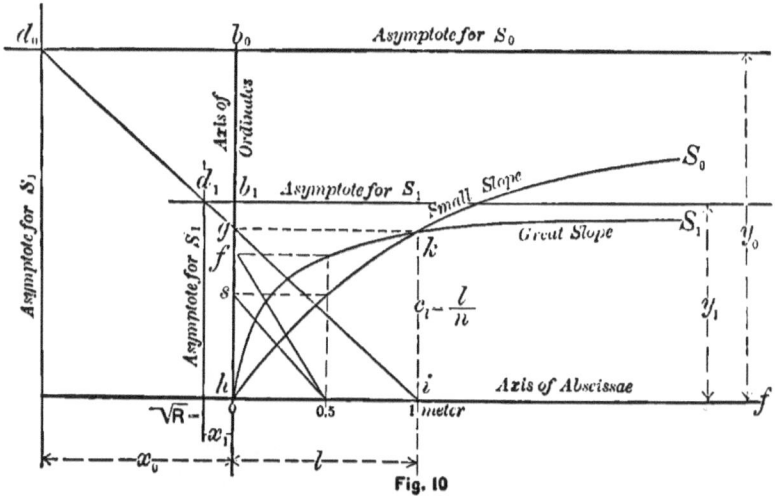

Fig. 10

As in Fig. 3, the abscissæ of the curves are the values of $\sqrt{R}$ and their ordinates are the values of c. From the conclusions derived from Fig. 9, namely, that when $\sqrt{R} = l = 1$ meter $= 1.811$ feet, difference of slope has

In order to exhibit this graphically, let hb_0 and hf, Fig. 10, be axes of co-ordinates, id_0 a straight line designating any desired degree of roughness of wetted perimeter and forming with the axis hb_0 of ordinates an angle b_0gd_0 whose tangent is $= n$. Further, let the abscissa $hi = gk = l = 1.00$ meter, and the ordinate $ik = hg = \dfrac{l}{n}$. See also Fig. A, Plate V.

In the expression $y = a + \dfrac{l}{n} + \dfrac{m}{S}$, the value y must plainly increase with a decrease of the slope S. Therefore, for a gentle slope, let $y_0 = hb_0$ and $x_0 = b_0d_0$, and for a steep slope, let $y_1 = hb_1$ and $x_1 = b_1d_1$. Hence, in accordance with our formula,

$$c = \frac{y}{1 + \dfrac{x}{\sqrt[\imath]{R}}},$$

the points d_1 and d_0 are the intersections of the asymptotes, of two equilateral hyperbolæ, running parallel with the axes of co-ordinates, the first (hS_0) of which exhibits the effect of a

little or no effect upon c, it follows that the two series of gaugings here represented will have equal values of $c (= c_l$, see foot-note, p. 37) when $R = 1$ meter; in other words, the two curves will intersect in a point k whose abscissa $\sqrt{R}$ is 1 meter. From the principle laid down in Art. 17, the centres d_1, d_0 (or intersections of asymptotes) of both curves must lie in a line id_0 drawn from i and intersecting the axis of ordinates in the point g whose ordinate is the same as that of k.

In Fig. A, Plate V, where the effect of variation of slope is not considered, and where, consequently, there is but one curve for each degree of roughness, it is immaterial what value is given to l, but in Fig. 10, which embodies the effect of slope, and in which, therefore, each degree of roughness has as many curves as there are slopes to be represented, it is obviously desirable that the coefficient of roughness, $n = \dfrac{l}{c_l}$ (see foot-note p. 37) should be independent of the slope and remain constant for a given degree of roughness. The authors therefore select for l that value of $\sqrt{R}$, viz., 1 meter, where c remains constant for all slopes. If another value, such as 0.5, of $\sqrt{R}$ had been chosen for l, we should have had two different values, hs and hf, of c_l and of $n (= \dfrac{l}{c_l})$ for the same degree of roughness in the two different slopes.—Trans.

4

gentle slope, and the second (hS_1) that of a steeper one. We see at a glance that when $\sqrt{R}$ *exceeds* 1.00^m the ordinates of the hyperbola, i.e., the values of c, *decrease* with an increase of slope, and that when $\sqrt{R}$ is *less* than 1.00^m the values of c *increase* with the slope.

We assume, then, that the variation of the coefficient c with the variation of the slope is an increase with *decrease* of slope, in streams where the mean radius R exceeds 1 meter, and an increase with *increase* of slope, in streams where the mean radius R is less than 1 meter; from which it follows that when the mean radius is $= 1.00^m$ the coefficient c does not vary with the slope.* Indeed, our formula makes the variation generally quite insignificant when R varies but little from 1 meter.

---

* The accompanying figure shows the variation of c with the slope, as given by the formula, for three different values of R, viz.: 1 foot, 3.28 feet ($= 1$

meter), and 10 feet; the character of the bed remaining constant. Compare the actual results plotted in Figs. 7 and 8. — *Trans.*

We have already intimated that while the opposite effects of change of slope upon the variation of c are apparent from and established by the results of the latest measurements, we must leave it to the scientists to explain this peculiar phenomenon. We were obliged to take cognizance of it in our formula, and we have done so in the simplest possible way, in conformity with the results of the experiments. Nevertheless, we shall enter no protest if others see fit to substitute another value, even a variable one, for l; but we believe that the correctness of the formula would not materially gain by such substitution.*

In order to ascertain the values of y for the ten Mississippi gaugings, as indicated by the results from the Seine, etc., we produce the ten straight lines, Fig. 9, Plate II, corresponding to the equation

$$\frac{1}{c} = \frac{1}{y} + \frac{x}{y'} \cdot \frac{1}{\sqrt{R}} .$$

Their points of intersection with the axis of ordinates will give us the values of $\frac{1}{y'}$. The values $\frac{1}{y'}$ and y, thus obtained, are as follows, arranged in the order of the slopes and their reciprocals ·

	H. & A.	G. & K.	s	$\frac{1}{s}$	$\frac{1}{y}$	y
Mississippi	No. 3	No. 9	.00000342	292400	.00178	561.8
"	" 4	" 10	.00000384	260417	.00257	389.1
"	" 2	" 8	.00001713	58377	.00648	154.3
"	" 1	" 7	.00002051	48757	.00762	131.2
"	" 8	" 1	.00002227	44903	.00733	136.4
"	" 9	" 2	.00003029	33014	.00824	121.4
"	" 7	" 5	.00004365	22910	.01035	96.6
"	" 10	" 3	.00004811	20785	.01136	88.0
"	" 6	" 4	.00006379	15676	.01369	73.0
"	" 5	" 6	.00006800	14706	.01465	68.3

---

* See Art. 41; and footnote, Appendix II.—*Trans.*

27. Determination of the constant value a in the expression $y = a + \dfrac{l}{n} + \dfrac{m}{S}$.

Having thus obtained from Plate II ten values of y, we plotted them in Fig. 11, Plate III, as ordinates, taking the corresponding values of $\dfrac{1}{S}$ as abscissæ. We now drew a straight line averaging the ten points as nearly as possible, and extended it to intersect the axis of ordinates at s. The height of s above the axis of abscissæ is plainly the value of y for the case $\dfrac{1}{S} = 0$, or $S = \infty$; in other words, it is the value of y_1 or $a + \dfrac{l}{n}$ in the equation

$$ y = y_1 + \frac{m}{S} = a + \frac{l}{n} + \frac{m}{S} , $$

of Art. 23. It also gives us the distance from the axis of abscissæ to the horizontal asymptote of the hyperbola giving the values of y (see Fig. 12, Plate III) when $n = .027$.

This plotting has given us the value $y_1 = a + \dfrac{l}{n} = 60$; [*] and we have already seen that the abscissa of the intersection of the straight lines in Plate II is $\dfrac{1}{\sqrt{R}} = l = 1$ meter, and its ordinate $\dfrac{1}{c} = \dfrac{1}{c_l} = n$ [†] $= 0.027$, from which we have $c_l = \dfrac{l}{n} = \dfrac{1}{.027} = 37$. Having thus ascertained the numerical

---

[*] For this particular set of gaugings only. For other cases, y_1, being $= a + \dfrac{l}{n}$, of course varies inversely with n. — *Trans.*

[†] When $\sqrt{R}$ is $= l$, c is $= c_l = \dfrac{l}{n}$ (see Fig. 10), so that if l is $= 1$ meter, c_l is then $= \dfrac{1}{n}$, and $\dfrac{1}{c_l} = n$. For English measure, $c_l = \dfrac{l}{n} = \dfrac{\sqrt{3.28}}{n} = \dfrac{1.811}{n}$.

— *Trans.*

PLATE III

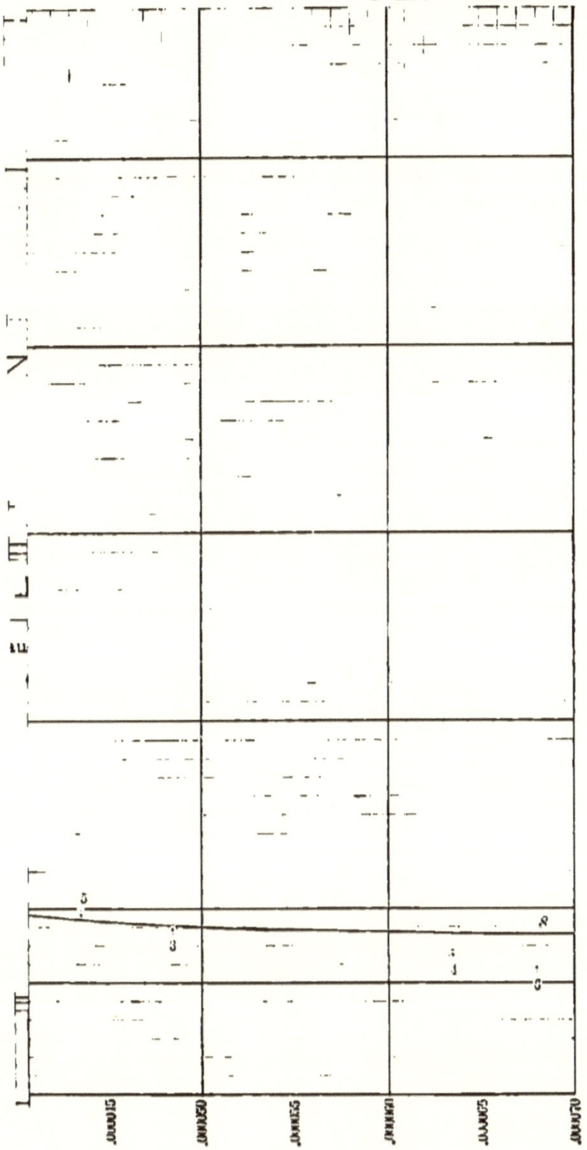

values of y_1 and $\dfrac{l}{n}$ for this particular case, we have for the value a, which is constant for *all* cases,

$$a = y_1 - \frac{l}{n} = 60 - 37 = 23 \ .$$

28. Determination of the constant value *m* in the expression $y = a + \dfrac{l}{n} + \dfrac{m}{S}$.

In the equation $y = y_1 + \dfrac{m}{S}$, *m* denotes the tangent of the angle *Fst* in Fig. 11, equal to that formed between the axis of abscissæ and the straight line *sF*, whose abscissæ are $\dfrac{1}{S}$ and whose ordinates are y; but if we take for the abscissæ the slopes S themselves, as in Fig. 12, instead of their reciprocals, $\dfrac{1}{S}$, then *m* is the square or constant which determines the equilateral hyperbola of the above equation. For the determination of this value it is necessary to assume a point through which the straight line, Fig. 11, (or the hyperbola, Fig. 12,)* should pass. We assumed a point F lying nearly midway between those of gaugings Nos. 9 and 10, as being farthest removed from the intersection s (Fig. 11), and therefore fixing the line *sF* as closely as possible.

The abscissa of this point is

$$= \frac{\text{abscissa No. 9} + \text{abscissa No. 10}}{2}$$

$$= \frac{.00000342 + .00000384}{2} = .00000363,$$

and in order to have it upon the straight line averaging the remaining values of y, and to approximate somewhat more

---

* The gaugings represented by these diagrams were selected for this determination because they embodied the *least slopes* on record, and thus gave the largest values of $\dfrac{m}{S}$. In the experiments of M. Bazin, $\dfrac{m}{S}$ is so small that a trifling want of accuracy in its determination would involve a considerable error in the value of *m*.—*Trans.*

closely to the point (No. 9) representing the least slope, we determined its ordinate to be $y = 487$.

But since $y = y_1 + \dfrac{m}{S}$. and since $y_1 = 60$ in this case, we have, for the distance from the assumed point to the horizontal asymptote, $\dfrac{m}{S} = 487 - 60 = 427$. The quantities $S = .00000363$ and $y - y_1 = 427$ form the sides of a rectangle, the area of which is equal to the constant of the hyperbola, and the value of which is thus found to be $m = 427 \times .00000363 = .00155$.

29. Determination of the coefficient n of roughness of wet perimeter.

Having thus determined the constants, a, l and m in our formula, we now proceed to determine the variable value n, which designates the degree of roughness of the wet perimeter. We wish to remark, however, that by this expression we understand not only the mere roughness of the surface, but also the irregularities and imperfections (Schadhaftigkeit) in the bed of the channel or river.

For instance, in the case of river-beds covered with boulders and detritus (Geschieben) we must not overlook the fact that when the water is low, and in general when the material forming the bed is not in motion, there is much less resistance to the flow than when it is moved during floods. In the first case we might compare the surface of the bed of the stream to that of an ordinary gravel-path or to that of rough rubble masonry, and the coefficient of roughness would be comparatively low. In the second case, each rolling stone presents alternately larger and smaller resisting surfaces to the current, and a considerable portion of the energy of the stream is absorbed in carrying the detritus forward, and the coefficient of roughness may become quite large. Bends in the stream also increase the resistance, thus diminishing the velocity and increasing the coefficient; and this will be the case even where the stream as a whole is quite straight, but where the *thalweg* passes occasionally from one side to the other, for here the particles of water have a lateral and varying as well as a forward and uniform motion. Thus, one and the same stream may furnish gaugings showing widely differing coefficients of roughness. In the Rhine, for instance, at Germersheim, $n = 0.023$; at Speyer, $n = 0.026$; and at Bâle, $n = 0.030$.[*]

It will thus be seen that the determination of the proper coefficient of roughness, in accordance with the circumstances and requirements of the problem, depends largely upon the sagacity and experience of the observer.

To obtain values of n graphically from actual gaugings, we may proceed as follows, Plate IV: Plot the values $\dfrac{1}{\sqrt{R}}$ as abscissæ, and those of $\dfrac{1}{c}$ as ordinates. Assuming a series of values of n, .009, .010, .011, etc., find for each the value y for the case when $S = \infty$, viz., $y_1 = a + \dfrac{l}{n}$, and its reciprocal $\dfrac{1}{y_1}$. Plot the latter upon the axis of ordinates, and the assumed values of n upon the ordinate for $\dfrac{1}{\sqrt{R}} = 1$ meter $= 1.811$ feet. Join each point $\dfrac{1}{y_1}$ with its corresponding point n, producing the lines, if necessary, to make them reach to the farthest point plotted.

These lines represent the values of n denoted at their intersections with the scale of n which is plotted upon the ordinate for $\dfrac{1}{\sqrt{R}} = 1$ meter. For each gauging, read the preliminary value of n indicated by the position of the point relative to these lines; and, taking its known value of S, find

$$y = a + \frac{l}{n} + \frac{m}{S}$$

$$= 41.6 + \frac{1.811}{n} + \frac{.00281}{S} \text{ for English measure,}$$

$$= 23 + \frac{1}{n} + \frac{.00155}{S} \qquad \text{for metric measure,}$$

---

[*] In the latter case the gaugings were made in a curve of the stream having a radius of about 900 meters.

and the corresponding reciprocal $\frac{1}{y}$. Lay off the latter upon the axis of ordinates, and draw from it a line through the point representing the gauging. The ordinate $\frac{1}{c}$ of the intersection of this line with the ordinate for $\frac{1}{\sqrt{R}} = 1$ meter is the proper value of n for the case.*

Since $ny - 1 = x$, the straight lines thus determining n, form, with the axis of abscissæ, angles whose tangents are $=$

$$ n - \frac{1}{y} = \frac{x}{y}. $$

---

* For example, Plate IV shows the application of this process to the Mississippi gauging No. 2 (plotted at q) and to Bazin's Series No. 8. For the former we have the preliminary value of $n = .016$, as given by its position with reference to the line ab; so that $y = a + \frac{1}{n} + \frac{m}{S} = 23 + \frac{1}{.016} + \frac{.00155}{.00003} = 137$, and $\frac{1}{y} = \frac{1}{137} = .0073$, which is to be plotted at e''. The line $e''q$, produced to K''', gives, on the scale of n, the value $n = .028$.

For, since oe'' is the value $\frac{1}{y}$ for this case, and since pq is the value of $\frac{1}{c}$, the line $e''K'''$ is that of the equation $\frac{1}{c} = \frac{1}{y} + \frac{x}{y} \cdot \frac{1}{\sqrt{R}}$.

As iK''' is the value of $\frac{1}{c_1}$ (or of $\frac{1}{c}$ for $\frac{1}{\sqrt{K}} = 1$ meter) and $oi = \frac{1}{l}$, we have, as explained in foot-note, page 48, $\dfrac{\frac{1}{c_1}}{\frac{1}{l}} = \frac{l}{c_1} = \frac{iK'''}{oi} = n =$ the tangent of the angle $K'''oi$.

For Bazin's Series 8, we have the preliminary value of $n =$ say $.0115$, then

$$ y = 23 + \frac{1}{.0115} + \frac{.00155}{.0052} = 108.7 $$

and $\frac{1}{y} = .00917$. This gives $n = .0115$. The slope here is so steep, and $\frac{m}{S}$ therefore so small, that the value y is but little affected by it, and the dotted line $e'K'$ drawn from $\frac{1}{y} = .00917$ through K' to the mean point of the series conforms so closely with those laid off upon the preliminary assumption, $S = \infty$, that the first and final values of n are practically identical. — *Trans.*

Determination IV.

1.5   2.0

For the gaugings that have come to our notice, n varies between 0.009 and 0.040.

30. Résumé. Final formula.

In our formula (4), p. 37,

$$c = \frac{y}{1 + \dfrac{x}{\sqrt{R}}},$$

we at first assumed, neglecting the effect of variation of slope, that $y = a + \dfrac{l}{n}$ and $x = an = ny - l$; so that

$$c = \frac{a + \dfrac{l}{n}}{1 + \dfrac{an}{\sqrt{R}}},$$

in which both values, y and x, vary with the coefficient n of roughness, while x also holds a certain relation to R.

The two values y and x, which vary with n, are thus seen to be related, not only to each other, but also to the mean radius R. This relation remains the same through all degrees of roughness, and fully expresses the variation of the coefficient c with such roughness.

With reference to the influence of variation of slope upon the variation of the coefficient c, we assumed

$$y = y_1 + \frac{m}{S},$$

in which $y_1 = a + \dfrac{l}{n}$.

From this we obtained

$$y = a + \frac{l}{n} + \frac{m}{S}$$

and

$$x = ny - l = \left(a + \frac{m}{S}\right)n,$$

and finally, from formula (4), the general formula (5), p. 43,

$$c = \frac{a + \dfrac{l}{n} + \dfrac{m}{S}}{1 + \left(a + \dfrac{m}{S}\right)\dfrac{n}{\sqrt{R}}} \ .$$

As remarked in Articles 25 and 26, we found that the transition from the effect of slope in large streams, where c *decreases* with increase of slope, to that in small streams, where c *increases* with the slope, is indicated by the intersection of straight lines whose abscissæ are the values of $\dfrac{1}{\sqrt{R}}$ and whose ordinates are the values of $\dfrac{1}{c}$, and that this intersection takes place in a point whose abscissa $\left(\dfrac{1}{\sqrt{R}}\right)$ is $= 1.00^m$. We thus determined the constant value $l = 1.00^m$.

By comparing the Mississippi results with those of other streams, we further obtained for ten different slopes the respective values of

$$y = y_1 + \frac{m}{S},$$

and from these determined the value of $y_1 = 60$.

But since

$$y_1 = a + \frac{l}{n},$$

and as in these cases $n = .027$ and $l = 1$ meter, we obtained, from

$$60 = a + \frac{1}{.027},$$

the constant value $a = 23$.

Further, from the product of S (= 0.00000363) and $y - y_1$ (= 427.0) we found the area m (= 0.00155) of the rectangle determining the equilateral hyperbola of the equation

$$y = y_1 + \frac{m}{S}.$$

Finally, the value n, denoting the degree of roughness of the wetted perimeter, was found to vary between 0.009 and 0.040.

Having thus developed the structure of our general formula, and ascertained the values of the constants, we obtain, by combining the results of these operations, the following general formula for the mean velocity of water in channels and rivers with uniform flow:

$$v = c \sqrt{RS},$$

in which

$$c = \frac{y}{1 + \frac{x}{\sqrt{R}}};$$

in which, again,

$$y = a + \frac{l}{n} + \frac{m}{S}$$

and

$$x = ny - l = \left(a + \frac{m}{S}\right)n;$$

and thus, finally,

$$v = \left(\frac{a + \frac{l}{n} + \frac{m}{S}}{1 + \left(a + \frac{m}{S}\right)\frac{n}{\sqrt{R}}}\right)\sqrt{RS}. \quad \ldots \quad (6)$$

The values a, l and m are constant, and n varies with the degree of roughness. If, therefore, we substitute in the formula the numerical values found for the constants, in metric measure, $a = 23$, $l = 1.00$, and $m = 0.00155$, we obtain, for such measure,

$$v = \left(\frac{23 + \frac{1}{n} + \frac{0.00155}{S}}{1 + \left(23 + \frac{0.00155}{S}\right)\frac{n}{\sqrt{R}}} \right) \sqrt{RS}.^{*} \qquad . \quad (7)$$

31. Determination of a few characteristic series of co-efficients of roughness of wet perimeter, to be used as mean or standard values.

With the values of n obtained from extensive experiments, and ranging from 0.009 (channel in carefully planed boards) to 0.0350 (Rhine in the Domleschger valley with detritus), we might construct at pleasure any number of categories of the same or similar degrees of roughness of wetted perimeter, i.e., for similar channels and rivers with approximately the same character of bottom and sides   But in view of the uncertainty which still exists in regard to the many phenomena in the movement of water and to the proper mathematical expression of these phenomena, and bearing in mind the unavoidable incompleteness of the gaugings, it appears preferable to adhere in general to M. Bazin's arrangement of the categories, especially as it seems well adapted to meet the requirements of practice.   M. Bazin's second category, embracing channels lined with boards, as well as with ashlar and brick masonry, we have, however, divided into two classes, because we found a decided difference between their results, and believed that a recognition of this difference, although not a

---

* For steep slopes, as will be seen by the diagrams on Plates VI to VIII, the variation of slope has but little effect upon the coefficient c. If we neglect it, as may be done in the case of sewer-pipes and other small channels, we have the simpler formulæ of Art. 20, viz.:

$$c = \frac{a + \frac{l}{n}}{1 + \frac{an}{\sqrt{R}}}. \qquad . \quad . \quad . \quad . \quad . \quad . \quad (8)$$

—Trans.

great one, must rather increase than diminish the usefulness of the formula in practice. We have also added a category for rivers with detritus, so that instead of four we have six categories, namely, in metric measure :

I. Channels lined with carefully planed boards or with smooth cement.

$$n = 0.010 ; \quad \frac{1}{n} = 100.00 ; \quad a + \frac{1}{n} = 123.$$

II. Channels lined with common boards.

$$n = 0.012 ; \quad \frac{1}{n} = 83.33 ; \quad a + \frac{1}{n} = 106.$$

III. Channels lined with ashlar or with neatly jointed brick-work.

$$n = 0.013 ; \quad \frac{1}{n} = 76.91 ; \quad a + \frac{1}{n} = 100.$$

IV. Channels in rubble masonry.

$$n = 0.017 ; \quad \frac{1}{n} = 58.82 ; \quad a + \frac{1}{n} = 82.$$

V. Channels in earth ; brooks and rivers.

$$n = 0.025 ; \quad \frac{1}{n} = 40.00 ; \quad a + \frac{1}{n} = 63.$$

VI. Streams with detritus or aquatic plants.

$$n = 0.030 ; \quad \frac{1}{n} = 33.33 ; \quad a + \frac{1}{n} = 56.$$

We need hardly observe that these six series represent only *mean* values.

In applying the formula, we are obliged to obtain the value of y by adding the values of a, $\frac{l}{n}$ and $\frac{m}{S}$. We therefore append tables,* giving values of $a + \dfrac{l}{n}$ and of $\dfrac{m}{S}$, from which we can determine the value y, and with it the value x, not only for our six categories, but also for any desired intermediate degree of roughness of perimeter, and for any slope that may occur in practice.

In designing semicircular artificial channels in rubble, represented by category IV, if they are to be substantially and carefully built and well maintained, we may assume $a + \dfrac{l}{n} = 100$. The values of n given for the other categories, I to III, are those for semicircular channels.†

We must observe, finally, that while M. Bazin's category I represents chiefly series No. 2 (rectangular channels lined with cement), our new category I represents the arithmetical mean of series Nos. 28, 29, 24, 2 and 25, conforming nearly to the results of series No. 24 (semicircular channels lined with cement). The curve for the values of c occupies in this case a higher position than in series No. 2, and represents nearly the maximum values of c obtained by Gauckler's formula, $\sqrt{v} = \alpha \sqrt[3]{R} \sqrt[4]{S}$ (category I).

32. Demonstration that the binomial and not the monomial form is the proper one in a general formula for the determination of the mean velocity of water.

In comparing Gauckler's very simple monomial formula with the general binomial formula herein recommended, we desire to add the following argument in favor of the latter.

If we give to Gauckler's formula,

$$\sqrt{v} = \alpha \sqrt[3]{R} \sqrt[4]{S} ,$$

the general form

$$v = \alpha' R'' S''' ,$$

---

* See Appendix, Tables II and III, which have been greatly extended and reduced to English measure.— *Trans.*

† In channels having a less favorable section, larger values of n should therefore be used.— *Trans.*

and, for a gentle slope, designate the slope S as S_0, the mean velocity v as v_0, and the coefficient c as c_0, but, for a steep slope, respectively S_1, v_1 and c_1, we obtain, for each pair of two cases with equal values of R and n, but with unequal slopes, the constant relation

$$\frac{v_0}{v_1} = \frac{S_0{}^x}{S_1{}^x} \, .$$

In other words, in all comparable cases with equal mean radii but with different slopes, the velocities vary as a certain given power of the slopes.

In our collection of reliable data we found about 250 cases, in each of which we could combine two gaugings with approximately equal values of R but with unequal slopes, and from these deduce the power to which the slope values must be raised in order to bring them into the same relation as the velocities. For this purpose we used the formula

$$\frac{v_0}{v_1} = \left(\frac{S_0}{S_1}\right)^x;$$

from which follows

$$x = \frac{\log v_0 - \log v_1}{\log S_0 - \log S_1}.$$

In this way we obtained the following approximate values of x :

In 40 cases, $x = 1$,

" 65 " $x = \dfrac{1}{1.5}$,

" 81 " $x = \dfrac{1}{2}$,

" 30 " $x = \dfrac{1}{2.5}$,

" 16 " $x = \dfrac{1}{3}$,

$$\text{In} \quad 8 \text{ cases, } x = \frac{1}{3.5},$$

$$\text{``} \quad 4 \quad \text{``} \quad x = \frac{1}{4},$$

$$\text{``} \quad 7 \quad \text{``} \quad x = \frac{1}{4.5}.$$

A great majority of the first 216 cases, in which x varied from 1 to $\frac{1}{2.5}$, are those of small channels and streams, whose mean radius R was less than 1.00 meter, while nearly all of the last 11 cases, where x varies from $\frac{1}{4}$ to $\frac{1}{4.5}$, are taken from the Mississippi and its tributaries.

It appeared, however, from this examination, as well as from the several newer formulæ and the results of general experience, that in any two comparable cases, having equal values of R but different slopes, the velocities are to each other as a variable and not as a constant power of the slope.

This variation of the power of the slope is embraced in the new general binomial formula,

$$v = \left(\frac{y}{1 + \dfrac{x}{\sqrt{R}}} \right) \sqrt{RS},$$

as will appear from the following explanation:

Suppose two cases, having the same degree of roughness and equal values of R, but different slopes. If we draw, as in Fig. 10, p. 48, for each of the two slopes S_0 and S_1, an equilateral hyperbola whose abscissæ are the values of $\sqrt{R}$, and whose ordinates are the values of c, we obtain, as has already been shown, two curves which intersect in a point whose abscissa l is $= 1$, and whose ordinate c_l is $= \frac{l}{n} = \frac{1}{n}$ (metric measure).

From the origin (h) of co-ordinates to the point (k) of intersection of the curves, in other words, so long as $R < 1.00$

meter, the curve for the gentle slope S_0 remains *below* that for the steep slope S_1, while beyond the point k of intersection, or when $R > 1.00$ meter, the reverse is the case.

When $R < 1.00$ meter, $\frac{c_0}{c_1}$ is < 1, and, since also $\frac{S_0}{S_1} < 1$, we may write

$$\frac{c_0}{c_1} = \left(\frac{S_0}{S_1}\right)^x;$$

and, remembering that R and n are the same in both cases, we may further write

$$\frac{v_0}{v_1} = \left(\frac{S_0}{S_1}\right)^x \sqrt{\frac{S_0}{S_1}} = \left(\frac{S_0}{S_1}\right)^{\frac{1}{2}+x}$$

But when $R > 1.00$ meter, and therefore $\frac{c_0}{c_1} > 1$, we have

$$\frac{c_0}{c_1} = \left(\frac{S_1}{S_0}\right)^y,$$

and consequently

$$\frac{v_0}{v_1} = \left(\frac{S_1}{S_0}\right)^y \sqrt{\frac{S_0}{S_1}} = \left(\frac{S_0}{S_1}\right)^{\frac{1}{2}-y}.$$

We thus see that in the first case, when $R < 1.00$ meter, the powers of S, namely, $\frac{1}{2} + x$, are greater than $\frac{1}{2}$, while in the second case, or when $R > 1.00$ meter, the powers of S, namely, $\frac{1}{2} - y$, are less than $\frac{1}{2}$.

The exponents x and y are, however, themselves variable. When, therefore, $x = \frac{1}{2}$, we have

$$\frac{v_0}{v_1} = \frac{S_0}{S_1},$$

because

$$\frac{v_0}{v_1} = \left(\frac{S_0}{S_1}\right)^{\frac{1}{2}+x};$$

a relation which, according to Bazin, may occur in small channels, as it did in 40 such cases of our investigations as above described.

When $y = \frac{1}{4}$, we have

$$\frac{v_0}{v_1} = \sqrt[4]{\frac{S_0}{S_1}} \cdot$$

This relation obtains in cases of large mean radius R and small slope S, as in that of the Mississippi.

Since we have thus shown that the ratio of the velocities to the powers of the slopes is not constant, but very variable, we cannot accept as correct the constant ratio of v to S contained in Gauckler's monomial formula.

33. Demonstration that the new general formula rightly embodies the law of the hyperbola.

In order to show that the new general formula properly represents the law of the hyperbola, already established for the two opposite variations of the value c with the variation of the slope, we assume a case in which R is constant and S is variable.

If in the general formula

$$c = \frac{\dfrac{l}{n} + a + \dfrac{m}{S}}{1 + \left(a + \dfrac{m}{S}\right)\dfrac{n}{\sqrt{R}}}$$

we divide by $a + \dfrac{m}{S}$, we obtain

$$c = \frac{\sqrt{R}}{n} + \frac{(l - \sqrt{R})\dfrac{\sqrt{R}}{mn^2}}{\dfrac{\sqrt{R}}{mn} + \dfrac{a}{m} + \dfrac{1}{S}} \; ;$$

and if we put

$$\frac{\sqrt{R}}{n} = A, \quad \frac{\sqrt{R}}{mn} + \frac{a}{m} = B, \quad \text{and} \quad (l - \sqrt{R})\frac{\sqrt{R}}{mn^2} = M,$$

we obtain

$$c = A + \frac{M}{B + \frac{1}{S}} \cdot$$

Considering c and $\frac{1}{S}$ as co-ordinates, this equation is seen to be that of an equilateral hyperbola.

When $\sqrt{R} < l$, M is positive; when $\sqrt{R} = l$, M is $= 0$; and when $\sqrt{R} > l$, M is negative.

In the first case, or when M is positive, we evidently obtain an equilateral hyperbola convex toward the axis of abscissæ, since c attains its greatest value, viz., $c = A + \frac{M}{B}$, when $\frac{1}{S} = 0$, and its least value, viz., $c = A$, when $\frac{1}{S} = \infty$.

In the second case, or when $M = 0$, we have $c = \frac{\sqrt{R}}{n} = \frac{l}{n}$, and thus a constant for all values of S; which indicates that the hyperbola has passed into a straight line running parallel with the axis of abscissæ.

In the third case, or when M is negative, we obtain an equilateral hyperbola concave toward the axis of abscissæ, for now the value of c is smallest $\left(A - \frac{M}{B}\right)$ when $\frac{1}{S} = 0$, and greatest (A) when $\frac{1}{S} = \infty$.

The same result appears if, instead of $\frac{1}{S}$, we plot the values S as abscissæ.

If we put

$$\frac{l+an}{n+an^2} = A, \qquad \frac{mn}{\sqrt{R}\left(1 + \dfrac{an}{\sqrt{R}}\right)} = B,$$

and

$$B\left(\frac{\sqrt{R}}{n} - A\right) = \frac{B\sqrt{R}}{n(\sqrt{R}+an)}(\sqrt{R}-l) = M,$$

we have

$$c = A + \frac{M}{B+S}.$$

This expression is also the equation of a hyperbola, whose abscissæ, however, are no longer the values of $\frac{1}{S}$, but those of S.

If $\sqrt{R} < l$, M is negative, and the formula gives an equilateral hyperbola concave toward the axis of abscissæ.

If $\sqrt{R} = l$, M is $= 0$, and the hyperbola merges into a straight line running parallel with the axis of abscissæ and passing through the point whose ordinate is $c = \dfrac{l}{n}$ and whose abscissa is $S = l$.

If $\sqrt{R} > l$, M is positive, and the hyperbola is convex toward the axis of abscissæ.

The following figures illustrate the three cases for both forms of the formula.

First Case. $\sqrt{R} < l$.   (Fig. 14.)

1. Form with abscissæ $= \dfrac{1}{S}$, M positive.

2. Form with abscissæ $= S$, M negative.

Second Case. $\sqrt{R} = l$.   (Fig. 15.)

1. Form with abscissæ $= \dfrac{1}{S}$, $M = 0$.

2. Form with abscissæ $= S$, $M = 0$.

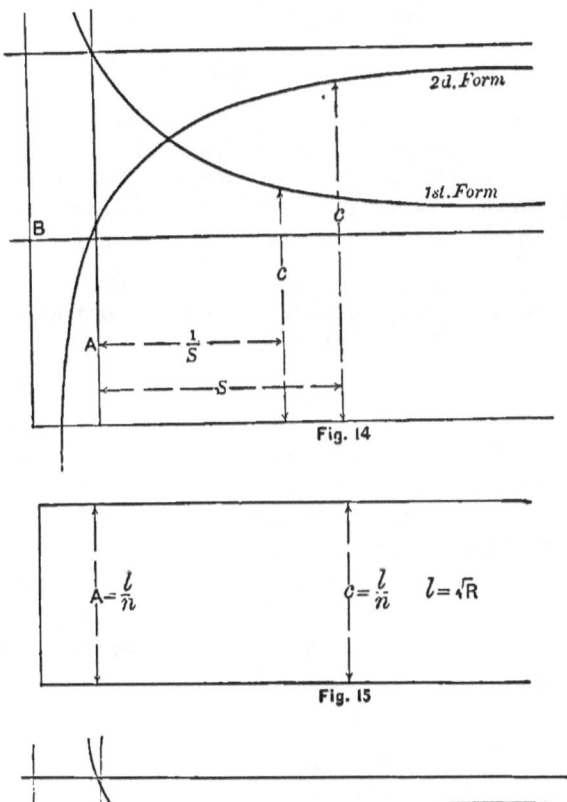

Fig. 14

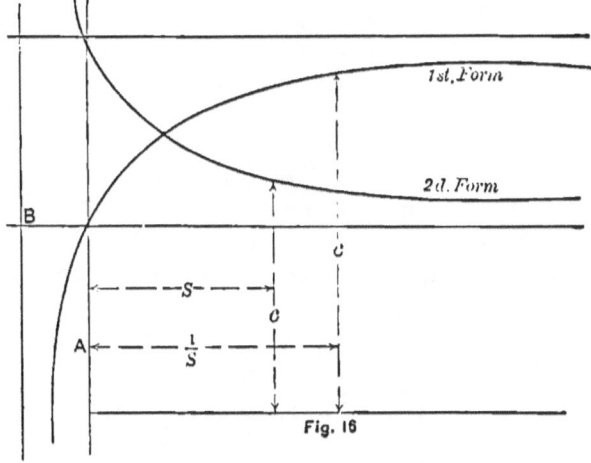

$$A = \frac{l}{n} \qquad c = \frac{l}{n} \qquad l = \sqrt{R}$$

Fig. 15

Fig. 16

Third Case. $\sqrt{R} > l.$ (Fig. 16.)

1. Form with abscissæ $= \dfrac{1}{S}$, M negative.
2. Form with abscissæ $= S$, M positive.

We have thus demonstrated that the new general formula rightly embodies the variation of the value c with the variation of the slope and in accordance with the law of the hyperbola.

34. Transformation of the new formula from the metric into other measures.

In order that the new formula may readily come into general use, we will here briefly note the method of its transformation into other measures.

Let α represent the length of the meter in any given unit of measure. (For instance, the meter being $= 3.2809 \ldots$ English feet, α in this case is $= 3.2809 \ldots$). We accomplish the transformation by simply multiplying each of the constant coefficients of the formula with $\sqrt{\alpha}$, while the coefficient n of roughness, being a tangent or ratio, remains the same for all measures. We thus have, in general,

$$c' = c_m \sqrt{\alpha},$$
$$y' = y_m \sqrt{\alpha},$$
$$x' = x_m \sqrt{\alpha},$$
$$a' = a_m \sqrt{\alpha},$$
$$l' = l_m \sqrt{\alpha},$$
$$m' = m_m \sqrt{\alpha},$$

in which c', y', etc., are the respective values in the given measure, while c_m, y_m, etc., are those for metric measure.

This gives, for English measure, as above, the general formula

$$v = \left(\frac{41.6 + \dfrac{1.811}{n} + \dfrac{0.00281}{S}}{1 + \left(41.6 + \dfrac{0.00281}{S}\right)\dfrac{n}{\sqrt{R}}} \right) \sqrt{RS},$$

in which

v = the mean velocity of the water;

R = the mean radius;

S = the slope of the water surface per unit of length;

n = coefficient of roughness of the wetted perimeter.

35. The simplicity of the new general formula for practical use.

The new general formula appears at first sight to be somewhat complicated for practical purposes, but if we consider the expression $c = \dfrac{y}{1 + \dfrac{x}{\sqrt{R}}}$, we see at once that its solution becomes a very simple matter as soon as we have determined the values y and x corresponding to various degrees of roughness and for a series of slopes, and arranged them in Tables.* But the determination of the coefficient c becomes even simpler by means of the following graphic process.

35a. Simple graphic determination of any one of the unknown values c, n, R, S, when the other three are given.

In Fig. A, Plate V, as explained on pages 37 and 38, we have endeavored to represent graphically the formula

$$c = \frac{y}{1 + \dfrac{x}{\sqrt{R}}} ,$$

neglecting the effect of slope and thus making $y = a + \dfrac{l}{n}$, and $x = an$.

But in our general formula the values y and x are made to include the effect of the slope, thus:

$$y = a + \frac{l}{n} + \frac{m}{S}$$

---

* See Appendix X, Tables II and III.

and

$$x = \left(a + \frac{m}{S}\right)u.$$

Here we see that y has *three* terms, of which one (a) is constant while the other two are variable. A third term, $\frac{m}{S}$, must therefore be introduced into the diagram.

We have already seen, page 43, that the variation of c, and also that of y, with difference of slope is represented by an equilateral hyperbola; and since, when $S = \infty$, $\frac{m}{S} = 0$, and when $S = 0$, $\frac{m}{S} = \infty$, it follows that the hyperbola is referred to its asymptotes.

In order to add to the diagram this hyperbola for the variation of y with the slope, i.e., for the values $\frac{m}{S}$, we extend the axis bh' of ordinates upward indefinitely, as also the lines gd', gd'', gd''', gd'''', Fig. B, Plate V. The asymptotes of the required hyperbola intersect at the point b,[*] and the hyperbola cc itself is easily constructed, because the constant[+] ($m = .00155$) which determines it is given.[‡]

The values y are now completely determined, because $bg = a$; gh', gh'', gh'''. etc. $= \dfrac{l}{n'}$, $\dfrac{l}{n''}$, $\dfrac{l}{n'''}$, etc.; and, for instance for slope S'', $bo = \dfrac{m}{S''}$.

In Fig. A. on the same Plate, in which the effect of slope is not considered, the intersections of asymptotes d', d'''', etc.,

---

[*] $gb = a = 23$. Hence b corresponds to a slope of $S = \infty$, or $\frac{m}{S} = 0$.

[+] See page 26.

[‡] On the other hand, if we take the reciprocals $\frac{1}{S}$ of the slopes as abscissæ, and the values $\frac{m}{S}$ as ordinates, we obtain a line sF, Fig. 11, Plate III, which for equal slopes gives the same ordinates $\left(\frac{m}{S}\right)$ as the hyperbola cc.

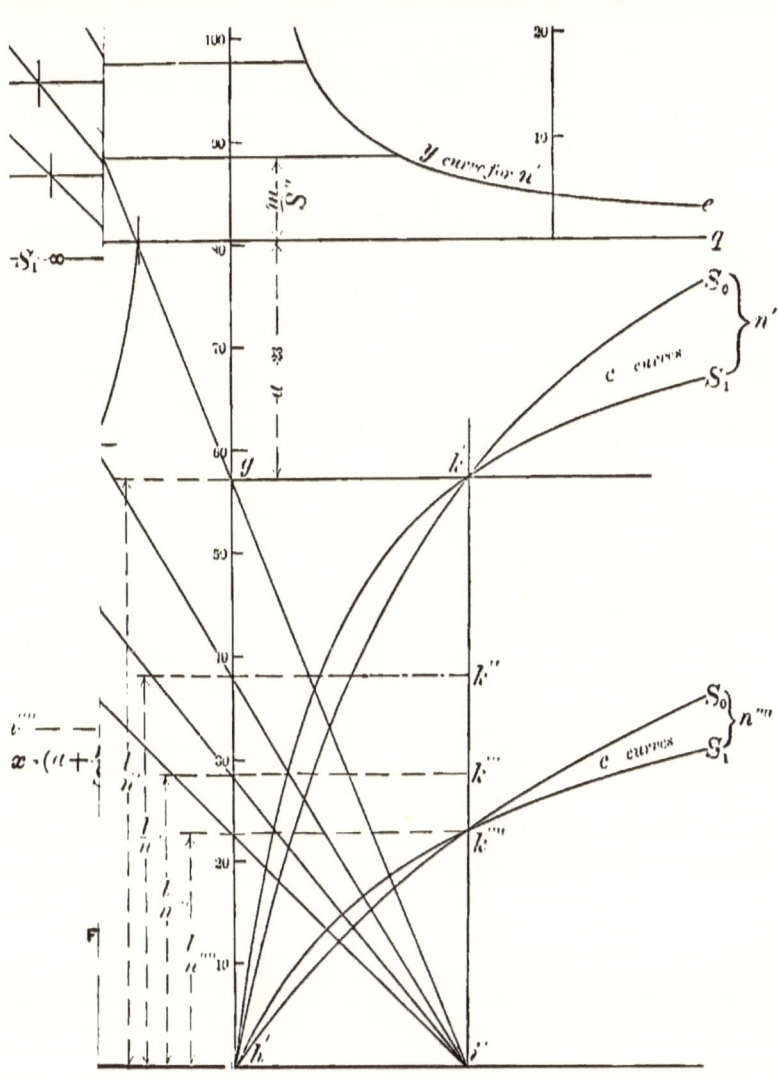

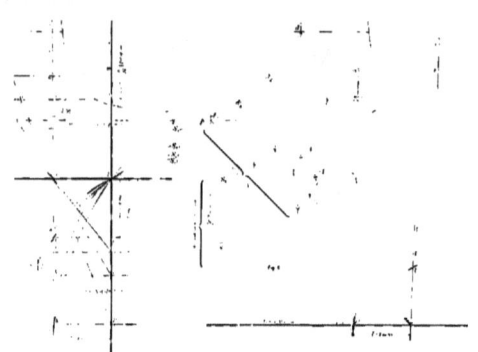

of the hyperbolæ $h'k$, $h''''k$, etc.,* giving the values of c, lie in the single horizontal line bd'''', corresponding to the horizontal asymptote pq of the curve cc, Fig. B; but in the latter figure they lie in the horizontal lines S_0, S_1, etc., corresponding to the different slopes, the heights of these lines above pq being determined by the values of $\dfrac{m}{S}$ given by the hyperbola cc.

Therefore the intersections of the asymptotes lie in the line gd' or gd'', etc., as in Fig. A, and at the same time in the horizontal lines S_0, S_1, etc., representing the several slopes. Thus, their horizontal distance from the axis of ordinates increases with the increase of roughness, and their vertical distance from the axis of abscissæ increases with decrease of slope.†

Examples.—1. Let $\sqrt{R} = 1.4$ meter, $S = S_0$, and $n = n'''$. Determine the coefficient c. (Fig. B.)

From the intersection d'' of the horizontal line S_0 with the radial line n''' draw a straight line $d''r'$ to the point r', corresponding to $\sqrt{R} = 1.4$ in the axis of abscissæ $h'''i'''$ for n'''. The line $d''r'$ cuts the axis of ordinates at a point c', 6.5 above g, and we have $c = h'''g + gc' = 29 + 6.5 = 35.5$.

2. Let $\sqrt{R} = 0.4$ meter, $S = S''$ and $n = n'$. Here the straight line cr'' intersects the axis of ordinates at -20, and we have $c = gh' - gc'' = 58 - 20 = 38$.

We may avoid these additions and subtractions by drawing the radial lines indicating the values of n from i', as in Fig. C, instead of from g, as in Fig. B, so that the angles whose tangents are respectively $= n'$, n'', n''', etc., shall have their apices in i'. In Fig. B we have a separate axis of abscissæ for each value of n, its distance gh', etc., from g being $= \dfrac{l}{n'}$, etc.; but

---

* Fig. B shows sixteen intersections of asymptotes, d', d'', etc., for as many c curves, hk, etc.; but to avoid confusion we show but two of these curves, viz.: for slope S_0, n' and n'''', and for slope S_1, n' and n'''.—*Trans.*

† But, since x is $= \left(a + \dfrac{m}{S}\right)n$, the horizontal distance x also increases with decrease of slope; and, since $y = a + \dfrac{l}{n} + \dfrac{m}{S}$, the vertical distance y increases with decrease of roughness.

the above modification leaves but the axis of abscissæ ($h'i'$) corresponding to the smallest value of n to be represented in the diagram.

The values of y remain unchanged by this modification; and, except for the first radial line, are now reckoned from a new axis ($h'i'$) of abscissæ. Hence the intersections d', etc., for a given slope no longer lie in a horizontal line, as in Fig. B, but in a curve $d''''d'$, etc., Fig. C,* which we shall call a slope curve.

Let us seek the equation of this curve. We know that

$$y = a + \frac{l}{n} + \frac{m}{S};$$

that

$$x = \left(a + \frac{m}{S}\right)n = ny - l;$$

and that, therefore,

$$n = \frac{x}{a + \frac{m}{S}}$$

and

$$x = \left(\frac{x}{a + \frac{m}{S}}\right)y - l.$$

We thus find the equation

$$y = \frac{(l + x)\left(a + \frac{m}{S}\right)}{x}$$

or

$$y = \frac{l\left(a + \frac{m}{S}\right)}{x} + a + \frac{m}{S}.$$

---

* The intersections lying along the first radial line n' remain in Fig. C the same as in Fig. B, because the end point, i', of that line has not been moved; but those on the next radial line n'' must be lower by a distance $= i''\, i'$, Fig. B, those on line n''' by a distance $= i'''\, i'$, and those on line n'''' by a distance $= i''''\, i'.$—*Trans.*

When $x = 0$, $y = \infty$; and when $x = \infty$, $y = a + \dfrac{m}{S}$

Here we again have the equation of an equilateral hyperbola whose vertical asymptote coincides with the axis of ordinates, and whose horizontal asymptote lies at a distance $y = a + \dfrac{m}{S}$ from the axis of abscissæ, and thus varies its position as the slope varies.

If we construct such hyperbolæ for a series of slopes, in accordance with the simple method already given, by means of the determining rectangles xy, and draw them through the radial lines indicating the values of n, we obtain points of intersection, each of which is common to a certain slope and to a certain degree of roughness. If now, in any given case, we draw a straight line, joining the point of intersection and the point in the axis of abscissæ corresponding to the value of $\sqrt{R}$, then the point where this line cuts the axis of ordinates gives us at once the desired value of c.

By this graphic method we may not only obtain the value c, but, having the four unknown quantities c, n, R and S, we may determine any one of them when the other three are known. This can best be illustrated by a few examples. See Plate VI, in metric measure.

1. For a canal in earth whose slope $S = 0.0002$, and whose $\sqrt{R} = 1.400$, to find the coefficient c in the formula $v = c\sqrt{RS}$.

The point of intersection of the curve for $S = 0.0002$ with the radial line of category V ($n = 0.025$) is a. The point in the axis of abscissæ indicating $\sqrt{R} = 1.400$ is b. The straight line ab cuts the axis of ordinates in the point c'', and c is $= 45.6$.

2. For a mill-race lined with boards, slope $S = 0.001$, and $\sqrt{R} = 0.400$, to find the coefficient c.

The curve for $S = 0.001$ cuts the radial line for category II ($n = 0.012$) in d. The point in the axis of abscissæ indicating $\sqrt{R} = 0.400$ is f. The straight line df cuts the axis of ordinates in the point c', and we have $c = 62$.

If the given slope falls between two of the curves of the diagram, we must, of course, take the point a or d between those two curves, and if the degree of roughness is intermediate between those of two adjoining radial lines, a similar modification must be made.

3. Let $c = 64.5$, $\sqrt{R} = 0.68$, $S = 0.001$; to find n.

From the point $\sqrt{R} = 0.68$ on the axis of abscissæ draw a straight line to the point $c = 64.5$ in the axis of ordinates, and extend it to intersect the slope curve $S = 0.001$. The point of intersection gives $n = 0.0138$.

4. Let $c = 50.5$, $n = 0.027$, $S = 0.00015$; to find $\sqrt{R}$.

From the intersection of radial line $n = 0.027$ with slope curve $S = 0.00015$ draw a straight line through the point $c = 50.5$ on the axis of ordinates, and extend it to the axis of abscissæ. Its intersection with the latter gives $\sqrt{R} = 2.338$.

5. Let $c = 52.0$, $n = 0.023$. $\sqrt{R} = 1.550$; to find S.

From the point $\sqrt{R} = 1.550$ on the axis of abscissæ draw a straight line through the point $c = 52.0$ on the axis of ordinates. By extending this line upward to the radial line $n = 0.023$, we find the slope curve $S = 0.0001$.

These examples illustrate the extreme simplicity of the process for determining any one of the four values c, n, R and S, when the others are given.*

Since n and S are the same for all systems of measures, the same diagram may be used for all systems, provided only that we first re-graduate the scales of $\sqrt{R}$ and c on the axes of co-ordinates in accordance with the desired system, bearing in mind that the unit of the new measure is found by putting $1 = \dfrac{1 \text{ meter}}{\sqrt{\alpha}}$, α being the ratio of the meter to the given unit.

For the English foot, $\alpha = 3.28109$. It thus appears that our diagram is of general practical utility, and is universally applicable. †

---

* Instead of using a ruler it will be found more convenient to stretch a black thread from the axis of abscissæ to the slope curves.— *Trans.*

† Inasmuch as the present translation will be consulted chiefly by American and English engineers, we have added (Plate VIII) a large scale diagram in English measure, and in Appendix V have shown the method of constructing it.— *Trans.*

PLATE VI.

‖RAM

ion of the values *c*, *n*, *R* and
Ganguillet and Kutter for
vers and other Channels.

$$= \left(\frac{a + \frac{l}{n} + \frac{m}{S}}{1 + \left(a + \frac{m}{S}\right)\frac{n}{\sqrt{R}}} \right) \} RS.$$

MEASURE.

ROOTS OF R

R	$\sqrt{R}$	R	$\sqrt{R}$	R	$\sqrt{R}$	R	$\sqrt{R}$
3.10	1.76	6.10	2.47	9.1	3.02	18.0	3.61
3.20	1.79	6.20	2.49	9.2	3.03	14.0	3.74
3.30	1.82	6.30	2.51	9.3	3.05	15.0	3.87
3.40	1.84	6.40	2.53	9.4	3.07	16.0	4.00
3.50	1.87	6.50	2.55	9.5	3.08	17.0	4.12
3.60	1.90	6.60	2.57	9.6	3.10	18.0	4.24
3.70	1.92	6.70	2.59	9.7	3.11	19.0	4.36
3.80	1.95	6.80	2.61	9.8	3.13	20.0	4.47
3.90	1.97	6.90	2.63	9.9	3.15	24.0	4.58
4.00	2.00	7.00	2.65	10.0	3.16	22.0	4.69
4.10	2.02	7.10	2.66	10.1	3.16	23.0	4.80
4.20	2.05	7.20	2.68	10.2	3.18	24.0	4.90
4.30	2.07	7.30	2.70	10.3	3.10	25.0	5.00
4.40	2.10	7.40	2.72	10.4	3.21	26.0	5.10
4.50	2.12	7.50	2.74	10.5	3.23	27.0	5.20
4.60	2.14	7.60	2.76	10.6	3.25	28.0	5.29
4.70	2.17	7.70	2.77	10.7	3.26	29.0	5.38
4.80	2.19	7.80	2.79	10.8	3.28	30.0	5.48
4.90	2.21	7.90	2.81	10.9	3.30	31.0	5.57
5.00	2.24	8.00	2.83	11.0	3.32	32.0	5.66
5.10	2.26	8.10	2.85	11.1	3.33	33.0	5.74
5.20	2.28	8.20	2.86	11.2	3.34	34.0	5.83
5.30	2.30	8.30	2.88	11.3	3.36	35.0	5.92
5.40	2.32	8.40	2.90	11.4	3.37	36.0	6.00
5.50	2.35	8.50	2.92	11.5	3.39	37.0	6.08
5.60	2.37	8.60	2.93	11.6	3.40	38.0	6.16
5.70	2.39	8.70	2.95	11.7	3.42	39.0	6.24
5.80	2.41	8.80	2.97	11.8	3.44	40.0	6.32
5.90	2.43	8.90	2.98	11.9	3.45	41.0	6.40
6.00	2.45	9.00	3.00	12.0	3.46	42.0	6.48

$$23 + \frac{1}{n} + \frac{0.001\ldots}{S}$$

$$23 + \frac{1}{n} + \frac{0.0\ldots}{\ }$$

$$1 + \left(23 + \frac{\ }{\ } \frac{0.00\ldots}{S}\right.$$

2,0   3,2   2,4   2,6   2,8   3,0

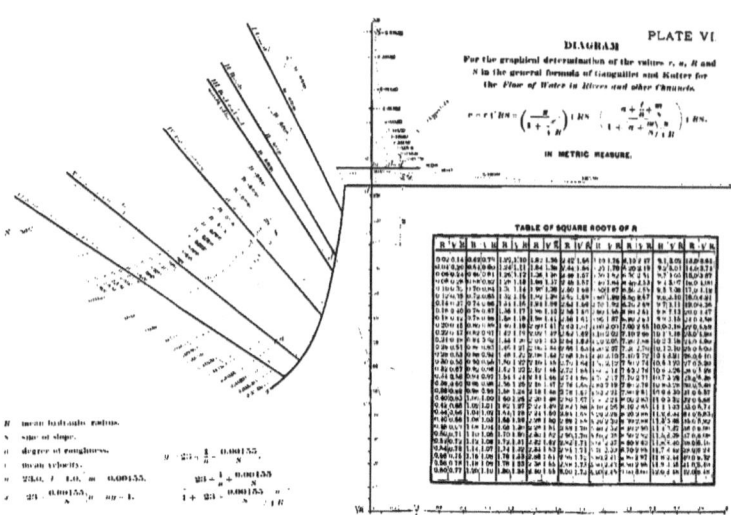

PLATE VI

DIAGRAM

For the graphical determination of the values c, u, R and
S in the general formula of Ganguillet and Kutter for
the Flow of Water in Rivers and other Channels.

$$c = c\sqrt{RS} = \left(\frac{R}{1+\frac{c}{\sqrt{R}}}\right) \sqrt{RS} \quad \left(\frac{a+\frac{l}{n}+\frac{m}{R}}{1+a+\frac{m}{n}\cdot\frac{n}{R}}\right)\sqrt{RS}.$$

IN METRIC MEASURE.

TABLE OF SQUARE ROOTS OF R

R = mean hydraulic radius.

S = sine of slope.

n = degree of roughness.

c = mean velocity.

$a = 23.0,\ l = 1.0,\ m = 0.00155.$

$c = 23 + \frac{0.00155}{S} + \frac{1}{n}, \quad ny = 1.$

$y = 23 + \frac{1}{n} + \frac{0.00155}{S}.$

$\frac{23 + \frac{1}{n} + \frac{0.00155}{S}}{1 + 23 + \frac{0.00155}{S} \cdot \frac{n}{\sqrt{R}}}.$

36. The correctness of the new general formula demonstrated by the results of 210 gaugings under widely different circumstances.

We have yet to show in how far our general formula accords with the results of observations by M. Bazin, by the American engineers Humphreys and Abbot, and by other authors. For this purpose we append a brief collection of such results, and remark in this connection, that, in view of the general character of our formula, it may appear permissible if the observations should fail to accord as closely as the several formulæ specially derived from them. Again, the values n of our six categories are not intended to be rigidly adhered to, but should in any particular case be modified according to its requirements, because they are merely mean values or suggestions intended to aid in the determination of the coefficients. M. Bazin gives definite coefficients for four categories only, and makes all intermediate cases subordinate to them.

We may be permitted to observe that our formula agrees more closely with the Mississippi observations than does that of Humphreys and Abbot.

To facilitate the comparison, we add in each case columns showing the differences between the results of the formulæ and those of the observations. The amounts in these columns are found by dividing the result of the formula by that of the gauging and deducting unity from the quotient. At the foot of each column in each series we give the arithmetical mean of the amounts. In the summary we give also means which are found by taking for each series the sum of the differences between the observed and the calculated results, and means found by taking the differences between the positive and negative differences. The comparison is thus made in three different ways.

In all three of them our formula is seen to give the best results, as will be evident from a glance at the summary. Out of 236* comparisons, 22 result in favor of Humphreys and Abbot, 49 in favor of that of Bazin, and 165 in favor of our own.

---

* See remark at foot of summary.

COMPARISON OF THE FORMULÆ OF

HUMPHREYS AND ABBOT, . . . (H. A.),
M. BAZIN, ... (B.),
GANGUILLET AND KUTTER, . . (G. K.).

(Metric measure.)

No.	$\sqrt{R}$	Slope, S	Mean Velocity.				Differences. Velocity measured / Velocity by formula -1.		
			Meas-ured.	By formula—					
				H. A.	B.	G. K.	H. A.	B.	G. K.

Bazin, Series No. 24. $n = 0.0100$.

No.	$\sqrt{R}$	Slope, S	Measured	H. A.	B.	G. K.	H. A.	B.	G. K.
1	0.334	0.0014243	0.921	0.323	0.914	0.909	− 1.85	− 0.01	− 0.01
2	0.391	"	1.135	0.378	1.103	1.135	− 2.06	− 0.03	0.00
3	0.429	"	1.267	0.415	1.289	1.289	− 2.05	− 0.03	+ 0.02
4	0.456	"	1.401	0.441	1.351	1.397	− 2.18	− 0.04	0.00
5	0.478	"	1.483	0.462	1.386	1.488	− 2.21	− 0.07	0.00
6	0.496	"	1.562	0.479	1.445	1.565	− 2.26	− 0.08	0.00
7	0.514	"	1.612	0.496	1.502	1.630	− 2.25	− 0.07	+ 0.02
8	0.528	"	1.681	0.510	1.547	1.698	− 2.29	− 0.09	+ 0.01
9	0.538	"	1.754	0.520	1.577	1.740	− 2.37	− 0.11	− 0.01
10	0.550	"	1.803	0.531	1.617	1.792	− 2.39	− 0.11	− 0.01
11	0.560	"	1.847	0.541	1.649	1.835	− 2.41	− 0.12	− 0.01
12	0.561	"	1.862	0.543	1.653	1.841	− 2.43	− 0.13	− 0.01
						Means:	2.22	0.07	0.01

Bazin, Series No. 2. $n = 0.0105$.

No.	$\sqrt{R}$	Slope, S	Measured	H. A.	B.	G. K.	H. A.	B.	G. K.
1	0.226	0.0050600	1.018	0.200	1.039	0.917	− 4.09	+ 0.02	− 0.10
2	0.277	"	1.338	0.368	1.358	1.740	− 2.63	+ 0.02	− 0.08
3	0.313	"	1.537	0.417	1.593	1.485	− 2.69	+ 0.04	− 0.04
4	0.338	"	1.731	0.443	1.749	1.655	− 2.91	+ 0.01	− 0.05
5	0.362	"	1.853	0.482	1.897	1.825	− 2.84	+ 0.02	− 0.01
6	0.380	"	1.984	0.506	2.009	1.952	− 2.92	+ 0.01	− 0.02
7	0.397	"	2.081	0.529	2.115	2.078	− 2.93	+ 0.02	0.00
8	0.412	"	2.171	0.549	2.209	2.183	− 2.96	+ 0.02	0.00
9	0.426	"	2.258	0.566	2.293	2.281	− 2.99	+ 0.02	+ 0.01
10	0.439	"	2.326	0.584	2.372	2.375	− 3.00	+ 0.02	+ 0.02
11	0.450	"	2.397	0.599	2.437	2.437	− 3.00	+ 0.02	+ 0.02
12	0.461	"	2.460	0.613	2.504	2.536	− 3.00	+ 0.02	+ 0.03
						Means:	3.00	0.02	0.03

Bazin, Series No. 26. $n = 0.0120$.

No.	$\sqrt{R}$	Slope, S	Measured	H. A.	B.	G. K.	H. A.	B.	G. K.
1	0.345	0.0015227	0.795	0.339	0.777	0.787	− 1.35	− 0.02	− 0.01
2	0.404	"	0.984	0.398	0.956	0.989	− 1.47	− 0.03	0.00
3	0.439	"	1.132	0.431	1.063	1.109	− 1.63	− 0.07	− 0.02
4	0.468	"	1.230	0.460	1.153	1.212	− 1.67	− 0.07	− 0.01
5	0.492	"	1.297	0.484	1.228	1.301	− 1.70	− 0.06	0.00
6	0.511	"	1.374	0.502	1.285	1.367	− 1.74	− 0.07	0.00
7	0.530	"	1.413	0.521	1.343	1.437	− 1.71	− 0.05	+ 0.02
8	0.542	"	1.486	0.533	1.379	1.483	− 1.79	− 0.08	0.00
9	0.556	"	1.524	0.547	1.421	1.534	− 1.79	− 0.07	+ 0.01
10	0.567	"	1.579	0.557	1.453	1.573	− 1.84	− 0.08	0.00
11	0.578	"	1.612	0.568	1.489	1.618	− 1.84	− 0.08	0.00
12	0.587	"	1.660	0.577	1.513	1.650	− 1.88	− 0.10	− 0.01
13	0.592	"	1.689	0.583	1.530	1.672	− 1.90	− 0.10	− 0.01
						Means :	1.64	0.07	0.01

COMPARISON OF THE THREE FORMULÆ—*Continued.*

No.	√R	SLOPE, S	MEAN VELOCITY.				DIFFERENCES. Velocity measured / Velocity by formula − 1.		
			Meas-ured.	By formula—					
				H. A.	B.	G. K.	H. A.	B.	G. K.

Bazin, Series No. 6. n = 0.0130.

No.	√R	SLOPE, S	Meas.	H. A.	B.	G. K.	H. A.	B.	G. K.
1	0.271	0.0022136	0.635	0.293	0.657	0.601	− 1.16	+ 0.04	− 0.06
2	0.333	"	0.819	0.300	0.887	0.817	− 1.28	+ 0.09	0.00
3	0.372	"	0.962	0.402	1.031	0.961	− 1.39	+ 0.07	0.00
4	0.401	"	1.076	0.434	1.142	1.076	− 1.48	+ 0.06	0.00
5	0.428	"	1.152	0.403	1.243	1.178	− 1.49	+ 0.08	+ 0.02
6	0.444	"	1.259	0.481	1.302	1.242	− 1.62	+ 0.03	− 0.01
7	0.463	"	1.324	0.501	1.373	1.319	− 1.64	+ 0.04	0.00
8	0.481	"	1.374	0.520	1.439	1.387	− 1.64	+ 0.05	+ 0.01
9	0.494	"	1.440	0.535	1.488	1.439	− 1.69	+ 0.03	0.00
10	0.508	"	1.487	0.550	1.536	1.495	− 1.70	+ 0.03	− 0.01
11	0.518	"	1.552	0.560	1.573	1.537	− 1.77	+ 0.01	+ 0.01
12	0.530	"	1.587	0.574	1.619	1.586	− 1.77	+ 0.02	0.00
						Means:	1.55	0.05	0.01

Bazin, Series No. 7. n = 0.0120.

No.	√R	SLOPE, S	Meas.	H. A.	B.	G. K.	H. A.	B.	G. K.
1	0.239	0.0048889	0.826	0.315	0.713	0.824	− 1.62	− 0.16	0.00
2	0.288	"	1.127	0.379	1.077	1.090	− 1.97	− 0.05	− 0.03
3	0.323	"	1.325	0.424	1.264	1.291	− 2.12	− 0.05	− 0.03
4	0.350	"	1.479	0.460	1.419	1.450	− 2.22	− 0.04	− 0.02
5	0.372	"	1.612	0.489	1.516	1.583	− 2.30	− 0.06	− 0.02
6	0.392	"	1.711	0.515	1.647	1.704	− 2.32	− 0.04	0.00
7	0.408	"	1.808	0.537	1.739	1.808	− 2.37	− 0.04	0.00
8	0.423	"	1.808	0.556	1.818	1.898	− 2.41	− 0.04	0.00
9	0.437	"	1.967	0.575	1.896	1.991	− 2.42	− 0.04	+ 0.01
10	0.449	"	2.045	0.590	1.960	2.045	− 2.47	− 0.04	0.00
11	0.461	"	2.102	0.606	2.032	2.142	− 2.47	− 0.03	+ 0.02
12	0.471	"	2.179	0.619	2.083	2.202	− 2.52	− 0.05	− 0.01
						Means:	2 27	0.05	0.01

Bazin, Series No. 8. n = 0.0115.

No.	√R	SLOPE, S	Meas.	H. A.	B.	G. K.	H. A.	B.	G. K.
1	0.211	0.0081629	1.074	0.317	0.894	0.938	− 2.39	− 0.20	− 0.15
2	0.265	"	1.348	0.398	1.229	1.315	− 2.39	− 0.09	− 0.02
3	0.297	"	1.594	0.445	1.457	1.556	− 2.58	− 0.09	− 0.03
4	0.323	"	1.776	0.484	1.632	1.758	− 2.67	− 0.09	− 0.01
5	0.346	"	1.902	0.519	1.804	1.944	− 2.67	− 0.05	+ 0.02
6	0.362	"	2.053	0.550	1.919	2.056	− 2.73	− 0.07	0.00
7	0.377	"	2.186	0.565	2.022	2.196	− 2.87	− 0.08	0.00
8	0.393	"	2.268	0.589	2.136	2.328	− 2.85	− 0.06	+ 0.03
9	0.406	"	2.357	0.609	2.231	2.440	− 2.87	− 0.06	+ 0.03
10	0.418	"	2.447	0.626	2.312	2.535	− 2.91	− 0.06	+ 0.04
11	0.429	"	2.518	0.644	2.397	2.633	− 2.91	− 0.05	+ 0.05
12	0.438	"	2.612	0.657	2.458	2.707	− 2.98	− 0.07	+ 0.04
						Means:	2.73	0.08	0 03

COMPARISON OF THE THREE FORMULÆ—*Continued.*

No.	√R	Slope, S	Measured.	By formula—			Velocity measured / Velocity by formula − 1.		
				H. A.	B.	G. K.	H. A.	B.	G. K.

Bazin, Series No. 3.   n = 0.0130.

No.	√R	Slope, S	Measured.	H. A.	B.	G. K.	H. A.	B.	G. K.
1	0.242	0.0050750	0 839	0.321	0.839	0.764	− 1.61	0.00	− 0.10
2	0.294	"	1.117	0.390	1.124	1.030	− 1.86	0.00	− 0.08
3	0.334	"	1.274	0.442	1.391	1.242	− 1 86	+ 0.09	− 0.03
4	0.359	"	1.440	0.476	1 487	1.386	− 2.03	+ 0.03	− 0.04
5	0.383	"	1.555	0.508	1.618	1.520	− 2.06	+ 0.04	− 0.02
6	0.406	"	1.626	0.538	1.749	1.651	− 2.02	+ 0.08	+ 0.01
7	0.421	"	1.731	0.559	1.834	1.741	− 2.10	+ 0.05	0.00
8	0.435	"	1.831	0.576	1.907	1.821	− 2.18	+ 0.04	0.00
9	0.451	"	1 874	0.598	1.999	1.916	− 2.13	+ 0.07	+ 0.02
10	0.461	"	1.973	0.611	2.055	1.976	− 2 23	+ 0.05	0.00
11	0.475	"	2.012	0.629	2.129	2.055	− 2.20	+ 0.06	+ 0.02
12	0.487	"	2.047	0.646	2.200	2.148	− 2.17	+ 0.07	+ 0.05
						Means:	2.04	0.05	0.03

Bazin, Series No. 39.   n = 0.0130.

No.	√R	Slope, S	Measured.	H. A.	B.	G. K.	H. A.	B.	G. K.
1	0.352	0.008100	1 746	0.526	1.837	1.710	− 2.32	+ 0.05	− 0.02
2	0.417	"	2.293	0.623	2.299	2.182	− 2.68	0.00	− 0.05
3	0.455	"	2.495	0.680	2.570	2.468	− 2.67	+ 0.03	− 0.01
4	0.483	"	2.666	0.722	2.767	2.680	− 2 63	+ 0.04	0.00
						Means.	2.50	0.03	0.02

Bazin, Series No. 32.   n = 0.0170.

No.	√R	Slope, S	Measured.	H. A.	B.	G. K.	H. A.	B.	G. K.
1	0.314	0.1007600	3.747	0.882	3.444	3.644	− 3.25	− 0.09	− 0.03
2	0.380	"	4.931	1.059	4.672	4.828	− 5.66	− 0.06	− 0.02
3	0.420	"	5.694	1.179	5.536	5.656	− 3.83	− 0.03	− 0.01
4	0.449	"	6.429	1.261	6.126	6.232	− 4.10	− 0.05	− 0 03
						Means:	3.71	0.06	0.02

Bazin, Series No. 33.   n = 0.0170.

No.	√R	Slope, S	Measured.	H. A.	B.	G. K.	H. A.	B.	G. K.
1	0.360	0.036856	2.757	0.787	2 610	2.707	− 2.50	− 0.06	− 0.02
2	0.435	"	3.494	0.951	3.529	3.588	− 2.67	+ 0.01	+ 0.03
3	0.477	"	4.131	1.043	4.036	4.109	− 2.96	− 0.02	0.00
4	0.510	"	4.595	1.115	4.510	4.530	− 3.12	− 0 02	− 0.01
						Means:	2.81	0.03	0.01

Kutter, Grünnbachschale.   n = 0.0175.

No.	√R	Slope, S	Measured.	H. A.	B.	G. K.	H. A.	B.	G. K.
1	0.329	0.082850	3 600	0.881	3.352	3.410	− 3.10	− 0.07	− 0.06
2	0.340	0.099270	4.062	0.953	3.877	3.931	− 3.26	− 0.05	− 0.03
3	0.344	0.106775	4.191	0.977	4.110	4.144	− 3.29	− 0 02	− 0.01
4	0.421	0.082850	4.737	1.127	5.042	4.957	− 3.20	+ 0.06	− 0.04
5	0.440	0.099270	5.574	1.233	5.886	5.789	− 3.52	+ 0.06	− 0.03
6	0.444	0.106775	5.844	1.262	6.210	6.094	− 3.63	+ 0.06	− 0.04
						Means:	3.33	c.05	0.03

COMPARISON OF THE THREE FORMULÆ—*Continued.*

No.	$\sqrt{R}$	SLOPE, S	MEAN VELOCITY.				DIFFERENCES.		
			Measured.	By formula—			$\dfrac{\text{Velocity measured}}{\text{Velocity by formula}} - 1.$		
				H. A.	B.	G. K.	H. A.	B.	G. K.

Strauss, Lauter Canal. $n = 0.0260.$

No.	$\sqrt{R}$	SLOPE, S	Meas.	H. A.	B.	G. K.	H. A.	B.	G. K.
1	0.744	0.0006640	0.642	0.632	0.635	0.648	− 0.01	− 0.01	+ 0.01

La Nicca, Canal at Marmels. $n = 0.02530.$

1	0.840	0.0005000	0.576	0.626	0.657	0.563	+ 0.09	+ 0.14	− 0.02

Legler, Linth Canal. $n = 0.0220.$

No.	$\sqrt{R}$	SLOPE, S	Meas.	H. A.	B.	G. K.	H. A.	B.	G. K.
1	1.252	0.000290	1.041	0.887	0.953	1.049	− 0.18	− 0.09	0.00
2	1.344	0.000300	1.170	0.950	1.071	1.174	− 0.23	− 0.09	0.00
3	1.405	0.000310	1.266	1.013	1.171	1.278	− 0.25	− 0.08	+ 0.01
4	1.473	0.000320	1.347	1.059	1.257	1.362	− 0.28	− 0.08	+ 0.01
5	1.514	0.000330	1.441	1.097	1.323	1.435	− 0.32	− 0.09	− 0.01
6	1.572	0.000340	1.500	1.153	1.410	1.526	− 0.30	− 0.06	+ 0.02
7	1.589	0.000340	1.542	1.160	1.436	1.550	− 0.33	− 0.07	0.00
8	1.621	0.000350	1.593	1.192	1.492	1.610	− 0.34	− 0.07	+ 0.01
9	1.644	0.000360	1.644	1.217	1.541	1.663	− 0.35	− 0.07	+ 0.01
10	1.673	0.000370	1.686	1.245	1.599	1.721	− 0.35	− 0.06	+ 0.02
						Means:	0.29	0.08	0.01

Dubuat, Canal du Jard. $n = 0.0250.$

No.	$\sqrt{R}$	SLOPE, S	Meas.	H. A.	B.	G. K.	H. A.	B.	G. K.
1	0.715	0.0000362	0.137	0.283	0.139	0.138	+ 1.01	+ 0.01	0.00
2	0.769	0.0000362	0.146	0.304	0.156	0.155	+ 1.09	+ 0.07	+ 0.06
3	0.791	0.0000458	0.185	0.332	0.185	0.185	− 0.80	0.00	0.00
4	0.887	0.0000651	0.320	0.407	0.260	0.268	+ 0.25	− 0.23	0.22
						Means:	0.77	0.08	0.07

Grebenau, Hübengraben. $n = 00235.$

1	0.423	0.0013000	0.434	0.433	0.323	0.435	0.00	− 0.34	0.00

Grebenau, Hockenbach. $n = 0.0245.$

No.	$\sqrt{R}$	SLOPE, S	Meas.	H. A.	B.	G. K.	H. A.	B.	G. K.
1	0.514	0.0007833	0.439	0.445	0.355	0.430	+ 0.01	− 0.24	− 0.02
2	0.518	0.0007966	0.446	0.451	0.302	0.441	+ 0.01	− 0.24	− 0.01
						Means:	0.01	0.24	0.01

Grebenau, Speyerbach. $n = 0.0250.$

1	0.668	0.0006667	0.556	0.585	0.527	0.578	+ 0.05	− 0.06	+ 0.04

COMPARISON OF THE THREE FORMULÆ—*Continued.*

No.	√R	Slope, S	Mean Velocity				Differences		
			Meas-ured.	By formula—			Velocity measured / Velocity by formula − 1.		
				H. A.	B.	G. K.	H. A.	B.	G. K.

Humphreys and Abbot, Mississippi. n = 0.0270.

No.	√R	Slope, S	Meas.	H.A.	B.	G.K.	H.A.	B.	G.K.
1	3.082	0.00012227	1.074	0.953	0.824	1.053	− 0.13	− 0.30	− 0.02
2	3.986	0.00003029	1.644	1.707	1.261	1.623	+ 0.01	− 0.34	− 0.04
3	4.181	0.00004811	1.926	1.866	1.673	1.972	− 0.03	− 0.15	+ 0.02
4	4.420	0.00000379	2.118	1.978	2.017	2.300	− 0.01	− 0.04	+ 0.01
5	4.435	0.00004365	2.080	2.102	1.700	2.063	− 0.01	− 0.22	− 0.01
6	4.481	0.00000800	2.121	1.874	2.143	2.393	− 0.13	+ 0.01	+ 0.13
7	4.685	0.00002051	1.807	1.819	1.231	1.845	0.00	− 0.47	+ 0.02
8	4.700	0.00001713	1.794	1.868	1.128	1.772	+ 0.04	− 0.59	− 0.01
9	4.734	0.00000342	1.229	1.308	0.508	1.209	+ 0.06	− 1.42	− 0.02
10	4.762	0.00000384	1.212	1.232	0.541	1.263	+ 0.02	− 1.24	− 0.04
						Means	0.05	0.48	0.04

Humphreys and Abbot, Bayou Plaquemine. n = 0.0300.

No.	√R	Slope, S	Meas.	H.A.	B.	G.K.	H.A.	B.	G.K.
1	2.161	0.00014372	1.207	1.089	1.378	1.197	− 0.11	+ 0.14	− 0.00
2	2.365	0.00020644	1.584	1.570	1.835	1.563	− 0.01	+ 0.16	− 0.01
						Means:	0.06	0.15	0.01

Humphreys and Abbot, Bayou Lafourche. n = 0.0200.

No.	√R	Slope, S	Meas.	H.A.	B.	G.K.	H.A.	B.	G.K.
1	1.950	0.00004384	0.850	0.827	0.670	0.874	− 0.03	− 0.27	+ 0.03
2	1.975	0.00003655	0.855	0.864	0.621	0.826	+ 0.01	− 0.38	− 0.04
3	1.993	0.00003731	0.866	0.872	0.636	0.847	+ 0.01	− 0.37	− 0.02
4	2.188	0.00004468	0.938	0.875	0.778	1.030	− 0.07	− 0.21	+ 0.09
						Means:	0.03	0.31	0.04

Ellet, Ohio River, Point Pleasant. n = 0.0210.

No.	√R	Slope, S	Meas.	H.A.	B.	G.K.	H.A.	B.	G.K.
1	1.431	0.00000334	0.767	0.776	0.650	0.763	+ 0.01	− 0.18	− 0.01

Buffon, Tiber at Rome. n = 0.0240.

No.	√R	Slope, S	Meas.	H.A.	B.	G.K.	H.A.	B.	G.K.
1	1.968	0.00013061	1.040	1.082	0.970	1.042	+ 0.04	− 0.07	0.00

Destrem, Great Nevka. n = 0.0250.

No.	√R	Slope, S	Meas.	H.A.	B.	G.K.	H.A.	B.	G.K.
1	2.304	0.00001487	0.624	0.466	0.477	0.624	− 0.34	− 0.31	0.00

Destrem, Neva. n = 0.0270.

No.	√R	Slope, S	Meas.	H.A.	B.	G.K.	H.A.	B.	G.K.
1	3.256	0.00001389	0.984	0.832	0.690	0.998	− 0.18	− 0.43	+ 0.01

COMPARISON OF THE THREE FORMULÆ—Continued.

No.	√R	Slope, S	Mean Velocity — Measured.	By formula— H. A.	B.	G. K.	Differences. $\frac{\text{Velocity measured}}{\text{Velocity by formula}} - 1.$ H. A.	B.	G. K.
			Brunings, Rhine delta in Holland. n = 0.0250.						
1	1.625	0.00022016	1.122	1.082	1.186	1.157	− 0.05	+ 0.06	+ 0.03
2	1.870	0.00011500	0.910	1.073	1.032	1.038	+ 0.13	+ 0.13	+ 0.14
3	1.948	0.00011056	0.918	1.101	1.062	1.069	+ 0.20	+ 0.16	+ 0.16
4	1.951	0.00022016	1.474	1.350	1.502	1.464	− 0.09	+ 0.02	− 0.01
5	2.213	0.00011500	1.310	1.277	1.272	1.274	− 0.03	− 0.03	− 0.03
6	2.260	0.00011056	1.210	1.283	1.271	1.300	+ 0.07	+ 0.05	+ 0.07
						Means:	0.10	0.07	0.07
			Schwarz, Weser. n = 0.0230.						
1	1.348	0.00018335	0.430	0.850	0.840	0.889	+ 0.98	+ 0.96	+ 1.07
2	1.387	0.00039856	1.246	1.072	1.288	1.340	− 0.16	+ 0.03	+ 1.08
3	1.393	0.00041100	1.580	1.089	1.316	1.378	− 0.45	− 0.20	− 0.15
4	1.435	0.00041067	1.503	1.119	1.370	1.431	− 0.33	− 0.10	− 0.06
5	1.628	0.00019168	1.058	1.053	1.109	1.168	0 00	+ 0.05	+ 0.10
6	1.696	0.00020000	1.239	1.112	1.200	1.247	− 0.11	− 0.03	0.00
7	1.745	0.00020000	1.338	1.142	1.238	1.305	− 0.17	− 0.08	− 0.02
8	1.791	0.00021668	1.450	1.207	1.336	1.400	− 0.20	− 0.08	− 0.03
9	1.837	0.00021668	1.581	1.235	1.378	1.443	− 0.20	− 0.15	− 0.03
10	1.961	0.00053103	2.416	1.684	2.351	2.405	− 0.43	− 0.03	0.00
11	2.017	0.00055035	2.409	1.734	2.470	2.532	− 0.39	+ 0.03	+ 0.05
						Means:	0.31	0.16	0.15
			Poirée, Seine at Paris. n = 0.0250.						
1	1.314	0.000127	0.638	0.735	0.673	0 675	+ 0.15	+ 0 06	+ 0.06
2	1.463	0.000133	0.630	0.863	0.705	0.797	+ 0.35	+ 0.13	+ 0.15
3	1.603	0.000135	0.737	0.940	0.912	0.901	+ 0.29	+ 0.24	+ 0.36
4	1.700	0.000140	1.027	1.011	1.005	1.491	− 0 02	− 0.02	− 0.04
5	1.824	0.000140	1.140	1.092	1.101	1.090	− 0.04	− 0.04	− 0.04
6	1.927	0.000140	1.163	1.163	1.179	1.173	0 00	+ 0.01	+ 0.01
7	2.102	0.000140	1.290	1.273	1.311	1.311	− 0.01	+ 0 02	+ 0.02
8	2 140	0.000140	1.375	1.296	1.342	1.342	− 0.06	− 0.02	− 0.02
9	2 203	0.000172	1.427	1.404	1.540	1.532	− 0.01	+ 0.08	+ 0.08
10	2.266	0.000131	1.463	1.349	1.390	1.403	− 0.09	− 0.05	− 0.04
11	2.367	0.000103	1.429	1.329	1.298	1.338	− 0.08	− 0.10	− 0.07
						Means:	0.98	0.06	0.08
			Emery, Seine at Poissy, etc. n = 0.0270.						
1	1.471	0.000090	0.704	0.784	0.670	0.621	+ 0.11	− 0.05	− 0.13
2	1.530	0.000087	0.705	0.808	0.689	0.646	+ 0.14	− 0 02	− 0.09
3	1.851	0.000057	0.720	0.880	0.715	0.704	+ 0.22	− 0.01	− 0.02
4	1.946	0.000060	0.719	0.938	0.781	0.772	+ 0.30	+ 0.09	+ 0.07
5	2.034	0.000050	0.723	0.932	0.752	0 762	+ 0.32	+ 0.04	+ 0.05
6	2.050	0.000054	0.791	0.994	0.806	0.812	+ 0.26	+ 0.02	+ 0.03
7	2.109	0.000062	0.887	1.085	0.923	0 924	+ 0.22	+ 0.04	+ 0.04
8	2.216	0.000067	0.945	1.141	0.992	0 994	+ 0.20	+ 0.05	+ 0.05
9	2.334	0.000075	1.015	1.208	1.087	1.083	+ 0.19	+ 0.07	+ 0.00
						Means:	0.22	0.04	0.06

COMPARISON OF THE THREE FORMULÆ—*Continued.*

No.	$\sqrt{R}$	Slope, S	Measured.	By formula— H. A.	B.	G. K.	Velocity measured / Velocity by formula − 1, H. A.	B.	G. K.
Leveillé, Saône at Raconnay. n = 0.0280.									
1	1.650	0.000040	0.488	0.718	0.515	0.496	+ 0.47	+ 0.06	+ 0.02
2	1.820	"	0.565	0.792	0.586	0.575	+ 0.40	+ 0.04	+ 0.02
3	1.881	"	0.582	0.819	0.610	0.604	+ 0.41	+ 0.05	+ 0.04
4	1.897	"	0.592	0.826	0.618	0.612	+ 0.40	− 0 04	+ 0.03
5	2.011	"	0.087	0.890	0.665	0.667	− 0.29	− 0.03	− 0.03
6	2.113	"	0.722	0.935	0.707	0.716	+ 0.30	− 0.02	− 0.01
7	2.197	"	0.725	0.970	0.739	0.757	− 0.34	+ 0.02	+ 0.04
						Means:	0.37	0.04	0.03
Dubuat, Haine. n = 0.0260.									
1	1.213	0.0000303	0.275	0.475	0.294	0.288	+ 0.73	+ 0.07	+ 0.05
2	1.224	0.0001653	0.730	0.732	0.694	0.661	0.00	− 0.05	− 0.10
3	1.322	0.0001559	0.629	0.779	0.753	0.715	+ 0.24	+ 0.20	+ 0.14
4	1.333	0.0000279	0.333	0.510	0.322	0.325	+ 0.53	− 0.04	− 0.02
						Means:	0.37	0.09	0.08
Strauss, Rhine at Speyer. n = 0.0260.									
1	1.722	0.0001120	0.887	0.971	0 913	0.882	+ 0.10	+ 0.03	− 0.01
Grebenau, Rhine at Germersheim. n = 0.0230.									
1	1.819	0.0002470	1.540	1.267	1.458	1.518	− 0.21	− 0.06	− 0.01
Grebenau, Rhine at Bâle. n = 0.0300.									
1	1.449	0.0012180	1.945	1.501	2.393	1.942	− 0.30	+ 0.23	0.00
Isar, n = 0.0300.									
1	0.752	0.002500	1.226	0.929	1.253	1.102	− 0.32	− 0.02	− 0.11
2	1.358	"	2.189	1.691	3.125	2.539	− 0.29	+ 0.43	+ 0.16
						Means:	0.32	0.22	0.13
Legler. Escher Canal. n = 0 0280.									
1	1.070	0.003000	1.938	1.324	2 426	2.004	− 0.46	+ 0.25	+ 0.03
2	1.160	"	2.340	1.439	2.733	2.951	− 0.63	+ 0.17	− 0.04
						Means:	0.54	0.21	0.03

COMPARISON OF THE THREE FORMULÆ—*Concluded.*

No.	$\sqrt{R}$	Slope, S	Mean Velocity Measured.	By formula— H.A.	B.	G. K.	Differences. Velocity measured / Velocity by formula -1. H. A.	B.	G. K.

La *Nicca*, *Plessur at Chur.* $n = 0.0270$.

No.	$\sqrt{R}$	Slope, S	Measured.	H.A.	B.	G. K.	H. A.	B.	G. K.
1	0.616	0.009650	1.830	0.969	1.750	1.811	— 0.89	— 0.05	— 0.19
2	0.844	"	3.045	1.351	2.984	2.788	— 1.25	— 0.02	— 0.00
3	1.029	"	3.108	1.719	4.095	3.781	— 1.81	+ 0 32	+ 0.22
4	1.045	"	4.140	1.744	4.426	3.858	— 1.37	+ 0.07	— 0.07
5	1.046	"	4.251	1.748	4.205	3.875	— 1.43	— 0.01	— 0.09
6	1.181	"	4.191	1.911	4.799	4.417	— 1.19	+ 0.14	+ 0.05
						Means	1.16	0.10	0.09

La *Nicca*, *Rhine in Rhine Forest.* $n = 0.0310$.

No.	$\sqrt{R}$	Slope, S	Measured.	H.A.	B.	G. K.	H. A.	B.	G. K.
1	0.356	0.014200	0.711	0.611	0.768	0.777	— 0.16	+ 0.08	+ 0.09
2	0.482	"	1.380	0.828	1 363	1.282	— 0.67	— 0.01	— 0.08
3	0.607	"	1.839	1.042	2.062	1.845	— 0.76	+ 0.12	0.00
						Means:	0 53	0.07	0.06

La *Nicca*, *Mösa in Misox.* $n = 0.0310$.

No.	$\sqrt{R}$	Slope, S	Measured.	H.A.	B.	G. K.	H. A.	B.	G. K.
1	0.548	0.011875	1.179	0.896	1.571	1.433	— 0.32	+ 0.33	+ 0.22
2	0.604	"	1.689	0.988	1.870	1.672	— 0.71	+ 0.11	— 0.01
3	0.682	"	2.313	1.115	2.311	2.006	— 1.08	0.00	— 0.15
						Means:	0.70	0.15	0.13

SUMMARY OF MEANS OF THE FOREGOING COMPARISONS.

H.A. signifies Humphreys and Abbot; B., Bazin; G.K., Ganguillet and Kutter.

Locality.	No. of Gaugings.	Arithmetical Mean of Differences by — Equation $\frac{v}{v_1}-1$ H.A.	B.	G.K.	Sums of Differences. H.A.	B.	G.K.	Differences of Differences. H.A.	B.	G.K.	Number of Best Results by — Equation $\frac{v}{v_1}-1$ H.A.	B.	G.K.	Sums of Differences. H.A.	B.	G.K.	Differences of Differences. H.A.	B.	G.K.
Bazin, Series No. 24. Cement	12	2.22	0.07	0.01	1.06	0.10	0.01	1.06	0.10	0.00			12			12			11
" 2 "	12	3.00	0.02	0.0	1.44	0.04	0.05	1.44	0.04	0.00		8	7		7	6		7	6
" 26. Boards	13	1.64	0.07	0.01	0.87	0.02	0.01	0.87	0.09	0.00			13			13			13
" 6. "	12	1.55	0.05	0.01	0.75	0.05	0.01	0.75	0.05	0.00	1	1	11		1	11	1		11
" 7. "	12	2.27	0.05	0.01	1.17	0.08	0.01	1.17	0.08	0.00			12			12			12
" 8. "	12	2.73	0.08	0.01	1.48	0.14	0.04	1.48	0.14	0.00		1	12		1	12			12
" 3. Brick	12	2.04	0.05	0.02	1.08	0.09	0.04	1.08	0.08	0.00		3	9		3	9		3	9
" 39. Ashlar	4	2.59	0.03	0.02	1.66	0.07	0.05	1.66	0.07	0.04		1	3		1	3	1	3	3
" 32. Rubble	4	3.71	0.66	0.02	4.10	0.25	0.11	4.10	0.25	0.11		3	4			4		1	4
" 33. "	4	2.81	0.03	0.01	2.77	0.09	0.06	2.77	0.07	0.01	1	1	6		1	6			3
Grünnbachschale. Rubble	6	3.33	0.05	0.0	3.59	0.25	0.17	3.59	0.08	0.17		1	6		1	6	1		6
Lauter Canal. Earth	1	0.01	0.01	0.01	0.01	0.01	0.01	0.01	0.01	0.01			1			1			1
Canal at Marmels. Coarse detritus	1	0.09	0.14	0.01	0.05	0.08	0.06	0.05	0.08	0.01	1			1					1
Linth Canal. Gravel	10	0.29	0.08	0.01	0.33	0.10	0.06	0.34	0.10	0.01		1	10		1	10			10
Canal du Jard	4	0.79	0.05	0.0	0.13	0.02	0.0	0.13	0.01	0.01	1	1	4	1	1	4	1	1	4
Hübengraben. Earth	1	0.00	0.34	0.0	0.00	0.11	0.08	0.00	0.11	0.01		1	1		1	1		1	1
Hockenbach. "	2	0.01	0.24	0.0	0.01	0.08	0.01	0.01	0.08	0.01	2		1		2	1		2	1
Speyerbach. "	1	0.05	0.66	0.0	0.03	0.03	0.02	0.03	0.03	0.02		1			1				
Mississippi. Mud, uneven	10	0.05	0.48	0.04	0.08	0.44	0.07	0.04	0.40	0.03	4	2	5	3	3	5	3		5
Bayou Plaquemine	2	0.06	0.15	0.01	0.06	0.21	0.02	0.06	0.21	0.02	1		2	1	1	2	1	2	1
Bayou Lafourche	4	0.03	0.11	0.04	0.02	0.20	0.04	0.02	0.20	0.02	4			4			4		1

SUMMARY OF MEANS OF THE FOREGOING COMPARISONS—Continued.

Locality.	No. of Gaugings.	Arithmetical Mean of Differences by— Equation $\frac{v}{v_1}-1$ H.A.	B.	G.K.	Sums of Differences. H.A.	B.	G.K.	Differences of Differences. H.A.	B.	G.K.	Number of Best Results by— Equation $\frac{v}{v_1}-1$ H.A.	B.	G.K.	Sums of Differences. H.A.	B.	G.K.	Differences of Differences. H.A.	B.	G.K.
Ohio River	1	0.01	0.18	0.01	0.04	0.12	0.0	0.01	0.12	0.0	1								1
Tiber, at Rome	1	0.04	0.07	0.04	0.04	0.07	0.0	0.03	0.07	0.0	1								1
Nevka	1	0.34	0.31	0.04	0.10	0.15	0.0	0.16	0.15	0.0			1			1			1
Neva	1	0.18	0.43	0.01	0.15	0.20	0.01	0.15	0.26	0.01	1		1			1			2
Rhine Delta (Brunings)	6	0.10	0.07	0.07	0.10	0.07	0.07	0.03	0.06	0.0	1	4	4		3	2	1	3	3
Weser (Schwarz)	11	0.31	0.16	0.15	0.34	0.13	0.1	0.26	0.03	0.02		3	7		3	7		3	7
Seine at Paris	11	0.68	0.09	0.08	0.68	0.06	0.07	0.01	0.01	0.0	5	6		4	5		4	5	3
Seine at Poissy, etc.	9	0.22	0.04	0.04	0.18	0.03	0.05	0.18	0.07	0.01		7			1	7		7	7
Saône at Raconnay	7	0.37	0.04	0.0	0.23	0.02	0.0	0.2	0.01	0.02	2	2		2	1		2	6
Ilaine	4	0.37	0.0	0.08	0.13	0.05	0.04	0.13	0.02	0.0	1			1				3
Rhine at Speyer. Fine detritus	1	0.10	0.0	0.01	0.08	0.03	0.0	0.08	0.03	0.0	1					1		1
Rhine at Germersheim. Fine detritus	1	0.21	0.0	0.0	0.17	0.08	0.02	0.27	0.08	0.0						1		1
Rhine at Basle. Coarse detritus	1	0.30	0.2	0.04	0.41	0.45	0.0	0.44	0.45	0.0			1			1		1
Isar. Coarse detritus	2	0.30	0.12	0.0	0.40	0.47	0.24	0.40	0.48	0.01	1		1			2		2
Escher Canal. Coarse detritus (boulders)	2	0.54	0.2	0.0	0.76	0.44	0.08	0.7	0.44	0.01		1				2		2
Plessur. " "	6	1.16	0.1	0.0	1.55	0.34	0.3	1.53	0.28	0.0	3	4		2	4		2	4
Rhine in Rhine Forest. Coarse detritus "	3	0.51	0.0	0.0	0.48	0.10	0.08	0.48	0.09	0.01	2	3	1	2	1		2	1
Nilxa in Misox. " "	3	0.70	0.1	0.0	0.73	0.19	0.1	0.73	0.19	0.02	2	2		1	2		1	2
Totals	210	35.13	4.07	1.41	27.1	5.55	2.6	26.86	5.10	0.81	22	40	165	18	47	155	18	47	155
Means	1	0.99	0.13	0.09	0.70	0.14	0.05	0.69	0.13	0.02	2.56*			215*			215*	

* REMARK.—In cases where two of the formulæ give each a "best result," it is credited to both of them. Hence the "totals" somewhat exceed the number of gaugings.

37. Remarks upon the result of the foregoing comparison and upon the experiments themselves.

From the data contained in this table it appears: that the formula of Humphreys and Abbot frequently gives too great velocities where the slopes are very small, and invariably too small velocities where the slopes are great; that M. Bazin's formula is not applicable to large streams with very small slopes, and that the new general formula, on the contrary, gives useful values throughout. We thus see that the first two formulæ are not universally applicable, although that of M. Bazin can, if modified, be made so. We must observe, however, that while the foregoing comparison embraces the most important of over 700 available gaugings, a similar comparison of other observations would doubtless give a different numerical result, which, however, would still uphold the above conclusion. M. Bazin's formula would no doubt be more exact if it were not restricted to four categories with fixed coefficients α and β, and if their variations were considered for all possible cases. The fact that we have in a few instances obtained results from M. Bazin's formula which differ from those given in the "Recherches hydrauliques" is, as already observed, due to our different use of the slopes. For instance, for Series No. 2 we found $S = 0.00506$, instead of $S = 0.00490$, which is the mean slope of the entire channel.

The great diversity in the phenomena and effects of the flow of water, and the widely differing influences to which that flow is exposed, from differences in roughness, in form and size of channel or river-bed, in slope, etc., explain the impossibility of obtaining good results in all cases from a formula which, like that of Humphreys and Abbot, is deduced from gaugings relating to quite extreme and one-sided conditions, without reference to a comprehensive series of gaugings made in various streams of the greatest possible diversity of character. This, however, does not in the least detract from the great value of the service which Humphreys and Abbot have rendered to the science of hydraulics.

Their work will always maintain its high position in the

literature of this branch of science, and the results of the investigations and gaugings in the Mississippi will never cease to be of great importance and to demand our grateful acknowledgments.

In comparing the differences between the results of the observations and of the formulæ, we have not assumed that the former are necessarily correct and the latter alone in error; the records of the gaugings have many imperfections, as appears at once from a glance at the graphic representation of the values of c corresponding to analogous experiments.

The coefficient for determining the velocity of the water from the number of revolutions of Woltmann's current-meter is not easily found with great exactness, while Pitot's tube gives the velocities only at the moment of observation, and cannot determine the mean values of the variations of speed, such as oscillations, pulsations, which take place during a certain interval of time. This is an important defect of the instrument.

Gaugings made with single and double floats require a very accurate determination of the times of passage, and this is always a very delicate operation even with the use of the best stop-watches. If, in view of this difficulty, a repetition of the measurements is resorted to, we are confronted with the fact that the arithmetical mean time is not necessarily the true time, and that we can expect an approximately correct average only after the elimination of those results which vary widely from the mean. And when ascertaining only the surface velocities, as accurately as possible by means of floats, the mean velocity has yet to be determined by multiplication with a more or less doubtful coefficient. Or, if the velocities are measured at different depths in a sufficient number of vertical planes, and the area of the cross-section is found, even then each of these several operations is subject to so many inaccuracies that no hydraulician can feel assured that he has measured the velocity with mathematical accuracy, or that such measurement is possible. The best gaugings are those in which the volume of discharge can be directly determined; yet here, too, precise time-measurement is indispensable.

The greatest difficulty, however, lies in the exact deter-

mination of the slope, which is the sole cause of the flow
and necessarily a principal factor in the formulæ.

In rivers an additional resistance is caused by irregularities
of cross-section and by bends in the stream, and, in view of
the uniform flow assumed by the formulæ, that portion of the
slope which is required to overcome these resistances should
be deducted from the measured slope in order to obtain the
effective slope.

Along the banks of large streams the level of the surface
is not regular, but variable ; in the main channel it is generally
somewhat higher, and its slope is necessarily more regular and
better suited to serve as a basis for calculation, than that
along the banks. Aside from the accuracy or inaccuracy of the
leveling instruments, a precise determination of the slope is
rendered a most difficult task by the fact that the movement
of the water, even in regular reaches of channels and rivers,
prevents the surface-level at a given spot from remaining constant. Furthermore, the flow seems in general to partake of a
wave-like motion, so that with precisely the same height of
water the volume discharged through the same cross-section
in equal times is not quite constant ; in other words, the mean
velocity is variable.

In this connection, Bernard remarks : * " We observe great
irregularity in rivers ; their width, depth and slope change con-
tinually ; their velocity is never uniform, either near the
channel or at any other point. In the same cross-section, we
find a multitude of different currents, both at low and high
water. At high water the differences of velocity are more
decided, and the main current may be distinguished from the
others by having a higher elevation."

This being true, flowing water has really no uniform motion,
such as is assumed in the formulæ, and it must always be a
difficult task to execute precise measurements of the flow.
Hence, when observed velocities are stated with more than
three decimal places for meters per second, or more than two
decimal places for feet per second, we know that they affect a
degree of precision which is simply unattainable.

---

* " Nouveaux principes hydrauliques," 1787.

We therefore remark that the discrepancies between the results of the gaugings and of the formulæ, irrespective of the differences among the latter, are chargeable *not only to the formulæ but also more or less to the gaugings themselves.*

38. Concluding remarks.

In the foregoing treatise we have recited the method followed by us in our effort to establish a general formula for the determination of the mean velocity of water flowing with a uniform motion in channels and streams, a formula applicable alike to the flow in small artificial channels and to that in great rivers ; and we have shown how we embodied in it a relation between the coefficient *n*, designating the degree of roughness of wetted perimeter, and the other values in the formula, by introducing a *single* coefficient varying with the degree of roughness, so that our formula satisfies the conditions required to render it generally applicable. Besides the variation of the coefficient *c* with the value *R* and with the degree of roughness, our formula provides for its two opposite variations with the slope, a variation which is apparent from the recorded observations, but recognized by no other formula. Similarly, the variation of the exponent *x* in the equation

$$\frac{c_0}{c_1} = \left(\frac{S_0}{S_1}\right)^x,$$

which is likewise deduced from the observations, is given by none other.

We make no claim to the establishment of a new theory, but give merely an empirical formula, in which we supply what we regard as lacking in the formulæ of Bazin and of Humphreys and Abbot; and we herewith submit this endeavor to the criterion of science. We hope that in doing so we have contributed in a small degree to the advancement of the study of Hydraulics.

A hundred years ago Michelotti and Bossut had established the fundamental principle, to which Dubuat also subscribes, that formulæ for the expression of the flow of water must be deduced, not by abstract theorizing, but from the results of experiments. We have acted upon this principle, and leave to others the task of explaining the recently acquired facts by mechanical laws, and of constructing a new and satisfactory theory from the rich fund of accumulated experimental data.

SUPPLEMENT.

39. A more direct derivation of the formula.

When we wrote the foregoing treatise, some eight years ago, we gave an account of the conception and development of our formula. This proved to be somewhat voluminous. In order to satisfy those who prefer mathematical brevity, we add the following simple and comprehensive sketch of its derivation.

In the general formula

$$v = c \sqrt{RS},$$

the coefficient c increases with the value of R, decreases with the increase of the slope S when $R > 1.00^m$, increases with the increase of slope when $R < 1.00^m$, and varies with the roughness of the wetted perimeter of the channel. In order to express these variations we have in the first place followed the example of M. Bazin in choosing the binomial form. We put

$$c = \frac{y}{1 + \dfrac{x}{\sqrt{R}}},$$

in which y embraces the variations with the slope and with the roughness, and $-\dfrac{x}{\sqrt{R}}$ the variations with R. We used $\sqrt{R}$ instead of R, because we found that by so doing we obtained results more nearly in accordance with the facts. If we divide the above equation by y and take the reciprocals of the values thus obtained, we have

$$c = \frac{1}{\dfrac{1}{y}+\dfrac{x}{y}\cdot\dfrac{1}{\sqrt{R}}} \quad \cdots \quad \cdots \quad (1)$$

and

$$\frac{1}{c} = \frac{1}{y}+\frac{x}{y}\cdot\frac{1}{\sqrt{R}} , \quad \cdots \quad \cdots \quad (2)$$

in which $\dfrac{1}{\sqrt{R}}$ gives the abscissæ and $\dfrac{1}{c}$ the ordinates of a straight line forming with the axis of abscissæ an angle whose tangent is $\dfrac{x}{y}$, and in which $\dfrac{1}{y}$ gives the value of $\dfrac{1}{c}$ when $\dfrac{1}{\sqrt{R}} = 0$.

In order to connect the Mississippi results with those of European and other smaller rivers, we plot, for all the streams which may be classed under the same category, the values $\dfrac{1}{\sqrt{R}}$ as abscissæ and the corresponding values of $\dfrac{1}{c}$ as ordinates. Now, in order to satisfy equation (2), those of the resulting

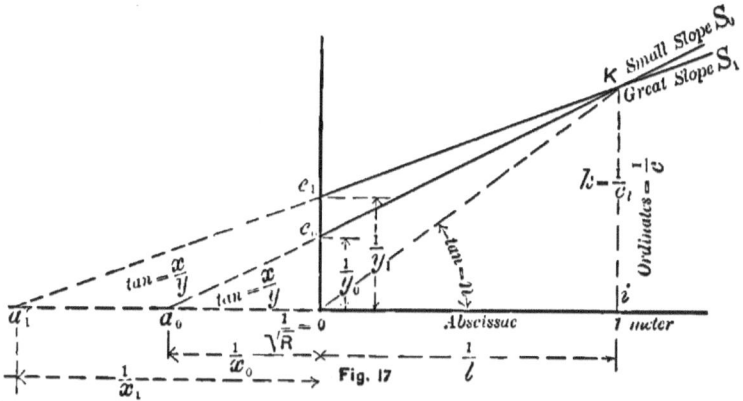

Fig. 17

points which correspond to similar slopes should lie in straight lines to be produced to the axis of ordinates. As this, however, is seldom more than approximately the case, we draw the straight lines so as to average, as nearly as possible, the points for each slope.

We of course obtain as many straight lines (Fig. 17) as there are degrees of slope in the experiments chosen. We have shown that these lines may be so drawn as to intersect each other in a single point, as indicated in the figure:

The values $\dfrac{1}{y}$ thus obtained determine the centers of the hyperbolæ corresponding to the several slopes; and the ordinate $\dfrac{1}{c}$ of the intersection K is common to all the lines.

If $\dfrac{1}{l}$ is the abscissa of the intersection, and k its ordinate, we have, from equation (2),

$$k = \frac{1}{y} + \frac{x}{y} \cdot \frac{1}{l} \quad \cdot \quad \cdot \quad \cdot \quad \cdot \quad \cdot \quad \cdot \quad \cdot \quad (3)$$

and

$$x = kly - l.$$

The ordinate k varies only with the roughness of the wetted perimeter and hence is constant for all slopes. We may consider $k \div \dfrac{1}{l}$ or kl as a tangent and therefore put $kl = n$, from which we have

$$x = ny - l. \quad \cdot \quad \cdot \quad \cdot \quad \cdot \quad \cdot \quad \cdot \quad \cdot \quad (4)$$

If we plot the reciprocals $\left(\dfrac{1}{S}\right)$ of the given slopes as abscissæ, and the corresponding values of y, obtained graphically from the above figure, as ordinates, as in Fig. 18, then, in order to express the variation of c with the variation of the slope in the formula, as explained in our treatise, we draw a straight line as nearly as practicable through the points obtained, and extend it to the axis of ordinates. The equation of this line has the form

$$y' = y_1 + \frac{m}{S}, \quad \cdots \quad \cdots \quad (5)$$

in which m is the tangent of the angle formed between the straight line and the axis of abscissæ, and y_1 is the distance of

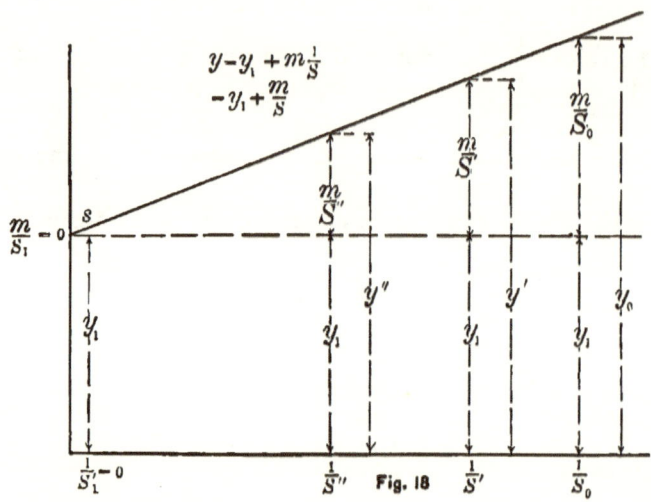

Fig. 18

the axis of abscissæ from the intersection of the straight line with the axis of ordinates. Since $\frac{1}{S}$, at the origin of the axis of abscissæ, is $= 0$, y_1 corresponds to a slope $S = \infty$. The variation of c with variation of slope may therefore be expressed in the general equation $c = \dfrac{y'}{1 + \dfrac{x}{\sqrt{R}}}$ by substituting, in accordance with (5) and (4), $y_1 + \dfrac{m}{S}$ for y', and $n\left(y_1 + \dfrac{m}{S}\right) - l$ for x, thus:

$$c = \frac{y_1 + \dfrac{m}{S}}{1 + \dfrac{n\left(y_1 + \dfrac{m}{S}\right) - l}{\sqrt{R}}}, \quad \cdots \quad \cdots \quad (6)$$

n and y_1, varying with the roughness of the wetted perimeter, while the other coefficients are constant. In order to express the mutual variation of n and y_1, we observe that, according to Bazin, x generally diminishes with increase of y_1. Hence, in order that x in equation (6) may diminish when y_1 increases, n must evidently decrease with x. Therefore the relation between x, n and y_1 is most simply expressed by

$$x_1 = an;$$

in which (for any given value of n) x_1 is the value of x for the case where $S = \infty$, and a is a constant; and from which, by (4),

$$an = ny_1 - l;$$

and thus

$$y_1 = \frac{l}{n} + a. \quad . \quad . \quad . \quad . \quad . \quad . \quad . \quad (7)$$

Substituting this value for y_1 in equations (5) and (4), we have

$$y' = \frac{l}{n} + a + \frac{m}{S}, \quad . \quad . \quad . \quad . \quad . \quad . \quad . \quad (8)$$

and

$$x = l + an + \left(\frac{m}{S}\right)n - l$$

or

$$x = \left(a + \frac{m}{S}\right)n; \quad . \quad . \quad . \quad . \quad . \quad . \quad . \quad (9)$$

and we thus obtain, for equation (1),

$$c = \frac{a + \dfrac{l}{n} + \dfrac{m}{S}}{1 + \left(a + \dfrac{m}{S}\right)\dfrac{n}{\sqrt{R}}}, \quad . \quad . \quad . \quad . \quad . \quad (10)$$

in which equation n expresses the degree of roughness of wetted perimeter, and is variable, while a, l and m are con-

stant coefficients.   By means of the graphic process indicated
by the above figures, we obtain

$$l = 1.00,$$

$$n = 0.027 \text{ for the Mississippi, etc.,}$$

$$m = 0.00155.$$

$$a = y_1 - \frac{l}{n} = 60 - \frac{1}{0.027} = 23.$$

The foregoing values are for metric measures, in which our
formula is

$$v = \left(\frac{23 + \dfrac{1}{n} + \dfrac{0.00155}{S}}{1 + \left(23 + \dfrac{0.00155}{S}\right)\dfrac{n}{\sqrt{R}}} \right) \sqrt{RS}. \quad . \quad . \quad (11)$$

40. General remarks on the coefficient of roughness n.*

We remarked in our treatise that the coefficient n must indicate not only the roughness of the material of the sides and
bottom of the channel, but also irregularities of profile, and,
generally, the conditions causing retardation of flow.   The
correctness of this view has been fully established.

Even in comparatively regular reaches of a river, the
position of the point of greatest depth often changes, being
found alternately near the left and near the right bank.   This
necessarily produces lateral movements of the water, which, in
combining with the forward movements due to the general
slope, cause increased resistances among the particles of water,
and increased retardation of flow.†

---

* See also Art. 29 and Appendix III.

† Hagen therefore errs in assuming that the velocity is constant for the
same slope when the mean radius is also constant.   (Handbuch der Wasserbaukunst, vol. ii. ¶ 65.)   The form of cross-section of a river may change
greatly while its mean radius remains the same, and in such cases the velocity
will be less than where the form of cross-section remains constant.   The
coefficient n of roughness should represent such resistance.

This and many other causes, such as the degree of turbidity of the water, eddies rising from the bottom, in short all causes of retardation of flow, as well as mere roughness of wetted surface, are covered by our n.

The variation of this coefficient in one and the same section of a channel has already been observed by Mr. Grebenau in the Rhine at Germersheim; and it has since appeared still more unmistakably from Mr. R. Gordon's gaugings of the Irawadi in Burmah. In this case n decreased as the depth increased; thus:

$$R = 6.393 \text{ to } 13.047;$$

$$n = 0.045 \text{ to } 0.029.$$

No such variation was observed in the case of the Mississippi;[*] but we have already shown in our treatise that, with a constant degree of roughness of wetted perimeter, the effect of such roughness is very marked in the smallest streams, such as M. Bazin's experimental canals, and is barely if at all perceptible in very large ones, such as the Mississippi. On the Irawadi the coefficient n of roughness decreases as the depth increases, and we may assume that if $R = \infty$ the coefficient n would be zero.

At any rate, this decrease of n with increase of depth is not a surprising phenomenon.

41. Development of a second general formula.[†]

With regard to the variation of c with variation of slope in small channels, namely, a decrease of c with decrease of slope when $R < 1.00^m$, we would observe that this variation was noticed chiefly in the wooden channels of Bazin, in which, however, there appeared also a number of cases of opposite character, namely, an *increase* of c with decrease of slope, as in large streams. The variations were not great, and Bazin neglected them in his formula because they seemed contradictory. In

---

[*] Later gaugings do show this variation   See Table 1.— *Trans.*

[†] For a third formula, by the same authors, see Appendix VI.

our formula, the increase of c with increase of slope when $R < 1.00^m$ is less than in M. Bazin's wooden channels.

If, in view of this contradiction between the results of M. Bazin's experiments as to the effect of slope, and, considering the smallness of that effect in small channels, we prefer to omit it and to show only the effect of slope in large streams, we obtain a different formula deduced as follows:

As in the foregoing, let

$$c = \frac{y}{1 + \dfrac{x}{\sqrt{R}}} = \frac{1}{\dfrac{1}{y} + \dfrac{x}{y} \cdot \dfrac{1}{\sqrt{R}}} \; ; \quad \cdots \cdots \quad (1)$$

$$\frac{1}{c} = \frac{1}{y} + \frac{x}{y} \cdot \frac{1}{\sqrt{R}} \cdots \cdots \cdots \cdots \cdots \quad (2)$$

Let us take the observations in the Mississippi and on other streams of similar character as to the bed of the channel, plot the observed values of $\dfrac{1}{\sqrt{R}}$ as abscissæ, and the corresponding values of $\dfrac{1}{c}$ as ordinates, draw straight lines averaging as nearly as possible those points which correspond to similar slopes, and produce them to the axis of ordinates. We thus obtain as many straight lines as there are slopes.

As but few comparable results of this kind exist, and as the points so obtained are widely scattered, it might be claimed that these straight lines may properly be drawn so that they shall not intersect at all,* but be parallel to each other, as in Fig. 19.

Under this assumption, the tangent $\dfrac{x}{y}$ of the angle between the straight lines and the axis of abscissæ remains the same for each category of roughness of wetted perimeter, even if y varies. We accordingly designate this tangent n and thus obtain, from (1),

---

* As they do in the first general formula.— *Trans.*

$$c = \cfrac{1}{\cfrac{1}{y} + \cfrac{n}{\sqrt{R}}} \quad \cdots \quad \cdots \quad \cdots \quad (3)$$

Plotting as ordinates the values y corresponding to the several slopes and given by the above figure, and as abscissæ

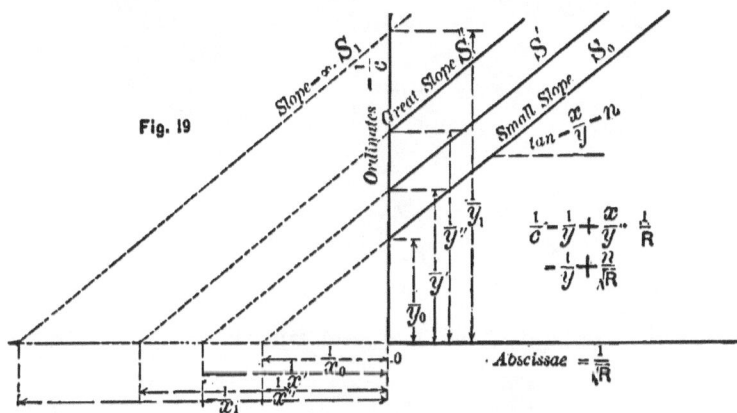

Fig. 19

the values $\dfrac{1}{S}$, and joining by a straight line the points so found, we obtain for this line, as in the case of the first formula, Fig. 18, the equation

$$y = y_1 + \frac{m}{S} \quad \cdots \quad \cdots \quad \cdots \quad (4)$$

In plotting this straight line we obtain the values of y_1 and of $\dfrac{m}{S}$. Substituting them in the general formula, we have

$$\frac{1}{c} = \cfrac{1}{y_1 + \cfrac{m}{S}} + \frac{n}{\sqrt{R}} \quad , \quad \cdots \quad \cdots \quad (5)$$

and

$$c = \cfrac{y_1 + \cfrac{m}{S}}{1 + \left(y_1 + \cfrac{m}{S}\right)\cfrac{n}{\sqrt{R}}} \quad \cdots \quad \cdots \quad (6)$$

This formula shows an increase of c with decrease of slope, and a variation of y_1 and n with that of roughness of the wetted perimeter.

The relation between y_1 and n, according to which x_1 decreases when y_1 increases, may be most simply expressed thus:

$$x_1 y_1 = a;$$

from which

$$x_1 = \frac{a}{y_1}\ ,$$

$$n = \frac{a}{y_1^2}\ ,$$

$$y_1 = \sqrt{\frac{a}{n}}\ .$$

Substituting this value for y_1 in equations (5) and (6), we find

$$\frac{1}{c} = \frac{1}{\sqrt{\frac{a}{n}+\frac{m}{S}}} + \frac{n}{1\,R}\ \cdot \qquad \cdots \quad (7)$$

and

$$c = \frac{\sqrt{\sqrt{\frac{a}{n}}+\frac{m}{S}}}{1 + \left(\sqrt{\frac{a}{n}}+\frac{m}{S}\right)\frac{n}{1\,R}} \quad \cdots \quad (8)$$

In this equation also, n expresses the degree of roughness[*] of the wetted perimeter, while a and m are constant coefficients. By means of the graphic process indicated above, we find, for metric measure,

$$m = 0.000719,$$

$$a = 150.66,$$

---

[*] The numerical values of n in this second formula of course differ from those in the first one. — *Trans.*

and thus obtain a second general formula :

$$v = \left(- \ - \frac{\sqrt{\dfrac{150.66}{n} + \dfrac{0.000719}{S}}}{1 + \left(\sqrt{\dfrac{150.66}{n} + \dfrac{0.000719}{S}}\right) \dfrac{n}{\dfrac{n}{R}}} \right) \sqrt{RS}. \quad . \quad . \quad (9)$$

This second formula assumes that the effect of slope in small streams is the same as in large ones, namely, an increase of c with decrease of slope : but it is nevertheless, as we see, too complicated for convenient every-day use. We have therefore represented it graphically for that purpose, and have included a diagram (Plate VII), that the reader may use either this or Plate VI (representing our first formula) as his judgment may dictate.

We have not as yet found reason to modify our first formula.* Still, we must not neglect to say that it contains a variation of the coefficient c which is open to some doubt, namely, a rapid decrease of c with decrease of slope in small channels with very smooth sides. Since, however, we are not in possession of experimental data for such channels with very light slopes, we are unable to investigate as to whether our misgivings are well founded.†

---

* Mr. Ganguillet writes (September, 1888) that he has made careful comparisons and finds that the second formula agrees less well with the gaugings than the first one.

† The authors here add some remarks, with a table and diagram, to show that the recent formulæ of Hagen, viz.,

$$v = 4.9 \ R^{\prime} \sqrt{S} \text{ for small streams,}$$

and

$$v = 3.34 \ \sqrt{R} \ \prime \sqrt{S} \text{ for large streams,}$$

are absolutely useless as general formulæ, because they give for streams with great slopes only $\frac{1}{8}$ to $\frac{1}{4}$ of the measured velocities, and for others a proportionately great error. Believing that this negative discussion can be of little interest to our readers, we have omitted it from the present work.—*Trans.*

PLATE VII.

...RAM

...of the values *c*, *n*, *R* and *S* in
...of Ganguillet and Kutter.

$$\left.\frac{\dfrac{n}{S}}{\dfrac{n}{\sqrt{R}}}\right)\ \sqrt{RS}.$$

(See p. 103.)

...150.66, *m* = 0.000719.

...raulic radius.
...pe.
...roughness.
...city.

...RE ROOTS OF R

$\sqrt{\bar R}$	R	$\sqrt{\bar R}$	R	$\sqrt{\bar R}$	R	$\sqrt{\bar R}$	R	$\sqrt{\bar R}$
1.56	3.10	1.76	6.10	2.47	9.1	3.02	13.0	3.61
1.56	3.20	1.79	6.20	2.49	9.2	3.03	14.0	3.74
1.57	3.30	1.82	6.30	2.51	9.3	3.05	15.0	3.87
1.57	3.40	1.84	6.40	2.53	9.4	3.07	16.0	4.00
1.58	3.50	1.87	6.50	2.55	9.5	3.08	17.0	4.12
1.59	3.60	1.90	6.60	2.57	9.6	3.10	18.0	4.24
1.59	3.70	1.92	6.70	2.59	9.7	3.11	19.0	4.36
1.60	3.80	1.95	6.80	2.61	9.8	3.13	20.0	4.47
1.61	3.90	1.97	6.90	2.63	9.9	3.15	24.0	4.58
1.61	4.00	2.00	7.00	2.65	10.0	3.16	22.0	4.69
1.62	4.10	2.02	7.10	2.66	10.1	3.16	23.0	4.80
1.62	4.20	2.05	7.20	2.68	10.2	3.18	24.0	4.90
1.63	4.30	2.07	7.30	2.70	10.3	3.10	25.0	5.00
1.64	4.40	2.10	7.40	2.72	10.4	3.21	26.0	5.10
1.64	4.50	2.12	7.50	2.74	10.5	3.23	27.0	5.20
1.65	4.60	2.14	7.60	2.76	10.6	3.25	28.0	5.29
1.66	4.70	2.17	7.70	2.77	10.7	3.26	29.0	5.38
1.66	4.80	2.19	7.80	2.79	10.8	3.28	30.0	5.48
1.67	4.90	2.21	7.90	2.81	10.9	3.30	31.0	5.57
1.67	5.00	2.24	8.00	2.83	11.0	3.32	32.0	5.66
1.68	5.10	2.26	8.10	2.85	11.1	3.33	33.0	5.74
1.69	5.20	2.28	8.20	2.86	11.2	3.34	34.0	5.83
1.69	5.30	2.30	8.30	2.88	11.3	3.36	35.0	5.92
1.70	5.40	2.32	8.40	2.90	11.4	3.37	36.0	6.00
1.70	5.50	2.35	8.50	2.92	11.5	3.39	37.0	6.08
1.71	5.60	2.37	8 60	2.93	11.6	3.40	38.0	6.16
1.71	5.70	2.39	8.70	2.95	11.7	3.42	39.0	6.24
1.72	5.80	2.41	8.80	2.97	11.8	3.44	40.0	6.32
1.73	5.90	2.43	8.90	2.98	11.9	3.45	41.0	6.40
1.73	6.00	2.45	9.00	3.00	12.0	3.46	42.0	6.48

Rubble Masonry

1.6   1.8   2.0   2.2   2.4   2.6   2.8   3.0

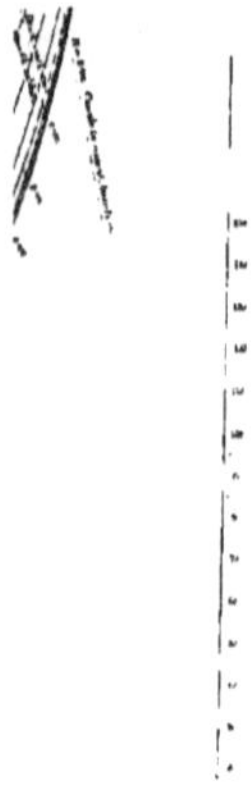

PLATE VII

DIAGRAM

For the graphical determination of the values c, n, R and S in the second general formula of Ganguillet and Kutter.

$$v = \left(\frac{a + \frac{l}{n} - \frac{m}{S}}{1 + \left(a + \frac{m}{S} \right) \frac{n}{\sqrt{R}}} \right) \sqrt{RS}.$$

See p. 103.

For metric measure: $a = 23$, $l = 1$, $m = 0.00155$.

R = mean hydraulic radius.
S = sine of slope.
n = degree of roughness.
v = mean velocity.

TABLE OF SQUARE ROOTS OF R

R	√R	R	√R	R	√R	R	√R	R	√R	R	√R	R	√R	R	√R	R	√R
[illegible]	[illegible]	[illegible]	[illegible]	[illegible]	[illegible]	[illegible]	[illegible]	[illegible]	[illegible]	[illegible]	[illegible]	[illegible]	[illegible]	[illegible]	[illegible]	[illegible]	[illegible]

APPENDICES.

I.

Limitations of the formula.*

Naturally our formula cannot apply to cases or conditions beyond the limits of existing gaugings and, still less, beyond possibilities. While it is true that the formula might give impossible velocities for a channel ten times larger than the Mississippi, with a fall almost infinitely small and with a bed having the highest degree of smoothness, yet this does not invalidate it, because such conditions nowhere occur. The formula rests only upon actual gaugings, and (which is most important) it embraces all *maximum* and *minimum* conditions *known up to the present time.*† Being an empirical formula, it is confined to the limits occurring in nature and makes no claim whatever to absolute perfection.

In spite of the large number of available gaugings, it cannot be denied that our knowledge of the elements and laws of the motion of water still needs extension and correction. It is therefore of the greatest importance to increase the collection of gaugings, and particularly is it highly desirable to have more reliable observations on large streams, such as the Amazon, etc., and likewise on very large and very small artificial channels.

---

* From " Bewegung des Wassers in Canälen und Flüssen," by W. R. Kutter. 1885.

† In the authors' collection of gaugings, c varies from 12.1 to 254.3 (English measure), and the width of the water surfaces ranges from 4 inches to 2740 feet.

II.

General laws. Examples.*

The general laws for the variation of the coefficient c, in the general formula $v = c \sqrt{RS}$, are as follows :

c increases :

I. *With the increase of the hydraulic depth* R, and most rapidly when R is small.

II. *With the decrease of the resistance to flow*, i.e., with the decrease of roughness of the perimeter, so that for constant values of R and S, c is greatest for the smoothest channel and smallest for the roughest channel, such as a mountain stream. This influence of roughness upon c is also greatest for the smallest value of R.

III. *With the decrease of S, if $R > 1$ meter*, and also in small channels if the wetted perimeter is very rough in comparison with the area of the cross-section.

IV. *With the increase of S, if $R < 1$ meter*, and if the wetted perimeter is smooth.†

---

* From " Bewegung des Wassers in Canälen und Flüssen," by W. R. Kutter. 1885.

† The seeming paradox, according to which the coefficient c has certain opposite variations with the slope, may be explained as follows :

The larger the water-way, the less will the direction of the movement of each particle of water be confined to that of the general current. In rivers we observe innumerable lateral currents and eddies, due both to a higher elevation of the water surface in the current and to natural irregularities of the bed. But in small channels with smooth beds there is less cause for such irregular movements. The larger the channel, therefore, the greater is the head consumed by these perturbations, and the smaller is the available slope left to generate the mean velocity in the cross-section

In rivers this loss will increase with the velocity or slope, because the conditions for quiet motion become less favorable, the water is more agitated and stronger lateral movements are produced, culminating in surface disturbances and eddies which retard the flow. A similar effect will appear also in small channels when the perimeter is very rough.

Therefore, in *large channels*, and in such small ones as have a very rough

In confirmation of the above principles we select the following interesting examples, all given in metric measure:

1. A comparison of Bazin's series Nos. 24 and 25, referring to semicircular channels in smooth cement, both having the same slope ($S = 0.0014$) for *the same values of R* ($R =$ about 0.1 to 0.3), shows a decrease in the values of c of about 7, simply because in series No. 25 the cement-mortar contained $\frac{1}{4}$ very fine river sand.

2. In Bazin's rectangular channels, 2 meters wide and lined with boards, there is a considerable increase in the values of c, for *the same values of R*, with the increase of the slope S. The average differences are:

   a. Between series No. 7 ($S = 0.005$) and No. 11 ($S = 0.008$) **2.5** to **7.0.**

   b. Between series No. 7 ($S = 0.005$) and No. 9 ($S = 0.0015$) **4.0** to **7·0.**

   c. Between series No. 9 ($S = 0.0015$) and No. 11 ($S = 0.008$) **8.0** to **11.0.**

When, in these channels, obstructions or resistances to the flow are introduced, such as laths nailed across the channel at short distances apart, or a lining of small or large pebbles held in place by cement, then the variation of c with the slope changes to the contrary, *i.e.*, c increases with the decrease of S. (Of course c increases also with the decrease in the size of the obstructions.) In the case of laths nailed crosswise, 0.01 meter apart, we find an increase of c with decrease of S ($S = 0.0090$

---

perimeter, the coefficient c should be expected relatively to increase with the *decrease* of slope.

On the other hand, in small and smooth channels, the loss of head due to lateral movements will decrease as the velocity or the slope increases, because such movements become less and less possible in a more rapid and confined current.

Therefore, in *small channels*, with smooth perimeter, the coefficient c should tend to increase with the *increase* of slope.

There are, however, exceptions to this contrary variation, and it is, furthermore, likely that the value l, instead of being a constant $= \sqrt[4]{1}$ meter, itself varies with the degree of roughness.—R. H.

to 0.0015), amounting, however, only to a difference of 0.5 to 1.0, for *the same values of R*. If the spaces between the laths are increased to 0.05 meter, the differences of *c* increase to 1.0 and 2.0.

The degree of roughness has even a greater effect upon *c* than that of the slope, just described. For the two cases, when the laths are 0.01 meter and 0.05 meter apart, and *R and S remain the same*, the differences of *c* increase up to 16.0. When the pebbles of the cemented gravel vary from 0.01 to 0.02 meter in diameter in one case, and from 0.03 to 0.05 meter in the other, and *R and S remain the same* in both instances, the differences of *c* increase to 8.0 and 10.5.

In comparing the gaugings of channels lined with boards with others having a greater degree of roughness, the following differences were found, for *equal values of R and S* :

(1) Channels with laths nailed crosswise, 0.01 meter apart :
$S = 0.0015$, difference of *c* :   **9.7**
$= 0.0059$,   "   "   **13.7**
$= 0.0085$,   "   "   **16.9**

(2) Channels with laths nailed crosswise, 0.05 meter apart :
$S = 0.0015$, difference of *c* :   **23.9**
$= 0.0059$,   "   "   **28.4**
$= 0.0085$,   "   "   **30.6**

(3) Channels lined with pebbles 0.01 to 0.02 meter in diameter, cemented to the perimeter :
$S = 0.0015$, difference of *c* : **12.4**
$= 0.0049$,   "   "   **19.6**

(4) Channels lined with pebbles 0.03 to 0.05 meter in diameter, cemented to the perimeter :
$S = 0.0049$, difference of *c* :

It is observed that these differences of *c* increase with *S*; which signifies that the degree of roughness exercises a greater influence in retarding the flow, the more the slope is increased. It is also seen how great an effect even a very insignificant variation of roughness has, in small channels, upon the variation of c, and therefore upon the velocity.

3. In channels of brick and smooth ashlar masonry (Bazin) there is likewise an increase of c with an increase of S, *for the same values of R*, but in a less degree than in channels lined with boards.

4. The same phenomenon was observed also in channels of rubble masonry (Bazin).

5. In a very small channel of carefully planed boards, rectangular, and only 0.10 meter wide and about 20 meters long (Bazin, series Nos. 28 and 29) c increases, *for the same values of R*, with the increase of S. But after lining the same with canvas (series Nos. 30 and 31), c *increases* with the decrease of S. The average differences of c for *the same value of R* are :

   a. Between series Nos. 29 and 31 ($S = 0.015$), **29.0 to 30.0.**

   b. Between series Nos. 28 and 30 ($S = 0.005$ and 0.008), **20.0.**

   c. Between series Nos. 28 and 29, very smooth surface ($S = 0.005$ and 0.015), **7.0.**

   d. Between series Nos. 30 and 31, coarse canvas lining ($S = 0.008$ and 0.015), **3.0 to 4.5.**

In the cases of *a* and *b*, the great differences of c result solely from the character (roughness) of the wetted perimeter; in the cases *c* and *d*, solely from the change of slope.

If, in the case of the small channel mentioned above (Series 28 to 31), the values of c are plotted as ordinates, and the very small values of R as abscissæ, the resulting curves, when compared with the corresponding plottings for larger channels, clearly indicate the position of the origin of co-ordinates, and confirm the proposition that c varies most rapidly for the smallest values of R.

6. It was noticed, in general, that the semicircular form of section in artificial channels gave higher velocities than the rectangular form. For instance, in Bazin's channels lined with boards ($R = 0.1$ to 0.3 meter and $S = 0.0015$) the values of c were from **3.5** to **6.2** higher in the semicircular than in the rect-

angular section, for *the same values of R and S and for the same degree of roughness.*

The effect upon c of difference in form between different angular sections is very slight, if at all noticeable.

7. Finally, the gaugings of M. Bazin show a slight variation of the coefficient n with that of R, mainly an increase of n with an increase of R, sometimes, however, the reverse effect, but to a less degree; while in the Irawadi River in India this latter result is very marked.

III.

Concerning the coefficient of roughness n.*

The coefficient of resistance or roughness (n) can be found only by consulting cases where analogous physical conditions prevail, and for which its value has already been ascertained. In doing this, we must consider the effect of future contingencies upon the condition of the channel in question, such as the washing-in of detritus, the growth of aquatic plants, breaking down of the shores, building of dams, etc.; and it is therefore recommended to choose a value of n rather too large than too small. To aid in selecting the proper coefficient, we have appended a collection of reliable gaugings.† The values of n were generally obtained by using our diagram, but in important cases they were computed by the formula, which, reduced to n, reads:

$$n = \sqrt{\frac{W\bar{R}}{Bc} + \frac{1}{4}\left(\frac{c - B}{Bc}\right)^2 R} - \frac{1}{2}\left(\frac{c - B}{Bc}\right)\sqrt{R},$$

in which $R =$ mean radius,

$$B = a + \frac{m}{S},$$

$$S = \text{slope},$$

$$c = \text{coefficient} = \frac{\text{velocity}}{\sqrt{RS}},$$

---

* From "Bewegung des Wassers," etc. See also Arts. 29 and 40.
† See Table I, which covers a much larger field and has been made more useful for reference than the original Table.—*Trans.*

$a = 23$ for metric and 41.5 for English measure,

$m = 0.00155$ "   " 0.00281 "   "

$l = 1$ for   "   " 1.811 for "   "

To show the effect of the degree of roughness of the wetted perimeter upon the mean velocity, Mr. Kutter compiled the following Table from Bazin's gaugings in rectangular channels having the same width, depth, and slope, but differing in the roughness of the bed and sides, i.e., as regards the value n:

FIRST CASE.—$R = 0.200$; $S = 0.005$.

1.	Series No. 2.	Bottom and sides of cement, smoothed with trowel..	$v = 2.397$
2.	" " 22.	" " " " boards........................	2 089
3.	" " 7.	" " " " "	2.045
4.	" " 18.	" " " " "	1.981
5.	" " 3.	" " " " brick........................	1.874
6.	" " 4.	" " " lined with pebbles from 0.01 to 0.02 meter in diameter..........	1.350
7.	" " 5.	" " " lined with pebbles from 0.03 to 0.05 meter in diameter..........	1.086

Thus, with the same width, depth, and slope, we find a difference of 1.311 meters per second in the velocity.

SECOND CASE.—$R = 0.250$; $S = 0.0015$.

1.	Series No. 24.	Bottom and sides of cement, smoothed with trowel.	$v = 1.562$
2.	" " 25.	" " " " " with one third fine sand	1.463
3.	" " 26.	" " " " boards........................	1.207
4.	" " 9.	" " " " "	1.234
5	" " 21.	" " " " "	1.228
6.	" " 12.	" " " boards, with laths 0.027 meter wide, nailed crosswise 0.01 meter apart...............	1.014
7.	" " 15.	" " " boards, with laths 0.027 meter wide, nailed crosswise 0.05 meter apart...............	0.674

This shows a difference of 0.888 meter per second in the velocity, with the same width, depth, and slope.

IV.

To compute the velocity from the formula.*

We give below an example of the practical application of the formula, indicating incidentally the great advantage of using the *diagram* (Plate VIII) for this purpose.

By measurement it was found that

area of cross-section $= 20,074$ square feet,

wet perimeter $= 1686$ feet,

mean radius, $R \quad = \dfrac{\text{area}}{\text{perimeter}} = 11.88$ feet,

Slope, S, $\quad = 0.000040393$.

To compute the mean velocity v from the formula, it is first necessary to examine the values that have been found for the coefficient of roughness n in similar streams, and then to assume one which will as nearly as practicable cover the case in question, always preferring a value rather too high than too low. Suppose this examination has led to the selection of a mean value of $n = 0.025$ (rivers and canals with regular channel).

Substituting these values in the formula, we have :

$$v = \left(\frac{\dfrac{1.811}{0.025} + 41.6 + \dfrac{0.00281}{0.000040393}}{1 + \left(41.6 + \dfrac{0.00281}{0.000040393}\right)\dfrac{0.025}{\sqrt{11.88}}} \right) \sqrt{11.88 \times 0.000040393.}$$

First, we compute the value within the large parenthesis (c, in the formula $v = c\sqrt{RS}$).

We add, for the *numerator :*

1.	log. 1.811	$=$	10.2579185
	$-$ log. 0.025 '	$=$	-8.3979400

$$1.8599785 = 72.440$$

---

* From " Bewegung des Wassers in Flüssen und Canälen," by W. R. Kutter. Berlin, 1885.

2. The second term $= 41.6$

3. $\log. \ 0.00281 \quad = \quad 7.4487063$
   $- \log. \ 0.000040393 = - 5.6063061$

$$1.8424002 = 69.565$$

Giving the numerator the value   183.605

For the *denominator* we first add the second and third terms of the numerator, viz.,

$$41.6 + 69.565 = 111.165,$$

and take out the log. of 111.165 $= 2.0459681$

Then we find

$$\log. \ 0.025 = \quad 8.3979400$$
$$- \tfrac{1}{2} \log. \ 11.88 = - 0.5374082$$

$$7.8605318 = 7.8605318$$

The log. of the product of the two factors therefore is   9.9064999
     The numerical value of which is $= 0.80631$
     Add to this   1.00000

and we have the denominator $= 1.80631$

$$\text{Therefore } c = \frac{183.605}{1.80631} = 101.64 \ *$$

Now we find for the factor $\sqrt{RS}$
   $\log. R \ (11.88) \quad = 1.0748164$
   $\log. S \ (0.000040393) = 5.6063061$

$$6.6811225$$

Of this we take $\tfrac{1}{2}$, and find

$$\sqrt{RS} = 0.21906$$

---

* With the diagram this value of c may be found in less than half a minute.

The computed mean velocity is, therefore,

$$v = 101.64 \times 0.021906 = \underline{2.23} \text{ feet.}$$

The measured mean velocity in the Danube at Szob in Hungary, which is the case covered by the above example, is 2.25 feet, making a difference of 0.02 feet, which is due to our assuming the value of n a little too high. In order to obtain the velocity 2.25 feet we should have assumed $n = 0.247$ instead of 0.0250.

V.

Construction of the Diagram, Plate VIII.

Scales of 3 inches = 1 for the abscissæ and 0.4 foot = 100 for the ordinates will be found convenient.

Multiply values of n from 0.008 to 0.025 by 200, and lay off the products upon a horizontal line ef drawn through the ordinate 200 from the vertical line at $\sqrt{R} = 1.811$ in the axis of abscissæ. (See Fig. 20.)

Multiply values of n from 0.025 to 0.050 by 100, and lay off these products upon a horizontal qs drawn through the ordinate 100 from the same vertical line.

From the point $\sqrt{R} = 1.811$ in the axis of abscissæ draw the n lines through the points just laid off.

For drawing the slope curves, find from Table III the values of x and y for each curve and for each value of n.

Points for the slope curves are found at the intersections of the radial n lines with the vertical lines corresponding to the values of x, or with the horizontal lines corresponding to the values of y.

A slight addition to the diagram will render it further useful in finding the relation of mean to maximum velocities, if the coefficient c is known. (See Appendix VII and Plate VIII.)

The scale of c upon the axis of ordinates is retained, and the graduation of the axis of abscissæ between the values 0 and 1.0 is used as the scale for the ratios $\dfrac{v}{v_{max}}$.

From the point $\sqrt{R} = 1$, plot $-c$ (minus c) $= 25.4$ for English measure, as shown. Uniting this point with any value of

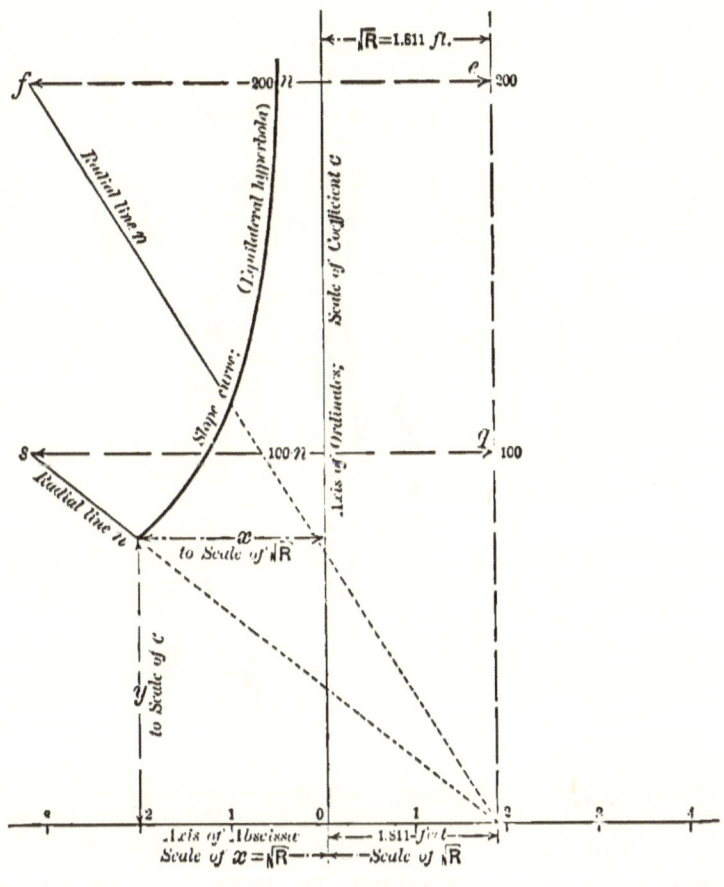

Fig. 20.

c on the axis of ordinates by a straight line, the corresponding values of $\dfrac{v'}{v_{max}}$ may be read off directly from the scale of abscissæ.

Another addition to Kutter's diagram, proposed by Mr. Hering,[*] enables us to read the velocity from the diagram.[†]

Find the square root of the reciprocal of each slope

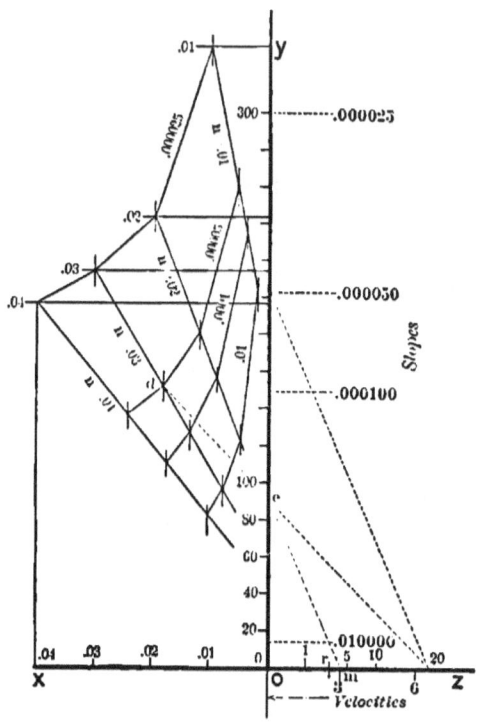

to be embraced in the diagram $= \sqrt{\dfrac{1}{\text{slope per unit of length}}}$

Lay off these square roots on the axis oy of ordinates, using the scale of c already laid off upon it. In our figure we have so proportioned the two scales that $\dfrac{c}{\sqrt{\dfrac{1}{S}}} = \dfrac{1.5}{1}$. *Mark* the dividing points with the *slopes S*.

---

[*] Transactions of the American Society of Civil Engineers, January 1879.
[†] See Trautwine's Civil Engineer's Pocketbook, p 279b (1888).

On oz lay off the velocities to be embraced in the diagram, using the scale of square roots of R already laid off on oz, and making

$$\frac{\text{velocity}}{\sqrt{R}} = \frac{c}{\sqrt{\dfrac{1}{S}}}.$$

1st. Having R, S, and n; to find v.   For example, let $R =$ 20 ft., $S = .00005$, $n = .03$. From $R = 20$ draw d–20 to the intersection d of curve .00005 with radial line $n = .03$. Then d–20 cuts oy at c, where $c = 96$. With a parallel ruler join $R = 20$ with $S = .00005$ on oy. Draw a parallel line through $c = 96$. It cuts oz at m, giving the required velocity 3.03 ft. per second.

2d. Having R, S, and v; to find n. For example, let $R =$ 20 ft., $S = .00005$, $v = 3.03$ ft. per sec. With a parallel ruler join $R = 20$ and slope .00005 on oy. Draw a parallel line through $v = 3.03$. It cuts oy at c, where $c = 96$. Through $R = 20$ and $c = 96$, draw d-20 to cut curve .00005. The point d of intersection, being on radial line $n = .03$, shows .03 to be the proper value of n.

3d. Having S, n, and v; to find R. For example, let $S = .00005$, $n = .03$, $v = 3.03$ ft. per sec. *Assume* a value of R, say 10 ft. Find curve .00005 and radial line $n = .03$. Join their intersection d with $R = 10$ ft. The connecting line cuts oy at $c = 82$. With a parallel ruler join $c = 82$ with $v = 3.03$. Draw a parallel line through slope = .00005 on oy. It cuts oz at $R = 27.3$, showing that a new trial is necessary, and with an assumed R *greater* than 10 ft. If R thus found is the same as the assumed one, the latter is correct.

4th. Having R, n, and v; to find S. For example, let $R =$ 20 ft., $n = .03$, $v = 3.03$ ft. per sec. *Assume* a slope (say .0001). Find its curve, and radial line $n = .03$. Join their intersection with $R = 20$, and note the value (89) of c where the connecting line cuts oy. With a parallel ruler join $c = 89$ with $v = 3.03$. Draw a parallel line through $R = 20$. It cuts oy at slope .000058, showing that a new trial is necessary, and with an assumed S *flatter* than .0001. If R is 3.28 ft. or 1 meter, the diagram gives the correct S at the first trial, no matter what S

was assumed at starting. With any other R, if the diagram gives the same S as that assumed, the latter is correct.

VI.

A modification of Bazin's formula.

A series of coefficients obtained directly from actual gaugings of different channels are much more valuable to the practical engineer than coefficients representing general averages from wide ranges, because the exactness of the former depends solely upon the correctness of the gaugings, while that of the latter depends greatly upon judgment.

Holding this view, Kutter[*] divided the coefficients of Bazin's formula into twelve classes instead of four, believing that the latter are both too few in number and placed at intervals far too large. As the original formula has the disadvantage of two variable coefficients, he further improved it by reducing them to one.

As published in 1871, the Bazin formula thus modified reads,

$$v = c\sqrt{RS}, \quad \text{and} \quad c = a - \frac{ab}{\sqrt{R}+b} \,,$$

in which for English measure $a = 181$ and b is a coefficient varying between 0.22 for very smooth channels, and 4.42 for streams carrying detritus and coarse gravel.

Mr. Kutter appends a table of actual gaugings, giving both the coefficient of the class to which it belongs and the amount of deviation from that coefficient in each case. But as this formula is hardly likely to come into general use, we do not reproduce the table, but simply give his list of the twelve classes, with the values of the variable coefficient b, adding a description of the nature of the channel to which they respectively refer, condensed from the above-mentioned table.

---

[*] "Die neuen Formeln," etc.

Class I, $b = 0.22$. Well planed planks in rectangular section, and neat cement in semicircular section.

" II, $b = 0.27$. Neat cement in rectangular section, and with one third sand in semicircular section.

" III, $b = 0.36$. Unplaned planks, semicircular section.

" IV, $b = 0.49$. Same, rectangular and triangular sections.

" V, $b = 0.63$. Smooth ashlar and brickwork.

" VI, $b = 0.81$. Good rubble masonry.

" VII, $b = 1.01$. Dry rubble masonry.

" VIII, $b = 1.30$. Dry rubble in bad condition.

" IX, $b = 1.68$. Masonry side walls and earth beds, also small channels in earth.

" X, $b = 2.21$. Canals and brooks with uniform section.

" XI, $b = 3.02$. Canals and rivers in alluvial ground.

" XII, $b = 4.42$. Creeks and rivers carrying detritus and coarse gravel.

VII.

To find the mean from the surface or maximum velocities.

When it is practicable to measure only the surface or maximum velocities, the following ratios or coefficients serve to determine the mean velocity:

1. *According to Prony.*

$$v = v_{max} \frac{v_{max} + 7.78}{v_{max} + 10.34}, \text{ for English measure,}$$

in which v is the mean and v_{max} the maximum velocity measured at the surface.

2. *According to Humphreys and Abbot.*

Humphreys and Abbot give for the variation of the velocity in the vertical plane the formula

$$v_x = v_{max} - \sqrt{bv}\left(\frac{\pm d_x \mp d_{max}}{D}\right)^2,$$

in which v_x is the velocity at the depth d_x; v_{max} is the greatest velocity in the vertical plane found to be at the depth d_{max}; v is the mean velocity in the cross-section of the river; D is the total depth of the water; b is a coefficient which is $= 0.1856$ for English measure, when $D > 30$ feet. For less values b is

more accurately $= \dfrac{1.69}{\sqrt{D + 1.5}}$.

3. *According to Bazin.*

Bazin's formula for the variation of the velocity in a vertical plane is

$$v_x = v_{max} - a \sqrt{RS}\left(\frac{d_x}{D}\right)^2,$$

in which, in addition to the notation under 2, a is a coefficient $= 20.1$ for metric and 36.3 for English measure. R is the mean radius and S the slope, as elsewhere.

This formula applies only when the maximum velocity is near the surface, *i.e.*, when $d_{max} < 0.2D$ and when $\dfrac{v}{v_{max}}$ varies between 0.80 and 0.90, but agrees well with the author's own gaugings and with those made by others on the Saône, Seine, and Garonne.

From sixty-one series of gaugings Bazin deduced the ratio between maximum and mean velocities with reference to the character of the channel, and found $v_{max} = v + 14 \sqrt{RS}$, metric measure. From this he deduced

$$\frac{v}{v_{max}} = \frac{1}{1 + 14\sqrt{\dfrac{RS}{v^2}}} ;$$

or, as $v = c \sqrt{RS}$, and therefore $\dfrac{1}{\sqrt{\dfrac{RS}{v^2}}} = c$, we find in metric measure, $\dfrac{v'}{v_{max}} = \dfrac{1}{1 + \dfrac{14}{c}}$;

in English measure, $\dfrac{v'}{v_{max}} = \dfrac{1}{1 + \dfrac{25.4}{c}}$.

As this is the equation of an equilateral hyperbola, a very simple means of finding the values $\dfrac{v'}{v_{max}}$ is obtained, by applying this equation to the graphical representation of the new general formula. (See Appendix V, p. 114.)

A series of these values is given below.*

VALUES OF THE RATIO $\dfrac{v'}{v_{max}}$ $\left(\dfrac{\text{mean velocity}}{\text{maximum velocity}}\right)$

to be used in obtaining mean velocities from maximum velocities when the value of the coefficient c in the formula $v = c \sqrt{RS}$ is given.

c	$\dfrac{v'}{v_m}$	c	$\dfrac{v'}{v_m}$	c	$\dfrac{v'}{v_m}$	c	$\dfrac{v'}{v_m}$
2	0.06	46	0.64	90	0.78	134	0.84
4	0.13	48	0.65	92	0.78	136	0.84
6	0.19	50	0.66	94	0.79	138	0.84
8	0.24	52	0.67	96	0.79	140	0.84
10	0.29	54	0.68	98	0.79	142	0.85
12	0.32	56	0.69	100	0.80	144	0.85
14	0.36	58	0.69	102	0.80	146	0.85
16	0.39	60	0.70	104	0.80	148	0.85
18	0.42	62	0.71	106	0.81	150	0.85
20	0.44	64	0.72	108	0.81	155	0.86
22	0.46	66	0.72	110	0.81	160	0.86
24	0.48	68	0.73	112	0.81	165	0.87
26	0.50	70	0.73	114	0.82	170	0.87
28	0.52	72	0.74	116	0.82	175	0.88
30	0.54	74	0.74	118	0.82	180	0.88
32	0.56	76	0.75	120	0.82	185	0.88
34	0.57	78	0.75	122	0.83	190	0.88
36	0.59	80	0.76	124	0.83	195	0.89
38	0.60	82	0.76	126	0.83	200	0.89
40	0.61	84	0.77	128	0.83		
42	0.62	86	0.77	130	0.83		
44	0.63	88	0.77	132	0.84		

* From " Bewegung des Wassers," etc., p. 134.

For the case when the values of the mean radius R and the degree of roughness n are given, instead of those for c, Mr. Kutter has appended the following table,* deduced from Bazin's experiments, for directly obtaining a value for the relation of $\dfrac{v}{v_{max}}$.

Given, for instance, the maximum velocity of the surface, $v_{max} = 2.46$ feet, and $R = 0.58$ feet, with $n = 0.025$, we take from the table $\dfrac{0.62 + 0.58}{2} = 0.60$, and obtain for the mean velocity $v = 2.46 \times 0.60 = 1.48$ feet.

$$\text{VALUES OF THE RATIO } \frac{v}{v_{max}} \left(\frac{\text{mean velocity}}{\text{maximum velocity}} \right)$$

to be used in obtaining mean velocities directly from maximum velocities when the mean radius R and the degree of roughness n are given.

R feet.	For $n =$														
	0.010	0.012	0.014	0.016	0.018	0.020	0.022	0.024	0.026	0.028	0.030	0.035	0.040	0.045	0.050
0.05	0.78	0.71	....	....	....	....	....	....	....	....	....	....	....	....	....
0.10	0.81	0.74	....	....	....	....	....	....	....	....	....	....	....	....	....
0.15	0.82	0.77	0.72	....	....	....	....	....	....	....	....	....	....	....	....
0.20	0.83	0.79	0.75	0.70	....	....	....	....	....	....	....	....	....	....	....
0.25	0.83	0.81	0.77	0.72	0.67	....	....	....	....	....	....	....	....	....	....
0.30	0.83	0.82	0.77	0.73	0.68	....	....	....	....	....	....	....	....	....	....
0.35	0.84	0.82	0.78	0.74	0.69	0.65	0.59	0.53	0.48	0.44	0.40	....	....	....	....
0.40	0.84	0.83	0.78	0.75	0.70	0.67	0.63	0.58	0.52	0.45	0.43	....	....	....	....
0.45	0.84	0.83	0.79	0.75	0.71	0.68	0.64	0.59	0.55	0.50	0.46	0.40	....	....	....
0.50	0.84	0.83	0.79	0.76	0.72	0.69	0.65	0.60	0.57	0.52	0.48	0.42	....	....	....
0.55	0.84	0.83	0.79	0.76	0.73	0.70	0.66	0.61	0.58	0.53	0.50	0.43	....	....	....
0.60	0.84	0.83	0.79	0.77	0.73	0.70	0.67	0.62	0.59	0.54	0.51	0.45	....	....	....
0.65	0.85	0.83	0.80	0.77	0.74	0.71	0.68	0.63	0.60	0.55	0.52	0.46	....	....	....
0.70	0.85	0.84	0.80	0.77	0.74	0.71	0.68	0.64	0.61	0.56	0.53	0.47	....	....	....
0.75	0.85	0.84	0.80	0.77	0.75	0.72	0.68	0.65	0.61	0.57	0.54	0.48	....	....	....
0.80	0.85	0.84	0.80	0.77	0.75	0.72	0.69	0.65	0.62	0.58	0.55	0.49	....	....	....
0.85	0.85	0.84	0.81	0.78	0.75	0.72	0.69	0.66	0.62	0.59	0.56	0.49	....	....	....
0.90	0.85	0.84	0.81	0.78	0.76	0.73	0.69	0.66	0.63	0.60	0.57	0.50	....	....	....
0.95	0.85	0.84	0.81	0.78	0.76	0.73	0.70	0.67	0.63	0.61	0.58	0.50	0.40	....	....
1.00	0.85	0.84	0.81	0.78	0.76	0.73	0.70	0.67	0.64	0.61	0.58	0.51	0.41	....	....
1.10	0.85	0.84	0.81	0.79	0.77	0.74	0.71	0.68	0.65	0.62	0.59	0.52	0.43	....	....
1.20	0.85	0.84	0.81	0.79	0.77	0.74	0.72	0.68	0.65	0.63	0.60	0.53	0.44	....	....
1.40	0.85	0.84	0.82	0.79	0.78	0.75	0.73	0.70	0.66	0.65	0.61	0.55	0.47	....	....
1.60	0.85	0.84	0.82	0.80	0.78	0.76	0.74	0.71	0.67	0.66	0.63	0.57	0.50	0.40	....
1.80	0.85	0.84	0.82	0.80	0.79	0.77	0.74	0.72	0.68	0.67	0.64	0.58	0.52	0.43	....
2.00	0.85	0.84	0.82	0.80	0.79	0.77	0.75	0.72	0.69	0.68	0.65	0.59	0.53	0.45	0.36
2.50	0.85	0.84	0.83	0.81	0.79	0.78	0.76	0.74	0.71	0.70	0.67	0.62	0.57	0.51	0.44
3.00	0.85	0.84	0.83	0.81	0.80	0.78	0.77	0.75	0.72	0.71	0.68	0.64	0.60	0.55	0.51
4.00	0.85	0.84	0.83	0.81	0.80	0.79	0.78	0.76	0.74	0.73	0.71	0.67	0.63	0.60	0.57
5.00	0.85	0.84	0.83	0.82	0.81	0.79	0.78	0.77	0.75	0.74	0.72	0.69	0.65	0.63	0.60
6.00	0.85	0.84	0.83	0.82	0.81	0.80	0.79	0.78	0.76	0.75	0.73	0.70	0.67	0.64	0.62
8.00	0.85	0.84	0.83	0.82	0.81	0.80	0.79	0.78	0.76	0.75	0.74	0.72	0.69	0.66	0.64
10.00	0.85	0.84	0.83	0.82	0.81	0.80	0.79	0.78	0.77	0.76	0.75	0.73	0.71	0.68	0.66
12.00	0.85	0.84	0.83	0.82	0.81	0.80	0.79	0.78	0.77	0.77	0.76	0.74	0.72	0.70	0.69
14.00	0.85	0.84	0.83	0.82	0.81	0.80	0.79	0.78	0.78	0.77	0.76	0.75	0.74	0.72	0.71
16.00	0.85	0.84	0.83	0.82	0.81	0.81	0.80	0.79	0.78	0.78	0.77	0.77	0.75	0.74	0.73
18.00	0.85	0.84	0.83	0.82	0.81	0.81	0.80	0.79	0.79	0.78	0.78	0.77	0.77	0.76	0.75
20.00	0.85	0.84	0.83	0.82	0.81	0.81	0.80	0.79	0.79	0.79	0.79	0.78	0.78	0.78	0.77

* From " Bewegung des Wassers," etc., p. 133.

4. *According to Sundry Authors.*

VALUES OF THE RELATION $\dfrac{v}{v_{max}}\left(\dfrac{\text{mean velocity}}{\text{maximum surface velocity}}\right)$.

Belgrand, for the Seine.. (?) 0.62
Destrem, for the Neva... 0.78
Baumgärtner, for the Garonne................................... 0.80
De Prony, for small wooden channels.......................... 0.82
Boileau, for canals.. 0.82
Cunningham, for the Solani Aqueduct.......................... 0.82
Bazin, for small channels... 0.83
Swiss Engineers.. 0.84
Brunnings, for rivers.. 0.85
Humphreys and Abbot, for the Mississippi (mean)...............0.79 to 0.82
    "   "   Ohio.............................0.78 " 0.80
    "   "   Yazoo............................0.66 " 0.84
    "   "   Bayou Plaquemine................0.83 " 0.85
    "   "   " La Fourche ....0.79 " 0.80

VIII.

Velocities beyond which a gradual destruction of the bed will take place.*

It may be useful to state here at what velocities a stream begins to destroy the bed of its channel.

Dubuat gives the following values. The first column indicates the velocities (v_b) at the bottom; the second gives the mean velocity of the cross-section according to the formula of Bazin:

$$v = v_b + 6\sqrt{RS}\ \text{(meters)},$$
$$v = v_b + 10.9\sqrt{RS}\ \text{(Engl. feet)};$$

or, taking a mean value, *i.e.*, a constant average coefficient of c in the formula $v = c\sqrt{RS}$, he finds

$$v = 1.31\ v_b.$$

---

* The data under this head are mainly from Kutter's work on " Bewegung des Wassers," etc. They have been extended and verified, however, from other sources.

The third column contains the maximum surface velocity, likewise according to a formula of Bazin :

$$v = v_{max} - 14 \sqrt{RS} \text{ (meters)},$$
$$v = v_{max} - 25.4 \sqrt{RS} \text{ (Engl. feet)};$$

or, taking a mean value,

$$v = 0.83 v_{max} .$$

Nature of Material forming the Bed.	Bottom Velocity v_b feet per sec.	Mean Velocity v feet per sec.	Maximum Surface Vel. v_{max} feet per sec.
River mud, clay, specific gravity = 2.64............	0.25	0.33	0 40
Sand, the size of anise-seed, specific gravity = 2.55.	0.35	0.46	0.55
Clay, loam, and fine sand..	0.50	0.66	0.79
Sand, the size of peas, specific gravity = 2.55.....	0.60	0.79	0.95
Common river sand, specific gravity = 3.36	0.70	0.92	1.10
Sand, the size of beans, specific gravity = 2.55....	1.07	1.40	1.69
Gravel........	2.00	2.62	3.15
Round pebbles. 1″ diam., specific gravity = 2.61.	2.13	2.79	3.36
Coarse gravel, small cobblestones....	3.00	3.93	4.73
Angular stones, flint, egg size, spec. gravity = 2.25.	3.23	4.23	5.09
Angular broken stone.....................	4.00	5.24	6.30
Soft slate, shingle..............................	5.00	6.55	7.86
Stratified rock....................................	6.00	7.86	9.43
Hard rock..................................	10.00	13.12	15.75

Whether and how far these velocities are reliable, we* have not been able to determine ; yet they are based upon the observations of eminent hydraulicians. The slope is of no consequence in this matter, but the depth of the water may have some influence. For the same character of bed and the same velocity, the scouring effect would probably be greater in deep than in shallow channels, owing to the greater pressure of the water. But this difference will not be material, and the velocity will always be the main controlling element. The above figures appear to us rather too small than too large, and thus err on the side of safety.

Bazalgette found the following velocities to move the bodies described :

---

* Ganguillet and Kutter.

Fine clay.......................0.25 feet per second.
Sand...........................0.50   "
Coarse sand....................0.66   "
Fine gravel ....1.00   "
Pebbles 1 inch diameter.........2.00   "
Stones of egg size............ ....3.00   "

Blackwell showed by experiments made for the British Metropolitan Drainage Commission that the specific gravity has a marked effect upon the velocities necessary to move bodies, as follows:

Nature of Bodies.	Specific Gravity.	Velocity in feet per second.
Coal.............................	1.26	1.25 to 1.50
Coal.............................	1.33	1.50 " 1.75
Brickbat.........................	2.00	1.75 " 2 00
Piece of chalk...................	2.05	
Oolite stone.	2.17	
Brickbat.....	2.12	2 00 " 2.25
Piece of granite.................	2 66	
Brickbat.........................	2.18	2.25 " 2.50
Piece of chalk...................	2.17	
Piece of flint...................	2.66	2.50 " 2.75
Piece of limestone...............	3.00	

Chailly has derived the following formula for the velocity which is just sufficient to set bodies in motion:

$$v = 3.13 \sqrt{ag} \ (\text{meters}).$$

$$v = 5.67 \sqrt{ag} \ (\text{Engl. measure}).$$

in which a is the average diameter of the body to be moved, and g its specific gravity.[*]

---

[*] From the above experiments of Blackwell, it appears that v varies rather more nearly as g than as $\sqrt{g}$.

IX.

A simple method of ascertaining the discharge of rivers.

BY PROF. A. R. HARLACHER AND H. RICHTER.

[From *Minutes of Proceedings of the Institution of Civil Engineers*, vol. xci p. 397.]

In order to ascertain the discharge of a river by this method, a cross-section of it must be surveyed, and the velocity of the current in the same be measured. The velocity may be accurately observed by a current-meter, and for an exact calculation of the discharge must be measured in a sufficient number of vertical lines distributed all over the cross-section, and in several points of each line from the surface to the bottom. In rivers of moderate velocity and depth, such observations can be made with comparative facility and promptness; but in more rapid rivers, and of greater depth, they require much time and great pains. This, of course, also holds good in ascertaining the discharge of rivers of moderate size at the time of flood, when the observations are, however, unfavorably influenced by the water level being commonly subject to frequent changes, for which reason the measurements should then be hurried as much as possible.

In case of the want of requisite measuring-appliances, it is expedient to measure the surface-velocity only; and then, of course, the discharge can only be calculated by means of certain proportional numbers.

  * * * * * * * *

It is impossible to form a direct estimate of the mean velocity at a cross-section by the observed surface-velocities; but there is a possibility of calculating the discharge by finding a certain relation between the mean velocity v'_m in the verticals of a cross-section and the surface-velocity v'_s. For this purpose the authors have calculated the proportion $p = \dfrac{v'_m}{v'_s}$ for about three hundred vertical curves of velocity in twenty-eight measurements of discharge in Bohemian rivers, and in the Danube at Vienna. In all these measurements Harlacher's current-

meter was used. The mean surface-velocity v_{ms} in a certain
cross-section was obtained by taking the measured v_s in the
relative points of the level of the water as ordinates, and by
laying from shore to shore a continuous curve through the
points thus obtained, and dividing the area enclosed by this
curve and the level of the water by the width of the latter. In
the same manner the mean of all the v_m could be obtained.

From a calculation of all the v_m and v_s, for each of the
twenty-eight measurements, the following values of the proportion p were obtained : 0.79 once, 0.82 twice, 0.83 six times, 0.84
six times, 0.80 five times, 0.86 once, 0.87 twice, 0.88 three
times, 0.89 once, and 0.91 once. Supposing the cross-section to
have been taken, and the velocities to have been measured, on
calculating the discharge, by the application of the mean value
of p, a quantity will be obtained varying but very slightly from
the discharge computed from all the velocities measured in the
verticals of the section in question. In the different cross-
sections of the rivers where these surveys were made, the highest velocity varied from 0.60 meter to 3.00 meters per second,
the greatest depth from 0.80 meter to 8.00 meters, and the
greatest width from 50 to 420 meters; the smaller velocities,
however, were measured only in the sections of moderate
depth. The nature of the bottom was very variable; for the
most part the greatest value of p occurred with a sandy bottom,
whereas the smaller values were found with gravel bottoms, the
gravel being of the size of the fist in bottoms of the roughest
nature. The proportion p in rivers not varying much in size,
velocity, depth and nature of bottom, from the above-mentioned limits, may be taken at 0.85.

An almost identical result has been obtained from measurements of velocity in other places. Thus in two hundred vertical curves of velocity surveyed by Swiss engineers the mean
value of p was found to be 0.835. In the measurements taken
a few years ago in Holland, in the Rhine and its branches, the
value of p was ascertained to be 0.87, and the probable error
of that value, ascertained by the application of the method
of least squares, was proved to be insignificant.

The authors have used bridges, from which the surface-velocity was measured by an electric current-meter let down on a small line. One great advantage in this mode of measurement is that neither boats nor any other appliances are wanted. Of course, only bridges with wide spans, those with iron superstructures, are suitable, and a proper position of the piers, lest the motion of the water in their vicinity may be affected by eddies.

The velocities having been measured all along the reach of the river at a sufficient number of points, 1, 2, 3, . . . of the

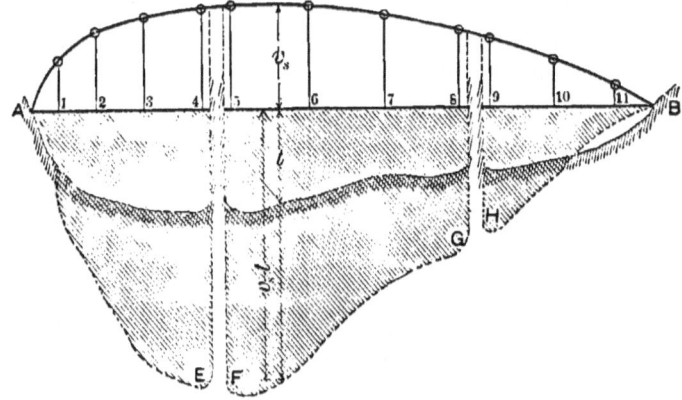

section ACB between the piers of a bridge, the curve of the surface-velocity ADB may be drawn. By calculating for the single points 1, 2, 3, ... and for a sufficient number of intermediate points, to be chosen in accordance with the formation of the bottom, the product of the surface-velocity v_s by the corresponding depth t, and by plotting the values $v_s t$ as ordinates, the points are obtained by which the curves AE, FG, and HB, bordering the hatched surface, are determined. The content of these surfaces multiplied by the proportion $p = 0.85$ gives the volume of water passed through the section. The authors have taken successfully more than seventy measurements by the above method in Bohemian rivers, many of them being in the Elbe and the Moldau.

TABLES FOR PRACTICAL USE.

THE following Tables will facilitate the use of the Ganguillet and Kutter formula for the uniform flow of water in rivers and smaller channels, viz.,

$$v = \left(\frac{a + \frac{l}{n} + \frac{m}{S}}{1 + \left(a + \frac{m}{S}\right)\frac{n}{\sqrt{R}}} \right) \sqrt{RS} = \left(\frac{y}{1 + \frac{x}{\sqrt{R}}} \right) \sqrt{RS} = c \sqrt{RS},$$

in which

      v = mean velocity;

      R = mean hydraulic radius;

      S = sine of slope;

      n = coefficient of roughness of perimeter;

      c = coefficient dependent upon slope, mean radius, and roughness of perimeter;

a, l, m = numerical constants;

$$y = a + \frac{l}{n} + \frac{m}{S};$$

$$x = \left(a + \frac{m}{S}\right) n = ny - l.$$

From **Table I.**, by consulting cases similar to the one in hand, a proper value for n may readily be selected. See Arts. 29 and 40, also Appendix III, and introduction to the table.

In **Table II.** the values of $a + \dfrac{l}{n}$ and of $\dfrac{m}{S}$ are given for all practical cases, from which the values of y and x may be easily computed when n and S are known.

Table III. contains the values of y and x for a large number of values of n and S.

Table IV. contains approximate values of c for a number of values of n and S.

For the very simple **graphical method** of determining, for any case, the coefficient c, or any of the other elements if a sufficient number of them are given, see p. 74, and Plate VIII, at the end of the book.

In **Table V.** are found the **equivalents of English and metric measures** as far as they relate to the flow of water.

TABLE I.

(English Measure.)

THE following table contains the elements of

Over 1200 Gaugings with Deduced Values of n.

Although the Ganguillet and Kutter formula was elaborated from gaugings made in open channels, yet when applied also to pipes running full under pressure it gives results that are fairly satisfactory; and as no other general formula for pipes offers better services, we have deemed it both useful and interesting to include in this table a number of such experiments. They are given as Class A, while Class B refers to open channels and rivers.

The gaugings are grouped in subdivisions or categories, according to the character of the material forming the perimeter or bed, beginning with the smoothest surfaces; and the series for each case are arranged in the order of the slopes, or, where these are constant or nearly so, in the order of the mean radii, beginning in each case with the smallest values.

The data have been taken directly from original sources as far as they were accessible to us. The elements given are: surface width, greatest depth, mean radius, slope, velocity, coefficients c and n. The number of the series of the gaugings as assumed by the respective authors is also frequently given for purposes of identification. The nature of the channel and of its perimeter, also the method of gauging, are described as fully as the available information permitted. It has been difficult, and in many cases impossible, to obtain a satisfactory description, and in some instances assumptions had to be made for purposes of classification. In the categories for rivers and canals there may be and probably are some cases which should have been placed in the category containing channels with masonry sidewalls or paved embankments. Subsequently to the completion of the table it was found that Fanning's experiment with a cement-lined pipe and H. Smith, Jr.'s, experiment with the Cherokee pipe were erroneously classed as old pipe, instead of as new wrought-iron pipe.

The values of n have been ascertained chiefly from the diagram, but occasionally by calculation, and they are believed to be correct within one or two points in the fourth decimal.

Ganguillet and Kutter assume the coefficient n to be a constant quantity, and in their publications give only its average value for the gaugings which they quote. It will be noticed, however, from our collection, that this coefficient varies slightly for the same channel, whether it has small or large dimensions. The series being arranged in the order of slopes and mean radii, this variation is generally found to possess some regularity, and for any given case it is practicable to select the most suitable value for similar conditions with more confidence than if averages alone were given.

It will also be seen from the table, that the variation of the coefficient c is not only much greater than that of n, but much more complex, owing to the fact that it embodies the combined effects of several variations, dependent respectively on slope, mean radius, roughness of perimeter and configuration of channel, etc., so that it would be almost hopeless to attempt to arrange the data into series from which satisfactory values of c may be directly assumed for a given case. In Ganguillet and Kutter's formula the variations of c with slope and mean radius have to a large degree been given mathematical expression, so that the practical engineer is much better able to exercise his judgment, because he is substantially confined to the consideration of the character of the perimeter and configuration of the bed.

In Articles 29 and 40, and in Appendix III, the nature of this coefficient n is fully explained. It covers " not only the mere roughness of the surface, but also the irregularities and imperfections in the bed of the channel or river;" it includes, further, the effect of loss of head or energy, in moving detritus or silt along the bed, in shifting the main current or channel from one side of the bed to the other, and in forming eddies or other lateral and irregular currents; in short, it embodies all conditions causing retardation of flow, the relative effect of which must be left to judgment.

It should further be borne in mind that *n* is to some extent relative. For the same general nature of the perimeter it decreases as the depth or mean radius increases, because the disturbances of the current throughout the water-section become relatively less, particularly when the channel has a rough or irregular perimeter. On the other hand, in streams carrying pebbles or coarse detritus *n* is comparatively small for a low stage and slight velocity, but larger for a higher velocity which is capable of moving the pebbles along the bed, and which consequently consumes more energy. During the rising and falling of a river having the same character of bed, the same slope and mean radius, the velocities often differ, in which case *n* alone can embody the corresponding variation. A change of slope in the channel causes an acceleration and retardation of the velocity for some distance above and below, which must also change the value of *n* at such points from that which it would have for a uniform slope.

In very smooth and regular channels or pipes *n* decreases as the slope increases if the course is straight and if there are no obstructions, but increases with the slope if the course is irregular and in the presence of obstructions. In rough and irregular channels or rivers *n* usually increases with the slope, because with a corresponding increase of velocity the current becomes more disturbed, produces stronger lateral currents, and thereby consumes more energy than in comparatively smooth channels or pipes without obstructions, where the particles of water maintain a direction more nearly parallel with the axis of the stream, and where accordingly the variation is generally found to be reversed.

As, however, these variations of *n* in the same channel are usually slight compared with those depending directly upon the character of the wetted perimeter and configuration of the bed, it is rarely necessary to give them much consideration.

Class A. Pipes,

DESCRIPTION OF PIPE. METHOD OF GAUGING.	AUTHORITY.
I. Glass	
Glass Pipe. Funnel mouthpiece.	H. Smith, Jr., 1886.
Glass Pipe. Straight.	Darcy, 1851.*
II. Tin and	
Lead Pipe in Hamburg (Lager platz).	Iben, 1875.
New Lead Pipe. Straight.	Darcy, 1851.
Lead Pipe. Straight. Velocity determined from known volume.	Bossut, 1771.*
Tin Pipe. Straight.	do.
Tin Pipe. Straight.	do.
Lead Pipe.	W. A. Provis, 1838.

* See H. Smith, Jr., "Hydraulics," for experiments of Darcy, Bossut, and Couplet.

under Pressure.

Length in Feet.	Diameter in Feet.	Mean Hydraulic Radius, in Feet, R.	Hydraulic Gradient or Slope per Thousand, $1000\,S$	Mean Velocity in Feet per Second, v	Coefficient in Formula $v = c\sqrt{RS}$, c	Coefficient of Roughness, n
Pipe.						
64	0.0764	0.0191	25.01	1.955	89.5	.0073
	"	"	50.77	2.945	94.6	.0072
	"	"	75.30	3.685	97.2	.0070
	"	"	102.06	4.383	99.3	.0069
	"	"	129.18	5.009	100.8	.0068
147	0.1630	0.0407	0.96	0.502	80.3	.0091
	"	"	7.71	1.591	89.8	.0086
	"	"	57.62	4.849	100.1	.0081
	"	"	111.91	6.916	102.4	.0080
Lead Pipe.						
350.3	0.082	0.0205	50.56	2.70	85.0	.0078
	"	"	64 61	3.16	87.0	.0077
	"	"	112.36	4.72	98.5	.0071
	"	"	216.29	6.88	104.0	.0068
	"	"	348.31	9.11	107.9	.0067
172	0.0886	0.0221	0.44	0.213	68.3	.0086
	"	"	8.14	1.089	81.1	.0082
	"	"	54.36	3.350	96.5	.0074
	"	"	146.32	5.509	96.8	.0074
53	0.0888	0.0222	6.24	1.086	92.2	.0075
	"	"	18.59	1.979	97.4	.0073
192	0.1184	0.0296	5.40	1.116	88.2	.0082
	"	"	10.76	1.678	94.0	.0079
64	"	"	15.08	2.075	98.2	.0077
32	"	"	26.94	2.946	104.3	.0074
32	"	"	52.98	4.310	108.8	0072
63	0.1184	0.0296	113.4	6.143	106.0	.0073
126	"	"	113.5	6.150	106.1	.0073
189	"	"	113.4	6.157	106.2	.0073
100	0.125	0.0313	29.17	3.090	102.3	.0072
80	"	"	36.46	3.396	100.3	.0075
60	"	"	48.61	3.903	100.1	.0075
40	"	"	72.92	4.759	99.7	.0076
20	"	"	145.83	6.150	91.1	.0079

Class A. Pipes,

DESCRIPTION OF PIPE. METHOD OF GAUGING.	AUTHORITY.
	Tin and Lead
New Lead Pipe. Straight.	Darcy, 1851.
Tin Pipe. Straight. Velocity determined from known volume.	Bossut, 1771.
Pipe at Versailles. For the first 320 feet in length, stoneware; for the remaining 7163 feet, lead; in fairly good condition. One rather abrupt bend and several easy bends. Discharge determined by a measuring vessel.	Couplet, 1732.*
	III. Earthen
Earthenware Pipe. Flowing partly under a slight head.	Bidder, 1853.
	IV. Wooden
Wooden Pipe. Closely jointed. Rectangular; 1.574 feet wide by .98 feet deep. Weir measurement.	Darcy and Bazin, 1859.
Wooden Pipe. Poplar; closely jointed. Rectangular; 2.624 feet wide by 1.64 feet deep. Weir measurement.	Darcy and Bazin, 1857.

* See H. Smith, Jr., " Hydraulics," for experiments of Darcy, Bossut, and Couplet.

under Pressure.

Length in Feet.	Diameter in Feet.	Mean Hydraulic Radius, in Feet, R	Hydraulic Gradient or Slope per Thousand, $1000\,S$	Mean Velocity in Feet per Second, v	Coefficient, in Formula $v = c\sqrt{RS}$, c	Coefficient of Roughness, n

Pipe—Continued.

172	0.1345	0.0336	0.82	0.394	75.0	.0090
	"	"	7.78	1.404	86.8	.0085
	"	"	56.00	4.318	99.5	.0078
	"	"	158.82	7.562	103.5	.0076
192	0.1785	0.0446	5.30	1.455	94.6	.0086
96	"	"	10.01	2.115	100.1	.0084
64	"	"	14.19	2.596	103.2	.0082
32	"	"	23.88	3.583	109.7	.0079
32	"	"	46.48	5.233	114.9	.0076
7483	0.444	0.111	0.066	0.1787	65.9	.0110
	"	"	0.135	0.2801	72.5	.0111
	"	"	0.199	0.3664	78.0	.0110
	"	"	0.250	0.4269	81.0	.0109
	"	"	0.285	0.4632	82.4	.0108
	"	"	0.297	0.4728	82.4	.0108

wave Pipe.

2310	1 5	0.375	2.50	3.581	117.0	.0111

Pipe.

145.73		0.319	0.533	1.230	94.3	.0124
		"	1.067	1.778	96.4	.0124
		"	1.733	2.276	96.8	.0123
		"	2.733	2.939	99.5	.0121
		"	3.867	3.529	100.5	.0120
		"	6.267	4.349	97.3	.0124
		"	7.267	4.625	96.1	.0125
		"	8.800	5.307	100.2	.0121
230.58		0.505	0.475	1.666	107.6	.0122
		"	1.076	2.519	108.1	.0123
		"	1.899	3.372	108.9	.0122
		"	2.911	4.225	110.2	.0122
		"	4.272	5.068	109.1	.0123
		"	5.063	5.527	109.3	.0123
		"	5.760	5.914	109.7	.0123
		"	6.614	6.373	110.3	.0122

Class A. Pipes,

DESCRIPTION OF PIPE. METHOD OF GAUGING.	AUTHORITY.
	V. New Wrought
Wrought Iron Pipe. Experiments of N. Y. Gaslight Co. Straight. Two elbows or a return would reduce delivery 2% to 4%. Quantity of discharge measured.	Rowland,* 1883.
New Wrought Iron Galvanized Pipe. Straight.	Ehmann,† 1878–79.
New Wrought Iron Pipe. Coated with asphalt. Funnel mouthpiece.	H. Smith, Jr., 1886.
New Wrought Iron Pipe. Not coated. Straight. Discharge measured with great accuracy.	Darcy, 1851.
New Wrought Iron Riveted Pipe. Coated with asphalt. Straight	Do.
New Iron Riveted Pipe at Versailles. Easy curves.	Couplet, 1832.

* See Brush, Trans. Am. Soc. C. E.

† See Iben, Druckhöhenverlust.

under Pressure.

Length in Feet.	Diameter in Feet.	Mean Hydraulic Radius. in Feet, R	Hydraulic Gradient or Slope per Thousand, $1000\,S$	Mean Velocity in Feet per Second, v	Coefficient, in Formula $v = c\sqrt{RS}.$ c	Coefficient of Roughness, n
Iron Pipe.						
31.0	0.0833	0.0208	6258.06	36.10	100.0	.0070
31.0	"	"	8935.49	43.40	100.6	.0057
31.0	"	"	10741.93	48.10	101.7	.0069
63.5	"	"	3055.12	26.70	105.8	.0067
63.5	"	"	4362.20	32.10	106.6	.0067
63.5	"	"	5244.10	36.60	110.7	.0066
97.0	"	"	2000.00	19.90	97.5	.0071
97.0	"	"	2855.67	24.50	100.5	.0071
97.0	"	"	3432.99	27.20	101.7	.0070
301.8	0.0842	0.021	7.61	1.11	87.1	.0077
	"	"	29.35	2.13	85.9	.0078
	"	"	113.04	3.71	77.2	.0082
	"	"	225.00	5.80	84.5	.0076
	"	"	239.13	5.90	83.2	.0077
about 60	0.0873	0.0218	26.93	2.220	91.6	.0075
	"	"	52.19	3.224	95.5	.0074
	"	"	103.38	4.761	100.2	.0071
	"	"	130.64	5.443	101.9	.0070
372	0.0873	0.0218	0.33	0.190	70.7	.0084
	"	"	10.15	1.207	81.1	.0082
	"	"	43.48	2.612	84.8	.0080
	"	"	105.71	4.203	87.5	.0078
	"	"	309.52	7.166	87.2	.0078
	0.1296	0.0324	0.22	0.205	76.9	.0086
	"	"	3.36	0.858	82.3	.0086
	"	"	23.89	2.585	92.9	.0082
	"	"	123.15	6.300	99.8	.0078
	"	"	224.08	8.521	100.0	.0077
365	0.2710	0.0677	0.27	0.328	76.7	.0100
	"	"	2.03	1.171	99.9	.0088
	"	"	12.20	3.117	103.4	.0085
	"	"	40.70	6.148	117.1	.0081
	"	"	106.54	10.535	124.0	.0078
	"	"	156.05	12.780	124.3	.0077
1825	0.533	0.133	0.146	0.2447	55.5	.0144
	"	"	0.255	0.3518	60.3	.0142

Class A. Pipes,

DESCRIPTION OF PIPE. METHOD OF GAUGING.	AUTHORITY.
	New Wrought Iron
New Wrought Iron Riveted Pipe. Coated with asphalt. Straight.	Darcy, 1851.
Sheet Iron Riveted Pipe at North Bloomfield. Funnel mouthpiece, 7.8 feet long. Velocity measured by weir.	H. Smith, Jr., 1876.
New Wrought Iron Riveted Pipe. Coated with asphalt. Straight.	Darcy, 1851.
Sheet Iron Riveted Pipe at North Bloomfield. Coated with asphalt. Funnel mouthpiece, 12 feet long. Velocity measured by weir.	H. Smith, Jr., 1876.
Same. Funnel mouthpiece, 14.8 feet long.	Do.
Sheet Iron Double-riveted Pipe at Texas Creek. Coated with asphalt. Easy curves. Velocity measured by weir and orifices.	Do.
Sheet Iron Riveted Pipe at Humbug, Cal. Velocity measured by flow through standard apertures	Do.
Wrought Iron Flume at Holyoke. Flume made of rings about 4.5 feet long, riveted with lap joints. Each ring consisted of three plates, lapped and riveted; thickness of plates, .03 feet. Section nearly circular. Velocity measured by Venturi water meter.	Herschel, 1887.

under Pressure.

Length in Feet.	Diameter in Feet.	Mean Hydraulic Radius, in Feet, R	Hydraulic Gradient or Slope per Thousand, $1000\,S$	Mean Velocity in Feet per Second, v	Coefficient, in Formula $v = c\sqrt{RS}$, c	Coefficient of Roughness, n
Pipe—Continued.						
365	0.6430	0.1607	0.20	0.591	104.1	.0097
"	"	"	1.29	1.529	106.2	.0100
"	"	"	5.80	3.530	115.6	.0095
"	"	"	12.00	5.509	125.4	.0090
"	"	"	29.70	9.000	130.2	.0088
"	"	"	121.56	19.720	141.0	.0083
abt. 700	0.911	0.228	8.50	4.712	107.1	.0108
"	"	"	13.34	6.094	110.6	.0106
"	"	"	16.95	6.927	111.5	.0105
"	"	"	25.59	8.059	113.4	.0104
"	0.9105	"	33.09	10.021	115.5	.0102
365	0.9350	0.234	0.70	1.296	101.3	.0110
"	"	"	4.33	3.808	121.6	.0098
"	"	"	11.90	6.673	126.5	.0096
"	"	"	28.07	10.522	129.9	.0094
abt. 700	1.056	0.264	6.68	4.595	109.4	.0109
"	"	"	14.28	6.962	113.4	.0106
"	"	"	22.19	8.646	113.0	.0106
"	"	"	33.18	10.706	114.4	.0105
abt. 700	1.229	0.307	5.02	4.383	111.6	.0110
"	1.230	"	10.97	6.841	117.8	.0106
"	"	"	12.27	7.314	119.1	.0105
"	"	"	16.46	8.462	119.0	.0105
"	"	"	24.70	10.593	121.6	.0104
"	"	"	32.31	12.090	121.3	.0104
abt. 4440	1.416	0.354	66.72	20.143	131.1	.0099
abt. 1200	2.154	0.538	16.41	12.605	134.1	.0106
152.9	8.58	2.145	0.0079	0.50	121.9	.0127
"	"	"	0.0320	1.00	120.6	.0134
"	"	"	0.0837	1.50	111.9	.0148
"	"	"	0.1557	2.00	109.4	.0154
"	"	"	0.2453	2.50	109.0	.0155
"	"	"	9.3584	3.00	108.2	.0157
"	"	"	0.4991	3.50	107.0	.0159
"	"	"	0.6619	4.00	106.2	.0160
"	"	"	0.8470	4.50	105.6	.0160

Class A. Pipes,

DESCRIPTION OF PIPE. METHOD OF GAUGING.	AUTHORITY.
	VI. New Cast
Cast Iron Pipe at Hahnwald. Asphalted; two years in use. · Many but easy curves, and several other irregularities. No incrustations. Observations were made of two stretches of the same pipe, this experiment being made in the lower part of the main, having a 3% grade.	Ehmann,* 1878–79.
Cast Iron Pipe at Hahnwald. Asphalted; two years in use. Many easy curves, and several other irregularities. No incrustations. This pipe includes the previous one, and had a heavy grade for the other 875.8 feet.	Do.
New Cast Iron Pipe.	Darcy, 1851.
Cast Iron Main at Stuttgart (Neckar St.). About ⅔ length was 9 years in use, and ¼ about 1 year. No incrustations noticeable in either stretch. Two stop-valves and six branches on the line.	Ehmann, 1878–79.
Cast Iron Pipe at Hamburg (Bill Strasse). 2½ years in use.	Iben,† 1875.
New Cast Iron Pipe at Hamburg (Wenden Strasse).	Do.

* For Ehmann's Experiments, see Iben, Druckhöhenverlust. They are said to have been made with great care. Discharges were measured by volumes, and pressures were taken at numerous points along the lines.

† For Iben's Experiments, see Iben, Druckhöhenverlust.

under Pressure.

Length in Feet.	Diameter in Feet.	Mean Hydraulic Radius in Feet, R	Hydraulic Gradient or Slope per Thousand, $1000\,S$	Mean Velocity in Feet per Second, v	Coefficient. in Formula $v = c\sqrt{RS}$, c	Coefficient of Roughness, n
Iron Pipe.						
1262.5	0.164	0.041	1.67	0.61	73.7	.0096
"	"	"	24.95	2.43	76.0	.0096
"	"	"	31.34	2.75	76.8	.0096
"	"	"	35.71	2.95	77.1	.0095
2138.6	0.164	0.041	3.15	0.84	73.9	.0097
"	"	"	6.38	1.22	75.4	.0096
"	"	"	9.74	1.52	75.9	.0096
"	"	"	13.71	1.80	75.9	.0096
"	"	"	15.66	1.93	76.3	.0095
"	"	"	20.25	2.20	76.4	.0096
366	0.2687	0.0672	0.20	0.289	78.8	.0096
"	"	"	5.31	1.841	97.5	.0091
"	"	"	22.55	3.888	99.9	.0089
"	"	"	99.04	8.160	100.0	.0089
"	"	"	170.72	10.712	100.0	.0089
3614.6	0.331	0.083	0.29	0.31	63.3	.0120
"	"	"	1.13	0.77	79.6	.0107
"	"	"	2.35	1.18	84.5	.0104
"	"	"	3.76	1.57	88.9	.0100
"	"	"	6.43	2.06	89.2	.0100
1889.3	0.334	0.083	3.65	1.43	82.2	.0105
"	"	"	25.87	3.52	76.0	.0111
"	"	"	36.11	4.10	74.9	.0112
"	"	"	41.15	4.32	73.9	.0114
896.8	0.334	0.083	15.73	3.47	96.1	.0096
"	"	"	31.09	4.86	95.7	.0096
"	"	"	42.06	5.80	98.3	.0093
"	"	"	48.64	6.17	97.2	.0094

Class A. Pipes,

DESCRIPTION OF PIPE. METHOD OF GAUGING.	AUTHORITY.
	New Cast Iron
New Cast Iron Pipe at Hamburg (Grindell Alley). Coated with tar.	Iben, 1876.
New Cast Iron Pipe at Hamburg (Deseniss St.). Coated with tar.	Do.
New Cast Iron Pipe.	Darcy, 1851.
New Cast Iron Pipe at Hamburg (Haller Strasse).	Iben, 1875.
New Cast Iron Pipe at Hamburg (Schoen St.). Coated with tar.	Iben, 1876.
New Cast Iron Main at Hamburg (Repsold St.). Coated with tar.	Do.
New Cast Iron Pipe.	Darcy, 1851.

Cast Iron Main at Stuttgart.
    About four years in use.
    Asphalted and in good condition.
    One bend of curved pipes.
    No valves or branches.
	Ehmann, 1878–79.

under Pressure.

Length in Feet.	Diameter in Feet.	Mean Hydraulic Radius, in Feet, R	Hydraulic Gradient or Slope per Thousand, $1000\,S$	Mean Velocity in Feet per Second, v	Coefficient, in Formula $v = c\sqrt{RS}$, c	Coefficient of Roughness, n

Pipe—Continued.

Length in Feet.	Diameter in Feet.	Mean Hydraulic Radius	Hydraulic Gradient	Mean Velocity	Coefficient c	Coefficient n
397	0.335	0.084	0.66	1.00	124	.0078
	"	"	5.62	2.10	97	.0094
	"	"	9.75	2.80	97	.0095
	"	"	20.50	4.30	105	.0089
	"	"	33.72	5.50	104	.0091
415	0.335	0.084	1.98	1.00	79	.0108
	"	"	4.11	1.70	92	.0098
	"	"	6.56	2.10	90	.0099
	"	"	7.83	2.30	90	.0099
	"	"	11.07	2.50	91	.0098
366	0.4495	0.1124	0.24	0.489	94.1	.0097
	"	"	4.75	2.503	108.4	.0094
	"	"	22.25	5.023	112.5	.0091
	"	"	98.52	11.942	113.5	.0091
	"	"	167.56	15.397	112.2	.0091
1088	0.498	0.125	11.46	3.36	89.4	.0109
	"	"	14.17	3.90	94.7	.0105
1073	0.499	0.125	4.59	2.00	82	.0116
	"	"	11.62	3.30	87	.0112
	"	"	16.21	3.90	88	.0110
	"	"	22.32	4.80	92	.0107
	"	"	30.27	5.30	87	.0112
930	0.499	0.125	3.53	2.30	111	.0093
	"	"	14.83	4.30	101	.0101
	"	"	27.52	5.30	90	.0109
	"	"	34.23	6.00	92	.0108
	"	"	50.46	7.10	90	.0109
	"	"	68.10	8.70	95	.0104
365	0.6168	0.1542	0.27	0.673	104.2	.0096
	"	"	3.68	2.487	104.4	.0100
	"	"	22.50	6.342	107.7	.0100
	"	"	109.80	14.183	109.0	.0099
	"	"	145.91	16.168	107.8	.0100
810	0.662	0.166	0.377	0.73	92.7	.0108
	"	"	0.850	1.12	94.7	.0109
	"	"	1.332	1.45	97.9	.0107
	"	"	1.883	1.69	96.0	.0109
	"	"				

Class A. Pipes,

DESCRIPTION OF PIPE. METHOD OF GAUGING.	AUTHORITY.
	New Cast Iron
Cast Iron Main at Stuttgart. About four years in use. Asphalted and in good condition. Several bends of large radius and made of curved pipe. No valves or branches.	Ehmann, 1878–79.
Cast Iron Main at Stuttgart. One year in use; perfectly clean. Several easy horizontal curves, and one vertical curve with summit at which air was allowed to escape before each experiment. Three valves on the line. Simultaneous observations along two stretches of the same main 2300.9 feet apart.	Do.
New Cast Iron Pipe at Hamburg (Uhlenhorst). (Author acknowledges some unknown obstruction.)	Iben, 1875.
New Cast Iron Main at Hamburg (Röhrendamm St.). Coated with tar.	Iben, 1876.
New Cast Iron Pipe at Hamburg (Laeisz St.). Coated with tar.	Do.
New Cast Iron Force Main at Bonn. Coated with asphalt. Alignment direct, with easy curves. Possibly some air in pipes. Discharge determined from reservoir contents. Static pressure, 155 feet.	Iben, 1880.
Cast Iron Pipe at Dantzig. Five years old; in good condition. Coated with asphalt. Nearly straight. Descent, 155 feet. Velocity determined from reservoir contents and pressure gauges.	Lampe,* 1869–71.

* See Iben. Druckhöhenverlust.

under Pressure.

Length in Feet.	Diameter in Feet.	Mean Hydraulic Radius, in Feet, R.	Hydraulic Gradient or Slope per Thousand, 1000 S	Mean Velocity in Feet per Second, v	Coefficient, in Formula $v = c\sqrt{RS}$, c	Coefficient of Roughness, n
Pipe—Continued.						
1131	0.826	0.206	0.0174	0.20	105.9	.0080
"	"	"	0.0319	0.27	105.9	.0082
"	"	"	0.0783	0.40	99.7	.0097
"	"	"	0.1880	0.62	99.7	.0103
"	"	"	0.3280	0.83	100.9	.0107
"	"	"	0.4060	0.94	102.9	.0104
1046.3	0.829	0.207	0.213	0.29	43.7	.0197
"	"	"	0.392	0.72	79.9	.0128
"	"	"	0.781	1.14	89.7	.0119
"	"	"	1.339	1.51	90.7	.0119
"	"	"	2.150	1.90	90.1	.0120
"	"	"	3.223	2.31	89.4	.0122
"	"	"	4.596	2.68	86.9	.0124
5612.1	1.000	0.25	0.82	1.35	94.3	.0119
"	"	"	3.10	2.37	85.5	.0130
"	"	"	4.21	2.77	85.4	.0131
1795	1.001	0.25	1.46	1.60	85	.0131
"	"	"	1.83	2.10	97	.0118
"	"	"	2.19	2.60	112	.0104
"	"	"	3.84	3.80	121	.0099
"	"	"	6.03	4.80	125	.0097
580	1.001	0.25	0.04	0.40	123	.0079
"	"	"	0.60	1.30	109	.0107
"	"	"	1.49	2.20	112	.0104
"	"	"	2.84	3.00	114	.0104
"	"	"	7.00	4.80	116	.0103
"	"	"	11.22	6.10	114	.0105
17,684	1.004	0.251	1.21	1.553	89.3	.0126
"	"	"	1.95	2.104	95.1	.0120
"	"	"	2.60	2.620	102.6	.0114
"	"	"	3.62	3.096	102.7	.0114
abt. 26,000	1.373	0.343	0.594	1.577	110.5	.0112
"	"	"	1.376	2.479	114.1	.0110
"	"	"	1.630	2.709	114.6	.0110
"	"	"	1.950	3.090	119.4	.0107

Class A. Pipes,

DESCRIPTION OF PIPE. METHOD OF GAUGING.	AUTHORITY.
	New Cast Iron
New Cast Iron Pipe.	Darcy, 1851.
New Cast Iron Pipe at Hamburg (Sternschanze). Coated with tar.	Iben, 1876.
New Cast Iron Force Main at Hackensack, N. J. Large number of summits, angles, and curves, of which there are four right angles and ten quadrants of 30 feet radius. Quantity measured at pumps, 5% slip. Static head, 165 feet.	Brush, 1882–87.
New Cast Iron Force Main at Philadelphia, Pa. One quarter turn; other curves 25 feet radius. Two check-valves, whose weight is deducted from pressure on gauge. Quantity measured at pumps, 5% slip. Static head, 324.2 feet.	Darrach, 1878.
Cast Iron Force Main at Philadelphia, Pa. Two years old. Curves, 25 feet radius. Four check-valves on line, the weight of which is deducted from pressure in gauge. Quantity measured at pumps, 5% slip. Static head, 167.3 feet.	Do.
New Cast Iron Pipe, Sudbury Conduit. Coated with asphalt. Horizontally straight; very easy vertical curves. Velocity measured by weir.	Stearns, 1885.

under Pressure.

Length in Feet.	Diameter in Feet.	Mean Hydraulic Radius, in Feet, R	Hydraulic Gradient or Slope per Thousand, $1000\ S$	Mean Velocity in Feet per Second, v	Coefficient, in Formula $v = c\sqrt{RS}$, c	Coefficient of Roughness, n

Pipe—Continued.

365	1.6404	0.4101	0 45	1.472	108.4	.0116
,,	,,	,,	1.20	2.602	117.3	.0111
"	"	"	2.10	3.416	116.4	.0112
"	"	"	2 60	3.674	112.5	.0115
3514	1.667	0.417	0.12	0.70	105	.0112
,,	,,	"	0.48	1.60	110	.0116
"	"	"	0.76	1.90	109	.0118
"	"	"	1.21	2.50	109	.0119
75,000	1.667	0.417	0.733	2.00	114.4	.0112
,,	,,	"	0.880	2.24	117.0	.0110
"	"	"	1.026	2 36	114.1	.0113
"	"	"	1.187	2.52	113.3	.0114
"	"	"	1.333	2.68	113.7	.0113
"	"	"	1.493	2.76	110.6	.0117
"	"	"	1.640	2.92	111.7	.0124
"	"	"	1.800	3.00	109.5	.0127
4000	2.500	0.625	0.39	1.60	102.8	.0131
"	"	"	0.46	1.74	102.9	.0132
"	"	"	0.53	1.87	103.0	.0132
"	"	"	0.60	2.00	103.3	.0132
"	"	"	0.67	2.14	104.6	.0129
20,200	2.500	0.625	0.310	1.47	105.5	.0128
,,	,,	"	0.38	1.62	105.9	.0128
"	"	"	0.44	1.76	106.2	.0128
"	"	"	0.50	1.91	107.7	.0127
"	"	"	0.57	2.06	109.4	.0126
"	"	"	0.63	2.20	110.7	.0124
"	"	"	0.70	2.35	112.6	.0123
"	"	"	0.76	2.50	114.6	.0121
"	"	"	0.83	2.64	116.2	.0119
"	"	"	0.89	2.79	118.4	.0118
"	"	"	0.95	2.94	120.4	.0116
"	"	"	1.02	3.08	122.1	.0114
"	"	"	1.08	3.23	124.2	.0113
1747	4.00	1.00	0.318	2.616	146.7	.0105
"	"	,,	0.711	3.738	140.1	.0109
"	"	"	1.221	4.965	142.1	.0108
"	"	"	1.849	6.195	144.1	.0107

Class A. Pipes,

DESCRIPTION OF PIPE. METHOD OF GAUGING.	AUTHORITY.
	New Cast Iron
Cast Iron Pipe at Loch Katrine. Coated with asphalt; in good condition. Several easy bends.	Jas. M. Gale, 1869.
	VII. Old
Old Cast Iron Pipe.	Darcy, 1851.
Same. Cleaned.	Do.
Cast Iron Pipe.	Do.
Same. Cleaned.	Do.
Old Cast Iron Pipe at Hamburg (Koppel). Nineteen years in use. Very heavily incrustated.	Iben, 1876.
Old Iron Pipe at Versailles. Much incrustated. Two abrupt and several easy bends. Velocity determined by a measuring vessel.	Couplet, 1732.
Old Cast Iron Pipe at Hamburg (Schulweg). Thirteen years in use. Heavily incrustated.	Iben, 1876.

under Pressure.

Length in Feet.	Diameter in Feet.	Mean Hydraulic Radius, in Feet, R	Hydraulic Gradient or Slope per Thousand, $1000\ S$	Mean Velocity in Feet per Second, v	Coefficient, in Formula $v = c\sqrt{RS}.$ c	Coefficient of Roughness, n

Pipe—Continued.

3¾ miles	4.00	1.00	0.947	3.458	112.4	.0134

Iron Pipe.

375	0.1178	0.0294	0.25	0.167	61.7	.0095
"	"	"	1.83	0.426	58.1	.0105
"	"	"	15.25	1.250	59.0	.0105
"	"	"	41.55	2.077	59.4	.0105
375	0.1194	0.0298	0.71	0.371	80.5	.0085
"	"	"	1.80	0.617	84.1	.0084
"	"	"	14.41	1.972	95.1	.0079
"	"	"	39.66	3.392	98.1	.0077
366	0.2608	0.0652	0.65	0.403	62.0	.0120
"	"	"	7.25	1.463	67.3	.0115
"	"	"	16.10	2.224	68.7	.0115
"	"	"	45.35	3.747	68.9	.0115
366	0.2628	0.0657	0.54	0.633	85.2	.0096
"	"	"	7.23	2.014	92.4	.0094
"	"	"	15.57	2.835	88.6	.0096
"	"	"	44.73	5.007	93.4	.0094
373	0.335	0.083	1.50	0.30	25	.0247
"	"	"	14.70	0.70	20	.0292
"	"	"	32.30	1.00	20	.0292
"	"	"	72.01	1.60	21	.0284
"	"	"	120.42	2.10	21	.0284
"	"	"	150.36	2.40	21	.0284
1898	0.355	0.0888	0.421	0.1836	30.0	.0212
"	"	"	0.982	0.3166	33.9	.0200
"	"	"	1.450	0.4086	36.0	.0194
899	0.499	0.124	7.66	0.80	26	.0268
"	"	"	11.31	1.30	34	.0221
"	"	"	16.78	1.50	34	.0221
"	"	"	19.33	1.70	34	.0221
"	"	"	22.25	1.80	34	.0221
"	"	"	24.44	1.90	34	.0221

Class A. Pipes,

Description of Pipe. Method of Gauging.	Authority.
	Old Iron
Old Cast Iron Pipe at Hamburg (Schulweg). Nineteen years in use Very heavily incrustated.	Iben, 1876.
Old Cast Iron Pipe at Paris.	Darcy, 1851.
Same. Cleaned.	Do.
Cast Iron Main at Stuttgart. Six years in use. Slight mud deposits, occasionally 0.016 feet in depth. It has a large number of easy curves horizontally, but a regular grade. Simultaneous observations along two stretches of the same main; 2300.9 feet apart.	Ehmann, 1878-79.
Old Cast Iron Pipe at Paris. Carefully cleaned.	Darcy, 1851.
Old Cast Iron Pipe at Hamburg (Rotherbaum). Twelve years in use. Slightly tuberculated.	Iben, 1876.
Old Cast Iron Pipe at Hamburg (Glacis Chaussée). Two years in use. Slightly incrustated.	Do.
Old Cast Iron Pipe at Hamburg (Hamm). Fourteen years in use. Slightly incrustated.	Do.

under Pressure.

Length in Feet.	Diameter in Feet.	Mean Hydraulic Radius, in Feet, R	Hydraulic Gradient or Slope per Thousand, $1000\,S$	Mean Velocity in Feet per Second, v	Coefficient, in Formula $v = c\sqrt{RS},$ c	Coefficient of Roughness, u

Pipe—Continued.

Length in Feet.	Diameter in Feet.	Mean Hydraulic Radius	Hydraulic Gradient	Mean Velocity	Coefficient c	Coefficient of Roughness
910	0.499	0.124	9.67	0.80	23	.0296
"	"	"	18.98	1.30	26	.0269
"	"	"	25.78	1.50	27	.0270
"	"	"	31.15	1.70	27	.0262
"	"	"	34.73	1.80	27	.0262
"	"	"	36.88	1.90	27	.0262
365	0.7979	0.1995	0.94	1.007	73.6	.0138
"	"	"	4.73	2.320	75.5	.0137
"	"	"	22.90	5.075	75.1	.0138
"	"	"	41.05	6.801	75.2	.0138
"	"	"	130.81	12.576	75.3	.0138
365	0.8028	0.2007	0.52	0.912	89.3	.0117
"	"	"	4.98	3.113	98.5	.0113
"	"	"	20.35	6.247	97.7	.0114
"	"	"	37.30	8.438	97.5	.0114
"	"	"	113.43	14.754	97.8	.0114
1098.8	0.829	0.207	0.203	0.29	44.7	.0192
"	"	"	0.364	0.72	82.9	.0123
"	"	"	0.937	1.14	81.9	.0128
"	"	"	1.558	1.51	83.3	.0127
"	"	"	2.322	1.90	86.7	.0124
"	"	"	3.719	2.31	83.2	.0128
"	"	"	4.818	2.68	84.9	.0127
365	0.9744	0.2436	0.28	0.800	96.9	.0114
"	"	"	1.19	1.765	103.7	.0112
"	"	"	5.37	3.789	104.8	.0112
"	"	"	23.05	7.841	104.6	.0112
"	"	"	40.70	10.308	104.1	.0112
541	1.000	0.250	2.24	1.79	75.7	.0143
"	"	"	2.84	2.03	76.2	.0142
2149	1.001	0.250	0.26	0.60	74	.0138
"	"	"	0.41	0.80	81	.0132
"	"	"	0.81	1.20	85	.0129
"	"	"	1.28	1.60	92	.0122
"	"	"	2.99	2.40	86	.0129
7179	1.001	0.250	0.42	0.70	71	.0147
"	"	"	1.65	1.60	78	.0139
"	"	"	4.44	2.70	80	.0137
"	"	"	9.43	3.90	80	.0138

Class A. Pipes,

Description of Pipe. Method of Gauging.	Authority.
	Old Iron
Old Cast Iron Pipe at Hamburg (Carolinen St.). Fifteen years in use. Rather heavily incrustated.	Iben, 1876.
Old Cast Iron Pipe at Hamburg (Strohhaus). Twenty-two years in use. Very heavily incrustated.	Do.
Cast Iron Pipe at Versailles. Used for some time.	Couplet, 1732.
Cast Iron Pipe at Crawley. Thirty years old. With incrustations.	Jas. Leslie, 1855.
Cast Iron Pipe at Versailles. Used for some time. Several easy bends.	Couplet, 1732.
Cast Iron Main at Jersey City. Tuberculated.	Bailey,* 1867.
Old Cast Iron Pipe at Hamburg (Heidenkampsweg). Twenty-five years in use. Heavily incrustated.	Iben, 1876.
Wrought Iron Cement-lined Force Main. No short bends, but two large Y branches, two small blow-off branches, and three stop-valves.	Fanning, 1880.

* See Fanning, " Treatise on Hydraulics." etc.

under Pressure.

Pipe—Continued.

Length in Feet.	Diameter in Feet.	Mean Hydraulic Radius, in Feet, R.	Hydraulic Gradient or Slope per Thousand, $1000\ S$	Mean Velocity in Feet per Second, v	Coefficient, in Formula $v = c\sqrt{RS}$, c	Coefficient of Roughness, n
1808	1.001	0.250	0.65	0.90	67	.0154
"	"	"	3.76	1.80	58	.0177
"	"	"	6.12	2.30	59	.0175
"	"	"	7.73	2.60	58	.0178
1736	1.001	0.250	1.08	0.80	50	.0197
"	"	"	4.29	1.50	47	.0207
"	"	"	10 91	2.40	45	.0215
"	"	"	23.86	3.50	46	.0212
3837	1.066	0.266	3.345	2.087	69.9	.0155
44,400	1.25	0.312	5.086	3.403	86.9	.0136
3837	1.599	0.400	3.313	3.478	95.6	.0132
29,715	1.667	0.416	0.947	1.438	72.4	.0166
4403	1.667	0.416	1.55	1.60	64	.0182
"	"	"	4.83	2.70	60	.0193
"	"	"	8.85	3.60	59	.0196
"	"	"	14.33	4.50	58	.0200
8171	1.667	0.416	0.23	0.949	97.4	.0124
"	"	"	0.44	1.488	109.8	.0115
"	"	"	0.73	1.925	110.7	.0116
"	"	"	1.04	2.320	112.0	.0116
"	"	"	1.34	2.597	110.1	.0117
"	"	"	1.58	2.867	111.7	.0115
"	"	"	1.99	3.271	113.5	.0114
"	"	"	2.28	3.439	111.7	.0116
"	"	"	2.72	3.741	111.1	.0117
"	"	"	3.00	3.920	110.8	.0118
"	"	"	3.13	4.000	110.7	.0118
"	"	"	3.20	4.040	110.6	.0118

Class A. Pipes,

DESCRIPTION OF PIPE. METHOD OF GAUGING.	AUTHORITY.
	Old Iron
Cast Iron Force Main at Philadelphia, Pa. Eleven years old. One quarter turn. Quantity measured at pumps, 5% slip. Static head, 313. feet.	Darrach, 1878.
Wrought Iron Pipe at Cherokee. Inverted syphon with 887 feet depression. Five years in use. Velocity measured by flow through standard orifices.	H. Smith, Jr., 1886.
Cast Iron Force Main at Philadelphia, Pa. Nine years old. One curve of short radius. Quantity measured at pumps, 5% slip. Static head, 190 feet.	Darrach, 1878.
Cast Iron Force Main at Philadelphia, Pa. Seven years old. Curves 25 feet radius; one T near discharge. Quantity measured at pumps, 5% slip. Static head, 118.4 feet.	Do.
Cast Iron Force Main at Philadelphia, Pa. Seven years old. Curves 25 feet radius. Quantity measured at pumps, 5% slip. Static head, 100 feet.	Do.

under Pressure.

Length in Feet.	Diameter in Feet.	Mean Hydraulic Radius, in Feet, R	Hydraulic Gradient or Slope per Thousand, 1000 S	Mean Velocity in Feet per Second, v	Coefficient, in Formula $v = c\sqrt{RS},$ c	Coefficient of Roughness, n

Pipe—Continued.

Length in Feet.	Diameter in Feet.	Mean Hydraulic Radius	Hydraulic Gradient	Mean Velocity	Coefficient c	Coefficient n
4320	1.667	0.416	3.88	2.71	67.4	.0175
"	"	"	4.55	3.01	69.2	.0172
"	"	"	5.21	3.31	71.0	.0168
"	"	"	5.88	3.61	72.9	.0166
"	"	"	6.55	3.91	74.8	.0162
"	"	"	7.22	4.21	76.8	.0158
"	"	"	7.89	4.51	78.7	.0155
"	"	"	8.56	4.81	80.6	.0153
"	"	"	9.22	5.11	82.4	.0149
12,800	2.43	0.607	11.72	10.78	127.8	.0111
4400	2.500	0.625	0.92	1.070	44.7	.0269
"	"	"	1.05	1.205	47.0	.0258
"	"	"	1.18	1.340	49.3	.0248
"	"	"	1.31	1.475	51.5	.0238
"	"	"	1.44	1.610	53.6	.0229
"	"	"	1.58	1.745	55.6	.0224
"	"	"	1.71	1.880	57.6	.0218
"	"	"	1.84	2.015	59.4	.0212
"	"	"	1.97	2.150	61.3	.0206
"	"	"	2.10	2.285	63.1	.0202
12,400	3.000	0.750	1.05	1.00	35.7	.0342
"	"	"	1.07	1.11	39.2	.0315
"	"	"	1.09	1.22	42.7	.0294
"	"	"	1.12	1.33	46.1	.0273
"	"	"	1.14	1.44	49.4	.0257
"	"	"	1.16	1.55	52.6	.0245
"	"	"	1.19	1.66	55.8	.0236
"	"	"	1.21	1.77	59.0	.0222
"	"	"	1.23	1.88	62.1	.0213
"	"	"	1.26	2.00	65.1	.0203
3700	3.000	0.750	0.93	1.58	59.7	.0218
"	"	"	1.09	1.74	60.9	.0216
"	"	"	1.25	1.89	61.8	.0214
"	"	"	1.40	2.05	63.2	.0208
"	"	"	1.56	2.21	64.6	.0204
"	"	"	1.72	2.37	66.1	.0201

Class A. Pipes,

DESCRIPTION OF PIPE. METHOD OF GAUGING.	AUTHORITY.

Old Iron

Cast Iron Pipe (Croton Main) **at New York.** Heavily tuberculated. Three easy curves.	Kirkwood, 1867.

VIII. Brick

Dorchester Bay Tunnel (near Boston). Inverted syphon. Hard brick, well pointed, covered with sewage slime. Not known whether tunnel had deposit. One quarter turn of about 10 feet radius, and one angle $23\frac{1}{4}°$. Velocity measured in reservoir. In 1st, 2d, and 3d gaugings, water consisted of sewage only. In 4th, 5th, and 6th gaugings, water consisted of $\frac{1}{4}$ sewage and $\frac{4}{4}$ salt water.	Clarke,* 1885.

* See H. Smith, Jr., " Hydraulics."

under Pressure.

Length in Feet.	Diameter in Feet.	Mean Hydraulic Radius in Feet, R	Hydraulic Gradient or Slope per Thousand, $1000\ S$	Mean Velocity in Feet per Second, v	Coefficient, in Formula $v = c\sqrt{RS}$, c	Coefficient of Roughness, n

Pipe—Continued.

Length in Feet.	Diameter in Feet.	Mean Hydraulic Radius	Hydraulic Gradient or Slope	Mean Velocity	Coefficient	Coefficient of Roughness
11,217	3.000	0.750	1.802	3.000	81.6	.0168

Conduit.

Length in Feet.	Diameter in Feet.	Mean Hydraulic Radius	Hydraulic Gradient or Slope	Mean Velocity	Coefficient	Coefficient of Roughness
7166	7.500	1.875	0.0414	0.965	109	.0147
	"	"	0.0726	0.929	80	.0199
	"	"	0.0790	0.998	82	.0195
	"	"	0.5135	3.769	121	.0138
	"	"	0.5547	3.798	118	.0141
	"	"	0.5812	3.929	119	.0140

Class B. Open Channels,

Location and Description of Channel. Method of Gauging.	Authority.	Author's No. of Series.
		I. Channels Lined
Test Channel. Neat cement. Semicircular.	Darcy and Bazin,* "Recherches Hydrauliques," Paris, 1865.	24— 1 2 3 4 5 6 7 8 9 10 11 12
Test Channel. Two-thirds cement and one-third very fine sand. Semicircular.	Do.	25— 1 2 3 4 5 6 7 8 9 10 11 12
Test Channel. Neat cement. Rectangular.	Do.	2— 1 2 3 4 5 6 7 8 9 10 11 12
Channel at Dijon. Roughly cemented.	Quoted by Kutter.	

* In Darcy and Bazin's experiments, measurements were made with floats, Darcy's improved Pitot's tube, or by measuring in advance the quantity fed to channel.

Creeks, and Rivers.

Surface Width in Feet.	Greatest Depth in Feet.	Mean Hydraulic Radius in Feet, *R*	Slope of Water Surface per Thousand, 1000 *S*	Mean Velocity per Second in Feet, *v*	Coefficient. in Formula $v = c \sqrt{R S}$, *c*	Coefficient of Roughness, *n*

with Cement.

2.874	0.59	0.366	1.5	3.02	128.9	.0102
3.294	0.83	0.503	"	3.72	135.0	.0103
3.563	1.03	0.605	"	4.16	138.0	.0104
3.707	1.18	0.682	"	4.60	143.7	.0103
3.832	1.34	0.750	"	4.87	145.1	.0103
3.924	1.47	0.809	"	5.12	147.1	.0103
3.970	1.61	0.867	"	5.29	146.7	.0104
4.049	1.72	0.915	"	5.51	148.8	.0104
4.075	1.83	0.949	"	5.75	152.5	.0102
4.095	1.94	0.992	"	5.91	153.3	.0102
4.101	2.05	1.029	"	6.06	154.2	.0102
4.098	2.08	1.034	"	6.11	155.1	.0101
2.913	0.61	0.379	1.5	2.87	120.5	.0108
3.360	0.88	0.529	"	3.43	122.0	.0113
3.616	1.09	0.635	"	3.87	125.3	.0114
3.760	1.24	0.700	"	4.30	132.1	.0110
3.891	1.41	0.787	"	4.51	131.3	.0113
3.963	1.54	0.839	"	4.80	135.3	.0111
4.029	1.69	0.900	"	4.94	134.5	.0113
4.068	1 80	0.941	"	5.20	138.3	.0111
4.088	1.92	0.983	"	5.38	140.1	.0110
4.095	1.98	1.006	"	5.48	141.0	.0109
4.095	2.04	1.022	"	5.55	141.7	.0109
4.095	2.09	1.038	"	5.66	143.5	.0108
5.94	0.18	0.168	4.9	3.34	116.5	.0096
"	0.28	0.251	"	4.39	125.1	.0098
"	0.36	0.322	"	5.04	120.9	.0101
"	0.43	0.375	"	5.68	132.4	.0100
"	0.50	0.430	"	6.02	132.4	.0103
"	0.56	0.474	"	6.51	135.1	.0103
"	0.63	0.518	"	6.83	135.5	.0104
"	0.69	0.558	"	7.12	136.2	.0104
"	0.76	0.595	"	7.41	137.2	.0105
"	0.80	0.632	"	7.63	137.2	.0106
"	0.86	0.665	"	7.86	137.8	.0107
"	0.91	0.696	"	8.07	138.2	.0106
		0.407	0.940	2.081	106.4	.0120

Class B. Open Channels,

Location and Description of Channel. Method of Gauging.	Authority.	Author's No. of Series.

Channels Lined with

Mill Race at Idria, Hungary. Cement plaster over rubble masonry. Trapezoidal, bottom width, 3.30 feet.	Rittinger,* 1855.	
Dhuys Aqueduct, near Paris. Cement surface. Rectangular.	Quoted by Kutter.	
Sudbury Conduit in Massachusetts. Plaster of pure cement over brickwork. Sectional shape, see Category III. 490 feet long.	Fteley and Stearns,† 1880.	

II. Channels Lined with

Test Channel. Carefully planed boards. Rectangular.	Darcy and Bazin, "Recherches Hydrauliques," Paris, 1865.	29—1 2 3 4 5
Same.	Do.	28—1 2 3 4 5 6 7
Flume in Venezuela. Very hard wood, sawed quite smooth. Rectangular.	Proc. Engr's Club of Phila., vol. i. p. 36.	

* See Bornemann, "Der Civil Ingénieur," 1869. Rittinger's experiments were made under instructions of the Austrian government. Stretches were at least 120 feet long, straight or nearly so, with slope, cross-section, and velocity approximately uniform. Velocity was obtained from cubic measurement in tanks or other vessels. Slopes and mean radii given in the table are averages for total length.

† See "Hydraulics," by H. Smith, Jr.

Creeks, and Rivers.

Surface Width in Feet.	Greatest Depth in Feet.	Mean Hydraulic Radius in Feet, R	Slope of Water Surface per Thousand, $1000 S$	Mean Velocity per Second in Feet, v	Coefficient, in Formula $v = c\sqrt{RS}$, c	Coefficient of Roughness, n

Cement—Continued.

	2.04	0.977	0.5	2.523	114.1	.0130
		0.984	0.100	1.148	115.3	.0124
	3.071	1.863	0.1606	2.529	146.2	.0114
	3.575	2.048	0.1596	2.672	147.9	.0114
	3.768	2.111	0.1580	2.805	153.6	.0111

Boards or Canvas.

0.328	0 037	0.030	15.2	1.87	87.5	.0084
"	0.058	0.043	"	2.30	90.0	.0087
"	0.078	0.053	"	2.68	94.4	.0089
"	0.097	0.061	"	3.00	98.5	.0089
"	0.134	0.074	"	3.56	106.4	.0088
0.328	0.04	0.029	4.7	0.00	76.5	.0090
"	0.08	0.052	"	1.30	83.0	.0096
"	0.11	0.066	"	1.58	89.4	.0097
"	0.14	0.075	"	1.74	92.7	.0097
"	0.17	0.084	"	1.94	97.6	.0095
"	0.20	0.091	"	2.11	102.1	.0094
"	0.22	0.003	"	2.16	103.2	.0097
0.58	0.25	0.134	3.0	2.3	114.7	.0093

Class B. Open Channels,

Location and Description of Channel. Method of Gauging.	Authority.	Author's No. of Series.

Channels Lined with Boards

Location and Description of Channel. Method of Gauging.	Authority.	Author's No. of Series.
Mill Race at Berne. Sawed boards. Rectangular. Floats and also known quantity of water.	Kutter, 1865.	
Two Small Wooden Channels.	Dubuat.	
Race of Schattberg Stamp Mill in Hungary. Wooden trough. Trapezoidal; bottom width, 1.04 feet.	Rittinger,* 1855.	
Race of Josefistoll Stamp Mill in Hungary. Wooden trough. Rectangular; bottom width, 2.58 feet.	Do.	
Mill Race at Idria, Hungary. Wooden trough. Rectangular; bottom width, 1.22 feet.	Do.	
Mill Race at Schemnitz, Hungary. Wooden trough. Semi-octagonal; bottom width, 0.81 feet.	Do.	
Test Channel. Planed boards. Semicircular.	Darcy and Bazin, " Recherches Hydrauliques," Paris, 1865.	26 —1 2 3 4 5 6 7 8 9 10 11 12 13

* See footnote Category I.

Creeks, and Rivers.

Surface Width in Feet.	Greatest Depth in Feet.	Mean Hydraulic Radius in Feet, R	Slope of Water Surface per Thousand, $1000\,S$	Mean Velocity per Second in Feet, v	Coefficient in Formula $v = c^4\,\overline{R}\overline{S}$, c	Coefficient of Roughness, n

or Canvas—Continued.

2.95	0.06	0.118	17.00	3.969	88.5	.0110
1.53		0.198	0.71	1.075	91.1	.0115
		0.259	0.10	1.509	92 9	.0110
	0.24	0.159	34.3	8.261	111.9	.0098
	0.26	0.173	"	8.213	106.6	.0104
	0.38	0.237	"	10.111	112.1	.0105
	0.41	0.246	"	10.635	115.8	.0103
	0.11	0.097	24.6	3.376	69.1	.0125
	0.23	0.202	"	6.054	85.9	.0125
	0.30	0.245	"	9.156	118.3	.0102
	0.35	0.277	"	8.705	106.2	.0113
	0.42	0.317	"	9.502	107.6	.0115
	0.51	0.363	"	10.501	111.1	.0115
	0.68	0.323	2.0	2.787	109.7	.0112
	0.41	0.264	0.5	1.084	94.3	.0119
	0.49	0.303	"	1.289	104.8	.0112
	0.66	0.371	"	1.644	120.7	.0105
	0.73	0.396	"	1.891	134.4	.0097
3.16	0.63	0.390	1.5	2.61	107.8	.0117
3.62	0.88	0.537	"	3.23	113.8	.0119
3.89	1.07	0.632	"	3.71	120.6	.0117
4.08	1.24	0.717	"	4.04	123.0	.0118
4.24	1.40	0.796	"	4.25	123.2	.0119
4.33	1.53	0.850	"	4.51	125.8	.0118
4.43	1.68	0.921	"	4.64	124.7	.0121
4.48	1.79	0.964	"	4.87	128.2	.0119
4.53	1.92	1.015	"	5.00	128.2	.0119
4.56	2.02	1.054	"	5.18	130.3	.0119
4.59	2.14	1.096	"	5.29	130.4	.0119
4.59	2.24	1.129	"	5.45	132.3	.0118
4.59	2.29	1.145	"	5.54	133.5	.0118

Class B. Open Channels,

Location and Description of Channel. Method of Gauging.	Authority.	Author's No. of Series.

Channels Lined with Boards

Location and Description of Channel. Method of Gauging.	Authority.	Author's No. of Series.
Test Channel. Unplaned boards. Rectangular.	Darcy and Bazin, " Recherches Hydrau-liques," Paris, 1865.	20— 1 2 3 4 5 6 7 8 9
Test Channel. Unplaned boards. Rectangular.	Do.	19— 1 2 3 4 5 6 7 8 9 10 11
Test Channel. Unplaned boards. Rectangular.	Do.	18— 1 2 3 4 5 6 7 8 9 10 11 12
Test Channel. Unplaned boards. Rectangular.	Do.	11— 1 2 3 4 5 6 7

Creeks, and Rivers.

Surface Width in Feet.	Greatest Depth in Feet.	Mean Hydraulic Radius in Feet, R	Slope of Water Surface per Thousand, $1000\,S$	Mean Velocity per Second in Feet, v	Coefficient, in Formula $v = c\sqrt{RS}$, c	Coefficient of Roughness, n

or Canvas—*Continued.*

1.58	0.34	0.237	6.0	3.57	94.5	.0120
"	0.44	0.281	"	4.00	97.3	.0122
"	0.50	0.304	"	4.20	98.3	.0123
"	0.53	0.317	"	4.23	97.1	.0125
"	0.62	0.347	"	4.67	102.3	.0122
"	0.70	0.372	"	4.94	104.6	.0121
"	0.79	0.393	"	5.11	105.3	.0122
"	0.87	0.412	"	5.26	105.7	.0123
"	0.95	0.431	"	5.49	107.9	.0121
2.63	0.26	0.214	4.3	2.85	94.0	.0119
"	0.39	0.299	"	3.47	96.9	.0124
"	0.50	0.304	"	4.14	104.6	.0121
"	0.60	0.412	"	4.54	107.8	.0120
"	0.71	0.461	"	4.91	110.4	.0120
"	0.81	0.490	"	5.12	110.5	.0123
"	0.90	0.535	"	5.41	112.7	.0121
"	0.99	0.563	"	5.60	113.9	.0121
"	1.17	0.618	"	5.92	114.9	.0123
"	1.33	0.662	"	6.23	116.7	.0123
"	1.50	0.700	"	6.48	118.1	.0123
3.93	0.27	0.235	4.9	3.37	99.1	.0116
"	0.41	0.341	"	4.43	108.3	.0116
"	0.55	0.428	"	5.05	110.2	.0119
"	0.67	0.498	"	5.54	112.3	.0120
"	0.78	0.558	"	5.94	113.7	.0121
"	0.89	0.612	"	6.26	114.3	.0123
"	1.00	0.661	"	6.50	114.2	.0125
"	1.10	0.703	"	6.76	115.3	.0125
"	1.19	0.741	"	7.00	116.1	.0125
"	1.29	0.777	"	7.20	116.7	.0126
"	1.37	0.808	"	7.42	118.0	.0125
"	1.46	0.839	"	7.59	118.4	.0126
6.50	0.15	0.146	8.39	3.54	101.1	.0104
"	0.24	0.224	"	4.57	105.4	.0109
"	0.37	0.334	"	6.00	113.4	.0111
"	0.49	0.424	"	6.89	115.5	.0115
"	0.59	0.500	"	7.57	116.8	.0117
"	0.68	0.565	"	8.19	118.9	.0118
"	0.77	0.621	"	8.74	121.0	.0117

Class B. Open Channels,

LOCATION AND DESCRIPTION OF CHANNEL. METHOD OF GAUGING.	AUTHORITY.	Author's No. of Series.

Channels Lined with Boards

LOCATION AND DESCRIPTION OF CHANNEL. METHOD OF GAUGING.	AUTHORITY.	Author's No. of Series.
Test Channel. Unplaned boards. Rectangular.	Darcy and Bazin, 1865.	10— 1 2 3 4 5 6 7
Test Channel. Unplaned boards. Rectangular.	Do.	9— 1 2 3 4 5 6 7
Test Channel. Unplaned boards. Rectangular.	Do.	8— 1 2 3 4 5 6 7 8 9 10 11 12
Test Channel. Unplaned boards. Rectangular.	Do.	7— 1 2 3 4 5 6 7 8 9 10 11 12

Creeks, and Rivers.

Surface Width in Feet.	Greatest Depth in Feet.	Mean Hydraulic Radius, in Feet, R	Slope of Water Surface per Thousand, 1000 S	Mean Velocity in Feet per Second, v	Coefficient, in Formula $v = c\sqrt{RS}$, c	Coefficient of Roughness, n

or Canvas—Continued.

6.52	0.18	0.172	5.9"	2.99	93.7	.0114
"	0.28	0.255	"	3.98	102.7	.0115
"	0.43	0.370	"	5.23	111.1	.0116
"	0.55	0.472	"	6.06	114.8	.0117
"	0.67	0.554	"	6.69	117.0	.0119
"	0.77	0.623	"	7.24	119.3	.0119
"	0.87	0.686	"	7.71	121.1	.0119
6.51	0.30	0.276	1.5	1.80	88.3	.0130
"	0.46	0.406	"	2.37	96.3	.0131
"	0.72	0.590	"	3.10	104.2	.0132
"	0.92	0.720	"	3.63	110.4	.0130
"	1.10	0.824	"	4.05	115.1	.0128
"	1.27	0.912	"	4.41	119.1	.0127
"	1.44	0.995	"	4.66	120.4	.0128
6.53	0.15	0.147	8.24	3.52	101.4	.0104
"	0.25	0.231	"	4.42	101.4	.0114
"	0.32	0.289	"	5.23	107.1	.0114
"	0.38	0.341	"	5.83	109.8	.0115
"	0.45	0.393	"	6.24	109.7	.0117
"	0.50	0.431	"	6.74	113.1	.0117
"	0.54	0.466	"	7.17	115.8	.0117
"	0.60	0.500	"	7.44	115.2	.0118
"	0.65	0.541	"	7.73	115.8	.0119
"	0.69	0.572	"	8.03	116.9	.0119
"	0.74	0.604	"	8.26	117.1	.0120
"	0.78	0.630	"	8.57	119.0	.0119
6.53	0.20	0.188	4.9	2.71	89.3	.0120
"	0.30	0.272	"	3.70	101.2	.0117
"	0.38	0.342	"	4.35	106.2	.0118
"	0.46	0.402	"	4.85	109.4	.0119
"	0.53	0.453	"	5.29	112.2	.0119
"	0.60	0.504	"	5.61	113.0	.0120
"	0.66	0.547	"	5.93	114.5	.0120
"	0.72	0.587	"	6.23	116.1	.0120
"	0.78	0.625	"	6.45	116.4	.0122
"	0.83	0.662	"	6.71	117.8	.0121
"	0.89	0.698	"	6.90	117.9	.0122
"	0.94	0.727	"	7.15	119.8	.0122

Class B. Open Channels,

LOCATION AND DESCRIPTION OF CHANNEL. METHOD OF GAUGING.	AUTHORITY.	Author's No. of Series.
	Channels Lined with Boards	
Test Channel. Unplaned boards. Rectangular.	Darcy and Bazin, " Recherches Hydrauliques," Paris, 1865.	6— 1 2 3 4 5 6 7 8 9 10 11 12
Test Channel. Unplaned boards. Triangular. Sides inclined at 45°.	Do.	23— 1 2 3 4 5 6 7 8 9 10 11 12
Test Channel. Unplaned boards. Trapezoidal. One side vertical, the other inclined at 45°. Bottom width, 3 10 feet.	Do.	22— 1 2 3 4 5 6 7 8 9 10 11 12

Creeks, and Rivers.

or Canvas—Continued.

Surface Width in Feet.	Greatest Depth in Feet.	Mean Hydraulic Radius in Feet, R	Slope of Water Surface per Thousand, $1000\ S$	Mean Velocity per Second in Feet. v	Coefficient, in Formula $v = c\sqrt{RS}$, c	Coefficient of Rough-ness, n
6.53	0.26	0.240	2.08	2.08	93.2	.0122
"	0.41	0.363	"	2.09	97.8	.0129
"	0.53	0.453	"	3.16	102.8	.0128
"	0.63	0.528	"	3.53	106.5	.0128
"	0.73	0.601	"	3.78	106.9	.0130
"	0.81	0.648	"	4.13	112.5	.0126
"	0.90	0.704	"	4.34	113.5	.0127
"	0.99	0.759	"	4.51	113.5	.0128
"	1.08	0.801	"	4.72	115.8	.0128
"	1.14	0.846	"	4.88	116.3	.0128
"	1.20	0.880	"	5.00	119.0	.0126
"	1.28	0.922	"	5.21	118.9	.0128
1.85	0.92	0.327	4.9	4.13	103.1	.0120
2.39	1.19	0.422	"	5.02	110.4	.0118
2.79	1.40	0.494	"	5.56	113.0	.0119
3.10	1.55	0.549	"	6.03	116.2	.0119
3.38	1.69	0.597	"	6.36	117.6	.0119
3.64	1.82	0.643	"	6.59	117.3	.0121
3.86	1.93	0.683	"	6.83	118.0	.0122
4.07	2.03	0.719	"	7.03	118.4	.0123
4.26	2.13	0.752	"	7.23	119.0	.0122
4.43	2.22	0.783	"	7.40	119.5	.0124
4.61	2.30	0.814	"	7.54	119.4	.0124
4.75	2.37	0.839	"	7.75	120.9	.0123
3.40	0.30	0.257	4.9	3.58	100.7	.0117
3.56	0.46	0.361	"	4.71	112 1	.0114
3.70	0.60	0.450	"	5.29	112.7	.0118
3.83	0.72	0.517	"	5.79	115.1	.0118
3.93	0.83	0.570	"	6.25	118.2	.0118
4.04	0.94	0.624	"	6.51	117.7	.0120
4.13	1.03	0.665	"	6.85	120.0	.0119
4.22	1.12	0.707	"	7.05	119.8	.0121
4.30	1.20	0.740	"	7.37	122.4	.0119
4.39	1.28	0.775	"	7.57	122.9	.0119
4.46	1.36	0.807	"	7.76	123.4	.0120
4.54	1.44	0.837	"	7.93	123.8	.0120

Class B. Open Channels,

Location and Description of Channel. Method of Gauging.	Authority.	Author's No. of Series.

Channels Lined with Boards

Test Channel. Unplaned boards. Polygonal. 6.56 1.64 3.29 15° 	Darcy and Bazin, " Recherches Hydrau- liques," Paris, 1865.	21— 1 2 3 4 5 6 7 8 9 10 11 12
Test Channel. Smooth boards, covered with stout canvas. Rectangular. The lining rounded the lower corners to some extent, and caused notable undulations in the surface.	Do.	30— 1 2 3 4 5 6
Test Channel. Smooth boards, covered with stout canvas. Rectangular.	Do.	31— 1 2 3 4 5 6 7 8 9
Wooden Flume near Boston. About 2500 feet long; straight. Square section, 6x6 feet, with plank laid lengthwise. In 1st and 2d gaugings water consisted of sewage only, in 3d of ¼ sewage and ¾ salt water.	Clarke, 1885.*	

* See H. Smith, Jr., " Hydraulics," 1886.

Creeks, and Rivers.

Surface Width in Feet.	Greatest Depth in Feet.	Mean Hydraulic Radius in Feet, R	Slope of Water Surface per Thousand, 1000 S	Mean Velocity per Second in Feet, v	Coefficient in Formula $v = c^1 \sqrt{RS}$, c	Coefficient of Roughness, n

or Canvas—Continued.

4.08	0.40	0.334	1.5	2.30	107.0	.0117
4.54	0.63	0.485	"	2.93	108.5	.0124
4.87	0.79	0.586	"	3.35	113.0	.0124
5.18	0.95	0.673	"	3.62	113.8	.0126
5.44	1.08	0.744	"	3.85	115.4	.0126
5.70	1.21	0.809	"	4.03	115.7	.0128
5.92	1.32	0.864	"	4.20	116.7	.0128
6.11	1.41	0.911	"	4.39	118.9	.0127
6.31	1.51	0.959	"	4.51	119.0	.0128
6.49	1.60	1.002	"	4.64	119.7	.0128
6.49	1.69	1.047	"	4.76	120.2	.0128
6.49	1.77	1.097	"	4.87	120.1	.0129
0.31	0.05	0.038	8.1	0.72	40.7	.0148
"	0.06	0.046	"	0.89	46.1	.0142
"	0.08	0.055	"	1.11	52.5	.0136
"	0.11	0.067	"	1.33	56.9	.0135
"	0.15	0.078	"	1.51	59.8	.0135
"	0.27	0.102	"	1.88	65.3	.0134
0.31	0.04	0.031	15.2	0.69	31.8	.0163
"	0.05	0.040	"	0.82	33.2	.0166
"	0.07	0.051	"	1.19	42.8	.0154
"	0.08	0.054	"	1.25	43.7	.0152
"	0.11	0.066	"	1.55	49.0	.0148
"	0.11	0.067	"	1.62	50.7	.0147
"	0.15	0.079	"	1.91	55.0	.0144
"	0.19	0.089	"	2.12	57.6	.0144
"	0.23	0.095	"	2.23	58.7	.0143
6.00		1.41	0.427	2.87	117	.0136
		1.45	0.435	2.94	117	.0136
		1.50	0.843	4.80	135	.0120

Class B. Open Channels,

Location and Description of Channel. Method of Gauging.	Authority.	Author's No. of Series.

III. Channels Lined with Brickwork.

Chazilly Canal. Section extremely regular; sides of ashlar; large-sized stones, smoothly dressed.	Darcy and Bazin, "Recherches Hydrauliques," Paris, 1865.	39— 1 2 3 4
Spillway of Grosbois Reservoir. Ashlar, with cement joints; bottom, not as smooth as sides, partly damaged, and covered with light very sticky and slimy deposit. Nearly rectangular.	Do.	32— 1 2 3 4
Grosbois Canal. Face stones, set in mortar, are more regular than bottom; joints are not damaged; no deposit. Sides nearly vertical; flat segmental invert.	Do.	45— 1 2 3 4
Test Channel. Brickwork, fairly smooth. Rectangular.	Do.	3— 1 2 3 4 5 6 7 8 9 10 11 12

Creeks, and Rivers.

Surface Width in Feet.	Greatest Depth in Feet.	Mean Hydraulic Radius in Feet, R	Slope of Water Surface per Thousand, $1000\,S$	Mean Velocity per Second in Feet, v	Coefficient, in Formula $v = c\sqrt{RS}$, c	Coefficient of Roughness, n

or Dressed Ashlar Masonry.

4.04	0.50	0.41	8.1	5.73	100.0	.0129
4.10	0.78	0.57	"	7.52	111.0	.0126
4.14	1.00	0.68	"	8.19	110.0	.0130
4.18	1.20	0.77	"	8.75	111.0	.0132
5.98	0.36	0.324	101.0	12.20	67.9	.0168
6.01	0.55	0.467	"	16.18	74.5	.0168
6.03	0.71	0.520	"	18.68	77.2	.0170
6.07	0.84	0.602	"	21.09	81.6	.0167
6.35	1.66	0.98	0.305	1.32	77	.0185
6.40	2.21	1.20	0.308	1.90	95	.0161
6.46	2.75	1.40	0.331	2.12	96	.0165
6.50	3.12	1.60	0.347	2.47	105	.0154
6.27	0.20	0.192	4.9	2.75	89.7	.0121
"	0.31	0.284	"	3.66	98.3	.0122
"	0.41	0.365	"	4.18	98.8	.0127
"	0.49	0.424	"	4.72	103.7	.0126
"	0.57	0.481	"	5.10	105.1	.0128
"	0.65	0.540	"	5.33	103.7	.0131
"	0.71	0.582	"	5.68	106.3	.0130
"	0.77	0.620	"	6.01	109.0	.0129
"	0.85	0.668	"	6.15	107.4	.0132
"	0.90	0.697	"	6.47	110.8	.0130
"	0.97	0.739	"	6.60	109.7	.0132
"	1.04	0.779	"	6.72	108.7	.0134

Class B. Open Channels,

LOCATION AND DESCRIPTION OF CHANNEL. METHOD OF GAUGING.	AUTHORITY.	Author's No. of Series.

Channels Lined with Brickwork or

Sudbury Conduit in Massachusetts.
Hard brick, smooth surface, with mortar-joints well made; surface carefully scraped clear of foreign substances.
Bottom slope, per thousand, about 0.16.
Length, 600 feet.
Velocity, obtained from weir measurements, made with great care.

Fteley and Stearns.[*]
1880.

Sudbury Conduit in Massachusetts.
Hard brick, smooth surface, with mortar-joints well made; fairly clean.
Cross-section same as above.
Bottom slope, per thousand, about 0.189.
Velocity, obtained from weir measurements, made with great care.
The first nine measurements were made in the lower section, 4200 feet long; the second nine measurements were made in the upper section, 5294 feet long.

Do.

* See H. Smith, Jr., "Hydraulics," 1886.

Creeks, and Rivers.

Surface Width in Feet.	Greatest Depth in Feet.	Mean Hydraulic Radius, in Feet, R	Slope of Water Surface per Thousand, 1000 S	Mean Velocity in Feet per Second, v	Coefficient, in Formula $v = c\sqrt{RS},$ c	Coefficient of Roughness, n

Dressed Ashlar Masonry—Continued.

1.415	1.016	0.0140	0.443	117.3	.0108
1.187	0.858	0.0246	0.550	119.8	.0103
1.404	1.008	0.0383	0.789	126.9	.0106
1.328	0.957	0.0746	1.064	125.9	.0112
1.076	0.778	0.0983	1.098	125.6	.0110
1.175	0.850	0.1115	1.241	127.5	.0111
0.820	0.577	0.1596	1.149	119.7	.0110
0.939	0.673	0.1633	1.298	123.9	.0111
0.719	0.493	0.1640	1.079	120.0	.0113
1.233	0.891	0.1701	1.569	127.4	.0114
1.224	0.885	0.1715	1.577	128.0	.0114
1.055	0.762	0.1742	1.423	123.6	.0114
1.041	0.751	0.1803	1.439	123.6	.0114
1.518	1.078	0.1928	1.827	126.7	.0119
2.014	1.372	0.1909	2.131	131.6	.0120
2.037	1.385	0.1922	2.139	131.1	.0120
2.513	1.625	0.1923	2.351	133.0	.0122
2.519	1.628	0.1924	2.372	134.0	.0121
3.010	1.843	0.1888	2.564	137.5	.0121
3.561	2.049	0.1929	2.720	137.2	.0123
4.012	2.192	0.1895	2.831	138.9	.0123
4.552	2.333	0.1922	2.926	138.2	.0125
1.505	1.071	0.1893	1.844	129.5	.0116
2.003	1.367	0.1901	2.143	133.0	.0118
2.023	1.378	0.1901	2.155	133.2	.0118
2.499	1.619	0.1899	2.366	134.9	.0120
2.499	1.619	0.1921	2.395	135.8	.0120
3.002	1.840	0.1903	2.572	137.5	.0121
3.548	2.044	0.1901	2.731	138.6	.0122
4.008	2.190	0.1886	2.834	139.5	.0122
4.541	2.330	0.1889	2.937	140.0	.0123

Class B. Open Channels,

Location and Description of Channel. Method of Gauging.	Authority.	Author's No. of Series.

Channels Lined with Brickwork or

Sudbury Conduit in Massachusetts. Hard brick, smooth surface, with mortar-joints well made; fairly clean. Cross-section same as above. Bottom slope, per thousand, about 0.189. Surface slope varies considerably, hence cross-sections and flow are not uniform. Values given are averages. The first fifteen measurements were made in the lower section, 4200 feet long; the second fifteen measurements were made in the upper section, 5294 feet long.	Fteley and Stearns, 1880.	
Sudbury Conduit in Massachusetts. Bottom of concrete; sides for 4362 feet rough rockwork, and for 252 feet brickwork with plaster of cement.	Do.	
Roquefavour Aqueduct, Marseilles Canal. Bottom of neat cement; sides brick, carefully jointed. Nearly rectangular.	Darcy and Bazin, "Recherches Hydrauliques," Paris, 1865.	1—1

Creeks, and Rivers.

Surface Width in Feet.	Greatest Depth in Feet.	Mean Hydraulic Radius in Feet, R	Slope of Water Surface per Thousand, $1000 \, S$	Mean Velocity per Second in Feet, v	Coefficient, in Formula $v = c\sqrt{RS}$, c	Coefficient of Roughness, n

Dressed Ashlar Masonry—Continued.

	3.971	2.179	0.0493	1.432	138.1	.0119
	4.348	2.284	0.0668	1.716	138.9	.0122
	2.811	1.759	0.1043	1.820	134.4	.0121
	2.212	1.478	0.1445	1.912	130.9	.0121
	2.735	1.727	0.1548	2.198	134.5	.0122
	3.177	1.909	0.1631	2.406	136.4	.0122
	2.065	1.400	0.1795	2.071	130.6	.0121
	4.574	2.338	0.1860	2.909	139.5	.0123
	2.002	1.366	0.1998	2.161	130.8	.0120
	3.963	2.177	0.2006	2.888	138.2	.0123
	2.463	1 602	0.2041	2.416	133.6	.0121
	3.440	2.006	0.2070	2.792	137.0	.0123
	2.940	1.814	0.2082	2.630	135.3	.0122
	3.713	2.099	0.2411	3.098	137.7	.0123
	4.390	2.294	0.2600	3.386	138.6	.0124
	4.672	2.359	0.0334	1.207	136.0	.0122
	4.972	2.417	0.0488	1.497	137.9	.0122
	3.319	1.963	0.0625	1 512	136.5	.0119
	2.561	1.648	0.0948	1.616	129.3	.0122
	2.998	1.838	0.1155	1.983	136.1	.0120
	3.369	1.981	0.1356	2.255	137.6	.0121
	2.192	1.468	0.1466	1.931	131.6	.0120
	4.602	2.343	0 1793	2.889	141.0	.0122
	3.878	2.151	0.2102	2.955	139.0	.0122
	3.266	1.943	0.2389	2.957	137.3	.0122
	1.799	1.251	0.2553	2.448	137.0	.0114
	2.245	1.495	0.2580	2.687	136.8	.0118
	2.707	1.714	0.2602	2.886	136.6	.0120
	2.881	1.789	0.4604	4.103	142.9	.0117
	3.437	2.005	0.4913	4.407	140.4	.0120
	3.44	2.211	0.2813	1 975	79.2	.0211
7.4	2.5	1.504	3.72	10.26	137.1	.0119

Class B. Open Channels,

LOCATION AND DESCRIPTION OF CHANNEL. METHOD OF GAUGING.	AUTHORITY.	Author's No. of Series.
Channels Lined with Brickwork or		
Aqueduct de Crau, Canal de Craponne. Hammer-dressed ashlar; very smooth. Rectangular.	Darcy and Bazin, " Recherches Hydrau-liques," Paris, 1865.	1—2
Tail Race of Grosbois Reservoir. Ashlar, with cement joints. Sides smoother than bottom, the joints of which were partly damaged, especially in the lowest part; bottom (slope, 0.12 feet) covered with light, very sticky, slimy deposit. Nearly rectangular.	Do.	33—1 2 3 4
Solani Right Aqueduct in Burmah. Floor of bricks, laid flat and fairly regular; sides of good masonry. In fairly good order. Rectangular section with lower corners slightly rounded. Velocity determined by one-inch tin tube floats.	Cunningham, Roor-kee, 1880.	125 (1)* 124 (1) 121 (2) 119 (7) 117 (2) 115 (1) 113 (1)
Solani Left Aqueduct. Nearly same as above.	Do.	105 (2) 103 (4) 101 (3)
Solani Right Aqueduct (Left Closed). Same as above.	Do.	139 (2) 138 (1) 137 (1) 136 (1) 135 (1) 132 (2) 131 (2)
IV. Channels Lined with		
Test Channel. Lined with pebbles $\frac{3}{4}$ to $\frac{7}{8}$ inch diameter, held in place with cement. Semicircular.	Darcy and Bazin, " Recherches Hydrau-liques," Paris, 1865.	27— 1 2 3 4 5 6 7 8 9 10

* Figures in parentheses indicate number of gaugings averaged.

Creeks, and Rivers.

Surface Width in Feet.	Greatest Depth in Feet.	Mean Hydraulic Radius, in Feet, R	Slope of Water Surface per Thousand, $1000\ S$	Mean Velocity in Feet per Second, v	Coefficient, in Formula $v = c\sqrt{RS}$, c	Coefficient of Roughness, n
Dressed Ashlar Masonry—Continued.						
8.5	3.0	1.774	0.84	5.55	125.0	.0133
6.0	0.49	0.424	37.0	9.04	72.2	.0169
6.1	0.77	0.620	"	11.46	75.7	.0175
6.1	0.97	0.745	"	13.55	81.6	.0170
6.1	1.16	0.852	"	15.08	84.9	.0170
85.0	2.0	1.95	0.203	1.61	86.8	.0187
85.0	3.5	3.26	0.195	2.43	96.4	.0188
85.0	5.6	5.00	0.240	3.43	99.0	.0196
85.0	6.2	5.43	0.245	3.74	102.6	.0192
85.0	7.1	6.14	0.220	3.67	99.9	.0201
84.4	7.8	6.63	0.198	3.86	106.5	.0190
84.3	8.2	6.88	0.228	3.85	97.2	.0211
84.0	8.6	7.19	0.222	3.70	92.6	.0224
82.5	9.4	7.65	0.207	3.87	97.3	.0215
82.2	9.9	7.94	0.189	4.06	104.8	.0200
85.0	2.66	2.52	0.151	2.20	112.8	.0153
"	2.88	2.72	0.145	2.54	127.9	.0137
"	3.13	2.94	0.200	2.51	103.5	.0171
"	3.12	2.94	0.208	2.79	112.8	.0157
"	3.18	2.99	0.253	3.20	116.4	.0154
"	3.96	3.65	0.473	4.83	116.2	.0159
"	4.60	4.20	0.025	1.24	121.0	.0161
Laths or Pebbles held in place.						
3.1	0.7	0.454	1.5	2.17	78.0	.0159
3.4	0.9	0.546	"	2.50	82.0	.0160
3.5	1.1	0.619	"	2.69	82.0	.0163
3.7	1.2	0.681	"	2.93	84.0	.0163
3.8	1.3	0.731	"	3.05	84.0	.0165
3.8	1.4	0.784	"	3.22	85.0	.0166
3.9	1.5	0.826	"	3.33	84.0	.0169
4.0	1.7	0.900	"	3.54	85.0	.0170
4.0	1.9	0.968	"	3.73	85.0	.0171
4.0	2.0	1.012	"	3.95	88.0	.0169

Class B. Open Channels,

Location and Description of Channel. Method of Gauging.	Authority.	Author's No. of Series.

Channels Lined with Laths or

Location and Description of Channel. Method of Gauging.	Authority.	Author's No. of Series.
Test Channel. Lined with pebbles $\frac{5}{8}$ to $\frac{7}{8}$ inch diameter, held in place with cement. Rectangular.	Darcy and Bazin, " Recherches Hydrauliques," Paris, 1865.	4— 1 2 3 4 5 6 7 8 9 10 11 12
Test Channel. Lined with pebbles $1\frac{1}{4}$ to $1\frac{1}{2}$ inches diameter, held in place with cement. Rectangular.	Do.	5— 1 2 3 4 5 6 7 8 9 10 11 12
Test Channel. Boards, with wooden laths, 1 x $\frac{5}{8}$ inch, nailed crosswise on bottom and sides of flume, $\frac{3}{4}$ inch apart. Rectangular.	Do.	12—1 2 3 4 5 6 7
Same.	Do.	13—1 2 3 4 5 6 7

Creeks, and Rivers.

Surface Width in Feet.	Greatest Depth in Feet.	Mean Hydraulic Radius in Feet, R	Slope of Water Surface per Thousand, 1000 S	Mean Velocity per Second in Feet, v	Coefficient, in Formula $v = c\sqrt{RS}$, c	Coefficient of Roughness, n

Pebbles held in place—Continued.

Surface Width in Feet.	Greatest Depth in Feet.	Mean Hydraulic Radius in Feet, R	Slope of Water Surface per Thousand, 1000 S	Mean Velocity per Second in Feet, v	Coefficient, in Formula $v = c\sqrt{RS}$, c	Coefficient of Roughness, n
6.0	0.27	0.250	4.9	2 16	61.7	.0170
"	0.41	0.357	"	2.95	70.5	.0166
"	0.53	0.450	"	3.40	72.5	.0170
"	0.63	0.520	"	3.84	76.1	.0168
"	0.73	0.588	"	4.14	77.2	.0170
"	0.82	0.644	"	4.43	78.8	.0171
"	0.91	0.700	"	4.64	79.3	.0173
"	0.99	0.746	"	4.88	80.7	.0173
"	1.06	0.785	"	5.12	82.6	.0170
"	1.15	0.832	"	5.26	82.4	.0173
"	1.23	0.871	"	5.43	83.1	.0173
"	1.30	0.910	"	5.57	83.4	.0174
6.11	0.32	0.291	4.9	1.70	47.5	.0215
"	0.48	0.417	"	2.43	53.8	.0212
"	0.61	0.510	"	2.90	58.0	.0209
"	0.73	0.587	"	3.27	61 1	.0206
"	0.84	0.656	"	3.56	62.8	.0207
"	0.93	0.712	"	3.85	65.2	.0204
"	1.03	0.772	"	4.03	65.5	.0206
"	1.13	0.823	"	4.23	66.6	.0205
"	1.21	0.867	"	4.43	68.0	.0205
"	1.29	0.909	"	4.60	69.0	.0204
"	1.37	0.940	"	4.78	70.3	.0203
"	1.46	0.987	"	4.90	70.4	.0205
6.43	0.33	0.302	1.5	1.65	77.4	.0148
"	0.51	0.442	"	2.17	84.5	.0149
"	0.89	0.634	"	2.86	91.0	.0150
"	1.02	0.775	"	3.33	94.0	.0150
"	1.23	0.889	"	3.68	97.0	.0151
"	1.42	0.956	"	3.98	99.0	.0152
"	1.62	1.076	"	4.19	99.0	.0154
6.43	0.22	0.205	5.9	2.50	71.8	.0146
"	0.33	0.302	"	3.34	79.0	.0147
"	0.51	0.442	"	4.40	86.2	.0145
"	0.67	0.552	"	5.08	89.0	.0148
"	0.80	0.643	"	5.63	91.4	.0150
"	0.92	0.716	"	6.14	94.5	.0150
"	1.05	0.790	"	6.48	94.8	0151

Class B. Open Channels,

Location and Description of Channel. Method of Gauging.	Authority.	Author's No. of Series.
Channels Lined with Laths or		
Test Channel. Boards, with wooden laths, 1 x ⅞ inch, nailed crosswise on bottom and sides of flume, ⅝ inch apart. Rectangular.	Darcy and Bazin, " Recherches Hydrau- liques," Paris, 1865.	14—1 2 3 4 5 6 7
Test Channel. Boards, with wooden laths, 1 x ⅜ inch, nailed crosswise on bottom and sides of flume, 2 inches apart. Rectangular.	Do.	15—1 2 3 4 5 6 7
Same.	Do.	16—1 2 3 4 5 6 7
Same.	Do.	17—1 2 3 4 5 6 7
V. Channels Lined		
Mill Race at Diemerstein, Bavaria. Sandstone masonry. Rectangular section. Velocity determined from known quantity of water.	Strauss. See Grebenau, " Zu- sätze," etc; 1867.	
Mill Race at Felsö-Bánya Hungary. Dry rubble walls, paved. Nearly semicircular; top width. 1.64 feet.	Rittinger,* 1855.	

* See Bornemann, " Civil Ingenieur," 1869.

Creeks, and Rivers.

Surface Width in Feet.	Greatest Depth in Feet.	Mean Hydraulic Radius in Feet, R	Slope of Water Surface per Thousand, 1000 S	Mean Velocity per Second in Feet, v	Coefficient. in Formula $v = c \sqrt{RS}$, c	Coefficient of Roughness, n

Pebbles held in place—Continued.

6.40	0.19	0.182	8.9	2.85	70.8	.0144
"	0.30	0.273	"	3.75	76.4	.0148
"	0.46	0.403	"	4.92	82.4	.0150
"	0.59	0.499	"	5.77	86.8	.0150
"	0.71	0.582	"	6.38	88.9	.0151
"	0.83	0.658	"	6.86	89.9	.0154
"	0.94	0.726	"	7.26	90.5	.0156
6.43	0.43	0.378	1.5	1.28	53.7	.0205
"	0.66	0.550	"	1.68	58.6	.0209
"	1.02	0.777	"	2.21	64.8	.0207
"	1.33	0.942	"	2.55	67.8	.0207
"	1.61	1.073	"	2.81	70.1	.0207
"	1.91	1.197	"	2.97	70.0	.0212
"	2.18	1.299	"	3.11	70.5	.0214
6.44	0.29	0.264	5.9	1.91	48.3	.0207
"	0.44	0.384	"	2.56	53.7	.0208
"	0.67	0.553	"	3.37	59.0	.0209
"	0.87	0.686	"	3.88	61.0	.0213
"	1.05	0.791	"	4.31	63.1	.0214
"	1.21	0.882	"	4.65	64.5	.0215
"	1.38	0.965	"	4.91	65.1	.0217
6.40	0.25	0.232	8.86	2.21	48.7	.0200
"	0.39	0.350	"	2.85	51.2	.0213
"	0.60	0.509	"	3.75	55.8	.0215
"	0.78	0.628	"	4.37	58.6	.0217
"	0.94	0.725	"	4.85	60.5	.0218
"	1.09	0.812	"	5.22	61.5	.0220
"	1.22	0.885	"	5.57	62.9	.0220

with Rubble Masonry.

1.08		0.308	1.4	1.378	66.1	.0167
	0.55	0.272	3.1	1.115	38.4	.0248
	0.70	0.345	"	1.250	38.2	.0263

Class B. Open Channels,

LOCATION AND DESCRIPTION OF CHANNEL. METHOD OF GAUGING.	AUTHORITY.	Author's No. of Series.
		Channels Lined with
Tail Race at Staukau, Hungary. Dry rubble walls, paved. Semicircular.	Rittinger, 1855.	
Aqueduct for Libeth Ironworks, Hungary. Dry rubble walls, paved. Nearly rectangular.	Do.	
Mill Race at Schmöllnitz, Hungary. Sides of dry rubble; bed of natural rock. Rectangular; width, 2.02 feet.	Do.	
Head Race at Kapnikbanya, Hungary. Dry rubble walls, paved. Trapezoidal; bottom width, 2.16 feet.	Do.	
Tail Race at Kapnikbanya, Hungary. Dry rubble walls, paved. Trapezoidal; bottom width, 2.51 feet.	Do.	
Conduit between Mill Ponds at Nagyar, Hungary. Dry masonry. Trapezoidal; bottom width, 1.71 feet.	Do.	
Grosbois Canal. Roughly-hammered stone masonry.	Darcy and Bazin, " Recherches Hydrauliques," Paris, 1865.	1—5 6 3 4
Grosbois Canal. Masonry in rather bad order; some mud and broken stones on bottom in many places. No grass. Shape, see Series 45, Category III.	Do.	46—1 2 3 4
Same.	Do.	44—1 2 3 4
Grosbois Canal. Stony bottom ; one slope protected by rock. Trapezoidal. Very little vegetation.	Do.	40—1 2 3 4

Creeks, and Rivers.

Surface Width in Feet.	Greatest Depth in Feet.	Mean Hydraulic Radius, in Feet, R	Slope of Water Surface per Thousand, 1000 S	Mean Velocity in Feet per Second, v	Coefficient, in Formula $v = c\sqrt{RS}$, c	Coefficient of Roughness, n

Rubble Masonry—Continued.

Surface Width in Feet.	Greatest Depth in Feet.	Mean Hydraulic Radius, in Feet, R	Slope of Water Surface per Thousand, 1000 S	Mean Velocity in Feet per Second, v	Coefficient, in Formula $v = c\sqrt{RS}$, c	Coefficient of Roughness, n
	0.42	0.289	2.5	1.257	46.8	.0217
	0.50	0.359	"	1.491	49.8	.0217
	0.69	0.419	"	1.643	50.8	.0220
	0.24	0.213	4.5	1.324	42.8	.0215
	0.65	0.439	"	2.396	53.9	.0214
	0.81	0.426	"	2.432	52.0	.0224
	0.88	0.472	3.1	1.470	38.7	.0284
	1.31	0.576	"	1.932	45.7	.0259
	0.26	0.213	3.8	1.369	48.\	.0196
	0.45	0.344	"	1.529	50.6	0212
	0.35	0.278	3.6	1.502	47.5	.0212
	0.47	0.351	"	1.928	54.2	.0201
	0.56	0.403	"	2.104	55.2	.0206
	0.28	0.212	21.0	3.305	40.5	.0193
	0.59	0.358	"	6.150	70.9	.0164
	1.20	0.535	"	7.510	71.3	.0178
3.9	1.6	0.88	12.1	7.58	73.5	0192
3.6	1.5	0.84	14.0	8.36	77.3	0182
3.5	1.2	0.71	29.0	11.23	78.4	.0175
3.5	0.9	0.62	60.0	13.93	72.5	.0181
6.8	1.5	0.88	0.648	1.47	62	.0222
6.9	2.0	1.23	0.671	2.02	70	.0212
6.9	2.4	1.40	0.683	2.34	76	.0204
7.0	2.7	1.50	0.683	2.78	87	.0183
6.8	1.6	1.07	0.30	1.12	62	.0226
6.9	2.4	1.38	0.35	1.69	77	.0199
7.0	2.9	1.57	0.33	1.92	84	.0187
7.0	3.3	1.71	0.30	2.18	96	.0169
9.1	1.7	1.05	0.036	1.08	34	.0385
11.2	2.3	1.37	0.936	1.37	38	0375
12.4	2.6	1.52	0.957	1.56	41	.0364
13.4	2.9	1.64	0.964	1.71	43	0355

Class B.   Open Channels,

LOCATION AND DESCRIPTION OF CHANNEL. METHOD OF GAUGING.	AUTHORITY.	Author's No. of Series.
	Channels Lined with	
Spillway of Level No. 52, Grosbois Canal. Roughly-hammered masonry, set dry, quite well-preserved but covered with slime and grass. Trapezoidal; flat.	Darcy and Bazin, "Recherches Hydrauliques," Paris, 1865.	34—1 2 3 4 5
Same. Stonework scraped and cleaned with great care, previous to experiments.	Do.	35—1 2 3 4 5
Canal at Thun, Switzerland. Bed cemented; sides of good rubble masonry. Very regular reach. Current meter.	Epper, 1884.	
Gerbebach schale, at Merligen, near Lake Thun. Like Grünnbach schale (see below). Semicircular; top width, 15.7 feet; depth, 6.2 feet; radius, 7.87 feet; length, 500 feet.	Kutter, 1867.	1 2 3 4 5
Lugibach schale, in Bernese Oberland. Dry rubble masonry of large stones; old. Rectangular; bed slightly curved, six inches depression.	Do.	
Gontenbach schale, at Gonten, near Lake Thun. Dry rubble masonry of large stones. New and well built. Semicircular; radius, 10.82 feet; length, about 1200 feet. Surface-floats; mean velocity from Bazin's formula.	Do.	1 2 3 4
Grünnbach schale at Merligen, near Lake Thun. Dry rubble masonry of large stones; six years old; bed somewhat damaged. Semicircular; top width 20.3 feet and depth 6.4 feet for upper stretch; but top width 26.4 feet and depth 7.15 feet for lower stretch. Length, 1200 feet. Nos. 4-6 were gauged during a freshet, the water being turbid and carrying gravel and stones. Velocity measured with surface-floats and stones by frequent repetitions.	Do.	1 2 3 4 5 6

Creeks, and Rivers.

Surface Width in Feet.	Greatest Depth in Feet.	Mean Hydraulic Radius in Feet, R	Slope of Water Surface per Thousand, $1000\,S$	Mean Velocity in Feet per Second, v	Coefficient in Formula $v = c\sqrt{RS},$ c	Coefficient of Roughness, n

Rubble Masonry—Continued.

10.3	1.2	0.86	14.6	4.19	37.5	.0341
11.2	1.6	1.09	"	5.75	45.7	.0306
12.8	2.1	1.38	"	7.20	50.7	.0295
14.1	2.5	1.59	"	8.27	54.3	.0285
14.8	2.7	1.69	"	8.99	57.2	.0275
10.2	1.2	0.70	14.2	5.66	56.6	.0230
10.5	1.3	0.93	"	7.36	64.0	.0220
11.8	1.8	1.23	"	8.94	67.7	.0221
12.8	2.1	1.39	"	10.12	71.9	.0215
13.1	2.3	1.49	"	11.26	77.4	.0203
		2.417	0.15	1.584	83.1	.0206
3.80	0.30	0.19	111.7	8.472	57.4	.0172
"		"	137.5	8.905	54.3	.0178
"		"	167.9	9.131	50.7	.0188
"		"	185.2	9.427	49.6	.0192
"		"	237.2	10.145	47.2	.0197
5.9		0.32	34.0	6.560	63.0	.0177
6.00	0.50	0.32	42.350	9.446	80.5	.0146
		0.32	46.425	10.409	85.4	.0138
7.00	0.57	0.37	42.350	9.889	82.5	.0147
		0.37	46.425	10.972	83.6	.0145
8.00	0.55	0.36	82.85	11.808	68.6	.0169
		0.38	99.27	13.323	68.4	.0170
7.40	0.60	0.39	106.775	13.746	67.3	.0175
10.60	0.90	0.58	82.85	15.537	70.6	.0183
		0.61	99.27	18.283	72.8	.0180
9.00	1.0	0.65	106.775	19.168	72.8	.0182

Class B. Open Channels,

LOCATION AND DESCRIPTION OF CHANNEL. METHOD OF GAUGING.	AUTHORITY.	Author's No. of Series.
	Channels Lined with	
Alpbach schale at Meiringen. Like Grünnbach schale (see above). Very old and very much damaged. Radius, 8.46 feet.	Kutter, 1867.	4 3 2 1
Saxetenbach schale in Bernese Oberland. Dry rough rubble masonry. Rectangular; bed curved, with 16 inches depression at center.	Do.	
	VI. Channels in Earth	
Mill Race at Pricbram, Hungary. Masonry sidewalls ; clay bottom ; very regular. Trapezoidal; bottom width, 1.88 feet.	Rittinger, 1855. See Bornemann. "Civil Ingenieur," 1869.	
Mill Race at Göllnitz, Hungary. Dry rubble walls; earth bottom. Rectangular; bottom width, 1.55 feet.	Do.	
Mill Race at Pricbram, Hungary. Dry rubble sidewalls; earth bottom; very irregular. Trapezoidal; bottom width, 2.07 feet.	Do.	
Aqueduct at Diosgyör, Hungary. Dry rubble sidewalls; earth bed. Rectangular; width, 2.09 feet.	Do.	
Mill Race at Diosgyör, Hungary. Dry rubble sidewalls; clay bed. Rectangular; width, 4.15 feet.	Do.	
Race at Stamp Mill, Veröspatak, Hungary. Masonry sidewalls; earth bed. Trapezoidal; bottom width, 2.07 feet.	Do.	
Race at Stamp Mill, Bezbanya, Hungary. Masonry sidewalls; bed of sand and gravel. Trapezoidal; bottom width, 2.58 feet.	Do.	

Creeks, and Rivers.

Surface Width in Feet.	Greatest Depth in Feet.	Mean Hydraulic Radius, in Feet, R	Slope of Water Surface per Thousand, 1000 S	Mean Velocity in Feet per Second, v	Coefficient, in Formula $v = c\sqrt{RS}$, c	Coefficient of Roughness, n
Rubble Masonry—Continued.						
8.02	1.18	0.73	22.920	7.970	53.9	.0242
		0.73	27.200	8.040	60.5	.0220
		0.73	27.647	8.197	57.6	.0228
		0.69	32.000	8.010	53.9	.0238
25.6		0.58	30.000	7.970	60.1	.0208
with Masonry Sidewalls.						
	0.54	0.373	1.0	1.127	58.4	.0191
	0.66	0.425	"	1.254	60.8	.0190
	0.33	0.233	2.0	0.468	21.7	.0364
	0.47	0.296	"	0.854	35.1	.0269
	0.74	0.385	"	1.144	41.2	.0255
	0.41	0.316	2.2	0.389	14.8	.0560
	0.44	0.336	"	0.588	21.6	.0406
	0.70	0.472	"	0.953	29.6	.0350
	0.80	0.548	"	1.135	32.7	.0337
	0.86	0.560	"	1.190	33.9	.0328
	0.90	0.506	"	1.269	36.0	.0312
	0.61	0.384	2.8	1.376	42.0	.0250
	0.82	0.458	"	1.515	42.3	.0260
	1.27	0.572	"	2.219	55.5	.0220
	0.63	0.487	4.0	2.403	54.5	.0217
	1.14	0.736	"	2.750	50.7	.0253
	1.66	0.924	"	3.323	54.8	.0250
	0.56	0.217	5.0	1.505	45.7	.0205
	0.78	0.258	"	1.581	41.7	.0236
	0.28	0.242	5.0	0.782	22.5	.0360
	0.35	0.282	"	1.191	31.7	.0291
	0.56	0.407	"	1.956	43.4	.0249
	0.73	0.483	"	2.134	43.4	.0260
	0.90	0.501	"	3.475	65.6	.0192

Class B. Open Channels,

Location and Description of Channel. Method of Gauging.	Authority.	Author's No. of Series.

Channels in Earth with

Ten Mill Races in Freiberg. Dry walls and clay bed, sometimes covered with mud, fine sand, and occasionally with some vegetation. Nos. 8 and 9 had bottom covered with much vegetation. Nos. 1–9 had trapezoidal sections; No. 10 was rectangular. Current meter.	Bornemann, 1854–59.	1 2 3 4 5 6 7 8 9 10
Chazilly Canal. Right sidewall of masonry, set in mortar, almost vertical; left sidewall dry stone work, somewhat inclined; bed in earth. No vegetation.	Darcy and Bazin, 1865.	42—1 2 3 4
River Tauber, in Baden. Banks paved. Regular.	Ammon, 1867. Quoted by Kutter.	1 2 3
Aar Canal, near Stegmatt Bridge, Switzerland. Bed regular; coarse gravel. Shore slopes rip-rapped. Surface-floats.	Quoted by Kutter.	
Mill Race at Thun, Switzerland. Rubble sidewalls and earth bed.	Do.	
River Aar, below Thun. Gravel bed; rip-rap along the shores. Fairly regular reach. No detritus at time of gauging. Current meter. Slope determined in 1884, and when stage was about four inches lower than in 1883.	Epper, 1883.	
River Aa, near Kermattbridge, Switzerland. Gravel bed; sidewalls ashlar masonry. Very regular reach. No detritus at time of gauging. Current meter.	Epper, 1885.	

Creeks, and Rivers.

Surface Width in Feet.	Greatest Depth in Feet.	Mean Hydraulic Radius, in Feet, R.	Slope of Water Surface per Thousand, $1000\ S$	Mean Velocity in Feet per Second, v	Coefficient, in Formula $v = c\sqrt{RS}$, c	Coefficient of Roughness, n

Masonry Sidewalls—Continued.

		1.680	0.0394	0.91	112.0	.0137
		1.355	0.1201	0.89	70.2	.0208
		1.366	0.1353	0.93	68.3	.0208
		1.241	0.2423	1.40	80.8	.0183
		1.010	0.4905	1.60	71.5	.0198
		0.859	0.5205	1.50	70.9	.0193
		0.944	0.9404	1.73	55.1	.0236
		1.173	0.6860	1.14	40.2	.0342
		1.215	1.0926	1.24	34.0	.0420
		0.688	0.7553	1.11	48.5	.0254
8.5	1.3	1.00	0.525	1.01	44	.0306
9.5	2.0	1.36	0.450	1.38	50	.0265
9.8	2.4	1.54	0.462	1.58	59	.0256
10.2	2.7	1.67	0.487	1.74	61	.0256
		1.66	2.000	3.897	67.3	.0234
		1.71	1.900	3.788	66.4	.0240
		2.82	0.200	2.007	84.2	.0208
		2.00	1.75	3.510	38.2	.0310
		2.42	0.150	1.574	83.1	.0216
		3.866	0.565	3.303	60.6	.0258
		1.948	3.9	4.976	57.1	.0284

Class B. Open Channels,

Location and Description of Channel. Method of Gauging.	Authority.	Author's No. of Series.
	Channels in Earth with	
River Aa, near Sarnen. Bed of gravel and mud; sidewalls of good rubble masonry. Regular reach. No detritus. Current meter.	Epper, 1885.	
Rhône at Porte de Sex. Gravel bed; slopes with smooth pavements. Very regular reach. Detritus.	Epper, 1887.	
Inner Aar, near Thun. Banks and partly the bed carefully paved. No detritus. Surface-floats.	Quoted by Kutter.	
Outer Aar, near Thun. Banks and partly the bed lined with stones. No detritus. Surface-floats.	Trechsel. 1825. See Kutter, "Die neue Theorie," etc., 1868.	
River Aar at Interlaken. Banks protected by sloping walls of rough rubble masonry.	Quoted by Kutter.	
Solani Embankment, Main Site. Sides of masonry, with steps 14″ tread and 9″ rise, lowest step has 4′ rise. Steps broken and sunken in many places, but are still fairly uniform. Bed of clay and boulders, very irregular, with frequent bars made of brick and boulders to prevent scour. No. 163, three steps immersed. No. 166, one step immersed. Nos. 173–181, no steps immersed. One-inch tin rod floats.	Cunningham, Roorkee, 1880.	181 (1)* 180 (2) 175 (5) 173 (5) 166 (1) 163 (6) 162 (5) 160 (6) 158 (2) 155 (6) 151 (5) 153 (6)

* The figures in parenthesis indicate the number of gaugings for which an average is given.

Creeks, and Rivers.

Surface Width in Feet.	Greatest Depth in Feet.	Mean Hydraulic Radius in Feet, R	Slope of Water Surface per Thousand, $1000 S$	Mean Velocity per Second in Feet, v	Coefficient, in Formula $v = c \sqrt{RS}.$ c	Coefficient of Roughness, n

Masonry Sidewalls—Continued.

Surface Width in Feet.	Greatest Depth in Feet.	Mean Hydraulic Radius in Feet, R	Slope of Water Surface per Thousand, $1000 S$	Mean Velocity per Second in Feet, v	Coefficient, in Formula c	Coefficient of Roughness, n
		3.398	0.64	3.496	74.5	.0245
		3.152	1.002	4.184	73.9	.0243
		5.44	0.625	5.182	88.9	.0222
		6.62	1.872	5.707	51.2	.0410
		6.69	0.585	4.166	67.9	.0305
150.0	1.5	1.69	0.090	0.44	35.7	.0380
"	2.3	2.26	0.148	0.87	45.9	.0355
"	3.9	3.86	0.088	1.35	73.2	.0260
"	4.1	4.07	0.215	1.79	60.5	.0315
152.3	5.6	5.39	0.155	2.40	83.0	.0241
157.0	6.8	6.18	0.171	3.05	93.8	.0218
159.3	7.6	6.78	0.221	3.39	87.5	.0237
161.3	8.2	7.26	0.214	3.22	81.7	.0258
164.0	9.1	7.84	0.215	3.43	83.6	.0256
166.3	9.9	8.42	0.217	3.58	83.6	.0260
168.7	10.7	8.96	0.227	3.71	82.3	.0267
170.1	11.0	9.34	0.227	4.02	87.3	.0251

Class B. Open Channels,

Location and Description of Channel. Method of Gauging.	Authority.	Author's No. of Series.

Channels in Earth with

Solani Embankment, Jaoli Site. Bed in earth; bottom very rough; side slopes 1 to 2; bricks set in mud. One-inch tin rod floats.	Cunningham, Roorkee, 1880.	217 (6)* 216 (9) 215 (10) 214 (8) 212 (6)
Solani Embankment, Belra Site. Similar to Jaoli Site.	Do.	205 (6) 204 (14) 202 (7) 201 (5)
Elbe at Magdeburg. Embankment walls. Current meter. Gaugings at low and high water.	"Handbuch der Hydraulic," Fischer, 1835. Quoted by Kutter.	1 2

VII. Small Rivers and Canals having

Experimental Channel. Wooden trough containing loose river sand, which, with a constant flow of water, was allowed to form a stable bed before measurements were taken. About 12 feet long; rectangular. Volume of discharge carefully determined. Slope ordinates measured to within $\frac{1}{300}$ inch on four or five parallel lines. Three forms of sections, *a*, *b*. and *c*, were used. Width and maximum depth are approximate.	Seddon in Journ. Assn. Eng. Soc., Feb. 1886.	*a* 3 4 5 6 7 *b* 3 4 5 6 7 *c* 3 4 5 6 7
Mill Race at Magura, Hungary. Sides of earth; bottom paved with broken stone.	Rittinger, 1855. See Bornemann, "Civil Ingenieur," 1869.	

* The figures in parenthesis indicate the number of gaugings for which an average is given.

Creeks, and Rivers.

Surface Width in Feet.	Greatest Depth in Feet.	Mean Hydraulic Radius in Feet, R	Slope of Water Surface per Thousand, $1000\,S$	Mean Velocity per Second in Feet, v	Coefficient in Formula, $v = c\sqrt{RS},$ c	Coefficient of Roughness, n

Masonry Sidewalls—Continued.

190.9	6.8	6.32	0.140	2.63	88.4	.0234
191.2	7.0	6.53	0.144	2.70	88.1	.0237
191.5	7.3	6.79 •	0.145	2.80	89.2	.0235
191.8	7.6	7.05	0.146	2.81	87.6	.0240
192.3	8.1	7.46	0.160	2.94	85.1	.0250
187.3	8.6	7.96	0.208	3.07	75.4	.0289
187.5	8.7	8.21	0.198	3.01	74.7	.0294
188.0	9.5	8.72	0.200	3.12	74.7	.0297
188.4	9.6	9.02	0.191	3.17	76.4	.0292
315	9.84	8.61	0.254	3.772	80.4	.0270
315	13.12	13.20	0.363	5.346	76.9	.0304

Fairly Regular Channels, in Earth.

		0.04652	3.5	0.86	67.4	.0107
0.57	0.065	0.04448	3.7	0.87	67.8	.0106
0.57	0.065	0.04535	4.1	0.84	61.6	.0114
0.57	0.065	0.04553	5.2	0.83	54.0	.0124
		0.04362	6.2	0.86	52.3	.0126
		0.04276	4.5	0.83	59.8	.0114
0.65	0.060	0.04292	4.8	0.82	57.1	.0118
0.65	0.060	0.04421	5.4	0.80	51.8	.0128
0.66	0.056	0.04180	6.3	0.83	51.1	.0126
		0.04235	7.2	0.81	46.4	.0136
		0.03162	7.9	0.93	58.9	.0107
0.83	0.040	0.03190	8.0	0.89	55.7	.0111
0.87	0.040	0.03181	8.6	9.88	53.2	.0116
0.91	0.036	0.02928	9.7	0.91	54.0	.0111
		0.02808	11.3	0.91	51.1	.0114
	0.53	0.403	3.2	2.895	80.6	.0151
	1.04	0.661	''	3.629	78.9	.0169
	1.31	0.834	''	3.580	69.4	.0199
	1.63	0.915	''	4.017	74.1	.0191

Class B. Open Channels,

Location and Description of Channel. Method of Gauging.	Authority.	Author's No. of Series.

Small Rivers and Canals having Fairly

Location and Description of Channel. Method of Gauging.	Authority.	Author's No. of Series.
Mill Race at Mittelwald Iron Works in Hungary. Loamy soil. More or less irregular.	Rittinger, 1855. See Bornemann, " Civil Ingenieur," 1869.	
Mill Race at Schemnitz, Hungary. Shallow ditch in sandy soil. More or less irregular.	Do.	
Mill Race at Flachau, Hungary. Shallow ditch in earth.	Do.	
Hubengraben, in Rhenish Bavaria. Creek. Current meter.	Grebenau, 1866.	
Hockenbach. Creek. Current meter.	Do.	2 3
Grosbois Canal. Earth; no vegetation. Trapezoidal; bottom width, 6.5 feet.	Darcy and Bazin, 1865.	49–1 2 3 4
Mill Race at Kagiswyl, Switzerland. Reach very regular. Side slopes in earth; bed covered with fine gravel. Current meter.	Epper, 1885.	
Mill Race. Rod floats.	Legler.	
Speyerbach. Creek.	Grebenau, 1866.	4
Lauter Canal, at Neuburg, on the Rhine. Earth; no detritus. Current meter.	Strauss. See Grebenau, " Zusätze," etc.	1
Saalach, in Bavaria. From Stauffenegg to the river Salzach. Detritus. Reichenbach's tube.	Roff, 1854. See Grebenau, " Zusätze," etc.	4 1 7 10 12

Creeks, and Rivers.

Surface Width in Feet.	Greatest Depth in Feet.	Mean Hydraulic Radius in Feet, R	Slope of Water Surface per Thousand, $1000\,S$	Mean Velocity in per Second in Feet, v	Coefficient in Formula $v = c\sqrt{RS}$, c	Coefficient of Roughness, n
	0.41	0.315	4.1	1.322	36.8	.0265
	0.56	0.411	"	2.189	53.3	.0212
	0.69	0.496	"	2.109	46.8	.0246
	0.37	0.315	2.7	1.500	51.4	.0206
	0.60	0.494	"	1.552	42.5	.0266
	0.72	0.596	"	1.934	48.2	.0252
	0.55	0.467	2.0	1.953	63.9	.0187
	0.86	0.703	"	2.149	58.7	.0220
		0.587	1.300	1.424	51.2	.0236
		0.866	0.778	1.440	55.2	.0241
		0.879	0.797	1.463	55.0	.0243
10.7	1.4	0.96	0.250	0.89	57	.0236
11.9	1.9	1.32	0.275	1.34	70	.0212
14.1	2.5	1.57	0.246	1.36	69	.0222
15 7	2.9	1.78	0.275	1.47	66	.0240
		1.040	1.754	2.817	65.8	.0218
		1.387	1.255	3.139	75.3	.0204
		1.410	1.200	3.221	78.3	.0198
14.8		1.11	1.000	2.20	65.7	.0220
		1.463	0.667	1.824	58.1	.0258
29.5		1.820	0.664	2.106	61.0	.0262
		1.54	0.875	2.073	56.5	.0269
		1.31	1.100	2.240	58.8	.0253
		1.91	1.242	3.077	63.0	.0256
		1.98	1.240	3.335	68.2	.0240
		2.16	3.600	5.474	64.3	.0259

Class B.   Open Channels,

Location and Description of Channel. Method of Gauging.	Authority.	Author's No. of Series.
Small Rivers and Canals having Fairly		
Canal du Jard, in France. Earth; no detritus. Mean velocity deduced from maximum surface velocities.	Dubuat, 1779.	1 2 3 4
Marmel Canal. Detritus; coarse gravel.	La Nicca, 1839.	
Gürben Canal, near Belp, Switzerland. Regular reach; detritus.	Quoted by Kutter.	1
Canal in England. Surface floats. Mean velocity by De Prony's ¹⁄₀ rule.	Watt. See Humphreys and Abbot.	
Canal at Réaltore. Bottom covered with mud. Nearly trapezoidal.	Darcy and Bazin, 1865.	1—7
River Lech, below Augsburg, Bavaria. Current meter.	Von Gumpenberg, 1854 *	1
Main, near Aschaffenburg. Earth.	Quoted by Kutter.	
River Salzach, in Bavaria. From Geisenfelden to Burghausen. Current meter.	Reich, 1855. See Grebenau, "Zusätze," etc.	1 3 2 5 4
Solani Embankment (Kamehera Reach). Earth; banks newly dressed to slopes from 1 : 1 to 1½ : 1; bed very rough. One-inch tin rod floats.	Cunningham, Roorkee, 1880.	222 (15)† 223 (11) 224 (12) 225 (14)
River Haine, in Belgium. Earth; no detritus. Surface floats; mean velocity determined by Dubuat's formula.	Dubuat, 1782.	22 17 40 46
River Arve, near Caronge, Canton Geneva.	Quoted by Kutter.	

* Grebenau, "Zusätze," etc.

† Figures in parenthesis indicate number of gaugings averaged.

Creeks, and Rivers.

Regular Channels, in Earth—Continued.

Surface Width in Feet.	Greatest Depth in Feet.	Mean Hydraulic Radius in Feet, R	Slope of Water Surface per Thousand, $1000\,S$	Mean Velocity per Second in Feet, v	Coefficient in Formula $v = c\sqrt{RS}$, c	Coefficient of Roughness, n
		1.68	0.0362	0.449	57.6	.0253
		1.94	0.0362	0.479	57.0	.0268
		2.05	0.0458	0.607	62.6	.0249
		2.58	0.0651	1.069	82.5	.0206
		2.31	0.500	2.263	66.4	.0253
		2.38	2.000	4.789	69.5	.0245
18	4	2.43	0.0631	1.134	91.5	.0184
19.7	4.5	2.87	0.43	2.54	73.2	.0244
153	3.6	3.16	1.150	4.950	81.8	.0220
		3.94	0.400	3.05	76.7	.0244
		3.45	0.280	2.686	86.2	.0213
		4 96	0.290	3.510	92.3	.0212
		3.52	0.348	3.618	103.2	.0176
		5.20	0.410	5.004	109.7	.0177
		5.00	0.607	5.543	100.3	.0193
65.2	5.3	4.50	0.291	2.82	78.8	.0244
64.8	5.1	4.37	0.297	2.79	77.4	.0245
64.3	4.8	4.18	0.304	2.74	78.3	.0240
64.0	4.6	4.07	0.306	2.71	76.8	.0244
about 50	about 9	5.83	0.0279	1.093	85.7	.0253
"	" 8	4.83	0.0303	0.902	74.6	.0275
"	" 9	5.74	0.1559	2.064	69.0	.0299
"	" 8	4.92	0.1653	2.305	84.0	.0235
		5.50	0.450	3.706	74.6	.0265

Class B. Open Channels,

Location and Description of Channel. Method of Gauging.	Authority.	Author's No. of Series.
Small Rivers and Canals having Fairly		
River Reuss, near Mellingen. Sandy bed.	Quoted by Kutter.	
Linth Canal at Biäschen, Canton Glarus. Gravel. Trapezoidal, slightly rounded.	Do.	
Linth Canal at Grynau. Earth; no detritus. Trapezoidal, slightly rounded. Rod floats; gaugings very carefully made.	Legler. See Kutter, " Die neue Theorie," etc.	
Solani Embankment (15th Mile, New Site). Earth; side slopes, 1½ : 1; bed quite uniform. One-inch tin rod floats.	Cunningham, Roorkee, 1880.	197 (1)*
Solani Embankment (15th Mile, Old Site). Earth; side slopes about 2½ to 1 ; bed rather irregular. One-inch tin tubes.	Do.	192 (6)*
VIII. Rivers and Canals, more or less Irregular,		
Ditch at Felsö-Bánya, Hungary. Earth; irregular.	Rittinger,† 1855.	
Lütschine, near Upper Grindelwald Glacier. Very coarse detritus. **Lütschine, near Lower Grindelwald Glacier.** Very coarse detritus.	Quoted by Kutter.	

* Figures in parenthesis indicate number of gaugings averaged.
† See Bornemann, " Civil Ingenieur," 1869.

Creeks, and Rivers.

Regular Channels, in Earth—Continued.

Surface Width in Feet.	Greatest Depth in Feet.	Mean Hydraulic Radius in Feet, R	Slope of Water Surface per Thousand, $1000\,S$	Mean Velocity per Second in Feet, v	Coefficient in Formula $v = c\sqrt{RS}$, c	Coefficient of Roughness, n
		6.95	0.150	3.018	93.2	.0224
113.2		4.0	0.800	4.264	75.5	.0247
		6.5	0.410	4.166	80.7	.0253
		5.14	0.29	3.414	88.4	.0222
		5.93	0.30	3.830	90.8	.0220
		6.48	0.31	4.152	92.6	.0219
		7.12	0.32	4.418	92.6	.0222
		7.52	0.33	4.753	95.4	.0218
123.0	10.8	8.09	0.34	4.920	93.8	.0224
		8.28	0.34	5.058	95.3	.0220
		8.62	0.35	5.225	95.1	.0222
		8.87	0.36	5.392	95.5	.0222
		9.18	0.37	5.530	94.9	.0224
184.2	9.7	8.35	0.220	3.93	92.8	.0228
174.9	10.0	8.64	0.231	3.93	89.1	.0242

with Detritus, Vegetation, or other Obstructions.

Surface Width in Feet.	Greatest Depth in Feet.	Mean Hydraulic Radius in Feet, R	Slope of Water Surface per Thousand, $1000\,S$	Mean Velocity per Second in Feet, v	Coefficient in Formula $v = c\sqrt{RS}$, c	Coefficient of Roughness, n
	0.56	0.348	1.1	0.548	28.0	.0332
	0.68	0.391	"	0.570	27.5	.0348
		0.38	53.000	2.329	16.5	.0520
		0.38	72.500	2.034	12.1	.0670

Class B. Open Channels,

Location and Description of Channel. Method of Gauging.	Authority.	Author's No. of Series.

Rivers and Canals, more or less Irregular, with

Landquart, in Canton Graubunden. Very coarse detritus.	Quoted by Kutter.	
Emme, near Emmermatt. Irregular; coarse detritus. Surface floats.	Do.	
Lütschine, near Eybridge. Coarse detritus.	Do.	
Mösa, in Misox, Canton Graubunden. Coarse detritus. Rod floats, probably.	La Nicca, 1839.*	1 2 3
Grosbois Canal. Earth; some vegetation. Trapezoidal; bottom width, 6.3 feet.	Darcy and Bazin, 1865.	50—1 2 3 4
Grosbois Canal. Earth; some vegetation. Nearly arc of a circle.	Do.	48—1 2 3 4
Grosbois Canal. Earth (stony); but little vegetation. Trapezoidal; bottom width, 3.9 feet.	Do.	37—1 2 3 4
Grosbois Canal. Earth; bottom and sides of mud; some vegetation in spots. Trapezoidal.	Do.	47—1 2 3 4
Grosbois Canal. Earth (stony); but little vegetation. Trapezoidal; bottom width, 4.4.	Do.	41—1 2 3 4

* See Kutter, " Die neue Theorie," etc. La Nicca's gaugings are said to have been carefully made, although, probably on account of several conversions of measures, there are some slight errors in the figures. The original publication was not accessible to us.

Creeks, and Rivers.

Detritus, Vegetation, or other Obstructions—Continued.

Surface Width in Feet.	Greatest Depth in Feet.	Mean Hydraulic Radius in Feet, R	Slope of Water Surface per Thousand, $1000 \, S$	Mean Velocity per Second in Feet, v	Coefficient in Formula $v = c\sqrt{RS}$, c	Coefficient of Roughness, n
		0 62	10.000	1.738	21.9	.0490
		1.19	5.000	3.510	45.4	.0310
		1.34	3.325	3.214	48 0	.0305
		0.99	11.875	3.867	35.7	.0369
		1.20	"	5.540	46.3	.0308
		1.53	"	7.587	56.1	.0274
10.5	1.5	1.05	0.310	0.82	45	.0298
11.4	2.1	1.42	0.290	1.26	62	.0242
13.8	2.7	1.65	0.330	1.30	56	.0277
15.5	3.1	1.85	0.330	1.41	57	.0278
9.5	1.5	0.99	0.555	0.96	41	.0322
10.7	2.1	1.30	0.555	1.48	55	.0264
11.9	2.5	1.56	0.525	1.57	55	.0278
13.5	2.9	1.71	0.515	1.75	59	.0267
9.1	1.5	0.96	0.792	1.23	45	.0299
11.4	2.0	1.20	0.808	1.67	53	.0270
12.6	2.4	1.41	0.858	1.81	52	.0287
13.3	2.7	1.56	0.842	2.00	55	.0277
9.9	1.7	1.09	0.464	0.82	36	.0366
11.2	2.2	1.38	0.450	1.32	53	.0279
12.5	2.7	1.63	0.479	1.43	51	.0300
14.0	2.9	1.71	0.493	1.68	58	.0271
10.1	1.6	1.04	0.445	0.96	45	.0303
12.0	2.3	1.38	0.450	1.27	51	.0289
13.2	2.7	1.57	0.455	1.40	52	.0290
14.3	3.0	1.71	0.441	1.51	55	.0284

Class B. Open Channels,

LOCATION AND DESCRIPTION OF CHANNEL. METHOD OF GAUGING.	AUTHORITY.	Author's No. of Series.

Rivers and Canals more or less Irregular, with

LOCATION AND DESCRIPTION OF CHANNEL. METHOD OF GAUGING.	AUTHORITY.	Author's No. of Series.
Grosbois Canal. Earth; covered with vegetation at many points. Trapezoidal; bottom width, 4.3 feet.	Darcy and Bazin, 1865.	43—1 2 3 4
Grosbois Canal. Earth; covered with vegetation at many places. Trapezoidal; bottom width, 3.7 feet.	Do.	36—1 2 3 4
Chazilly Canal. Earth (stony); little vegetation. Trapezoidal; bottom width, 3.9 feet.	Do.	38—1 2 3 4
Simme Canal, Canton Berne. Very coarse gravel and detritus. Surface floats; mean velocity from Bazin's formula.	Wampfler, 1867. See Kutter, " Die neuen Formeln," etc.	3 4 2 1
River Isar, Bavaria. Coarse gravel and detritus. Gaugings at low and high water.	Quoted by Grebenau, 1867, in " Zusätze," etc.	
Plessur, near Chur. Coarse gravel and detritus. Mean velocity deduced from surface velocities and also rod floats.	La Nicca, 1839.	1 2 3 4 5 6
Saare, near Laupen Bridge, Canton Berne. Irregular bed; coarse detritus.	Quoted by Kutter.	
Rhine, in the Rhine Forest. Coarse gravel and detritus. Mean deduced from surface velocities and rod floats, probably.	La Nicca, 1839.	1 2 3
Rhine, in the Domleschger Valley. Coarse gravel and detritus. Mean deduced from surface velocities and rod floats, probably.	Do.	1 7 13

Creeks, and Rivers.

Surface Width in Feet.	Greatest Depth in Feet.	Mean Hydraulic Radius in Feet, R	Slope of Water Surface per Thousand, $1000\,S$	Mean Velocity per Second in Feet, v	Coefficient in Formula $v = c\sqrt{RS}$, c	Coefficient of Roughness, n

Detritus, Vegetation, or other Obstructions—Continued.

Surface Width in Feet.	Greatest Depth in Feet.	Mean Hydraulic Radius in Feet, R	Slope of Water Surface per Thousand, $1000\,S$	Mean Velocity per Second in Feet, v	Coefficient in Formula $v = c\sqrt{RS}$, c	Coefficient of Roughness, n
10.1	1.7	1.06	0.420	0.89	42	.0322
12.3	2.4	1.41	0.470	1.18	46	.0320
13.5	2.8	1.60	0.470	1.31	47	.0320
14.7	3.1	1.76	0.450	1.39	49	.0316
10.5	1.9	1.14	0.678	0.91	33	.0411
12.9	2.5	1.42	0.633	1.28	43	.0341
14.2	2.9	1.61	0.644	1.45	45	.0337
15.2	3.2	1.74	0.622	1.65	50	.0310
8.9	1.5	0.96	0.957	1.24	41	.0322
11.0	2.0	1.18	0.929	1.70	51	.0278
12.1	2.4	1.41	0.993	1.80	48	.0307
13.0	2.6	1.54	0.986	1.96	50	.0303
		1.82	6.500	4.920	45.1	.0350
		1.87	7.000	5.373	46.9	.0338
		1.36	11.600	5.491	43.6	.0335
		1.32	17.000	5.993	39.8	.0361
153	2.0	1.86	2.500	4.021	59.0	.0271
172	6.7	6.05	2.500	7.180	58.4	.0352
		1.25	9.650	6.002	54.7	.0266
		2.33	"	9.988	66.4	.0255
		3.48	"	10.194	66.4	.0275
		3.58	"	13.579	72.8	.0253
		3.59	"	13.943	74.8	.0246
		4.58	"	13.746	65.4	.0294
		2.70	3.333	4.559	48.1	.0360
		0.42	14.200	2.332	30.3	.0337
		0.76	"	4.526	43.4	.0292
		1.21	"	6.032	46.0	.0309
		0.25	5.775	1.250	32.8	.0272
		1.32	7.735	4.753	47.0	.0310
		2.95	7.959	7.419	48.3	.0366

Class B. Open Channels,

Location and Description of Channel. Method of Gauging.	Authority.	Author's No. of Series.
Rivers and Canals more or less Irregular, with		
Rhine, at the Tardes Bridge, Canton Graubünden. Coarse detritus.	Quoted by Kutter.	
Tessin, opposite Giubiasco. Reach quite irregular. Bed of gravel, with occasional boulders; shallow near shores. Current meter.	Epper, 1888.	
Limmat, near Zürich. Irregular bed; very little detritus.	Quoted by Kutter.	
Engstligen, near Frutigen, Canton Berne. Bed very irregular, with very coarse detritus.	Do.	
Chesapeake and Ohio Canal Feeder. Near Georgetown, D. C. In bad order.	Humphreys and Abbot, 1859.	18 17
Escher Canal, near Lake Walen, Canton Glarus. Coarse gravel and detritus. Road floats.	Legler. See Kutter, " Die neuen Formeln," etc.	1 2
River Salzach, Bavaria. From Bergheim to Wildshut. Detritus. Current meter.	Reich, 1855. See Kutter, " Die neuen Formeln," etc.; also Grebenau, " Zusätze," etc.	3 2 5 8 1 7 4 6
Zihl, near Gottstatt, Canton Berne. Bed very irregular. Mud or fine detritus. Current meter.	Trechsel, 1825. See Kutter, " Die neue Theorie," etc.	1 2 3
Kander, near Frutigen, Canton Berne. Bed irregular. Very coarse detritus.	Quoted by Kutter.	
Scheuss Canal, near Biel. Earth, somewhat stony.	Do.	

Creeks, and Rivers.

Surface Width in Feet.	Greatest Depth in Feet.	Mean Hydraulic Radius in Feet, R	Slope of Water Surface per Thousand, $1000\ S$	Mean Velocity per Second in Feet, v	Coefficient, in Formula $v = c\sqrt{RS}$ c	Coefficient of Roughness, n

Detritus, Vegetation, or other Obstructions—Continued.

		2.92	6.000	4.231	31.9	.0485
		2.962	0.254	1.663	60.6	.0291
		3.160	2.750	5.346	57.4	.0313
		3.31	22.200	8.856	32 6	.0550
23	7.5	3.66	0.6985	2.723	53.8	.0342
23	7.6	3.70	0.6985	3.032	59.0	.0310
		3.76	3.000	6.986	65.7	.0283
		4.42	3.000	8.364	72.6	.0263
		3.68	0.662	3.543	71.7	.0258
		3.53	0.940	3.480	60.3	.0306
		4.20	0.940	4.034	63.9	.0298
		7.39	1.120	5.786	63.4	.0337
		3.51	1.550	4.100	55.4	.0333
		4.64	1.550	4.671	67.5	.0287
		3.87	1.796	4.448	53.4	.0352
		4.26	1.796	5.150	58.8	.0326
		3.52	0.400	2.296	61.0	.0300
		5.02	0.460	3.706	77.1	.0253
		5.53	0.810	4.625	69.1	.0290
		4.12	9.180	8.692	44.7	.0430
21.3		4.35	1.850	5.445	60.8	.0314

Class B. Open Channels,

Location and Description of Channel. Method of Gauging.	Authority.	Author's No. of Series.

Rivers and Canals, more or less Irregular, with

Location and Description of Channel. Method of Gauging.	Authority.	Author's No. of Series.
Aar, near Aarberg. Detritus in small quantities.	Trechsel, 1825. (See Kutter, "Die neue Theorie," etc.)	
Aar, at Berne. Irregular bed. Detritus in small quantities.	Quoted by Kutter.	1 2 3
Aar, near Thalgut. Irregular bed. Detritus.	Trechsel, 1825. (See Kutter, "Die neue Theorie," etc.)	
Aar, near Büren. Irregular bed. Sand and mud. Current meter.	Do.	
Schanzengraben, near Zürich. Earth; but little detritus.	Quoted by Kutter.	
Ohio River, at Point Pleasant, W. Va.	C. Ellet, 1858.*	
Pannerden Canal, in Holland.	Quoted by Kutter.	1 2
Weser. Earth. Do., near Vlotow, at low water. Do., near Hausberg. Do., near Vlotow, at high water.	Schwarz. (See Grebenau, "Zusätze," etc.)	1 5 2 4 3 6 7 8 9 10 11
Tiber at Rome. Rod floats, 5.6 to 12.5 feet long, in twelve longitudinal planes. Length for slope determination, 804 feet.	Buffon, 1821. (See Humphreys and Abbot.)	

* See Humphreys and Abbot.

Creeks, and Rivers.

Surface Width in Feet.	Greatest Depth in Feet.	Mean Hydraulic Radius in Feet, R.	Slope of Water Surface per Thousand, 1000 S	Mean Velocity per Second in Feet, v	Coefficient in Formula $v = c\sqrt{RS}$, c	Coefficient of Roughness, n

Detritus, Vegetation, or other Obstructions—Continued.

Surface Width in Feet.	Greatest Depth in Feet.	Mean Hydraulic Radius in Feet, R.	Slope of Water Surface per Thousand, 1000 S	Mean Velocity per Second in Feet, v	Coefficient in Formula $v = c\sqrt{RS}$, c	Coefficient of Roughness, n
		6.69	0.787	5.642	77.8	.0263
		3.12	1.270	4.198	66.6	.0270
		6.10	1.270	6.134	69.7	.0292
		4.22	0.461	2.821	63.7	.0300
		7.07	0.800	5.150	68.6	.0305
		7.78	0.993	7.511	85.3	.0250
		4.58	1.776	5.445	61.0	.0320
		7.06	1.776	6.77	60.5	.0348
		11.5	0.100	2.21	65.2	.0385
		14.9	0.100	3.38	87.8	.0284
		16.8	0.120	4.23	94.1	.0264
		7.81	0.090	1.706	64.6	.0353
1073	8	6.72	0.0933	2.515	100.4	.0210
551		8.66	0.220	3.67	84.0	.0257
		10.23	0.224	4.20	87.7	.0254
		5.96	0.1834	1.410	42.7	.0502
		8.70	0.1917	3.470	84.7	.0257
		6.31	0.3986	4.087	81.3	.0250
		6.75	0.4107	4.950	93.6	.0216
344		6.49	0.4110	5.182	101.0	.0198
371	13.12	9.44	0.2000	4.064	93.2	.0234
		9.98	0.2000	4.389	97.9	.0224
		10.52	0.2167	4.756	99.2	.0222
		11.06	0.2167	5.186	105.5	.0207
430		12.61	0.5316	7.924	96.5	.0230
472		13.55	0.5504	7.902	91.9	.0241
243	15	9.46	0.1306	3.413	97.1	.0228

Class B. Open Channels,

Location and Description of Channel. Method of Gauging.	Authority.	Author's No. of Series.

Rivers and Canals, more or less Irregular, with

Location and Description of Channel. Method of Gauging.	Authority.	Author's No. of Series.
Theiss below Szolnok. Bed irregular, sand and much vegetation.	Quoted by Kutter.	
Elbe at Tetschen, Bohemia. Gentle curve in the river, rather steep banks; thalweg changes from centre to near concave shore; coarse gravel, with pebbles up to egg size; bed undulating; changes very slightly after freshets. Reach, 5740 feet long. Current meter.	Harlacher, 1877–79.	
Same. At high water. Reach, 1663 feet long. Surface floats.	Harlacher, 1881.	
Saône at Raconnay. Current meter. Slope measurements for 1, 2, and 3 are reported as doubtful.	Léveillé, 1858–9. (See Darcy and Bazin.)	1 2 3 4 5 6 7 8 9 10
Seine at Paris (between the bridges of Jena and Invalids). Reach fairly regular. Floats.	Villevert. Experiments under the direction of M. Poirée, 1851–2. (See Darcy and Bazin.)	1 2 3 4 5 6 7 8 9 10 11

Creeks, and Rivers.

Surface Width in Feet.	Greatest Depth in Feet.	Mean Hydraulic Radius in Feet, R	Slope of Water Surface per Thousand, $1000\,S$	Mean Velocity per Second in Feet, v	Coefficient in Formula $v = c\sqrt{RS}$, c	Coefficient of Roughness, n

Detritus, Vegetation, or other Obstructions—Continued.

Surface Width in Feet.	Greatest Depth in Feet.	Mean Hydraulic Radius in Feet, R	Slope of Water Surface per Thousand, $1000\,S$	Mean Velocity per Second in Feet, v	Coefficient in Formula $v = c\sqrt{RS}$, c	Coefficient of Roughness, n
		10.10	0.017	0.689	53.6	.0537
342.8	6.2	3.51	0.38	2.49	68.2	.0268
411.3	8.5	5.18	0.37	3.74	85.4	.0229
452.0	11.8	7.77	0.41	4.95	87.6	.0239
580.2	25.3	17.5	0.49	8.00	86.3	.0275
		3.88	0.040	0.564	45.3	.0425
		4.77	"	0.814	58.9	.0348
		7.06	"	0.988	58.7	.0399
		8.92	"	1.601	84.8	.0285
		10.87	"	1.854	88.9	.0286
		11.61	"	1.910	88.6	.0293
		11.81	"	1.942	89.3	.0292
		13.27	"	2.254	97.8	.0270
		14.64	"	2.369	98.0	.0277
		15.83	"	2.379	94.5	.0296
		5.66	0.127	2.093	78.1	.0263
		7.08	0.133	2.264	73.7	.0294
		8.43	0.135	2.418	71.7	.0315
		9.48	0.140	3.370	92.5	.0240
		10.92	0.140	3.740	95.6	.0238
		12.19	0.140	3.816	92.4	.0253
		14.50	0.140	4.232	94.0	.0255
		15.02	0.140	4.511	98.3	.0243
		15.93	0.172	4.682	89.5	.0272
		16.85	0.131	4.800	102.1	.0238
		18.39	0.103	4.689	107.6	.0233

Class B. Open Channels,

Location and Description of Channel. Method of Gauging.	Authority.	Author's No. of Series.

Rivers and Canals, more or less Irregular, with

Seine at Meulan, Triel, and Poissy. Floats used in all experiments, except Nos. 2 and 4, for which current meter was taken. Experiments Nos. 1 and 2 at Meulan; Nos. 3 and 4 at Triel; remainder at Poissy. Reaches fairly regular.	Bonnet. Experiments under the direction of M. Emmery, 1852–3. (See Darcy and Bazin.)	1 2 3 4 5 6 7 8 9
Rhine at Flurlingen, above the Rhine Falls. Reach slightly irregular. Bed of gravel. Channel near left bank. Water turbid at time of gauging. Current meter.	Epper, 1887.	
Rhine at Noll, below the Rhine Falls. Reach fairly regular. Bed of gravel, with occasional boulders ; shallow near shores. Water turbid at time of gauging. Current meter.	Do.	
Rhine at Bâle (near the bridge). Coarse detritus, coarse gravel. Current meter.	Grebenau, 1867.	
Rhine at Germersheim. Fine detritus and gravel. Current meter.	Do.	1 2 3
Rhine at Neuburg. Detritus.	Quoted by Kutter.	
Rhine at Pforz. Detritus.	Do.	
Rhine at Speyer. Fine detritus and gravel. Current meter, at a large number of points.	Strauss. (Grebenau, " Zusätze," etc.)	

Creeks, and Rivers.

Surface Width in Feet.	Greatest Depth in Feet.	Mean Hydraulic Radius in Feet, R	Slope of Water Surface per Thousand,' $1000\ S$	Mean Velocity per Second in Feet, v	Coefficient, in Formula $v = c\sqrt{RS}$, c	Coefficient of Roughness, n

Detritus, Vegetation, or other Obstructions—Continued.

		7.10	0.000	2.310	91.3	.0236
		7.68	0.057	2.313	89.5	.0245
		11.24	0.057	2.362	93.3	.0263
		12.43	0.060	2.359	86.4	.0295
		13.57	0.050	2.372	91.1	.0287
		14.20	0.054	2.595	93.6	.0278
		15.86	0.062	2.910	92.7	.0285
		16.85	0.067	3.101	92.4	.0288
		17.87	0.075	3.330	91.1	.0293
		6.732	0.1573	2.965	91.8	.0226
		7.00	0.1618	2.834	84.2	.0250
		6.89	0.928	6.363	79.6	.0259
		6.89	1.218	6.380	69.7	.0300
		10.85	0.247	5.051	97.2	.0230
		12.11	0.307	5.215	85.4	.0265
		17.27	0.349	6.101	78.7	.0303
		13.91	0.391	5.838	78.9	.0297
		13.94	0.357	5.642	79.8	.0294
1440		9.72	0.112	2.909	88.0	.0258

Class B. Open Channels,

LOCATION AND DESCRIPTION OF CHANNEL. METHOD OF GAUGING.	AUTHORITY.	Author's No. of Series.

Rivers and Canals, more or less Irregular, with

Rhine Delta, Holland.	Krayenhoff, 1812.	
Yssel Arm, at upper mouth. Reach about one mile.	(See Humphreys and Abbot.)	27
Below the Yssel. Reach over 8 miles.		26
Waal Arm, at upper mouth. Reach nearly 12 miles.		25
At Pannerden. Reach over 11 miles.		24
At Byland. Reach over 11 miles.		23
Rod floats; allowance made for resistance of bends.		
Slopes for Waal and Yssel are doubtful.		
Rhine Delta at Nymwegen.	Brunings.	1
Alluvial.	(Grebenau, "Zu-	2
Nos. 1 to 4, at ordinary water.	sätze," etc.)	3
Nos. 5 and 6 at high water.		4
(Slopes are doubtful, not being given by		5
Brunings. See Hülsse's Polyt. Central Bl., 1845, vol. 6, p. 308.)		6
Danube at Ravensburg.	Mathcis, 1858.	
Bed irregular; sand or fine gravel.	(See Kutter, "Die	
Current meter.	neuen Formeln," etc.)	
Danube at Szob.	Quoted by Kutter.	
Reach fairly regular.		
Sandy bed, probably.		
Danube below Sarengrad.	Do.	
Reach irregular.		
Sandy bed, probably.		
Danube at Budapest.	Do.	
Bed irregular.		
Sand or fine gravel.		
Bayou La Fourche (near upper mouth).	Humphreys and Ab-	15
Double floats.	bot.	14
		16
		13
Bayou Plaquemine (near upper mouth).	C. Ellet, 1851.	12
Double floats.	(See Humphreys and Abbot.)	11

Creeks, and Rivers.

Surface Width in Feet.	Greatest Depth in Feet.	Mean Hydraulic Radius in Feet, R	Slope of Water Surface per Thousand, $1000\,S$	Mean Velocity per Second in Feet, v	Coefficient in Formula $v = c\sqrt{RS}$, c	Coefficient of Roughness, n

Detritus, Vegetation, or other Obstructions—Continued.

Surface Width in Feet.	Greatest Depth in Feet.	Mean Hydraulic Radius in Feet, R	Slope of Water Surface per Thousand, $1000\,S$	Mean Velocity per Second in Feet, v	Coefficient in Formula $v = c\sqrt{RS}$, c	Coefficient of Roughness, n
321	abt. 9	5.96	0.11657	2.773	105.2	.0194
700	abt. 12	7.59	0.11744	2.917	97.7	.0220
1328	abt. 17	11.03	0.10438	3.165	93.1	.0252
557	abt. 17	11.20	0.09986	3.277	98.0	.0237
1155	20	16.45	0.09769	3.575	89.2	.0288
		8.66	0.2202	3.680	84.3	.0258
1685		11.54	0.1150	2.935	81.6	.0291
		12.44	0.1106	3.011	81.2	.0298
		12.48	0.2202	4.835	93.2	.0248
1709		16.17	0.1150	4.297	99.7	.0246
		16.75	0.1106	3.969	92.2	.0273
		5.77	0.536	3.762	67.3	.0300
		11.88	0.040	2.250	102.3	.0247
		14.25	0.058	2.493	86.9	.0287
		15.38	0.071	2.034	61.7	.0459
223	24	12.80	0.03655	2.807	129.7	.0195
"	24	13.04	0.03731	2.843	128.8	.0195
"	23	12.47	0.04384	2.789	119.3	.0205
"	27	15.71	0.04468	3.076	116.1	.0225
268	24	15.32	0.14372	3.959	84.4	.0292
292	28	18.35	0.20644	5.198	84.5	.0296

Class B. Open Channels,

Location and Description of Channel. Method of Gauging.	Authority.	Author's No. of Series.
Rivers and Canals, more or less Irregular, with		
Great Nevka, near St. Petersburg, Russia. Surface floats; mean velocity from De Prony's formula.	Destrem. (See Humphreys and Abbot.)	
Neva, in Russia. Surface floats; mean velocity from De Prony's formula.	Do.	
Missouri River, at St. Charles, Mo. Twenty-five miles above mouth. Reach about two miles long, including a bend and a bridge with four piers. River bed is sand. Double floats.	Missouri River Commission Report, 1879.	

Creeks, and Rivers.

Surface Width in Feet.	Greatest Depth in Feet.	Mean Hydraulic Radius in Feet, R	Slope of Water Surface per Thousand, $1000\,S$	Mean Velocity per Second in Feet, v	Coefficient in Formula $v = c\sqrt{RS}$, c	Coefficient of Roughness, n

Detritus, Vegetation, or other Obstructions—Continued.

Surface Width in Feet.	Greatest Depth in Feet.	Mean Hydraulic Radius in Feet, R	Slope of Water Surface per Thousand, $1000\,S$	Mean Velocity per Second in Feet, v	Coefficient in Formula $v = c\sqrt{RS}$, c	Coefficient of Roughness, n
881	21	17.42	0.01487	2.049	127.3	.0252
1218	50	35.42	0.01389	3.230	145.6	.0275
		5.65	0.1137	3.01	118.8	.0167
		6.80	0.1109	2.97	105.2	.0191
		8.40	0.1132	2.83	91.8	.0238
		8.15	0.1150	3.39	110.7	.0193
		8.07	0.1165	3.25	106.0	.0202
		8.05	0.1170	3.10	101.0	.0212
		11.50	0.1170	3.78	103.1	.0222
		10.70	0.1183	3.63	102.0	.0222
		8.35	0.1196	3.02	95.5	.0229
		8.05	0.1210	2.96	95.0	.0237
		12.00	0.1371	4.46	107.3	.0213
		12.10	0.1518	3.97	92.6	.0248
		11.60	0.1532	3.90	92.5	.0247
		11.60	0.1540	3.85	91.1	.0251
		7.72	0.1558	3.11	89.7	.0238
		14.1	0.1615	4.72	95.9	.0237
		15.4	0.1627	5.14	102.7	.0228
		13.0	0.1672	4.22	90.5	.0258
		14.7	0.1673	4.84	97.6	.0242
		14.7	0.1677	5.18	104.3	.0222
		14.6	0.1683	4.85	97.8	.0241
		15.4	0.1752	5.00	98.0	.0242
		15.4	0.1764	4.89	93.8	.0254
		12.5	0.1774	4.54	96.4	.0238
		11.4	0.1820	4.27	93.7	.0242
		12.9	0.1831	4.48	93.2	.0248
		12.5	0.1840	4.35	90.7	.0254
		13.1	0.1842	4.44	90.4	.0258
		11.5	0.1865	4.44	95.9	.0236
		17.8	0.1923	6.16	105.3	.0224
		16.7	0.2006	5.57	90.2	.0247
		13.5	0.2270	5.65	102.1	.0222
		17.7	0.2337	6.20	96.4	.0250
		13.9	0.2354	5.64	95.6	.0232
		14.5	0.2412	5.47	92.5	.0251
		14.7	0.2435	5.77	96.5	.0240
		13.4	0.2470	5.47	95.1	.0241
		14.9	0.2590	5.89	94.8	.0245

Class B.   Open Channels,

Location and Description of Channel. Method of Gauging.	Authority.	Author's No. of Series.

Rivers and Canals, more or less Irregular, with

Location and Description of Channel. Method of Gauging.	Authority.	Author's No. of Series.
Irawadi at Saiktha, Burmah. Bed mostly sand, with occasional shingle. The right bank rocky in places, but generally covered with sand. Straight reach, nearly five miles long. Channel and maximum depth are near the right bank, varying in the reach from ten to fifty feet below low-water stage. The values of R, S, and v are reductions to certain gauge readings of even feet made from curves averaging the observed values. The slopes are averages from frequent readings on both sides of river while rising. For very high and very low stages, the author says they may need correction. Double floats were used, but comparative measurements made in 1882 with electric meters show that the original velocities as recorded require about 10% reduction. This correction has been made.	Gordon, 1873.	
Mississippi River at New Madrid, Mo. Seventy-five miles below confluence with Ohio. The upper and lower mile of a five-mile reach are comparatively straight and uniform, but in the central three miles the channel changes from one side to the other and causes a number of perturbations. River bottom is sand. The table refers only to upper and lower mile reaches.	Mississippi River Com., 1887. (MS.)	6 5 4 1 3 2 6 4 5 3 1 2
Mississippi River at Fulton, Tenn. Bed, sand; reach nearly two miles; fairly straight and regular, though forming a basin with bars near upper and lower ends of reach. Double floats.	Miss. River Commission Report of 1881.	

Creeks, and Rivers.

Detritus, Vegetation, or other Obstructions—Continued.

Surface Width in Feet.	Greatest Depth in Feet.	Mean Hydraulic Radius in Feet, R	Slope of Water Surface per Thousand, $1000\,S$	Mean Velocity per Second in Feet, v	Coefficient. in Formula $v = c\sqrt{RS}$, c	Coefficient of Roughness, n
3395	35	16.28	0.00861	1.007	85.1	.0420
3528	37	17.52	0.01291	1.459	97.0	.0357
3710	39	18.49	0.01722	1.783	99.9	.0336
3930	41	19.88	0.02152	2.083	100.7	.0328
4208	43	19.99	0.02583	2.360	103.9	.0304
4605	45	20.40	0.03013	2.620	105.7	.0292
4780	47	21.13	0.03444	2.857	105.9	.0286
4820	49	22.07	0.03874	3.091	103.6	.0293
4859	51	24.70	0.04304	3.321	101.9	.0300
4899	53	26.42	0.04735	3.548	100.3	.0306
4938	55	28.11	0.05165	3.771	99.0	.0310
4970	57	29.80	0.05596	3.993	97.8	.0315
4976	59	31.68	0.06026	4.213	96.4	.0320
4982	61	33.57	0.06456	4.432	95.2	.0325
4988	63	35.44	0.06887	4.652	94.2	.0330
4994	65	37.31	0 07317	4.874	93.3	.0336
5002	67	39.16	0.07748	5.110	92.8	.0337
5011	69	41.01	0.08178	5.382	92.9	.0336
5025	71	42.82	0.08608	5.717	94.2	.0327
5045	73	44.47	0.09039	6.147	97.0	.0314
4970		17.90	0.142	3.380	67.0	.0403
4970		18.91	0.142	3.500	67.6	.0405
5100		23.66	0.124	3.862	71.3	.0403
5420		24.06	0.124	3.681	67.4	.0434
5650		29.53	0.128	4.077	66.3	.0469
5545		31.06	0.132	3.804	59.4	.0540
3375		23.90	0.08000	4.043	92.4	.0303
4030		24.10	0.08250	3.689	82.7	.0351
3300		24.70	0.08466	3.436	75.1	.0402
4120		29.91	0.11150	4.349	75.3	.0400
4050		31.72	0.11330	4.126	68.8	.0463
4130		37.96	0.12180	4.750	69.9	.0460
2465	39.5	29.6	0.01444	2.20	106.2	.0384
2467	40.0	30.4	0.01870	2.35	98.6	.0402
2463	40.0	30.4	0.01906	2.37	98.4	.0400
2501	42.0	32.9	0.02094	2.82	107.4	.0361
2569	51.0	40.1	0.04762	4.22	96.6	.0359
2563	49.5	39.3	0.04950	4.04	91.6	.0381
2582	52.5	41.1	0.05131	4.49	97.8	.0348
2598	69.0	53.5	0.06170	7.47	130.0	.0230
2615	68.0	53.7	0.07397	7.74	122.8	.0243

Class B. Open Channels,

Location and Description of Channel. Method of Gauging.	Authority.	Author's No. of Series.

Rivers and Canals, more or less Irregular, with

Mississippi River at Columbus, Ky.	Humphreys and Abbot, 1858.	5
Mississippi River above Vicksburg, Miss. Double floats.	Do.	8 9 7 10 6
Mississippi River at Carrolton, La. Bed, very fine sand; banks comparatively stable. A short, sharp bend of about 130° between two straight reaches, each about two miles in length. At the bend there was a powerful eddy. Local slopes varied greatly. The table contains the average slope over the entire distance, taken on other days from those on which the velocities were measured, but are believed to apply fairly well to the respective gaugings. The results at the mean stages of the river are considered the most trustworthy. Double floats.	Miss. River Commission Report of 1882.	
Mississippi River at Carrolton, La. Double floats. High water, 1851.	Humphreys and Abbot, 1851.	3 4 2 1

Creeks, and Rivers.

Surface Width in Feet.	Greatest Depth in Feet.	Mean Hydraulic Radius in Feet, *R*	Slope of Water Surface per Thousand, 1000 *S*	Mean Velocity per Second in Feet, *v*	Coefficient, in Formula $v = c\sqrt{RS}$, *c*	Coefficient of Roughness, *n*

Detritus, Vegetation, or other Obstructions—Continued.

2214	88	65.88	0.0680	6.958	103.9	.0327
2507	63	31.16	0.02227	3.523	133.8	.0307
2556	83	52.12	0.03029	5.558	139.9	.0253
2732	101	64.52	0.04365	6.825	128.6	.0267
2580	90	57.37	0.04811	6.319	120.3	.0283
2729	100	64.10	0.06379	6.950	108.7	.0308
2359	86	57.6	0.0097	2.95	124.8	.0452
2369	86	60.7	0.0097	3.35	139.3	.0400
2392	88	58.8	0.0105	3.52	141.7	.0378
2401	90	59.6	0.0112	3.58	138.6	.0383
2423	89	57.7	0.0112	3.73	146.7	.0354
2417	90	58.5	0.0112	3.91	152.8	.0333
2417	91	59.3	0.0112	4.05	157.2	.0322
2565	90	63.4	0.0127	5.08	179.0	.0261
2665	95	58.7	0.0136	5.33	185.6	.0229
2565	91	64.2	0.0137	4.54	153.1	.0320
2582	92	57.2	0.0139	4.46	158.2	.0290
2541	87	65.6	0.0142	5.13	168.1	.0276
2445	88	60.8	0.0143	4.39	148.9	.0318
2438	90	62.5	0.0143	3.89	130.1	.0397
2636	92	62.6	0.0165	5.24	163.0	.0267
2647	93	63.1	0.0165	5.90	182.9	.0218
2421	131	73.53	0.00342	4.034	254.4	.0295
2429	132	74.39	0.00384	3.978	235.3	.0267
2656	136	72.46	0.01713	5.887	167.1	.0273
2653	136	72.03	0.02051	5.929	154.3	.0277

TABLE II.

(English measure.)

This table contains the values of

$$a + \frac{l}{n}$$

for different degrees of roughness varying from $n = .0070$ to .050, and the values of

$$\frac{m}{s}$$

for different slopes varying from 0 to ∞, so that for any given case the value

$$y = \left(a + \frac{l}{n}\right) + \left(\frac{m}{S}\right)$$

in the general formula for the coefficient c,

$$c = \frac{y}{1 + \dfrac{x}{\sqrt{R}}} ,$$

may be found simply by addition.

The value of x may then be readily obtained from

$$x = ny - l.$$

The numerical values for the constants a, l, and m from which the Table is computed are:

$$a = 41.66;$$
$$l = 1.81132;$$
$$m = 0.0028075.$$

VALUES FOR $a + \frac{l}{n}$.

n	$a + \frac{l}{n}$	n	$a + \frac{l}{n}$	n	$a + \frac{l}{n}$	n	$a + \frac{l}{n}$
0.0070	300.42	0.0130	180.99	0.0190	136.99	0.0290	104.12
0.0075	283.17	0.0135	175.83	0.0195	134.55	0.0300	102.04
0.0080	268.07	0.0140	171.04	0.0200	132.23	0.0320	98.26
0.0085	254.76	0.0145	166.58	0.0205	130.01	0.0340	94.93
0.0090	242.92	0.0150	162.41	0.0210	127.91	0.0360	91.97
0.0095	232.33	0.0155	158.52	0.0220	123.99	0.0380	89.33
0.0100	222.79	0.0160	154.87	0.0230	120.41	0.0400	86.94
0.0105	214.17	0.0165	151.44	0.0240	117.13	0.0420	84.79
0.0110	206.33	0.0170	148.21	0.0250	114.11	0.0440	82.83
0.0115	199.17	0.0175	145.16	0.0260	111.33	0.0460	81.04
0.0120	192.60	0.0180	142.29	0.0270	108.75	0.0480	79.40
0.0125	186.57	0.0185	139.57	0.0280	106.35	0.0500	77.89

VALUES FOR $\frac{m}{S}$.

S	$\frac{m}{S}$	S	$\frac{m}{S}$	S	$\frac{m}{S}$	S	$\frac{m}{S}$
.000000	∞	.000028	100.27	.000062	45.28	.000300	9.36
.000001	2807.54	.000029	96.81	.000064	43.87	.000350	8.02
.000002	1403.77	.000030	93.58	.000066	42.54	.000400	7.02
.000003	935.85	.000031	90.57	.000068	41.29	.000450	6.24
.000004	701.88	.000032	87.74	.000070	40.11	.000500	5.62
.000005	561.51	.000033	85.08	.000072	38.99	.000600	4.68
.000006	467.92	.000034	82.57	.000074	37.94	.000700	4.01
.000007	401.08	.000035	80.22	.000076	36.94	.000800	3.51
.000008	350.94	.000036	77.99	.000078	35.99	.000900	3.12
.000009	311.95	.000037	75.88	.000080	35.09	.001000	2.81
.000010	280.75	.000038	73.88	.000085	33.03	.001250	2.25
.000011	255.23	.000039	71.99	.000090	31.19	.001500	1.87
.000012	233.96	.000040	70.19	.000095	29.55	.001750	1.60
.000013	215.96	.000041	68.48	.000100	28.08	.002000	1.40
.000014	200.54	.000042	66.85	.000110	25.52	.002500	1.12
.000015	187.17	.000043	65.29	.000120	23.40	.003000	0.94
.000016	175.47	.000044	63.81	.000130	21.60	.004000	0.70
.000017	165.15	.000045	62.39	.000140	20.05	.005000	0.56
.000018	155.97	.000046	61.03	.000150	18.72	.006000	0.47
.000019	147.77	.000047	59.73	.000160	17.55	.007000	0.40
.000020	140.38	.000048	58.49	.000170	16.51	.008000	0.35
.000021	133.69	.000049	57.30	.000180	15.60	.009000	0.31
.000022	127.62	.000050	56.15	.000190	14.78	.010000	0.28
.000023	122.07	.000052	53.99	.000200	14.04	.020000	0.14
.000024	116.95	.000054	51.99	.000220	12.76	.030000	0.09
.000025	112.30	.000056	50.14	.000240	11.70	.050000	0.06
.000026	107.98	.000058	48.41	.000260	10.80	.100000	0.03
.000027	103.98	.000060	46.79	.000280	10.03	∞	0.00

TABLE III.

(English measure.)

This table contains the values of

$$y \text{ and } x$$

in the general formula for the coefficient c,

$$c = \frac{y}{1 + \frac{x}{\sqrt{R}}},$$

for a large number of slopes and values of n.

They were mostly obtained by converting into English measure the values computed by Mr. Chas. H. Swan, C.E., and contained in the Trans. Am. Soc. C.E., 1880.

They may be used also for the purpose of plotting the slope- or grade-curves in the diagram, Plate VIII, y and x representing their coördinates. The construction of such a diagram is thereby rendered quite easy.

TABLE III.

Slope	n = 0.008 x	n = 0.008 y	n = 0.009 x	n = 0.009 y	n = 0.010 x	n = 0.010 y	n = 0.011 x	n = 0.011 y	n = 0.012 x	n = 0.012 y	n = 0.013 x	n = 0.013 y	n = 0.014 x	n = 0.014 y
0.000025														
0.000030											2.001	293.2	2.154	283.2
0.000035									1.622	286.2	1.758	274.6	1.892	264.5
0.000040					1.119	293.1	1.486	299.9	1.461	272.8	1.584	261.1	1.705	251.1
0.000045					1.039	285.1	1.339	286.5	1.341	262.7	1.453	251.1	1.566	241.2
0.000050					.977	278.9	1.229	276.6	1.247	254.9	1.352	243.4	1.455	233.4
0.000055					.927	273.9	1.144	268.7	1.173	248.6	1.271	237.0	1.368	227.1
0.000060					.883	269.4	1.075	262.4	1.111	243.5	1.204	232.0	1.298	222.0
0.000065			.796	289.6	.849	266.0	1.019	257.3	1.061	239.4	1.149	227.8	1.238	217.8
0.000070			.764	286.1	.816	262.7	.972	253.0	1.017	235.8	1.102	224.2	1.187	214.2
0.000075			.735	283.1	.791	260.2	.933	249.5	.981	232.7	1.062	221.1	1.144	211.1
0.000080			.711	280.4	.767	257.8	.899	246.4	.948	230.0	1.028	218.4	1.106	208.4
0.000085			.690	278.0	.746	255.7	.869	243.7	.921	227.6	.997	216.0	1.073	206.1
0.000090			.672	276.0	.728	253.9	.843	241.4	.896	225.6	.970	214.0	1.044	204.1
0.000095			.655	274.1	.711	252.2	.822	239.2	.874	223.8	.947	212.1	1.019	202.3
0.00010			.641	272.4	.697	250.8	.800	237.4	.854	222.2	.925	210.4	.996	200.5
0.00012	.557	296.1	.623	270.9	.650	246.1	.784	235.8	.836	220.6	.907	209.0	.976	199.0
0.00015	.519	291.4	.585	266.1	.603	241.4	.767	234.3	.780	216.0	.845	204.3	.910	194.5
0.0002	.483	286.7	.543	261.5	.557	236.8	.715	229.6	.724	211.3	.784	199.7	.845	189.8
0.0003	.445	282.2	.501	256.9	.510	232.1	.664	224.9	.668	206.6	.724	195.0	.780	185.1
0.0004	.407	277.5	.460	252.2	.487	229.8	.612	220.4	.612	201.9	.662	190.3	.713	180.4
0.0005	.389	275.1	.438	249.9	.472	228.3	.561	215.7	.585	199.6	.632	188.0	.681	178.0
0.0006	.378	273.7	.425	248.4	.463	227.4	.536	213.3	.567	198.1	.614	186.5	.661	176.6
0.0007	.371	272.8	.416	247.5	.456	226.7	.519	211.9	.556	197.2	.603	185.6	.648	175.7
0.0008	.366	272.1	.411	246.8	.451	226.2	.509	211.0	.548	196.7	.594	184.9	.639	174.9
0.0009	.362	271.4	.405	246.4	.447	225.8	.501	210.2	.541	196.1	.586	184.5	.632	174.6
0.0010	.358	271.1	.404	245.9	.445	225.6	.496	209.9	.538	195.8	.581	184.0	.626	174.2
0.0015	.355	270.9	.400	245.7	.431	225.2	.492	209.3	.534	195.4	.577	183.8	.623	173.9
0.0020	.344	269.4	.387	244.3	.424	224.2	.489	209.2	.516	194.0	.559	182.4	.603	172.4
0.0040	.338	268.7	.381	243.5	.422	223.5	.474	207.7	.509	193.2	.550	181.6	.592	171.7
0.0060	.337	268.5	.378	243.4	.420	223.3	.466	207.0	.505	193.0	.547	181.5	.590	171.5
0.0080	.336	268.3	.377	243.2	.420	223.1	.463	206.8	.503	192.9	.546	181.3	.588	171.3
0.0100	.335	268.3	.376	243.2	.416	223.1	.462	206.6	.503	192.6	.545	181.2	.586	171.1
0.1000	.333	268.0	.375	242.8	.416	222.7	.458	206.3	.500	192.6	.541	180.8	.583	171.0
1.0000	.333	268.0	.375	242.8	.416	222.7	.458	206.3	.500	192.6	.541	180.8	.583	171.0

TABLE III.—Continued.

Slope	n = 0.015 x	n = 0.015 y	n = 0.016 x	n = 0.016 y	n = 0.017 x	n = 0.017 y	n = 0.018 x	n = 0.018 y	n = 0.019 x	n = 0.019 y	n = 0.020 x	n = 0.020 y	n = 0.021 x	n = 0.021 y
0.000025	2.399	274.7	2.464	267.2	2.018	260.5	2.772	254.6	2.926	249.3	3.080	244.5	3.233	240.2
0.000030	2.027	255.9	2.162	248.4	2.298	241.8	2.435	235.9	2.570	230.6	2.705	225.8	2.840	221.5
0.000035	1.827	242.6	1.949	235.0	2.072	228.4	2.195	222.5	2.314	217.2	2.438	212.5	2.560	208.1
0.000040	1.676	232.5	1.788	225.1	1.900	218.5	2.014	212.5	2.124	207.3	2.236	202.6	2.349	198.1
0.000045	1.560	224.7	1.663	217.1	1.768	210.7	1.873	204.7	1.975	199.5	2.081	194.6	2.184	190.4
0.000050	1.466	218.6	1.564	211.0	1.662	204.4	1.759	198.6	1.858	193.1	1.955	188.3	2.054	184.1
0.000055	1.390	213.5	1.482	205.9	1.575	199.2	1.667	193.3	1.759	188.1	1.854	183.1	1.947	178.9
0.000060	1.327	209.2	1.414	201.6	1.502	195.1	1.591	189.1	1.680	183.9	1.768	178.9	1.858	174.8
0.000065	1.272	205.5	1.358	198.1	1.441	191.5	1.526	185.5	1.611	180.2	1.696	175.5	1.781	171.1
0.000070	1.225	202.5	1.307	194.9	1.388	188.3	1.472	182.4	1.553	177.1	1.634	172.2	1.716	168.1
0.000075	1.186	199.7	1.265	192.3	1.343	185.7	1.423	179.7	1.502	174.4	1.580	169.7	1.660	165.4
0.000080	1.151	197.4	1.225	190.0	1.303	183.4	1.381	177.3	1.457	172.1	1.535	167.3	1.611	163.0
0.000085	1.120	195.4	1.195	187.8	1.269	181.2	1.343	175.3	1.419	170.1	1.493	165.2	1.567	161.0
0.000090	1.091	193.6	1.166	186.0	1.238	179.3	1.310	173.5	1.383	168.2	1.455	163.4	1.529	159.0
0.000095	1.063	192.0	1.138	184.4	1.209	177.7	1.281	171.9	1.352	166.6	1.423	161.7	1.495	157.4
0.00010	1.036	190.5	1.115	182.9	1.186	176.3	1.254	170.4	1.325	165.0	1.394	160.3	1.464	155.9
0.00012	.976	185.8	1.041	178.2	1.106	171.5	1.171	165.7	1.234	160.5	1.300	155.6	1.365	151.2
0.00015	.905	181.1	.965	173.5	1.026	167.0	1.086	161.0	1.146	155.8	1.207	150.9	1.267	146.7
0.0002	.834	176.4	.891	169.0	.947	162.3	1.003	156.3	1.057	151.1	1.113	146.3	1.169	142.0
0.0003	.766	171.7	.816	164.3	.867	157.6	.918	151.6	.968	146.3	1.019	141.6	1.072	137.3
0.0004	.729	169.3	.778	161.9	.827	155.2	.876	149.2	.925	144.0	.974	139.3	1.021	134.9
0.0005	.710	168.1	.757	160.5	.804	153.8	.851	148.0	.898	142.5	.945	137.8	.992	133.5
0.0006	.695	167.2	.740	159.6	.787	152.9	.834	146.9	.880	141.6	.927	136.9	.972	132.6
0.0007	.684	166.4	.729	158.8	.776	152.1	.822	146.3	.867	140.9	.912	136.2	.959	131.9
0.0008	.677	165.9	.722	158.3	.767	151.8	.813	145.8	.858	140.6	.903	135.7	.948	131.5
0.0009	.672	165.5	.711	157.8	.760	151.2	.805	145.1	.851	140.2	.894	135.3	.939	131.0
0.0010	.666	165.2	.711	157.8	.755	151.1	.800	145.1	.843	139.8	.889	135.1	.934	130.8
0.0020	.646	163.7	.688	156.3	.731	149.6	.775	143.6	.818	138.4	.862	133.7	.903	129.3
0.0040	.635	163.1	.677	155.6	.720	148.9	.762	142.9	.804	137.7	.847	133.0	.889	128.6
0.0060	.632	162.8	.673	155.2	.715	148.7	.758	142.6	.800	137.5	.842	132.8	.883	128.4
0.0080	.630	162.7	.672	155.2	.713	148.5	.756	142.6	.798	137.3	.840	132.6	.851	128.2
0.0100	.628	162.5	.670	155.0	.713	148.5	.755	142.4	.796	137.3	.838	132.6	.880	128.2
0.1000	.624	162.5	.666	154.0	.705	148.2	.749	142.4	.791	137.1	.833	132.2	.874	127.9
1.0000	.624	162.5	.666	154.0	.705	148.2	.749	142.4	.791	137.1	.833	132.2	.874	127.9

TABLE III.—Continued.

Slope	n = 0.022 r	n = 0.022 r'	n = 0.023 r	n = 0.023 r'	n = 0.024 r	n = 0.024 r'	n = 0.025 r	n = 0.025 r'	n = 0.026 r	n = 0.026 r'	n = 0.027 r	n = 0.027 r'	n = 0.028 r	n = 0.028 r'
0.000025	236.3	3.357	232.7	3.541	229.4	3.695	226.4	3.849	223.0	4.003	221.1	4.157	218.7	4.311
0.000030	217.6	2.976	214.0	3.111	210.7	3.240	207.7	3.381	204.9	3.517	202.3	3.652	199.9	3.787
0.000035	204.2	2.682	200.6	2.803	197.4	2.925	194.3	3.047	191.6	3.169	189.0	3.291	186.6	3.413
0.000040	194.2	2.461	190.6	2.573	187.3	2.685	184.3	2.797	181.5	2.909	178.9	3.020	176.5	3.132
0.000045	186.4	2.289	182.8	2.393	179.5	2.497	176.5	2.602	173.7	2.706	171.1	2.810	168.7	2.914
0.000050	180.2	2.151	176.0	2.249	173.3	2.348	170.3	2.446	167.5	2.543	164.9	2.641	162.5	2.739
0.000055	174.9	2.039	171.5	2.131	168.2	2.224	165.2	2.318	162.4	2.411	159.8	2.504	157.0	2.596
0.000060	170.8	1.945	167.2	2.031	163.9	2.122	160.8	2.211	158.1	2.300	155.4	2.389	153.1	2.477
0.000065	167.2	1.867	163.5	1.952	160.3	2.035	157.4	2.121	154.5	2.206	151.9	2.291	149.5	2.376
0.000070	164.1	1.797	160.5	1.880	157.2	1.961	154.1	2.044	151.4	2.124	148.9	2.207	146.5	2.290
0.000075	161.4	1.739	157.8	1.818	154.5	1.895	151.6	1.978	148.7	2.055	146.2	2.135	143.8	2.215
0.000080	159.0	1.687	155.6	1.765	152.1	1.842	149.2	1.918	146.3	1.994	143.8	2.072	141.5	2.149
0.000085	157.0	1.642	153.4	1.716	150.1	1.792	147.1	1.867	144.4	1.941	141.8	2.016	139.5	2.092
0.000090	155.2	1.602	151.6	1.674	148.3	1.747	145.3	1.822	142.5	1.892	140.0	1.967	137.5	2.039
0.000095	153.6	1.566	150.0	1.636	146.7	1.709	143.6	1.779	140.9	1.851	138.4	1.923	135.9	1.994
0.00012	152.1	1.533	148.5	1.604	145.3	1.672	142.2	1.743	139.5	1.812	136.8	1.883	134.4	1.952
0.00015	147.4	1.439	143.8	1.495	140.6	1.560	137.5	1.625	134.8	1.691	132.2	1.756	129.7	1.822
0.0002	142.7	1.327	139.1	1.378	135.9	1.448	132.8	1.503	130.1	1.569	127.5	1.629	125.2	1.689
0.0003	138.1	1.225	134.4	1.280	131.1	1.336	128.2	1.392	125.4	1.448	122.8	1.502	121.2	1.558
0.0004	133.3	1.122	129.7	1.173	126.4	1.224	123.5	1.274	120.6	1.325	118.1	1.377	115.8	1.428
0.0005	131.0	1.070	127.5	1.119	124.1	1.167	121.2	1.216	118.3	1.265	115.8	1.314	113.4	1.363
0.0006	129.7	1.039	126.1	1.086	122.6	1.133	119.7	1.182	117.0	1.229	114.3	1.276	112.0	1.323
0.0007	128.6	1.019	125.2	1.064	121.2	1.111	118.8	1.158	115.4	1.204	113.4	1.251	111.1	1.296
0.0008	128.1	1.005	124.4	1.050	120.6	1.095	118.1	1.140	114.9	1.187	112.3	1.233	110.3	1.278
0.0009	127.5	.994	123.9	1.039	120.3	1.084	117.6	1.128	114.5	1.173	112.0	1.218	110.0	1.263
0.0010	126.8	.985	123.5	1.030	119.9	1.073	117.2	1.119	114.1	1.164	111.6	1.209	109.4	1.253
0.0020	125.4	.977	123.2	1.023	119.0	1.066	115.6	1.111	112.6	1.155	110.1	1.200	109.2	1.243
0.0040	124.6	.947	121.9	.990	118.5	1.034	114.9	1.075	112.1	1.119	109.4	1.162	107.8	1.205
0.0060	124.4	.932	121.2	.971	117.9	1.015	114.7	1.059	111.8	1.100	109.2	1.142	107.1	1.186
0.0080	124.3	.927	120.8	.968	117.6	1.010	114.5	1.052	111.8	1.095	109.1	1.137	106.9	1.178
0.0100	124.1	.923	120.6	.967	117.4	1.008	114.5	1.050	111.6	1.091	109.1	1.133	106.7	1.175
0.1000	124.1	.921	120.5	.963	117.2	1.006	114.1	1.048	111.4	1.090	108.8	1.131	106.7	1.173
1.0000	124.1	.916	120.5	.957	117.2	.999	114.1	1.041	111.4	1.082	108.5	1.124	106.3	1.166

TABLE III.—Continued.

Slope	n = 0.009 y	x	n = 0.010 y	x	n = 0.012 y	x	n = 0.014 y	x	n = 0.036 y	x	n = 0.098 y	x
0.000030	197.7	3.922	182.3	3.057								
0.000035	184.3	3.535	172.2	3.356	168.5	3.579						
0.000040	174.3	3.214	164.4	3.122	160.7	3.330	157.3	3.538				
0.000045	166.5	3.016	158.2	2.935	154.4	3.130	151.1	3.326	148.1	3.521	140.4	3.523
0.000050	160.3	2.837	153.1	2.782	149.3	2.967	146.0	3.152	143.0	3.338	136.1	3.362
0.000055	155.2	2.689	148.8	2.654	145.1	2.831	141.7	3.007	138.8	3.184	132.5	3.225
0.000060	150.9	2.565	145.2	2.546	141.5	2.715	138.1	2.885	135.2	3.055	129.4	3.103
0.000065	147.3	2.461	142.2	2.451	138.1	2.617	135.0	2.780	132.1	2.944	126.8	3.006
0.000070	144.2	2.372	139.5	2.373	135.4	2.531	132.4	2.689	129.4	2.847	124.4	2.917
0.000075	141.5	2.294	137.1	2.303	135.7	2.456	130.0	2.610	127.1	2.763	122.4	2.839
0.000080	139.3	2.225	135.1	2.240	133.4	2.399	128.0	2.549	125.0	2.689	120.5	2.769
0.000085	137.1	2.166	133.3	2.186	131.3	2.331	126.1	2.477	123.2	2.623	118.9	2.706
0.000090	135.3	2.111	131.7	2.136	129.4	2.278	124.5	2.421	121.5	2.561	117.4	2.651
0.000095	133.7	2.063	130.1	2.092	127.9	2.231	123.0	2.371	120.1	2.511	112.7	2.473
0.00012	132.2	2.023	125.5	1.952	126.4	2.081	118.3	2.211	115.4	2.342	108.1	2.295
0.00015	127.5	1.887	120.8	1.811	121.7	1.932	113.8	2.052	110.7	2.172	103.5	2.117
0.0002	122.6	1.750	116.1	1.671	117.0	1.781	109.1	1.894	106.0	2.005	98.7	1.937
0.0003	118.1	1.615	111.4	1.529	112.3	1.631	104.1	1.734	101.3	1.836	96.4	1.849
0.0004	113.6	1.479	109.1	1.459	107.6	1.557	102.0	1.654	99.1	1.752	94.9	1.796
0.0005	111.2	1.410	107.6	1.417	105.3	1.511	100.6	1.605	97.7	1.701	94.0	1.759
0.0006	109.8	1.370	106.7	1.300	104.0	1.482	99.7	1.575	96.8	1.667	93.3	1.734
0.0007	108.9	1.343	106.2	1.365	102.9	1.461	98.9	1.551	96.0	1.643	93.0	1.716
0.0008	108.2	1.323	105.6	1.354	102.4	1.444	98.6	1.535	95.5	1.625	93.0	1.700
0.0009	107.6	1.309	105.3	1.343	101.8	1.432	98.0	1.522	95.1	1.611	92.2	1.689
0.0010	107.3	1.298	104.0	1.331	101.5	1.423	97.8	1.511	94.8	1.600	92.2	1.636
0.0020	106.0	1.249	103.5	1.291	101.1	1.377	96.4	1.462	93.5	1.549	90.7	1.609
0.0030	105.6	1.227	103.1	1.271	99.7	1.354	95.9	1.439	92.8	1.524	90.0	1.600
0.0040	104.9	1.222	102.7	1.263	98.9	1.347	95.5	1.432	92.4	1.515	89.8	1.598
0.0050	104.5	1.216	102.5	1.260	98.7	1.343	95.3	1.428	92.3	1.511	89.6	1.593
0.0100	104.4	1.215	102.4	1.258	98.6	1.341	95.3	1.424	92.3	1.508	79.6	1.583
0.1000	104.2	1.207	102.1	1.249	98.4	1.333	94.9	1.416	92.0	1.499	79.2	1.582
1.0000	104.2	1.207	102.1	1.249	98.4	1.332	94.9	1.415	92.0	1.499	79.2	

TABLE III.—*Concluded.*

Slope.	n = 0.040		n = 0.042		n = 0.044		n = 0.045		n = 0.048		n = 0.050	
	y	r	y	r	y	r	y	r	y	r	y	r
0.000060	133.7	3.558	128.0	3.564								
0.000065	130.1	3.394	124.9	3.435	122.9	3.598						
0.000070	127.1	3.271	122.2	3.322	120.3	3.480						
0.000075	124.4	3.164	119.9	3.224	117.9	3.378	116.1	3.531				
0.000080	122.0	3.070	117.8	3.137	115.9	3.287	114.1	3.436				
0.000085	120.0	2.988	116.0	3.060	114.0	3.206	112.2	3.352	110.6	3.497		
0.000090	118.1	2.914	114.3	2.991	112.4	3.134	110.6	3.276	109.0	3.419		
0.000095	116.5	2.849	112.9	2.930	110.9	3.069	109.1	3.209	107.5	3.348	106.0	3.488
0.0001	115.1	2.790	108.2	2.733	106.2	2.863	104.4	2.993	102.8	3.123	101.3	3.254
0.00012	110.3	2.603	103.5	2.536	101.6	2.657	99.8	2.778	98.1	2.899	96.6	3.020
0.00015	105.7	2.415	98.8	2.340	96.9	2.451	95.1	2.563	93.4	2.674	91.9	2.786
0.0002	101.1	2.226	94.2	2.142	92.2	2.244	90.4	2.347	88.8	2.449	87.3	2.552
0.0003	96.4	2.041	91.9	2.044	89.8	2.142	88.0	2.238	86.4	2.337	84.9	2.435
0.0005	94.0	1.947	90.3	1.985	88.3	2.079	86.5	2.175	84.9	2.269	83.5	2.365
0.0006	92.6	1.891	89.4	1.947	87.1	2.039	85.6	2.131	84.0	2.224	82.6	2.318
0.0007	91.7	1.853	88.7	1.918	86.7	2.008	85.1	2.100	83.4	2.190	81.9	2.284
0.0008	90.9	1.827	88.3	1.896	86.3	1.987	84.5	2.077	82.9	2.168	81.3	2.258
0.0009	90.3	1.806	87.8	1.880	86.0	1.970	84.2	2.059	82.5	2.140	80.9	2.238
0.0010	90.0	1.790	87.6	1.867	85.6	1.955	83.8	2.044	82.2	2.133	80.7	2.224
0.0020	89.8	1.777	86.2	1.808	84.2	1.894	82.4	1.981	80.7	2.066	79.3	2.153
0.0040	88.3	1.721	85.4	1.777	83.4	1.863	81.6	1.949	80.0	2.034	78.6	2.117
0.0060	87.0	1.694	85.3	1.768	83.3	1.853	81.5	1.937	79.8	2.021	78.4	2.106
0.0080	87.4	1.683	85.1	1.763	83.1	1.849	81.3	1.932	79.6	2.016	78.2	2.100
0.0100	87.2	1.680	85.1	1.759	83.1	1.845	81.3	1.929	79.6	2.012	78.2	2.097
0.1000	87.0	1.676	84.7	1.750	82.7	1.835	81.0	1.918	79.3	2.001	77.8	2.084
1.0000	86.9	1.665	84.7	1.748	82.7	1.833	80.9	1.916	79.3	1.999	77.8	2.082

TABLE IV.

(English Measure.)

This table contains the values of the

coefficient c

in the general formula

$$v = c \sqrt{RS},$$

for a number of slopes and values of n, as given in "The Civil Engineer's Pocket-book," by John C. Trautwine.

SLOPE S	MEAN RADII R feet	COEFFICIENTS n OF ROUGHNESS.											
		.009	.010	.011	0.12	.013	.015	.017	.020	.025	.030	.035	.040
.000025	.1	65	57	50	44	40	33	28	23	17	14	12	10
	.2	87	75	67	59	53	45	38	31	24	19	16	14
	.4	111	97	87	78	70	59	51	42	32	26	22	19
	.6	127	112	100	90	81	69	60	49	38	31	26	22
	.8	138	122	109	99	90	77	66	55	43	35	30	25
	1	148	131	118	106	97	83	72	60	47	38	32	28
	1.5	166	148	133	121	111	95	83	69	55	45	38	33
	2	179	160	144	131	121	104	91	77	61	50	43	37
	3	197	177	160	147	135	117	103	88	70	59	50	44
	3.28	201	181	164	151	139	121	106	91	72	60	52	46
	4	209	188	172	158	146	127	113	96	78	65	56	49
	6	226	206	188	174	161	142	126	108	88	74	64	57
	8	238	216	199	184	171	151	135	117	96	82	71	63
	10	246	225	207	192	179	159	142	124	102	87	76	68
	12	253	231	214	198	186	165	149	129	107	92	81	72
	16	263	242	223	208	195	174	157	138	115	100	88	79
	20	271	249	231	215	202	181	164	144	121	106	94	84
	30	283	261	243	228	215	193	176	157	133	117	104	95
	50	297	274	257	241	225	207	190	170	147	130	117	107
	75	306	284	267	251	238	217	200	180	157	140	127	117
.00005	.1	78	67	59	52	47	39	33	26	20	16	13	11
	.15	91	79	69	62	56	46	39	31	23	19	16	13
	.2	100	87	77	68	62	51	44	35	26	21	18	15
	.3	114	99	88	79	71	59	50	41	31	25	21	18
	.4	124	109	97	88	79	66	57	46	35	28	24	20
	.6	139	122	109	98	90	76	65	53	41	33	28	24
	.8	150	133	119	107	98	83	71	59	46	37	31	27
	1	158	140	126	114	104	89	77	64	49	40	34	29
	1.5	173	154	139	126	116	99	87	72	57	47	40	34
	2	184	164	145	135	124	107	94	79	62	51	44	38
	3	198	178	161	148	136	118	104	88	71	59	50	44
	3.28	201	181	164	151	139	121	106	91	72	60	52	46
	4	207	187	170	156	145	126	111	95	77	64	56	49
	6	220	199	182	168	156	137	122	105	85	72	63	56
	8	228	206	189	175	163	144	129	111	91	78	68	61
	10	234	212	195	181	169	149	134	116	96	82	72	64
	12	238	217	200	185	173	153	138	120	99	86	75	68
	16	245	223	206	191	180	160	144	126	106	91	81	73
	20	250	228	211	196	184	165	149	131	110	96	85	77
	30	257	236	219	204	192	172	157	139	118	103	92	84
	50	266	245	228	213	201	181	165	148	127	112	101	93
	75	272	250	233	218	207	187	171	153	133	119	108	99

Slope S	Mean Radii R feet.	Coefficients n of Roughness.											
		.009	.010	.011	.012	.013	.015	.017	.020	.025	.030	.035	.040
.0001	.1	90	78	68	60	54	44	37	30	22	17	14	12
	.2	112	98	86	76	69	57	48	39	29	23	19	16
	.3	125	109	97	87	78	65	56	45	34	27	22	19
	.4	136	119	106	95	86	72	62	50	38	31	25	22
	.6	149	131	118	105	96	81	70	57	44	35	30	25
	.8	158	140	126	114	103	88	76	63	48	39	33	28
	1	166	147	132	120	109	93	81	67	52	42	35	31
	1.5	178	159	144	130	120	103	89	75	59	48	41	35
	2	187	168	151	138	127	109	96	81	64	53	45	39
	3	198	178	162	149	137	119	104	89	71	59	51	45
	3.28	201	181	164	151	139	121	106	91	72	60	52	46
	4	206	186	169	155	143	125	111	94	76	64	55	49
	6	215	195	178	164	152	134	119	102	84	71	61	54
	8	221	201	184	170	158	139	124	107	88	75	66	59
	10	226	205	188	174	162	143	128	111	92	78	69	62
	15	233	212	195	181	169	150	135	118	98	85	75	68
	20	237	216	200	185	173	154	139	122	102	89	79	71
	30	243	222	206	191	179	160	145	128	108	95	84	77
	50	249	227	211	197	185	166	151	134	114	100	91	83
.0002	.1	99	85	74	65	59	48	41	32	24	18	15	12
	.2	121	105	93	83	74	61	52	42	31	25	21	17
	.3	133	116	103	92	83	69	59	48	36	29	24	20
	.4	143	125	112	100	91	76	65	53	40	32	27	23
	.6	155	138	122	111	100	85	73	60	46	37	31	26
	.8	164	145	131	118	107	91	79	65	50	41	34	29
	1	170	151	136	123	113	96	83	69	54	44	37	32
	1.5	181	162	146	133	122	105	91	77	60	49	42	36
	2	188	170	154	140	129	111	97	82	64	54	45	40
	3	200	179	163	149	137	119	105	89	72	59	51	45
	4	205	185	168	155	143	125	111	94	76	63	55	48
	6	213	193	176	162	150	132	117	100	82	69	60	53
	8	218	198	181	167	155	137	122	105	87	73	64	57
	10	222	201	185	170	158	140	125	108	89	76	67	60
	15	228	207	190	176	164	145	131	113	95	82	72	65
	20	231	210	194	180	168	149	134	117	98	85	76	68
	30	235	215	198	184	172	154	139	122	103	89	80	73
	50	240	220	203	189	177	158	143	126	108	94	85	78

SLOPE S	MEAN RADII R feet	COEFFICIENTS n OF ROUGHNESS.											
		.009	.010	.011	.012	.013	.015	.017	.020	.025	.030	.035	.040
.0004	.1	104	89	78	69	62	50	43	34	25	19	16	13
	.15	116	101	90	80	71	59	50	40	29	23	19	16
	.2	126	110	97	87	78	65	54	44	32	25	21	18
	.3	138	120	107	96	87	73	62	50	37	30	24	21
	.4	148	129	115	104	94	79	68	55	42	33	27	23
	.6	157	140	126	113	103	87	75	62	47	38	31	27
	.8	166	148	133	121	110	93	81	67	51	42	35	30
	1	172	154	138	125	115	98	85	70	55	45	37	32
	1.5	183	164	148	135	124	106	93	78	61	50	42	37
	2	190	170	154	141	130	112	98	83	65	54	43	40
	3	199	179	162	149	138	119	105	89	71	59	51	45
	4	204	184	168	154	142	124	110	94	76	63	55	48
	6	211	191	175	161	149	130	116	99	81	69	60	53
	10	219	199	183	168	157	138	123	107	88	75	66	59
	20	227	207	190	176	164	146	131	115	96	83	73	66
	50	235	215	198	184	173	154	139	123	104	91	82	75
.0010	.1	110	94	83	73	65	54	45	36	27	21	17	14
	.2	129	113	99	89	81	66	57	45	34	27	22	18
	.3	141	124	109	98	89	74	63	51	39	30	25	21
	.4	150	131	117	105	96	80	69	56	43	34	28	24
	.6	161	142	127	115	104	88	76	63	48	39	32	27
	.8	169	150	134	122	111	94	82	68	52	42	35	30
	1	175	155	139	127	116	99	86	71	56	45	38	33
	1.5	184	165	149	136	124	108	93	78	62	50	43	37
	2	191	171	155	142	130	112	98	83	66	54	46	40
	3	199	179	163	149	138	119	105	89	71	59	51	45
	4	204	184	168	154	142	124	110	93	75	63	54	48
	6	211	190	174	160	149	130	116	99	81	68	59	52
	10	215	197	181	167	155	136	122	105	87	74	65	58
	20	225	205	188	175	163	144	129	113	94	81	72	65
	50	232	212	196	182	170	151	137	120	101	89	79	72
.0100	.1	110	95	83	74	66	54	46	36	27	21	17	14
	.15	122	105	93	83	75	62	52	42	31	24	20	17
	.2	130	114	100	90	81	67	57	46	34	27	22	19
	.3	143	125	111	100	90	76	64	52	39	31	25	22
	.4	151	133	119	107	98	82	70	57	44	35	29	24
	.6	162	143	129	116	106	90	77	64	49	39	33	28
	.8	170	151	135	123	112	95	82	68	53	43	35	31
	1	175	156	141	128	117	99	87	72	56	45	38	33
	1.5	185	165	149	136	125	107	94	79	62	51	43	37
	2	191	171	155	142	130	112	99	83	66	55	46	40
	3	199	179	162	149	138	119	105	89	71	59	51	45
	3.25	201	181	164	151	139	121	106	91	72	60	52	46
	4	204	184	167	154	142	123	109	93	76	63	55	48
	6	210	190	173	160	148	129	115	99	81	68	59	52
	10	217	196	180	166	154	136	121	105	86	74	65	58
	20	225	204	187	173	161	143	128	112	93	80	71	64
	50	231	210	194	181	168	150	135	119	100	87	73	71

TABLE V.

Metric Conversion Tables.

In the following table are grouped only those units which are likely to be employed in matters relating to the flow of water in open channels. The values[*] given are based upon the following:

$$\text{1 meter} = 39.37079 \text{ inches;}$$
$$\text{1 U. S. gallon} = 231 \text{ cubic inches;}$$
$$\text{1 Imperial gallon (British)} = 277.274 \text{ "}$$
$$\text{1 cubic centimeter of water} = 1 \text{ gram.}$$

To convert either of the coefficients c, a, l, or m, of the general formula, from metric into English measure, they must be multiplied by $\sqrt{3.2809} = 1.811325$.

To convert either of the coefficients from English into metric measure, they must be multiplied by $\dfrac{1}{\sqrt{3.2809}} = 0.552083$.

---

[*] See "Tables of Equivalents of Units of Measurement," prepared by Carl Hering (New York, 1888), from which most of the values are taken.

LENGTH.

				Log.
1 inch	=	2.53995	centimeters	0.404 8259
	=	0.0253995	meter	2.404 8259
	=	0.0833333	foot	2.920 8186
1 foot	=	30.4794	centimeters	1.484 0071
	=	0.304794	meter	1.484 0071
	=	0.0001894	mile	4.277 3661
1 yard	=	0.914384	meter	1.961 1284
1 mile	=	1609.3123	meters	3.206 6403
	=	1.6093123	kilometers	0.206 6403
	=	5280.	feet	3.722 6339
1 centimeter	=	0.393707	inch	1.595 1741
	=	0.032809	foot	2.515 9929
1 meter	=	39.370790	inches	1.595 1741
	=	3.280899	feet	0.515 9929
	=	1.093633	yards	0.038 8716

AREA.

1 square inch	=	6 451368	square centimeters	0 809 6518
1 square foot	=	928.997	square centimeters	2.968 0142
	=	0.0928997	square meter	2.968 0142
1 square yard	=	0 836097	square meter	1.922 2567
1 square centimeter	=	0.1550059	square inch	1.190 3482
1 square meter	=	10.764300	square feet	1.031 9858
	=	1.196033	square yards	0.077 7433

VOLUME.

1 cubic inch	=	16.38618	cubic centimeters	1.214 4777
	=	0.0163861	liter	2.214 4777
	=	0.0005787	cubic foot	4.762 4558
1 cubic foot	=	28315.313	cubic centimeters	4.452 0213
	=	28 315313	liters	1.452 0213
	=	0 0283153	cubic meter	2.452 0213
	=	1728.	cubic inches	3.237 5437
	=	7.48052	U. S. gallons	0.873 9317
	=	6.23210	British Imperial gallons	0.794 6344
1 cubic yard	=	0.764514	cubic meter	1.883 3852
1 U. S. gallon	=	3785 2079	cubic centimeters	3.578 0897
	=	3 7852079	liters	0.578 0897
	=	0.0037852	cubic meter	3.578 0897
	=	231.	cubic inches	2 363 6120
	=	0.1336806	cubic foot	1.126 0683
	=	0.833111	British Imperial gallon	1.920 7029
1 British Imperial gallon	=	4543.461	cubic centimeters	3.657 3868
	=	4 543461	liters	0.657 3868

				Log.
1 British Imperial gallon	=	0.0045435	cubic meter	3.657 3863
	=	277.274	cubic inches	2.442 9091
	=	0.16046	cubic foot	1.205 3654
	=	1.20032	U. S. gallons	0.079 2970
1 cubic centimeter	=	0.0610270	cubic inch	2.785 5223
1 liter	=	1000.	cubic centimeters	3.000 0000
	=	1.	cubic decimeter	0.000 0000
	=	61.027042	cubic inches	1.785 5223
	=	0.0353166	cubic foot	2.547 9787
	=	0.2641863	U. S. gallon	1.421 9103
	=	0.2200966	British Imperial gallon	1.342 6132
1 cubic meter	=	35.316585	cubic feet	1.547 9787
	=	264.1863	U. S. gallons	2.421 9103
	=	220.0966	British Imperial gallons	2.342 6132
	=	1.308022	cubic yards	0.116 6148

WEIGHT OF WATER.

1 cubic inch weighs	252.88	grains	2.402 9097
	0.036125	pound	2.557 8117
	16.386	grams	1.214 4777
1 cubic foot weighs	62.425	pounds	1.795 3553
	28.3153	kilograms	1.452 0213
1 U. S. gallon weighs	8.3448	pounds	0.921 4237
	3.7852	kilograms	0.578 0807
1 British Imperial gallon weighs	10.0165	pounds	1.000 7208
	4.5435	kilograms	0.657 3868
1 cubic centimeter weighs	15.4323	grains	1.188 4322
	1.	gram	0.000 0000
1 liter weighs	2.204672	pounds	0.343 3340
	1000.	grams	3.000 0000
1 cubic meter weighs	2204.672	pounds	3.343 3340
	1000.	kilograms	3.000 0000
1 pound measures	27.681414	cubic inches	1.442 1883
	0.016019	cubic foot	2.204 6447
	0.119833	U. S. gallon	1.078 5763
	0.099834	British Imperial gal.	2.999 2792
	453.59263	cubic centimeters	2.656 6660
	0.45359	liter	1.656 6660
	0.00045359	meter	4.656 6660
1 kilogram measures	61.027042	cubic inches	1.785 5223
	0.0353166	cubic foot	2.547 9787
	0.2641863	U. S. gallon	1.421 9103
	0.2200966	British Imperial gal.	1.342 6132
	1000.	cubic centimeters	3.000 0000
	1.	liter	0.000 0000
	0.001	cubic meter	3.000 0000

VELOCITY.

				Log.
1 foot per second	=	0.304794	meter per second	$\overline{1}$.484 0071
	=	0.681818	mile per hour	$\overline{1}$.833 6687
1 mile per hour	=	0.447032	meter per second	$\overline{1}$ 650 3384
	=	1.466666	feet " "	0.166 3313
1 meter per second	=	3.280899	feet " "	0.515 9929
	=	2.236977	miles per hour	0.349 6616

DISCHARGE.

1 cubic foot per second	=	28.315313	liters per second	1.452 0213
	=	0.0283153	cubic meter per second	$\overline{2}$.452 0213
	=	7.48052	U. S. gallons " "	0.873 9317
	=	6 23210	British Imp. gal. per sec.	0.794 6346
1 U. S. gallon per second	=	3.7852079	liters per second	0.578 0897
	=	0.0037852	cubic meter per second	$\overline{3}$.578 0897
	=	231.	cubic inches " "	2.363 6120
	=	0.1336806	cubic foot " "	$\overline{1}$.126 0683
	=	0.833111	British Imp. gal. per sec.	$\overline{1}$.920 7029
1 Brit. Imperial gal. p. sec.	=	4.543461	liters per second	0.657 3868
	=	0.004534	cubic meter per second	$\overline{3}$.657 3868
	=	277.274	cubic inches " "	2.442 9091
	=	0.16046	cubic foot " "	$\overline{1}$.205 3654
	=	1.20032	U. S. gallons " "	0.079 2970
1 liter per second	=	0.0353166	cubic foot " "	$\overline{2}$.547 9787
	=	0.2641863	U. S. gallon " "	$\overline{1}$.421 9103
	=	0.2200966	British Imp. gal. per sec.	$\overline{1}$.342 6132
1 cubic meter per second	=	35.316585	cubic feet per second	1.547 9787
	=	264.1863	U. S. gallons per second	2.421 9103
	=	220.0966	British Imp. gal. per sec.	2.342 6132

SLOPE.

Slope, S (Sine of Slope).	$\frac{1}{S}$	Feet per mile.	Inches per mile.
0.000001000 foot per foot......	1000000	0.00528	0.06336
0.000010000 " "	100000	0.0528	0.6336
0.000015783 " "	63360	0.08333	1.00000
0.000100000 " "	10000	0.528	6.336
0.000189394 " "	5280	1.000	12.000
0 001000000 " "	1000	5.28	63.36
0.010000000 " "	100	52.8	633.6
0.100000000 " "	10	528.	6336.

www.ingramcontent.com/pod-product-compliance
Lightning Source LLC
Chambersburg PA
CBHW030631030726
47497CB00006B/1731